DYING VOICES

Laura Wilson

ORION

An Orion Paperback

First published in Great Britain in 2000
by Orion
This paperback edition published in 2001
by Orion Books Ltd,
Orion House, 5 Upper St Martin's Lane,
London WC2H 9EA

Excerpt from 'Phizzog' in GOOD MORNING, AMERICA,
copyright 1928 and renewed 1956 by Carl Sandburg,
reprinted by permission of Harcourt, Inc.

'The Hippopotamus Song'
Words and music by Donald Swann and Michael Flanders
© 1952 Chappell Music Ltd
Warner/Chappell Music Ltd, London W6 8BS
Reproduced by permission of International Music Publications Ltd

A CIP catalogue record for this book
is available from the British Library.

ISBN 0 75284 328 1

Typeset at The Spartan Press Ltd,
Lymington, Hants
Printed and bound in Great Britain by
Clays Ltd, St Ives plc

To Michael,
who is the hero of this book
in more ways than one

Acknowledgements

I am very grateful to Judith Amanthis, Harriet Brittain, Hugh Davis, Tim Donnelly, Ruth Gavin, everyone at Gregory & Radice, Nigel Osborne, Derek Rimmer, Selina Walker, my parents June and William Wilson, and Jane Wood, for their encouragement, advice and support.

Prologue

It happened when I was on my way to work. It was an ordinary day; I was walking down the street and everything was completely normal. I wasn't really thinking about anything in particular, just meetings and decisions and what I ought to do first, when I suddenly heard a woman's voice. 'I love you, Dodie.' And I thought, that's my mother. Quite matter of fact. That's my mother, telling me she loves me.

I stopped. I don't know whether I physically turned round or not, but I saw – no, not saw, I sort of sensed . . . It's no good, I can't describe it exactly, but I had this very strong feeling – more than that, I *knew*. She was beside me. A beautiful young woman, standing there, smiling. 'Oh, Dodie,' she said, 'I do love you.' I felt so wonderful. Happy, proud, elated . . . I said, 'I love you, too.'

Then everything sort of clicked back into place. I thought, that cannot have happened. I don't believe in ghosts, and my mother doesn't exist any more. She's been dead for twenty years. She was kidnapped when I was eight, and they never found her body.

1

My name is Dodie Blackstock. Well, it's supposed to be Dorothy, but I hate it. And yes, it's *those* Blackstocks. Wolf Blackstock was my father. I'm the one who inherited all the money. My mother was his third wife. The one who was kidnapped.

I hate telling people. Sometimes – no, often – I lie. Because when they ask if I'm related, they expect me to say something like, 'No, but I wish I had his money,' and then we can talk about the kidnap and how weird that they never found her body, and that leads us on to the summer of 1976 and how hot it was. If you're about my age – I'm twenty-nine – I already know it was your best school holiday ever and that you went to the open-air pool every day and came back in the evening feeling as if the sun was inside you.

If I do tell the truth, I usually regret it. Because if you tell someone that your father was Wolf Blackstock and your mother was murdered by her kidnappers, you might just as well add, 'And by the way, I'm seriously screwed up,' because that'll be what they're thinking. I've had every sort of reaction, from total disbelief to a level of sympathy where they're almost ready to commit suicide on my behalf, and they've only known me five minutes. But the worst thing is the nice people, the ones who just say, 'God, that must have been terrible.' I just say, 'Yeah, well . . .' and talk about something else. But it's always uncomfortable. It's as if people feel guilty because they asked or they'd made a joke about it or something. And because they're fascinated by the money, of course.

People used to ask all the time. I used to think about

3

handing out flyers with my life story printed on them to save time. Father rich; mother kidnapped, body never found; university; the reason I actually work for a living instead of designing my own range of swimwear or prancing about in art galleries or whatever rich girls are supposed to do that passes for a job. Anyway, the life-story thing dropped off a bit because people were getting younger – well, they weren't, but you know what I mean. But last year, when my father died, it was all raked up in the obituaries and magazine articles and one of those TV programmes, so now everyone knows about it all over again.

I was eight when Mum was kidnapped. January 1976. The kidnappers wanted ten million pounds, but my father wouldn't pay. They dropped it to nine million, and then to eight million three months later, then seven, then two months after that they dropped it to six, before he agreed to part with a penny. You know the Pathé News videos they sell, one tape for each year? Well, if you get the one for 1976 you can see what happened. You'll find it in June, after the bit about the end of the Cod War. There's a man with fuzzy sideburns and a drip-dry shirt with a long pointy collar, crouching in some grass in front of a bush. The camera's a bit wobbly, and sometimes you catch sight of a bit of thatched roof poking up behind him.

At ten o'clock this evening, armed police stormed the cottage where kidnappers were said to be holding Susan Blackstock, wife of multi-millionaire property tycoon Wolf Blackstock, who was snatched from her car in January this year. Mr Blackstock, one of the richest men in Britain, was asked for ten million pounds in exchange for the safe return of his wife. The kidnappers, who are thought to be politically motivated, have not yet received any money. In a covert operation, police marksmen surrounded this quiet Suffolk cottage but when they

4

approached the house, the kidnappers fired on them. The police responded, and in the crossfire two policemen were injured and one man, thought to be the leader of the group, was killed. One of the officers, PC Timothy Corrigan, has subsequently died in hospital. Susan Blackstock was not in the house, and no traces of her have so far been found.

Then a voice-over will tell you that police arrested the third member of the gang at a house in Cricklewood, where items of women's clothing were discovered, but that despite a nationwide search, my mother's body was never found. Then it goes on to talk about record traffic jams to British coastal resorts and Dennis Howell being the Minister for Drought.

After that, half the journalists in the country must have descended on that village in Suffolk. One of the locals said it was like *Gunfight at the OK Corral* and a woman said she'd rung the police station when she heard the gunfire, and the sergeant said not to worry because the police were the ones doing the shooting. The other half of the journalists were doorstepping us, or that's what it felt like. We were down at Camoys Hall. That was my father's country house, which was where he lived most of the time and where I lived when I wasn't at school. It's got a great circle of gravel in front of it, made when the house was built so that carriages could turn round. I remember looking down at it from a top-floor window and not being able to see one speck of gravel, only the tops of journalists' heads. I spat, but nobody looked up.

Frankly, it would have been child's play to kidnap Mum from Camoys Hall, but she was taken from her car in London. My father wouldn't have dogs or guards or anything because he said he wouldn't be made a prisoner in his own house, so there were ordinary farm gates at the end of the driveway instead of electric ones. There was a notice saying PRIVATE PROPERTY, but the gates were usually open and anyone could have driven through them. Those journalists must have thought they'd died and gone to heaven, except that my father refused to talk to them, and they waited in front of the house every single day for almost three weeks while the search for Mum's body was going on. The reporters had vans, lighting, everything. By the end, there were blankets and even deckchairs. Most of the men had sunhats, and some of the women were lying on the brown grass of the front lawn with their tops rolled up, sunbathing. One of the newspapers ran a picture of them sitting around a picnic, playing cards. When they finally went, Joan, our housekeeper – actually she was a bit more than that, but I don't want to go into it now – and I tiptoed out of the front door to have a look and by the state of the grounds you'd have thought there'd been a garden party. Not a Buckingham Palace one, though. The following spring, our cook cut open one of the cabbages from the kitchen garden and found a used condom inside it.

I've got a photograph of the press conference that my father eventually gave. We're all standing on the porch at Camoys Hall. My father's in the front with Angela, his mistress – she had been sort of pensioned off when he married Mum, but she still lived at Camoys Hall – Des, Irene des Voeux, Joan and me. Irene des Voeux was the woman Mum was on her way to spend the weekend with when she was kidnapped. Des is Desmond Haigh-Wood. He's retired now, but he was my father's finance director and probably the closest thing he had to a friend. He had his own suite at Camoys Hall because he stayed with us so often. Des was always nice to me: I used to practise writing *Dodie Haigh-Wood*, and wish that he was my father instead of my real one.

I think the photo I've got must have been done just after the official picture was taken. Everyone's turning sideways to talk to each other and I'm obviously not meant to be there at all; they're in suits and I'm wearing shorts and a T-shirt and Joan's holding the top of my arm as if she's trying to hoick me back into the house. You can just about see my squint through my glasses, which are completely lopsided, and my hair is a mess – *plus ça change*. It looks as though Joan's been at my fringe with her nail scissors.

At that time, the police were still searching for my mother. I couldn't believe she was dead. I was sure they'd find her. I thought she'd manage to escape from the kidnappers, and that she was going to come and get me and take me away with her to somewhere lovely where we could live together. I couldn't believe she was just going to leave me with my father. I went on believing that for about three years, and then on and off until I was about fifteen. I couldn't talk about it to anyone. I knew they'd be sympathetic but pitying, because they didn't believe she was going to come back themselves. I never spoke to Angela anyway if I could help it, and the thought of talking to Joan about it was even worse because I liked her. I suppose I could have talked to Des, but I was frightened he'd say the same as the others and then I wouldn't be able to love him any more. And I didn't really talk to my father at all. I mean, I couldn't have gone to his study unless I was summoned. Nobody did that, not even Des.

Mum had to be officially declared dead in the end. They never found her body. Until last night, that is. June 14, 1996. They found it on an estate in Hackney, where they've been pulling down the tower blocks.

She's been dead for less than forty-eight hours.

2

Des once told me this story about soldiers in the Second World War. They're in Malaya or somewhere, fighting, and their commander – a man not known for his tact and sensitivity – gets a telegram to say that one of the men's mothers has died. He orders a parade and says, 'All those men with mothers still alive, take one pace forward. And where d'you think you're going, Private Smith?'

The policeman who told me about Mum was a bit like that. I told him my mother was already dead, and he said, 'Look, you *are* Dorothy Jane Blackstock, aren't you?' When I said yes, he said, 'Well, you're absolutely right, because she died yesterday. We've just found her body.' Then he asked me if I'd like to 'take a look at her', meaning would I come to the mortuary and identify her.

There was another policeman in the car with him. Neither of them looked old enough to shave, so they can't have remembered the kidnap and it was obvious no one had told them, or maybe they thought it didn't matter. At the mortuary, they had this person they said was my mother, on a trolley covered over with a sheet. I looked around to see if there was someone older, someone who'd remember what happened, a doctor or somebody I could talk to.

Someone in a white coat came and pulled the sheet down a bit, and one of the policemen said, 'Do you recognise her?'

I said, 'I'm sorry, I don't.'

'So you're saying that this isn't your mother?'

'I don't know. I'm sorry.' I mean, how was I meant to know? I suppose she did look vaguely familiar, but even if I'd seen the same face, alive, in a crowd of people – because she wasn't battered or anything – I wouldn't have shouted out, 'That's my mother!' My idea of Mum – the beautiful young woman whose voice I'd heard so clearly in my mind two days before – and this woman . . . I just couldn't bring them together. The woman's face just looked so . . . so nothing. So *dead*, I suppose.

I said, 'I haven't seen her for twenty years. I can't tell if it's her or not.' One of the policemen gave me a funny look, but they covered her up again. When we left the room, I asked,

'Why do you think she's my mother?' and they said she'd had a diary with her name in it: Susan Carrington. Then I asked them how they'd found me and they said my name was in the diary as well. In the section where you put personal details, where it says who to contact if there's an emergency, she'd written my name. She'd put 'daughter' beside it. That was why they kept calling me *Mrs* Blackstock all the time – they thought I was married, and Blackstock was my husband's name.

They took me into a little office with filing cabinets and a scuzzy grey carpet. I looked to see if there was a name on the door, just to get my bearings, but I couldn't see one. 'Did you leave home when you were very young?' one of them asked.

'No,' I said. 'It wasn't like that.' I suppose I should have explained, but I couldn't be bothered. I was angry because they didn't know, and they should have. I mean, they must have a computer or records or something where they look people up. Why should I do their work for them? And if it *was* Mum, why didn't they do their job in 1976 and find her while she was still alive? I couldn't stand having to go through it all again while they asked stupid prurient questions and just . . . I don't know, trampled over everything. I wanted to go home.

I was about to ask if I could when an older man in ordinary clothes poked his head round the door and motioned one of the uniforms outside. I heard them talking – not the words, though – and then the older one looked in again and told the other uniform to fetch me a cup of tea.

'Get younger all the time, don't they?' He came in and sat down. He said his name was Inspector Halstead. I don't think the others told me their names, or if they did I don't remember them. 'That must have been a terrible shock,' he continued. 'Miss Draycott obviously wasn't able to talk to you.'

I was about to ask him who Miss Draycott was, but then I

realised he meant Joan. She still lives at Camoys Hall. 'You've spoken to her?'

'Your name was in Miss Carrington's diary with a Cambridgeshire address. I spoke to Miss Draycott, and she told me where to reach you.'

'When was this?'

'This morning. She said she'd phone you straight away. She wanted to tell you herself.'

'Well she didn't. I was at home all the time, until your men came.'

He was sitting across from me, with his legs properly under the table. The uniform who'd asked me if I'd run away from home had parked his bum on the corner of the desk as if he was just making do with me until someone more interesting came along.

'Do you know about it?' I asked.

'You mean, about the kidnap? Yes.'

'Those others didn't. They didn't know anything. Anyway, why are you so sure it's her? It couldn't be some sort of hoax, could it?' I'm not sure what I was thinking, really – I suppose that someone might claim to be my mother, like that woman in America who claimed to be the Tsar's daughter. The woman in the mortuary had red hair, but it was darker than Mum's, and anyone can dye their hair. I didn't know if I wanted the woman to be Mum, but I didn't want her to be Minnie Bloggs who'd just been decanted from the mental home and was going round telling everybody that she was Susan Carrington, either.

'Well, we're not certain. Having said that, we think that she might have been homeless. A couple of the local shelters recognised the name and description, though they didn't know much about her. Both said she was quiet – not a talker. They didn't think she was anyone in particular. They didn't say that she'd gone round claiming to be kidnapped or anything. Mind you, a lot of them do in those places, so another one would hardly stand out.'

'They claim to be kidnapped?'

'You know, by aliens or something. The nutters.'

'Did they say she was a nutter?'

'God, no. Nothing like that. Sorry, I wasn't suggesting—'

'No, no, it's OK. Can we just . . . just be quiet for a moment? I need to think.'

He went over to one of the filing cabinets and picked at a dying spider plant while I sat there and tried to take it all in. Remember the Etch-a-Sketch toy? You'd twiddle the knobs and try to draw a house or something on the screen, but all you ended up with was a load of jagged lines. My mind was like that – nothing connected up or made sense. Except, he'd said the woman was homeless. If it was my mother, she was homeless. I might have passed her on the street and not recognised her. She might have asked me for money and been refused.

'Do the shelter people know who you think she is? Could they talk to the press? Surely the papers don't have to know if it's someone who *thought* they were my mother?'

'You needn't worry about that. As far as the shelter people are concerned, she was just another customer.'

'But if it is her, then the papers will have to know eventually, won't they?' God, why was I even asking? They'd have a field day, I knew they would. We both did.

'We'll have to release the information, yes. There's something else: she had a couple of plastic bags with clothes inside. There were some photographs in one of them. Do you want to see them?'

I didn't, but I knew I had to.

Inspector Halstead left the room and came back with three very small clear plastic bags, each with a photograph inside. He put them on the table in a row in front of me, face down. I didn't want to turn them over. When I heard Inspector Halstead say she was homeless, I knew I didn't want it to be her. I suddenly felt desperate to go home and forget all about it.

The photographs must have been handled a lot and fixed to walls because their edges were tatty and they were covered in Blu-tack marks and pin holes. Inspector Halstead turned one over and pointed at it. 'Do you recognise this?'

Shit. It was a photograph of me as a toddler, standing in a paddling pool in the garden at Camoys Hall, wearing a blue swimsuit with a white pleated skirt and waving a little red spade.

'That's me. I think I was about two. Joan – Miss Draycott – has the same picture.'

'And this one?'

The second one was black and white. My mother and father. It looked like a portrait; my father used to get them done for Christmas cards. Mum's sitting down and he's standing slightly behind with one hand on her shoulder. She's smiling, but it doesn't look natural, and her legs, which are sort of tucked in and crossed at the ankles, look as if they've been arranged by someone else. She's wearing a pale coat with a wraparound collar in black fur and big black buttons down the front, like a pierrot at an old-fashioned end-of-pier show. He's wearing a dark suit and looking handsome and glamorous. He was like Marilyn Monroe, my father. He could turn it on and off at will.

'I've never seen it before, but those are my parents.'

'This?' He turned over the third photograph.

It was a photograph of me in the middle of a group of people at a party. Not taken with my camera, because I don't own a camera. I usually leave when people start waving cameras about, partly because you never know where the negatives will end up, and partly because I don't understand this mania for recording everything as if it didn't really happen unless you've got a bunch of snaps mouldering away in an album somewhere. I remembered the photograph, because I can usually smell a camera at fifty paces and it was one of the few times when I didn't realise it until it was too late. I'm blurred and my pupils are red dots, so whoever took it must have been pissed.

'This was taken last Christmas. If that woman in there really *is* my mother, I don't see how she could have got hold of it.'

'Do you remember who took it?'

'It was just some man at a party. I didn't know him.'

'Whose party was it?'

'A friend of mine. Tony Hepworth. But I don't see—'

'Are you sure your mother – or someone calling herself your mother – has never tried to contact you?'

'Never. We all thought she was dead. *Everyone* thought she was dead. The *police* thought she was dead. There was a memorial service. There's a plaque in the church at Camoys Hall. My father remarried, for God's sake. Oh Christ, it *is* her in there, isn't it?' I felt the tea surge back into my throat and for a moment I thought I was going to throw up, but I managed to get it to go down again. 'I should look at her again, shouldn't I?'

'Do you want to?' He wasn't exactly shouting 'Result!' and punching the air with his fist, but I could tell he was pleased, even if he was trying to keep it out of his voice.

'I couldn't see her eyes. She had a brown mark in one eye. They're green, but one of them has a little brown patch. We used to do Cyclops – you know, the game where you get nearer and nearer to the other person's face until you can only see one eye – and I could always see it. She used to call it her birthmark. If I saw that, I'd know it was her.'

Inspector Halstead said he'd see what he could do and left me with one of the uniforms. I felt sick again. I looked at the sludge of sugar crystals at the bottom of the tea and tried not to think about them having to prise open her eyes. I kept getting this picture of the pathologist or whoever it was doing it with forceps or tongs or something. Inspector Halstead came back eventually and took me into the room.

The eyes seemed to be looking straight at me. Their

surface – the viscous humour or whatever it's called – had sort of congealed. They looked dull and shiny at the same time, like unmade jelly. But the brown patch was there. I'd know it anywhere.

'Yes,' I said. 'That's my mother.'

3

When I got home I sat on the sofa for a bit. Then I put on a video of *Grease*. I didn't want to watch it, in fact, I didn't even know I had it. It was the first one I saw when I opened the cupboard. Mum was forty-eight when she died. I worked it out. I'm the same age now as she was when she was kidnapped – when everyone thought she'd died. When I was twenty-eight I used to think, when it's my twenty-ninth birthday, I'll be older than she ever was. But I won't now, will I? Because she had twenty more years of life, and she didn't tell me.

The two uniforms brought me home. They asked if there was anyone I could get to 'come and sit with me' but I told them I wanted to be on my own. I asked Inspector Halstead how Mum had died, but he said they had to do tests and that they'd contact me when they knew more. I asked if he'd warn me before he told the press. I just wanted him to give me twenty-four hours to get to Camoys Hall before they did. I thought, I've got to talk to Joan. What's wrong with her? Why didn't she ring me?

I decided I wasn't going to think about it. I rewound the film and watched it again because I hadn't been following, but the second time was no better. You know when people die and you give their clothes to charity shops? That's what we did with Angela's clothes. She had cancer. My father paid for the clinic but he never went to see her because he hated

14

sick people. Sick people and mad people scared him. He was always afraid of catching what they had. Angela had lots of swirly, floppy clothes like caftans and djellabas, and Joan had them all washed and dry-cleaned and then she packed them up in suitcases with tissue paper. We took them into Cambridge one evening and left them in the doorway of the Sue Ryder shop because Joan couldn't face going in and handing them over. Joan even gave them Angela's fur coat. It was one of those slashed ones that Fendi used to do. I thought, if Mum had just told me where she was, I could have sent her that coat. Or I could have sent her the money to buy a coat. She could have come to live with me in my flat. All she was wearing when I saw her was a blue T-shirt, but I could only see the top half. I don't know what other clothes she had. Inspector Halstead told me that I could have her bags and things when the forensic lab had finished with them, so I suppose I'll find out. I could have helped her. If she'd come to me, I would have helped her.

She loved clothes. I've got lots of photographs of her from when she was a model, but my favourite is one from an article in *Harpers* called 'English Roses'. It was taken a week before she married my father. It's a bit like the girls-in-pearls thing they run in *Country Life*, except that the girls in these photographs are beautiful. There's a huge close-up of my mother's face running across two pages. Everything about her is glowing: her long, straight, strawberry-blond hair, high cheekbones and skin as delicate as a peach, with just a sprinkling of tiny cinnamon-coloured freckles across her nose. Her eyes are enormous, almond shaped and slightly slanted upwards. They're bright green except for the brown patch. You wouldn't know it was brown because the way they've lit her face makes it look golden.

Everyone said Mum was beautiful, even Angela, but she didn't think she was. If she was going out for the evening with my father, she'd sit at the dressing table for hours doing her make-up. I used to watch her. She'd be completely finished – stunningly beautiful – and she'd put her jewellery on and turn to me and say, 'What do you think?' I never knew what to say. I could have just sat and looked at her for *ever*. I'd always tell her she looked lovely, but she'd go straight back to the mirror and start scrubbing at her eyes with cold cream to get it all off so she could do it again. She'd apply her make-up five or six times before she was satisfied. Most of the time, the only reason she left the dressing table was because my father sent someone up to say that they were going to be late if she didn't come down. I used to think she redid the make-up because I wasn't saying the right thing, but now I know it wasn't that. It was almost as if, when she looked in the mirror, she saw something ugly.

Somebody once told me that redheads have fewer layers of skin than other people. It's not true, but if you'd seen my mother when she was alive you'd have believed it. That was part of the problem when I saw her body – not that the face was ugly or contorted or anything, although it didn't look much like I remembered – but it was her *skin*. It looked pasty and sort of thick. Perhaps dead people's skin always looks coarse. I wouldn't know because I've never seen a corpse before. I know this sounds horrible, but the skin was more like mine than hers. I mean, OK, I've got the hair and the freckles and the skinny body, but my skin always looks dull, as if I don't wash enough. And I have spots. Mum probably never had a single spot in her whole life, but I still get them even now I'm nearly thirty. Not the type that join up for the thin-crust pizza look, just big, individual, splotchy ones. I spend a fortune on skin cream, but most of the time, what with the blotches and the stick-figure arms and legs, I look like something that's just been dragged out of a plague pit.

Oh, *God*. I switched off the TV and curled up on the sofa, my back to the room. Why didn't she contact me? She wrote my name in her diary. She even wrote that I was her daughter. Surely she could have written a letter. God Almighty, it wasn't that hard. She even had the address of Camoys Hall in the diary. But she never even *tried*. She just went off and had her own life and left me with *him*. She must have had friends. Christ, there's probably a bunch of pissed-up old dossers out there somewhere who know more than I do about my own mother. The police know more than me. Everyone knows more than me. Why couldn't she just have been dead when we thought she was?

I didn't know how I felt about any of it. Jesus, how would you feel? Don't even try to answer that, because you can't. Well, I can't, either. No – actually, I can. I can tell you exactly how I felt. I hated her. I really *hated* her. I was upset, but more than that, I was so *angry*, not just with Mum, but with myself, with everyone. For letting it happen.

4

Joan wasn't answering her telephone, so I decided to drive up to Camoys Hall the following morning. I rang Mark, my boss, first, to ask for a couple of days off. I'm an editor – well, that's what it's called, although I'm more of a stylist, really. I work for an interiors magazine. My friend Tony thinks that all I do is drape muslin over things and throw cushions about. There's a bit more to it than that; not much, but a bit. Anyway, I like it. I'm good at it too, and I got the job because of me, not because of my family. Of course, it only took a couple of months before Mark put two and two together, but he'd met *me* first, if you see what I mean.

Mark was resigned about being phoned at home, and pissed off when I told him I needed the time away from the office.

'Is it a family thing?' he asked.

'I'm afraid so. I'm sorry, but I really do have to sort it out.'

'We'll manage, but give me a ring if you need any more time, yeah? I'd like to know sooner rather than later.'

'Thanks, Mark.'

'It's OK. But you'll call me, yeah?'

'I promise. Bye.'

All the way there in the car, I tried to kid myself that I'd be able to hang on to my job once the press found out about Mum, but I knew it wasn't true. They'd make my life impossible: I wouldn't be able to leave my flat, they'd pester me at the office . . . What am I going to do? I thought. Just when I was starting to make a life on my own, this had to happen. Because it matters so much to me, earning my own money. It means I can stand on my own two feet and be my own person. And I was so nearly there, so close . . .

I thought how ironic it was, Mum and I, both trying to have our own lives. Did she think she was free as well? Did she think she was going to do it all by herself? Except that she hadn't had my father funnelling money into her bank account for years, buttressing her with cash to make sure she'd never, ever be independent.

I suddenly found myself thinking about something that used to worry me a lot when I was younger, though I stopped thinking about it eventually because it seemed so improbable. It was this: I used to believe I'd met the kidnappers – before they took Mum, I mean. It was about a year before, so I must have been seven. I know it sounds absurd, but I'm sure that Mum and I were actually in their house. I wasn't allowed to go to the trial, so I never saw the kidnappers in the flesh, but I saw some of the newspaper photographs and they looked like the same people, only with different hair.

I never mentioned it to anyone. It seemed so ridiculous to

think that they might be the kidnappers, especially because they were the only studenty-looking people I'd ever met and you have to admit that students did all look pretty similar in the mid-seventies. Especially to me, because I'm so short-sighted that things look blurred even when they're close up. I never wore glasses as a child because Mum had read somewhere that they made your eyes lazy, so I used to get headaches all the time from peering at things. My father simply refused to acknowledge that there was a problem. Every time he saw me, he'd tell me to 'Take that sullen expression off your face.'

After a while I decided that they couldn't have been the kidnappers, that I must have made them up or dreamt them. Then a few months ago, by chance, I drove past the end of the street where I thought their house was. It's in north London, near Muswell Hill. I remembered it as a detached Victorian house with peeling paintwork, steps up to the front door and a big, weedy front garden. The houses in that street are certainly Victorian, but it's a terrace and they're quite small – no steps or front gardens. I suppose it could have been the wrong road.

I've tried to think why Mum and I would have been in that part of town, and the only thing I can come up with was the eye exercises. For my squint. Whenever we were staying at our house in London, Mum used to take me to see this elderly lady who lived in Muswell Hill and practised something called the Bates Method. She used to get me to rock backwards and forwards on the balls of my feet and wink at a stick with different coloured nails stuck into it. I can't remember how long I went to those classes, but they didn't make any difference.

We met the kidnappers because of a cat. Mum was driving down the main road and it ran straight out in front of the car. We didn't hear the bump but she must have hit it, because, when we stopped, it was lying at one side of the road as if the impact of the car had flung it there. Mum and I were bending over the cat to see if it was alive when a man came up to us. He didn't come out of the kidnappers' house, he was just walking past and he saw us. Mum didn't call out to him or wave, but he crossed over to our side of the road and squatted down beside the cat.

'I'm so sorry, is it yours?' Mum asked.

'Never seen it before.'

'Have you got a phone? I ought to ring a vet.'

'Yeah. All right.'

He looked quite ordinary. He had black hair down to his shoulders, and he was wearing dirty blue jeans and a brown skinny-rib polo neck. I think he might have been the man they called Steven Moody.

The cat seemed terrified. It wasn't moving but its sides were heaving and it was panting with its mouth open like a dog.

'Do you think we ought to move it?' Mum asked.

'Oh yes,' he said. 'You can't just leave it out here.'

I remembered that because Mum wasn't saying that we should go off and leave the cat, she was just asking if it should be moved, but he made it sound as if we were planning to abandon it. It was as if he was suddenly in charge, and Mum went along with it. She often did that – deferred to people.

'Let's be having you,' the man said to the cat, and scooped it up in his arms.

We followed him down the road and into the house. The kidnappers lived on the first floor. The landing was their hallway. I thought it had two rooms coming off it on either side, but when I saw the house again it looked too narrow for that. There was a shop-window mannequin in the hall. It was dressed in army fatigues with a helmet on its head. There were telephone directories piled up round its feet, and the Steven Moody man put the cat on the floor and started riffling through one of them to find the nearest vet.

I must have said something about the mannequin because he said, 'We got him for a play we were doing.'

All the doors were closed except one, and we could see a bunch of people – students, I thought – sitting around on beanbags and chairs and things. They saw us come in, but none of them moved or said anything until the Steven Moody man stuck his head round the door and asked one of them to fetch a blanket for the cat. It must have been stunned rather than hurt, because while Mum was arranging the Afghan rug they'd brought for it, the cat jumped up and shot into the sitting room. Mum and the man went after it. They made grabs through people's legs, but none of them took any notice, even when the cat shat behind the sofa.

I remember looking through the door and seeing Mum standing in the middle of all these people, begging to be allowed to clear up the mess. They kept saying, 'Look, it's cool,' and, 'No problem,' but she said, 'No, please, you must let me,' and, 'But we can't just *leave* it.' I could see that she was right about clearing it up, but I felt embarrassed for her because they were all just sitting there, looking at her as if she was mad to be making such a fuss. The cat was obviously fine, because it ran along the back of the sofa and jumped straight out of the window.

Mum gave up in the end and came out into the hall, but I could see it really bothered her.

One of the men got up and came after her. He said, 'Don't worry, it's a natural reaction to shock.' He fetched a cloth from the kitchen, and we followed him in there – to help, I suppose.

A girl wandered in after him and asked, 'Do you want a cup of tea?' I could tell she didn't like us. I remember thinking, she isn't doing this because she wants to. One of the others has told her to do it.

Mum said, 'It's very kind of you, but we're fine, really.'

'I was going to make one anyway.' She seemed irritated.

'It's not a problem.' Mum hadn't been rude or anything, but the kitchen was filthy and I could see she was horrified by it. She kept looking over at me to make sure I didn't say anything.

The girl turned to me. 'What about you? I mean, if you don't like tea, there's orange squash.'

'No, thank you.'

'Are you sure? It's no big deal.'

Mum answered for me. 'No, really, but thanks, anyway.'

The girl shrugged. 'Please yourself.'

I can't remember what the man with the cloth looked like, but I remember every detail about the girl. Maggie Hill. The newspapers said she'd got a scholarship to music college to study the cello. She was wearing a brown velvet trouser suit. The jacket had wide lapels and the trousers were flared. It was almost threadbare in places and one of the pockets was ripped. She had on brown platform boots with broad elastic bands stretched round them to keep the uppers and soles together. Her hair was frizzy, almost like an Afro except that it was blonde. There was far too much of it for her face, which was narrow and very pale. She had a pencil in one hand and she kept scratching her head with the pointed end.

When I saw the photos in the newspapers, Maggie Hill looked faint, like a ghost. She was the one I thought about the most, because she was a girl. I wondered if she'd been nice to Mum when the gang were holding her. Probably not, if the exchange in the kitchen was anything to go by. The newspapers said Maggie Hill was Mick Martin's girlfriend. Martin was the leader, the one who got killed in the raid. Judging from the photograph in the newspaper, he looked like Jim Morrison. I know I didn't see him, because I'd have remembered someone who looked like that.

Later on, when I was seventeen or eighteen, I used to get these awful thoughts about what might have happened if they'd . . . done anything to Mum. If they'd raped her. But when I tried to get a picture in my mind, I found I couldn't. I'd imagine her in a little room like a cell, all dark and dirty, with a horrible man looming over her. I went to the village school for a couple of years when I was seven or eight, and a policewoman came one day and showed us a film about not taking sweets from strangers and not getting into people's cars unless you knew who they were. It had this footage of a terrified little girl huddled up in an armchair in the corner of a room and an enormous man closing in on her and blocking out the light. I had no idea what the man was going to do to her, but I knew it was something terrible. That was what came into my mind when I tried to think about Mum. I just couldn't make myself think about it with real images that I'd thought of for myself. But I often wondered what Maggie Hill would have done if the men had tried anything. Would she have tried to stop them, or would she have laughed and encouraged them and felt glad because Mum was beautiful and rich and she was neither? When I pictured her standing in that grubby kitchen, raking at her frizzy yellow hair with a chewed pencil and asking me if I wanted orange squash, I could never decide.

I always wondered what they did with Mum. Was she locked up, or tied up, or what? It was worst when the kidnappers had been arrested and the police were trying to find her. I'd heard about the Lesley Whittle case, how the man who kidnapped her kept her in a drain, and I imagined Mum in a cavern under the ground somewhere, with people walking over the top and not knowing she was there. I used to have this nightmare that it was me in the cavern. I'd scream but nobody came to help me, and the space got smaller and smaller and I'd panic and thrash about, thinking I was suffocating. If we were having a meal, I'd imagine Mum locked in a room somewhere, starving to death. I used to think, if I could just give her this food . . .

At the trial, the kidnappers said they didn't know where Mum was. The prosecution claimed that they'd already killed her, which was what most people thought. Everyone at Camoys Hall thought it, although I never heard them say it in so many words. Except me. I didn't believe it, although when I was about eighteen, I started to think that if she hadn't reappeared after ten years, they must have killed her. It was so much harder without a body or something that showed she was definitely dead. But it wasn't true, was it? Because she was still alive.

I don't remember what happened after Mum refused the tea. I suppose we must just have left. I can't remember Mum giving them her name or telephone number, but she might have done, in case the cat was really hurt. And they must have realised Mum was rich, because she must have seemed so . . . well, so looked-after: her clothes, her hair, everything. Maggie Hill didn't look like that. She looked as if she'd never seen a bottle of hair conditioner in her life. And it wasn't as if Mum drove an old banger, either. She had a sports car, a Mercedes 280SL. It was a pinky-red colour called Russian red, and the seats were cream leather. If there wasn't much traffic about, I'd say to her, 'Go on, go as fast as you can,' and she always would. Once she did a hundred miles an hour down Royal Hospital Road in Chelsea, and she and Irene des Voeux used to have races up the motorway to Camoys Hall, and then they'd go *really* fast. You can't do that now because there are too many other cars, which is a pity. I'd have a go, though. If I had anyone to race with, I'd do it.

The day was too hot for it, but I'd deliberately dressed in a pair of jeans. If I'd come to Camoys Hall wearing jeans when my father was alive, Joan would have whisked me off up the back stairs to get changed 'before Wolfie catches sight of them'. He *hated* women in trousers; even if they were guests. I remember once, when I was about sixteen, Irene des Voeux came down to dinner in the most beautiful Thierry Mugler trouser suit. My father waited until everyone was seated – there must have been eight or ten people there – and then he sat back in his chair and stared at Irene without saying anything. There was this terrible long silence while everyone tried to figure out what was wrong and why they weren't getting any food. It was Joan who finally twigged. She walked round to Irene and whispered to her, and Irene went out and came back with a dress on. I never defied him. I wish I could tell you I'd come down to dinner wearing trousers, but I never did. Because everyone just did what he said. We all tiptoed round him. It was as if he was everywhere. You know how people say that when they were kids they thought that God could see them all the time, even when they were on the loo? Well it wasn't exactly that, but it was close. He just *pervaded* everything.

When I was older – before I stopped coming to Camoys Hall for good, that is – I had a car, and I used to drive up on a Friday night, after college. I was always late because I used to leave it till the last minute. I'd go haring along the motorway to be in time for dinner, and then the last bit was winding country lanes, one car's width and no passing places for miles, and I'd be belting down them, swapping the wheel from hand to hand, changing my clothes as I was going. Word of advice: don't try this with anything you have to pull over your head, especially if you're like me and don't wear a bra, because it scares people, and also because if you had a crash it would be a real bummer and definitely your fault.

I promised myself that I would park my car right outside the front porch. ('I do wish you wouldn't do that, Dodie. For heaven's sake, move that car before Wolfie sees it. You'll have to rake the gravel yourself. All the men have gone home.')

I pulled off the motorway and drove through the lanes past fields full of sheep, and pig housing-estates made of miniature Nissen huts. Camoys village itself is a jumble of jettied medieval cottages with a pub and a war memorial in the centre and a fringe of post-war pebble-dash. The long tree-lined drive up to Camoys Hall was striped with shadows. There were more potholes than I remembered and the house at the end looked vaster than ever. I was planning on accelerating and swerving to a halt smack in front of the doors, but driving into the house's enormous shadow took the wind out of my sails a bit. I stopped the car, got out and looked up at it. The sky was still blue, the sun was shining, but the honey-coloured stone walls looked grey in the shade and all the front windows were shuttered and barred. Paint was peeling from the downstairs window frames and grass was growing between the stone flags of the portico. It wasn't exactly going to rack and ruin, but it looked neglected. Unloved. I wondered how much money my father had left Joan for its upkeep.

She hadn't answered my calls. I didn't want to go in. I looked up at the cold, closed house and thought, I wish Des were here.

5

The front door was locked, so I had to go round the back. So much for the big entrance. The back door on the church side was locked as well, but I've got a key for that. It's in the older part of the house, where the kitchen is. I stood in the passage and shouted, but no one answered. I was trying not to feel angry that Joan hadn't rung to tell me about Mum and that she hadn't been there when I phoned. I mean, where else would she be, for God's sake? She never goes anywhere.

Going into the kitchens at Camoys Hall always used to make me feel like Arietty in *The Borrowers*: you know, titchy, because they are *mammoth*. They're a strange mixture of a National Trust Victorian reconstruction job with dressers and wooden draining boards, and how I imagine one of those places where they used to make up school dinners would look – full of big steel cookers and worktops. But it's not industrial *chic*, more the kind of thing you'd see in a factory in Russia. Half of it probably doesn't work any more because nobody's used it for about ten years. My father stopped entertaining after Virginia left – she was the wife after Mum – and Joan got rid of the kitchen staff after that. She bought a second-hand Baby Belling from someone in the village and did all the cooking herself. The poor little cooker looked sad alongside all the big metal stuff. Joan had left a cup and saucer on the big wooden table in the middle of the room and that was sad, too; to imagine her sitting there having tea all on her own and thinking about my father.

There was one of her lists on the table, tucked underneath the saucer. Joan's lists are famous. She does one every day, and they always start the same way: *Get up, bath, dress . . .* When she's done the thing, she ticks it off. My father used to say that Joan's list was the sum of her consciousness and he hoped he was on there somewhere, which was pretty disingenuous because at least half the entries were things she had to do for him, probably more. And, of course, Angela used to weigh in – any chance to take my father's side against Joan's. She'd say things like, 'Dear Joan, she's one of life's turnip diggers.'

I glanced at the paper on the table: *Book hair 40'c Fri. Ring Mrs Williams. Order flowers. Milk bill. Fruit and Veg. Woolite. Vol-au-vents . . .* Vol-au-vents? There wasn't anything about going out. Or about telephoning me. I shoved the list into my pocket, and I was just going to see if Joan had left anything nice to drink in one of the six fridges in the scullery next door when an enormous man erupted through the door behind me waving a meat cleaver and bellowing, 'Don't fucking move, you bastard!'

I froze. I understand now why rape victims say that they

didn't do anything – you know, scream or try to fight the man off – because I seized up like the Tin Man in *The Wizard of Oz*. I wanted to say, 'Please don't kill me,' or something, but I couldn't get the words out. Suddenly he was a blur, flying through the air towards me. I remember putting my hands up to cover my face, and thinking, Oh shit, and then I thought, I don't want Oh shit to be my last thought on earth, and then there was a tremendous crash and he completely disappeared. I think he must have caught his hip on the table because he shot off to one side and cannoned into the big oven which is built to withstand a nuclear holocaust and runs along one entire wall. The next thing I knew was that he had dropped the cleaver and rugby-tackled my legs, and we were both on the floor with me trying to crawl away from him on my hands and knees and him hanging on to my ankles.

'Stop, I need to talk to you,' he gasped.

I tried to kick him, but it didn't work. I might as well have had a concrete block tied to my feet.

'Let go of me!'

'I only want to talk to you, for God's sake.' He sounded indignant, as if I was the one being unreasonable.

'Just get off me, will you?'

'Dodie, please.'

Dodie? 'How do you know my name?'

His grip slackened enough for me to wrench my legs round and sit up, trying to get my breath back. He was sprawled face down on the floor, less than a foot away from me. He was easily as big as I'd first thought, with curly black hair. He was wearing a white T-shirt and those checked trousers that chefs wear. At least that gave him a reason for carrying a machete-sized meat cleaver in the first place, I thought, idiotically.

He raised his head and groaned. He had dark blue eyes, almost black, which looked more puzzled than mad. 'Christ, that hurt.' He sat up and rubbed his knee.

'I said, how do you know my name?'

'Joan told me. She showed me a picture. I've got to talk to you.'

'Bollocks. How did you get in, anyway?'

'Joan gave me a set of keys. Look, I won't do anything – I'll make you a bacon sandwich.'

'I don't want a bacon sandwich.'

'A cup of tea, then. I'll make you a cup of tea; and you can hold the knife if you want.' He picked it up off the floor and held it out to me. 'OK? I'm giving it to you. You can have it. You can hold it for as long as you want. Just listen to me. Please. For a minute.'

I took the knife. It weighed a ton, and my palms were stinging from where I'd put my hands out to save myself when I fell, but I thought I'd better hold on to it in case he changed his mind.

The man stood up, brushing the dust off his trousers, and looked down at me. 'I really do need to talk to you.'

'What about?'

'Tea first. Promise you won't do a runner?' He went into the scullery to fill the kettle. I suppose I could have tried to get out to the car – I even thought, they're going to ask me in court why I didn't run for it while I had the chance – but I didn't. I just sat there. Partly because I'd believed him when he'd said that Joan had given him the keys, partly because I didn't want to make him angry, and partly because, well, in my mind, I could see myself making a break for the car really clearly, but I couldn't actually get up and do it. Don't ask me why.

'I came back to feed the cat,' he called out conversationally.

'What cat?'

'Shaanti. Grey cat. Orange nose. Don't you remember?'

'I thought it had died.'

Shaanti had been Angela's cat. She found it in a lay-by during the five minutes she was into Indian mysticism, hence the name which is Sanskrit for love or peace or something. Joan used to call it Sea-shanty to annoy her. Joan had a dog, a Jack Russell called Malcolm, who died about a year ago. Typical, I thought, that Angela's cat should still be hanging around like some sort of familiar.

'How do you know her?'

'Joan?' He came back carrying a tray with mugs and glasses and a bottle. 'My mum knew her. We used to live in the village. When I came back to live round here, I came to see her. Because of Mum, really. Then she said, come again, so I did, and that was it.' He sat down beside me on the floor. 'Tea?'

'Thanks.'

'Can I have my knife back?'

'You said I could keep it.'

'You can if you want. I'll need it for tomorrow, though.'

'What for?'

'Work. I work in a restaurant.'

'Was that why you offered me a sandwich?'

'I suppose it was. Stupid really, but it was the first thing that came into my head. Besides, no one ever refuses my bacon sandwiches. Except you, that is.' He poured out two glasses of brandy and held one out to me. 'There you go.'

'I don't really want it.'

'Jesus! Stop saying you don't want things. You've had a shock. Just drink it.'

I put the tea down and had a sip of the brandy, then I put the glass on the floor on the other side of me, where he couldn't see it. He didn't look to see what I was doing, just drank his. He had nice muscles on his arms and chest. Not a washboard stomach, though. Not a pot belly, either, but just slightly round. He was hairy, but not out of control. And he was warm. He wasn't touching me or anything, but I could feel it. He was leaning against the oven with his chequered legs stuck out in front of him. Dirty pink espadrilles. I suddenly wanted him to like me. Nothing unusual about that – I want everyone to like me. Except that this time, the feeling was quite strong. That's what they say about kidnap victims, isn't it? They want to please their captors so they don't kill them or hurt them. I've often wondered if it was like that for Mum with those men. Did she . . . I took a sideways look at the man beside me, then glanced down at the knife on my lap. It suddenly occurred to me that practically everything in a kitchen is lethal: knives, forks, cheese wires, the bloody Baby Belling. I took another sip of the brandy. Stop it, said my brain. Talk to him. Make him like you. *Talk to him.*

'. . . quite bad, and they had to take her to hospital. I was going to see her later.'

'To see Joan?'

'Yes.' He looked at me worriedly. 'Do you understand?'

'I'm sorry. Can you say all that again?'

'She's been taken to hospital. There was a burglar, this morning. She came in and found him. Gave her a shock. She was in a bad way – I mean, she was still talking, just about, but they think she must have had a heart attack.'

Joan. Burglar. Heart attack. Hospital. *Oh God, this isn't fair, it isn't fair . . .*

'They?'

'The ambulance men.'

'But she was OK – when they left, I mean? Did they say how serious it was? Did they think she'd be all right?'

'They said they couldn't be sure. She just needed to get to the hospital.'

'What hospital? Where did they take her?'

'Addenbrooke's. I would have gone with them, but I thought I should see to the window.'

'What window?'

'He broke it getting in. The one in the passage, with the table underneath. I tried to ring you after I'd fixed it, but you must have been on your way here. She didn't know you were coming, did she?'

'No, she didn't. Did you call the police?'

'Don't worry, they've been here.' He was looking at me as if I'd accused him of something. 'They were all set to march me off to the nick, but Joan wouldn't let them.'

I felt I should apologise, so I said, 'It's just as well you were here, otherwise . . .' I levered myself off the floor. 'Look, I ought to go and see her.'

'I'm sorry about just now. The knife and everything. When I saw you, I thought the burglar must have come back.'

'It's OK. Thanks for telling me about Joan, anyway.'

'Are you going to be all right? Do you want me to take you to the hospital?' He was still sitting on the floor and he still looked nice, but what if he was lying and Joan was upstairs all trussed up with a gag on? I kept thinking about that bloody film; the one about not going off with strangers if they turned up at your school and offered you sweets and said your mum was ill and you had to come home with them.

'What's your name?' I asked.

'Henessey, Jimmy Henessey.' He lowered his voice slightly as if he was about to do a Sean-Connery-as-James-Bond impression. I'm sure he was going to, but he stopped himself. I almost laughed.

'What about your work?'

'They'll cope. I was going to go and see Joan as soon as I'd fed the cat.'

'Do you think she needs anything?'

'I've got some flowers. They're in my van. They can be from you, if you like.'

'That's kind of you, but it's OK. I meant more . . . a nightie or something. Perhaps I should go and get some stuff together for her. I won't be a minute.'

He didn't try and stop me when I ran out of the kitchen and up the narrow servants' stairs to Joan's bedroom, which overlooks the churchyard.

It was just the same: rosewood furniture with embroidered runners, old ladies' flowers in crystal vases, a bottle of Croft sherry on a little table by the window, armchairs with antimacassars and Camoys Hall's only TV. A portable black-and-white with a little round aerial. My father hated television, and Mum took her cue from him, but she knew Joan had one. She didn't tell my father about it, but I often wondered if he knew anyway but didn't fly into a rage because it was Joan's. Sometimes, if Mum wasn't around when Joan brought me home from the village school, we used to watch it together.

I kept expecting Joan to walk in. Her drawers were full of beautifully ironed and folded clothes and lavender bags and neat little rolls of underwear. I put one of her nighties into an overnight bag with a pair of tights, in case the hospital let her go. Pretty Polly. I didn't think they still made American Tan.

There was one drawer full of Joan's old lists. Hundreds – thousands, probably – of little pieces of paper covered in neat writing, with all the items ticked off. Everything Joan's ever done in her life must be on those lists. They're a bit like diaries, but with no thoughts or feelings, just things to do. Some of them must be historic, like the Silver Jubilee or the day she married my father. They were married in 1950. She didn't tell me, I read it in his obituary. Of course, I knew they'd been married, it wasn't a secret, but I didn't know when and I've never seen a photo or anything. There was a wife before Joan, a woman called Betty Carroll, who I hadn't known about at all. Mind you, it only lasted about a nanosecond, judging by the dates. Joan never told me about when she was married to my father. Perhaps she thought it wasn't fair because of Mum. People sometimes ask, 'Wasn't it weird, your father's ex-wife and ex-mistress living in the same house as you?' but when you're a child, you just accept things. It took me years – until I left home, really – to realise *quite* how different my life was from other

33

people's. Anyway, my parents would have been lost without Joan. She ran their lives. And mine. I thought, what if she dies? I couldn't imagine Camoys Hall without her. She can't die, I told myself. She's always been here and there are so many questions I want to ask her. And – this is going to sound silly – I thought, Joan loves me. She's never said so, but I know she does. Only Joan. In her dependable, old-fashioned, list-making way.

In the next drawer down, there was a bundle of pencils held together with an elastic band. One of them had a troll pencil-top with purple hair. It must have been mine originally. I suddenly felt a surge of emotion. Not because Joan had kept it because of me – I knew she hadn't. It was just the way she can't bear to waste anything. She saves elastic bands and brown paper bags, neatly folded. Even her lists are economical; when she's done all the things on one day's list, she turns the paper over and uses the other side for the next day. She once told me that it was because she grew up in the war, and she'd never lost the habit of saving things, even when rationing ended and there was plenty of everything.

I didn't cry. I brushed the troll's purple hair under my nose a couple of times so it tickled and put the bundle of pencils back in the drawer. I hardly ever used to cry, because Joan hated it. Mum used to cry sometimes and if Joan saw her, she'd go all panicky and say, 'Now stop it, Susan. Stop it at once!' She didn't know whether to hug Mum or shake her. I think it was partly because she was frightened that my father would find out Mum had been crying, or that Mum would tell him and he'd think that it was Joan's fault. Because there was constant vying for his attention, a sort of competition to be in his good books. They all did it: Joan, Angela, Irene des Voeux when she was here, even Mum, and she was his wife. Like children telling tales on each other. And on me. Especially Angela. She was always trying to buttonhole him for little secret chats, saying she was *so* concerned for my welfare when all she really wanted was to score a few points. Bitch. I got Joan's list from the kitchen table out of my pocket to put into the drawer with the others, but then I thought that she might like to see how far she'd got, so I put it in the overnight bag instead.

When I went back downstairs, Jimmy was waiting for me in the passage. 'We should go. I've got my van outside.'

I didn't know what to do. I mean, I'd sort of agreed that we'd go together, but I didn't know if I wanted to go with him or even if I wanted him to be there at all. I said, 'I think I'd like to go in my car.' At least I could pretend to be in control of things if I was driving my own car.

'Do you want me to come with you?'

'Do you mind?'

'Not at all. Let me get the flowers and I'll be right with you. Where's your car?'

'At the front.'

He opened the back door. It was getting dark, but I could see a battered white Transit van. He said, 'I bet yours is more comfortable. I bought it off my brother a few years back. For work, really. I had bikes before that. Got my first one when I was eighteen. Five hundred cc Norton. I thought I was . . . I don't know . . .'

'Evel Knievel?'

'Yeah, with the leathers and everything. I thought I was really cool, but every time I rode it through the village, the kids used to shout, "Get off and milk it!"' We walked round to the front of the house. 'Is this yours?' he asked as he saw my ancient Volkswagon Polo sitting in the drive.

'You sound surprised.' Even as I was saying it, I knew it wasn't fair. People always expect me to have a gorgeous car and designer clothes and a house to die for and all the rest of it, and they're puzzled that I don't. I felt the familiar wave of irritation at always having to explain everything. 'Jump in. It's open.'

'I thought you'd have something more—' Jimmy

stopped, looked embarrassed and busied himself with his seat belt.

I started the car. 'I can't afford anything better.' That was all the explanation he was going to get – for the time being, at least.

'Sorry, it's none of my business.'

Time to change the subject, I thought. 'Where did you live in the village?'

'Just down the lane from the Curtises.'

'The pig farmer? I know Carol and Jackie.'

'Yeah. Mr Curtis's piglets were always getting out and trashing our garden. My dad used to go berserk.'

Pond Lane. Thick dank hedges and grey box-houses built in the 1950s. We were just passing the end of it.

'Did you actually find Joan?'

'Yes.'

'Was the burglar still there?'

'He'd gone. Or she, I suppose. I had a look round, but there wasn't anyone there.'

'No van or car outside? He'd need something to take away the loot.'

'Depends what he was after. If it was small stuff, jewellery, he could have lost himself in the grounds and then gone over a wall.'

That was true. There's over a hundred acres and, apart from Camoys village, the nearest house is at least five miles away. 'Long walk, though, unless he had someone waiting for him. The buses aren't exactly frequent.'

'They're non-existent now. They cut the service.'

'So he – or she – must have meant to do it.'

Jimmy snorted. 'You mean some burglars do it by accident?'

'I mean, it wasn't an opportunist.'

'Like some villain who happens to be passing by, or a kid who's after car radios so he can go and buy drugs? You've been in London too long. Camoys Hall isn't your average semi. You have to turn off the road and go up half a mile of driveway before you *can* pass by. Anyway, don't they reckon that the people who do the big houses nick to order? Paintings, statues, that sort of stuff.'

'So where was the van? Those are big things. Anyway, the really good stuff was put into storage when my father died. Joan didn't want all the hassle.' *Joan.* 'Did she look really bad?'

'Quite bad.'

'Did he attack her?'

'I don't think he had time. All she said was that she saw someone, and then she felt the pain in her chest. You know she had a minor heart attack some time ago? At least, she made out that it was just a sort of blip – but it sounded like a heart attack to me.'

'I didn't know.'

'Didn't you?' Jimmy sounded surprised. 'Perhaps she didn't want to worry you. She kept saying it was nothing, but she had to spend quite a few days in hospital.'

'She didn't tell me. Not that we had much contact. She just used to write to me sometimes.'

'She was like that, wasn't she? Stiff upper lip. She probably thought it would be making a fuss if she mentioned it.'

'I suppose so.' She hadn't told me. I could feel tears waiting to ambush me, so I changed the subject again. 'Did they look in the grounds?'

'The police? Yeah, a couple of them went out there. I don't think it was much of a search as they only took about ten minutes. They went round the house too. Well, the back part. You know she keeps the front part locked, the connecting doors?'

No, I didn't. Great, I thought. Another person who knows more about my life than I do. My house, anyway. My hou— It really would be mine, if anything happened to Joan. Oh God, *please* let her be all right.

'They wanted to have a look, but I told them she never goes in there, it's always locked. Anyway, I don't know where she keeps the keys and they'd taken her off to hospital by then. She's probably got them with her.'

'What about fingerprints?'

'They wanted to come back to do those. They told me to ring to arrange a time, but now you're here . . .' He shrugged. 'They said they'd get a description off Joan once the hospital's sorted her out. But I wouldn't get your hopes up. There's not much the police can do. They said they didn't think anything was nicked. Joan probably disturbed the burglar when he was getting in through the window. That's where I found her, lying on the floor in the passage.'

'She was conscious, wasn't she? Properly conscious?'

'She seemed to be. I mean, she was coherent. Her chest was hurting. She'd bashed her leg and it was bleeding, and I think she was more upset about that than the chest thing. And she was flustered because of all the people, her hair was in a mess and her skirt was rucked up and she didn't want the ambulance men to see her like that. While we were waiting for them, she made me get her handbag so she could powder her nose.'

'Are you sure he didn't hit her?'

'Not absolutely positive, but I got the impression she saw him come through the window, then she felt the pain, and the next thing she knew she was on the floor. That's what the police thought, that she'd frightened him off. They said if it was a professional burglar, they don't want to hurt anyone because then they'll do less time if they're caught. Otherwise they can charge them with manslaughter, especially if they're carrying a knife or something.'

'You know you said you thought I was the burglar?'

'Yeah?'

'Well, how did you know it was me? Did Joan really show you photographs?'

'One or two. And you look like your mother.'

'In my dreams.' I could feel him looking at me. Good job it was dark.

'Nothing was messed up, and nothing missing – not as far as I could tell, anyway. I was burgled once. I was living with someone, and we came home from work and found the place had been turned upside down. My girlfriend's underwear was all over the floor.'

'Was it a pervert or something?'

'The police said they were looking for money and passports and stuff. Lisa thought *they* were the perverts. They certainly had a great time perving through her knickers. She was furious.'

'So what happened?'

'Nothing. We never heard from them again.'

'What did he take?'

'Not a lot. Nothing worth taking, really. Weren't you supposed to turn right back there?'

By the time we got up to the ward, Joan was dead. I realised later that it must have happened while we were in the hospital reception, watching a friendly but totally incompetent clerk failing to access her details on the computer. He kept telling us she hadn't been admitted, and we kept insisting she had, and by the time he'd located her – and explained about a hundred times why it wasn't his fault – and we'd finally managed to get there, she'd had another heart attack, and this time it was fatal.

6

I lifted my head off the floor and thought, where am I? Joan's sitting room came into focus. Sleeping bags on the floor. Unzipped. Sheet, blanket. Head on a cushion. Stupid, really. This house has enough beds – more beds than you can shake a stick at, Des would say. I remembered telling Jimmy that I didn't want to sleep in any bed in this house.

He'd been with me. He'd driven us back in my car. He'd come in . . . There was an empty brandy bottle on the mantelpiece. Hang on, I thought, how come I can see? I winked. First one eye, then the other. Still wearing my contact lenses. One, anyway. Now you see it, now you don't. And even when you do see it, it's blurred round the edges. Must have finished the brandy. Don't feel too bad, considering. Probably not been awake long enough to get the full effect. Jimmy must have gone. I bet he's one of those people who never get hangovers.

I looked around a bit more. Ashtray? OK, he smokes roll-ups. Clock: 8.20. Not bad. We must have got back here about eleven and sat up talking. Then he got out all the bedding. I remembered thinking it was a good job he was here because I wouldn't have known where it was kept. I must have gone to sleep after that. Jeans folded over the arm of a chair. They're mine. Must have taken them off at some point, and my socks . . . *and my knickers.* Oh no, that did not happen, I told myself. It *can't* have done. I mean, I hadn't taken a sleeping pill or anything, so I'd have woken up, wouldn't I? The brandy, though. We had drunk quite a lot . . . I couldn't see any evidence. There was nothing on me or the sleeping bag. No condoms or suspicious-looking wodges of tissue lying about either. He might have taken it with him, I suppose. I don't remember him kissing me, but then he wouldn't have needed to, would he? Not if I was out of it. I stared at the ceiling for a bit, hoping it would all go away, imagining the feature in *Cosmo*.

Are You An Old Slapper? Find Out With Our Multiple Choice Quiz.
You hope for great things when Mr Wonderful comes back to your place but overdo the brandy and crash out

on the sofa. When you wake up, he's gone. Now you want to know what, if anything, happened. Do you:

a) Assume yes and think, 'Wow! I scored.'
b) Sue him because he failed to give you the three multiple orgasms that are the minimum post-feminist requirement.
c) E-mail him immediately to find out?

Answer: It doesn't matter whether you chose a), b) or c). You are still an old slapper and your chances of forming a meaningful and lasting relationship with a man are NIL.

I hadn't even got his phone number, never mind his e-mail. I thought, he'll probably never speak to me again. That's what comes of trying to kid myself for one tiny second that any man could possibly be attracted to me for anything other than being Wolf Blackstock's daughter. Had 'er once, she was rubbish. Why do I expect anything else? It's always been like that, ever since the first time when I went to a hotel with a man called Andrew Collins. It was by the sea somewhere, near Chichester. I was supposed to be spending the weekend at home, revising for A-levels, but I'd told Joan that I needed to work in the school library. I'd met this man at some wedding and agreed to go away with him for the weekend. God knows why. I'd only talked to him for about ten minutes and I didn't even fancy him much. To get at my father, I suppose, although I was terrified he'd find out. I think it was really because I just wanted to do something for myself for once.

Anyway, it was a disaster. Andrew Collins was flash on the surface, like an under-engineered sports car, and older than me – thirty perhaps, thirty-five? He might as well have been a hundred, I felt so young and stupid. He talked about his work. He was a stockbroker. I couldn't think of anything to say. It was three weeks before my A-levels and all I could think about were my set texts and what would happen if anyone found out where I'd been. The hotel was one of those large Victorian family houses with flat-roofed bits added on that look like public loos. We ate in the dining room next to a table full of pissed middle management and their secretaries. They kept repeating 'two smart fellows, they felt smart' over and over again, except they'd get it wrong and it would come out as 'two smart fellows, they smelt farts' which was the idea, of course. Every time it happened, all the women had hysterics. The waiters kept trying to make them keep quiet, but they were too drunk to take any notice. Andrew and I had managed to race through every possible topic of conversation within about three minutes of sitting down, so by the time they were in full swing we didn't stand a chance. It wouldn't have been so bad if we could have caught each other's eye and laughed about it, but we couldn't. I could see that Andrew was trying to come across as Mr Suave Ladies' Man who'd done this a thousand times but actually he wasn't and hadn't – he'd never have chosen a hotel like that one if he had – and I didn't know what to do. I couldn't even say anything nice about the food and wine, because he must have known they were disgusting, and I felt so self-conscious about eating that I could hardly swallow anything. We skipped the pudding and coffee by unspoken consent and went up to our room. I made us coffee out of little packets of things and took my cup over to the window to avoid sitting on the bed. The room overlooked the car park, and just as Andrew came up behind me and put his arm around my waist, one of the secretaries from the works outing tottered across the tarmac and threw up into a bush.

I was a virgin, surprise, surprise. We got undressed – well, I got into bed partially clothed and wriggled around taking bits off and throwing them out so Andrew wouldn't be able to see what I looked like – and then I just lay there and waited for it to happen. I didn't want to touch him, and I didn't really want him to touch me, but I thought, at least

I'll have done it. I'll know what it's like. He was quite enthusiastic at first, and with the lights out and everything, I even thought for a moment that I might be enjoying it, but then I just sort of clammed up. Andrew was nice about it at first, but then, when he saw he wasn't going to get anywhere, he got angry. 'What's the matter with you?' he kept saying. At first I tried to answer, then I stopped trying because I was asking myself the same question.

Andrew had another go, but after a while he gave up and we lay in silence, side by side. The hotel must have shared its car park with the rugby club next door, because about an hour later people emerged and staggered around outside our window, singing, 'Balls to your partner, arse against the wall. If you don't get fucked on a Saturday night, you'll never get fucked at all.' I don't know if Andrew was still awake, but I remember lying there and thinking, that's me all right.

I never told anyone. Instead, I simply got on with my A-levels and erased the whole thing from my mind. But it happened over and over again – not the physical thing, but the feeling that men saw me as some sort of *passport*. Even if they didn't know who I was at the beginning, they always found out. Even when I explained that I didn't have that sort of lifestyle, it never did any good.

I groaned. Why did it always have to be so bloody difficult? Yes, all right, I wanted Jimmy to like me. Was that really so much to ask? I took off my T-shirt and bra and stood on one of the armchairs to see my reflection in the mirror over the mantelpiece. Well, part of it, anyway. The mid-section. Honestly, it's not surprising I'm a sexual disaster area. How does anyone manage to be thin *and* flabby at the same time? My skin's dead white, my stomach sticks out and my breasts are minute. Gnat bites. There used to be this old man in the village, Albert. I should think he's probably dead by now, but he used to be the Curtises' pig man. He stank, he had ramshackle brown teeth and

43

threadbare corduroys tied up with orange string, and he was always sidling up to young girls and trying to feel their tits. People in the village would say, 'Dirty old devil,' but nobody really minded, because he was pretty harmless. When I was fifteen, he did it to me. It was a rite of passage having your tits squeezed by Albert, but I was so stunned that I just stood there and let him stick his hand inside my T-shirt. After a moment, he said, 'Very nice, dear,' and took his hand out. I knew he was just being kind. He never tried it again. I couldn't really blame him; Mr Curtis's daughters, Jackie and Carol, could have given Samantha Fox a run for her money.

I stood on the arm of the chair to see my legs and cheer myself up a bit. Thin thighs. At least I got something right. And – bummer – the most enormous bruise, which I must have got from fighting with Jimmy. Then I noticed a piece of paper tucked behind the mirror. A note! I nearly broke my ankle jumping off the armchair.

Hope I didn't wake you. I'll come back this afternoon to see how you're doing. If you want to get in touch, my mobile number is 0140 9770398. Jimmy.
PS I'll bring some more brandy. You've run out.
PPS Nothing happened.

Isn't it stupid how, when people are kind to you, it makes you cry? I read Jimmy's note and immediately burst into tears. Not about what he'd written, but about everything – Joan, Mum, my eight-year-old self. For a second, I raised my head and caught a glimpse of my face in the mirror, two red eyes in troughs of wet mascara.

Joan would be disgusted, I thought. When they'd finally let me see her, I'd put her last list into her hand. It seemed so unfair that she couldn't finish doing all the things and tick them off.

A tidal wave of grief, sorrow and loneliness overwhelmed

44

me. Naked, clutching the drenched scrap of paper, I curled up on the rug and sobbed.

7

It was a shock seeing Joan's handbag on the kitchen table, as if she was going to bustle through from the scullery any minute, and put on her coat and scarf. But it was me who'd put the bag there, not Joan. I sat with it on my lap for a while. In the space of twenty-four hours, my entire world had disintegrated. I couldn't even kid myself about keeping my job. That was out of the question, because the money would be mine now: the Blackstock fortune – the money, the shares, the property – and with it, the responsibility. My father left everything in trust to Joan, to come to me on her death. 'Why did you have to die, Joan?' I asked out loud. 'Why *now*, for God's sake?'

The phone rang in Joan's sitting room. I thought it would be for her, but it was the doctor from the hospital to say that he had to tell the coroner about Miss Draycott, and did I know if she had expressed a preference for burial or cremation? I told him she was going in our churchyard, next to my father. My mother could go on the other side if they ever let me have her back. When Angela died, my father wouldn't let her be buried in the churchyard. When I asked Joan why, she said it was because Angela was Jewish, which I hadn't known. The doctor said that the funeral parlour couldn't take Joan's body in case the coroner wanted a post-mortem done, but that somebody would let me know what was happening.

I phoned the vicar and he said he'd see about the service. He told me the church at Camoys Hall hadn't been used for ages and volunteered his crack cleaning squad of ninety-year-old ladies. I'll have to hire professional cleaners, I thought. The vicar's lot would probably break themselves in half falling off ladders and then their families would sue me until the end of time. I'd have to find the key to the church first, though. I must get organised, I thought. What I need to do, in fact, is make a list.

Whenever Des saw Joan with a list in her hand, he used to sing, 'She's got a little list, she's got a little list,' like the Lord High Executioner's chorus in *The Mikado*. Then he'd say, 'Who's for the chop today, Joanie?' and she'd laugh and tell him not to be so silly. Joan and Des were friends from way back when she was married to my father. She used to fuss over Des and boss him and scold him and laugh even when he made terrible puns and corny jokes that she'd heard six million times before. Oh, God, I thought, *Des*. I should have told him last night.

It took about five goes to dial his number because I kept starting and not finishing and getting up and walking about and fiddling with things. I kept telling myself, the worst he can do is tell me to get lost, but it wasn't much help. I haven't actually seen Des since my father's funeral, and I didn't talk to him for more than a minute then because I left straight after the service. It was seeing Virginia that really did it. My father married her in 1980 and they separated about five years before he died, by which time she'd developed galloping anorexia. She turned up at his funeral looking like a skeleton wrapped in flesh-coloured clingfilm. The man she came with had to carry her into the church. I looked at her and thought, my father did that, and now everyone's going to spend the next three hours thanking God for the gift of his life and saying how great he was. I wanted to throw up.

I listened to the phone ring and prayed that Des would be in because I didn't think I'd ever get up the courage to try again. Then he answered.

'Des? It's Dorothy,' I said.

'Dodie!' He sounded really pleased. 'How are you? Wait a minute, let me get hold of a chair. The old legs aren't what they used to be.' He put the phone down.

I could imagine him in his pinstriped suit, dragging a chair across the carpet. I've known Des since I was a baby, and I've never seen him wearing anything but a suit. He probably sleeps in one. His shirts are always starched and white, and his hair and nails perfectly groomed, but the thing you really notice is his face. It's so asymmetrical it's almost Cubist. Even his eyebrows are lopsided – one curves upwards and the other downwards – his nose slaloms down the middle and his bottom teeth are crammed in any old how. I'm making him sound like Frankenstein's monster, but he isn't. He's got the kindest eyes of anyone I've ever met, and the sweetest smile.

It suddenly struck me how stupid it was that Des had got caught up in the anger I felt for my father. When I discovered about the secret payments to my account and wrote him a letter, he sent Des round to see me, so I had the row with him instead, which was stupid, because it wasn't his fault. And, of course, it didn't make any difference, because my father carried on sending me the money every month. But the anger I'd felt had obliterated all my good memories of Des, and I'd completely lost sight of how nice he is. I tried to work out how I was going to tell him about Joan and Mum. I felt as if I'd swallowed my tongue.

'Now I'm sitting comfortably, you may begin.'

'Oh, Des—' I started to cry again. Damn and blast and shit.

'Dodie? What's wrong, my old love?'

'I just—' I couldn't get the words out.

'Steady on, there's plenty of time. Have you got a handkerchief?'

'Tissue.'

'Good. Blow your nose. Go on, big blow. Now, tell me what's up.'

'Joan's dead,' I blurted. So much for breaking it gently. Des didn't say anything. 'She had a heart attack.'

There was another silence, and then he said, 'Oh dear.'

'There was a burglar, and he scared her, and she had a heart attack and they took her to hospital, and then she had another one and I wasn't in time. I didn't get there in time to see her before she died. I . . . Sorry, I can't help it . . . She was all on her own. She . . . I . . .' I was sobbing so much I could scarcely breathe, never mind speak. It felt as if I'd never be able to stop. The tissue was a sodden ball in my hand.

'Oh dear.'

'Des . . . I'm sorry . . . but there's something else as well.'

'Go on.'

'It's about Mum. The police, they found this body, and it had stuff with her name on, a notebook or something, and they asked me to identify it – the body. I didn't know if it was her or not, but I thought it was because the eyes looked right, she had that spot in her eye, and I spoke to the man in charge and he showed me—'

'Whoa! Slow down. Us golden oldies aren't as quick on the uptake as you young 'uns, you know. Are you saying that the police have found Susan's body?'

'Yes.'

'What was that you said about the eyes . . . a spot in the eyes?'

'Her birthmark, she had a mark—'

'I'm sorry, Dodie. I don't quite understand. You're saying that the body they found was . . . *fresh*?'

'Yes. She died a couple of days ago.'

'But surely . . . Where did they find her?'

'East London. Some builders found her when they were demolishing blocks of flats.'

'So when did the police get in touch with you?'

'Saturday. Then I went up to see Joan, and that's when

I found out about the burglar and the heart attack and everything.'

'I see.'

'And now there'll be the newspapers, and the journalists, and they'll all want to know things, and there's nothing I can tell them because I don't know anything! And nobody's going to believe me because the minute anyone is rich or famous or has a title or something, then it's all got to be a big conspiracy and everyone's got to be hiding something and it's in the public interest to know. They're never going to leave me in peace and I'll have to give up my job and there's all the stuff with the money and I'm all on my own and—' I sort of broke up after that.

Des didn't say much except 'Steady the Buffs' for the next few minutes, while I fished around for more tissues and tried to stop heaving. Then he asked, 'Where are you?'

'Camoys Hall.'

'You'll need to see Benny at some point – the sooner the better. Shall I fix something up?' Benny is Mr Bennington, our solicitor.

'Will you come with me?'

'If you want me to. I'll arrange it and we can have dinner afterwards. If you'd like, that is.'

'That's fine. If you don't mind.'

'Of course I don't mind. To be honest, Dodie, I'm just grateful that you still want to talk to me.'

I thought I'd better find Joan's address book before I did anything else as there were dozens of people I needed to ring. I ought to go home, I told myself, and get some clothes before Des and I go to see Benny. And my fax machine. And I might as well bring my television as well. I didn't have anything at Camoys Hall. The minute I'd stopped living there, Joan had turned my old room over to storage. Not that I'd have wanted to sleep in there, anyway. I decided to pick one of the big rooms where nobody had ever slept before and see if I could get hold of a double bed to put in it.

I went up to Joan's bedroom with an idea that I ought to sort out some clothes for her, but I just wandered around looking at things instead. I didn't know what her favourite clothes were any more. She used to wear things that weren't even fashionable in the seventies: labels like Jacqmar and Windsmoor, scarves with swirly patterns and suits from displays with names like 'The Peach Story'. They either came from Barkers in London – Angela always called it the poor man's Harrods to annoy her – or Pearson & Sheldrake's in Cambridge. Her most recent stuff came from M&S because Pearson & Sheldrake's closed down five years ago. I used to love going to that shop with her. They had a massive rocking horse in the children's clothes department and you could have smorgasbord for lunch from the cold table. I was really disappointed the first time I had real smorgasbord, because it was nothing like Pearson & Sheldrake's at all.

I opened the cupboard where Joan kept what she called her woollies and wondered if people ever get buried in hairy cardigans. It would have to be a new one, of course, not one of the ones she'd kept forever and darned massively on the elbows. One of her running battles with Angela was about heating. In the winter, Joan used to stump about in heavy tweeds and thick woolly tights while Angela wore long cotton ethnic things and complained about being cold. Angela would say to Joan, 'I don't know how you can *think*, all bundled up like that. I couldn't bear it,' and, 'No wonder you're so repressed, Joan. All those layers of clothes you insist on wearing.' But the real reason Angela wouldn't wear tights and things was that she wanted to show off her tan. She was always managing to pop her legs out of the slits in her flappy robes and jiggle them up and down under people's noses until they made comments about how brown she was. 'I'm a Leo. Child of the sun. I simply can't live without it. Wolfgang's always saying it's a shame we can't go and live abroad somewhere, but of course he has so many *obligations.*' She persuaded my father to buy her a home sunbed, and she used to grill herself under it for hours. Her face looked like a saddle by the end.

While I was looking for Joan's address book, I found a box of Lindt chocolate kittens. Joan always used to bring me up here and feed me one if my father had shouted at me. That's probably why I still get spots – all those hundreds of chocolate kittens working their way out of my system. She did it because she didn't want me to cry. I bit the head off one. It had a bow round its fat little chocolate neck. It was a bit stale, but the taste of chocolate and salty tears mixed together was appallingly familiar.

I found one of my fantasy menus stuck to the bottom of the chocolate box. Written in purple felt-tip so old it was almost invisible, it said: *Fish fings, backed baes, potted paes.* It wasn't dated, but I knew I must have written it during the summer before Mum was kidnapped, when she suddenly went funny about food and insisted on having a private kitchen where she could make things just for the two of us. It was one of the few times I remember Mum being really definite about something. She didn't usually have opinions about things, she just agreed with other people, especially if it was Joan or my father. But with the food thing, it was as if she suddenly knew her own mind. Except that she didn't, because she was having a nervous breakdown, something my father kept so quiet that even the eagle-eyed researchers from the hatchet-job TV programme couldn't spot it.

I remember Joan being against the kitchen idea. 'Wolfie, she's not herself. Besides, I doubt if she's ever cooked a meal in her life!' But my father wouldn't listen. He agreed to it like a shot. I suppose he thought it would help to isolate Mum and prevent whatever barminess she had from spreading to him; so he had a special kitchen built for her upstairs. The thing was, Mum had decided somewhere along the line that some foods were pure and good for you and some weren't, and that the impure ones had to be eradicated from our diet at all costs. I remember her sitting at the kitchen table with no make-up and chipped pink nail varnish like someone's fantasy of a schoolgirl, chewing the end of her biro and running her hands through her beautiful hair as she trawled through Joan's recipe books and crossed out all the stuff that she thought was bad for you: meat, fish, lard, salt, sugar, white flour – practically everything you can think of, in fact. If the recipe was for something really evil like toad-in-the-hole or steak and kidney pie, she'd scribble over it until the page looked like a black cartoon cloud.

The first time she announced that she was going to cook something, I was fascinated. I spent the whole morning peering round the kitchen door. 'Can I come in? Can I come in now? When will it be ready?'

'Not now, Dorothy. I'm busy.'

All she seemed to be doing was sitting at the table scribbling over things in one of the cookery books. When I eventually managed to catch her stirring something in a saucepan, I was so excited I nearly screamed. This was what other mothers did. They wore aprons and they cooked things in small kitchens! It was the photograph on the front cover of Joan's *Marguerite Patten Family Cookbook*, with the smiling glaze-haired mother in her twinset doling out bright yellow custard to her family over a blue Formica table. That was what life was supposed to be like. When I saw my mother bending over the cooker, I suddenly thought, we're going to be like other people. I didn't know how it would happen – just that all the arguments, the sycophancy, the secret agendas, the constant whispering, the eruptions of shouting and screaming, the sulks and the crying in locked rooms would all just disappear and my mother and I would somehow merge into the picture on the *Marguerite Patten Family Cookbook* and be happy for ever.

This marvellous state of euphoria lasted till lunchtime, when the two of us sat down at the kitchen table. Mum made a trumpet noise, 'Ta-daa! Here we are!' and proudly lifted the lid of the tureen. And there it was: sprigs of watercress floating in warm water.

'What is it?' I asked.

'Watercress soup.'

'It doesn't look like it.'

'Come on, pass your bowl.'

'Mum, this isn't watercress soup.'

'Yes, it is.'

'Was the recipe from here?' I picked up the book and looked at the list of ingredients. *1 large or 2 small bunches of watercress*. Through a dense cloud of blue biro scribble, I could read: *1lb potatoes, peeled and diced, 2½ pints chicken stock, 1 small onion, butter, salt, grated nutmeg, pepper, 2–3 tablespoons cream*. On the opposite page was a photograph of a blue and white striped dish of thick green liquid. 'This is what it's supposed to look like. You didn't put all the stuff in, did you?'

Mum turned the book towards her. 'I couldn't put all that in. It says chicken stock! Ugh! I'm not putting chicken stock in food.'

'But what's wrong with potatoes?'

'Far too coarse. That's what animals eat, potatoes.'

'Cream?'

'You can't mix cream with watercress.'

'Salt?'

'Salt's bad for you. But I did put in some pepper.'

'Oh well, that's all right then, isn't it?'

'Don't talk to me like that, Dorothy. I'm sure it'll be fine. Now, let me give you some before it gets cold.'

When I told Joan about the soup thing, she said, 'That can't have happened, dear,' but a couple of weeks later she went into Mum's kitchen to look for something and discovered her cheese-making experiment lined up on the window sill: ten bottles of milk in various stages of decomposition. If she caught it in time, Mum would sieve the separated milk through muslin to produce a quivery blue-white curd cheese which made me feel sick just looking at it. The rest of the bottles she left. Standing in the sun day after day, their contents went first yellow, then green, and finally, black.

Joan also discovered the weevils in the pantry and the rock-hard end of a coarse-grained grey loaf in the bread bin. Then she took me for a walk in the garden and asked me what I'd been eating for the past three months. Shock, horror. 'But you must have *protein*! I thought you'd been looking a bit peaky. How are you supposed to grow properly if you don't have meat?' This was music to my ears, of course, and it was how the fantasy menus got started. We had a special arrangement. Every morning, I was to write what I'd like for lunch on a piece of paper and stick it under Joan's door. After I'd picked my way through lunch with Mum, I trotted along the corridor to Joan's room and had a delicious second lunch, cooked by Joan according to my specifications. *Fish fings, backed baes, potted paes.* God, my spelling. *Backed baes* must be baked beans. I wondered what Joan made of *potted paes.* Peas from a tin, I suppose. I'd only ever eaten *fish fings* a couple of times at the Curtises', but they were my idea of heaven, and I suppose I thought *backed baes* and *potted paes* were what you had with them. To be honest, I'm not sure that the *fish fings* and *backed baes* did me any more good than Mum's watercress soup, but they tasted about five hundred times better. And there was Angel Delight from the village shop. Joan and I had a code name for Angel Delight. We called it 'holy pins', because I'd read somewhere about angels on a pinhead. In the end, it became a sort of all-purpose exclamation. Whenever Angela was going on about her latest spiritual fad, we'd say 'Holy pins!' to each other and roll our eyes. Angela always pretended not to notice, but it used to drive her up the wall.

*

A pessimistic fingerprint man came and dusted things in the passageway, and Jimmy and the glazier arrived together about half an hour later. The glazier did his stuff and I made tea for all of us; and then Jimmy and I went on a tour of the front of the house. I had the key from Joan's bag, but I'd been saving it till Jimmy came because I didn't want to go in there by myself. I didn't tell him that, though.

As I opened the connecting door, he said, 'I've never been through here. I don't think Joan had it open much.'

'No reason to, really. Her room's in the back bit and she didn't do any grand entertaining like my father.' I opened the door to the dining room. 'He used to have banquets in here.' The shutters were closed, and only a few slivers of sunlight shone across the vast acreage of dark glossy wooden table.

'You could seat fifty people round this, easy.' I couldn't see Jimmy's expression too well in the half-light, but he sounded impressed.

'Which restaurant do you work at?'

'The Artichoke.'

'That's a really good one!' I'd been there a couple of times with Des.

'You sound surprised.'

'I didn't mean to. Sorry. But it's a brilliant place.'

'Yeah, it's not bad. I'd like one of my own, though.'

Oh, great, I thought. He thinks I'm going to buy him a restaurant; that's why he's being so nice. It's probably why he was cosying up to Joan too, only now she's not here he's doing it to me.

'A couple more years and I can go it on my own. What's through here?'

'The billiard room. It shouldn't be locked.'

Perhaps he wasn't dropping hints, after all. If my friend Tony Hepworth, whose ex-boyfriend sold all his sex secrets to the *Sun* last year, thinks I'm paranoid, then maybe I really am. Tony's the heir to the Manifold car parts empire. He'd rung me up the week before to tell me he'd lost his licence, which is quite funny when you think about it. But Des did warn me about freeloaders years ago. He told me about one of the old ACME business codes for telegrams, ARPUK, which means, This person is an adventurer, have nothing to do with him. He said, 'You'll meet a lot of adventurers, Dodie, when you grow up.'

We went through the billiard room and into the hall. All the furniture was draped in dust sheets.

'Can we open the shutters?' Jimmy asked.

'If you like. We'll have to close them afterwards, though.'

'Seems a shame to keep it all shut up like this.'

'It's because the light fades the colours but a few minutes shouldn't hurt.'

The shutters were padlocked, and I couldn't find the right key. Jimmy came up behind me. 'Want some help?'

I handed over the bunch of keys. 'I don't know what half of these are.' God, he was so *warm*. I could feel it. He was wearing the chef's trousers again, with one of those trendy V-necked T-shirts in two colours. You always see them on skinny *Trainspotting* types, and he was really too muscular to wear it, but it looked great.

Jimmy drew back the shutters.

I have to say, the hall did look pretty impressive, in spite of the dust sheets. There's a huge expanse of marble floor and three beautiful marble pillars at each end, and pale yellow walls with white-painted half-circular niches for statues.

'It's like an ice palace or something. It should be full of people waltzing in great big Scarlett O'Hara dresses,' he said.

'Do you want to?' I hadn't meant to say that. It just came out.

'What?'

'Waltz.'

'I don't know how.'

'I do. Well, I didn't get as far as turns, but I know how to waltz in straight lines. We'll have to start in a corner, that's all. Come over here.' We got to the corner and then I remembered. 'Except it's no good, because I'll have to be the man, otherwise it won't work.'

Jimmy shrugged. 'I don't mind.'

'OK. Now, put one arm on my waist, here, and one on my shoulder, and I do the same. Now, everything I do, you do, except backwards. OK?'

'Sounds difficult.'

'No, it's not, honestly. It's much easier being the girl. Now, I'm going to move my leg literally into your leg, and you have to move yours – no, same leg, this one – backwards in order to avoid being trodden on.'

'I bet that's not how your dancing teacher explained it.'

'No, but she was an old bat and this makes more sense. Come on. ONE, TWO, THREE, one two three, one two three . . .'

It worked really well so we did it again, and then we tried it with Jimmy being the man which was fine, except that he kept trying to step round my feet instead of towards them. Then we stopped dancing and stood in the corner for a second with our hands still in position and he gave me a little hug, but he didn't try to kiss me or anything. I suddenly thought, dancing is like a prelude to sex, so now he probably thinks I'm one of those women who barks out orders all the time when they're in bed.

'Do you want to see upstairs?'

'Can I?'

'Why not? Let's go up the front stairs.' I opened the double doors to the staircase, which has a separate hall of its own. It's smaller than the front hall, but still pretty massive.

Jimmy looked at the portraits of bovine Georgians dotted round the walls. 'Are these all your ancestors?'

'They're someone's ancestors. I don't know whose. They

came with the house. My father bought it in the sixties. That one's my ancestor though – him at the top.' As you walk round the curve of the stairwell there's this very distinguished painting of a man in army uniform eyeballing you from across the landing. 'That's my Uncle Lawrence. It's by Graham Sutherland.'

'What was he, a field marshal or something? He's got enough medals.'

'I don't think he was that high ranking. The medals are for spying and stuff. You know, behind enemy lines. Service to your country or whatever.'

'Good for him. I used to love all those comics – Take that Fritz, *Gott im Himmel, Hande hoch, aiiee, banzai*, ur-ur-ur-u-ur.' Jimmy leant on the banisters and machine-gunned the portraits. 'I think I must have been about eight when I finally realised that the war wasn't actually going on any more. I was really disappointed.'

'It's funny they still had all that when we were growing up. How old are you, Jimmy?'

'Thirty-four. Thirty-five, nearly.'

'Wow, old. I'm twenty-nine. I had a little farm, you know, a plastic one, with cows and tractors and things. It had a land girl. That's what it said on the label in the shop, "land girl". I had to ask Joan what one was.' I looked up at Uncle Lawrence. 'His real name was Ludwig. After Beethoven.'

'No wonder he changed it to Lawrence.'

'Yeah. My father just shortened his to Wolf. From Wolfgang. Wolfgang Amadeus Blackstock. I didn't know about the Amadeus bit till I read his obituary.'

'Did your grandparents like German music, by any chance?'

'I suppose they must have. My grandmother was half-German, but my grandfather was English. They both died before I was born and I don't know much about them. I think she was probably quite domineering. I don't think my father had a very happy childhood.' I threw open the double doors to the ballroom.

Jimmy took a step backwards. 'God, it's massive!'

It was nicer than I remembered, although the enormous chandelier was furry with dust and there was soot-fall in front of both the giant marble fireplaces. The furniture that remained was sheeted, which was no end of an improvement. The ballroom has a row of windows that look out across the front lawn with an enormous central window in a pillared recess. I always used to imagine the slightly scratched soldier and his lady from the Quality Street tin where Joan kept her hairpins whirling across the floor to stand there, face to face in the moonlight, as the music came to an end.

I went across to the recess and dragged the dust sheet off the overblown brocade sofa. 'Let's sit this one out, shall we?'

'OK.' Jimmy plonked himself down beside me. 'What was he like, your father?'

'Oh . . . Forceful, good businessman, very sharp mind. He didn't inherit his money. He made it all himself – property, mainly. Cheap housing on bomb sites after the war, office blocks in central London, chunks of the City and West End, that sort of thing. He wasn't all sweetness and light – he had a hand in pulling down the Euston Railway Arch and the Coal Exchange and probably quite a few other bits of architectural heritage as well – but he wasn't a crook. You could say he was three parts mighty tycoon to one part Wizard of Oz.'

'What do you mean?'

'Just that. I think he was a bit of a charlatan in some ways. Remember the bit in the film where Toto gets behind the curtain and you see this little chap pulling strings like a Punch and Judy man? Well, I sometimes used to think, if I could get behind *his* curtain, then I'd find out who he really was. But it wasn't a curtain he had, it was more like the Great Wall of China, and I didn't know how to . . . you know, how to navigate it.' Whoops, I thought, now I've gone right off *piste* and he doesn't have a clue what I'm talking about. 'With your father, was it like that for you?'

Jimmy looked surprised. 'Not really. He was just a good bloke, my dad. After he died, I wished I'd asked him what it was like growing up during the war and doing National Service, but I didn't want to . . . pry . . . you know? We didn't talk about anything much, but we got on. And he was sensible about things. When I said I wanted to work in a restaurant, my brothers were saying what a poncey thing to do, and I thought Dad was going to hit the roof, but he didn't. He thought for a bit and then he said that all the famous chefs were men, and if that was what I wanted, I should go for it.'

'Did you ever cook for him?'

'Sometimes. Had to be simple, though. He was a meat and potatoes man. But even if he didn't like it, he'd finish it, and I always knew if he'd really liked it because he'd ask if there was any more.' He looked down at the bunch of keys in his hand and fiddled with them a bit. Then he said, 'My dad . . . If he hadn't been my dad, I mean, if I'd just met him in a pub or somewhere, I'd have liked him anyway.'

'That's a really nice thing to say. I wish I could say that about mine.'

'It's different,' Jimmy said. 'Yours was much older, wasn't he? That must have made it more difficult. And they didn't make a *Public Image* programme about my father.' He fiddled with the bunch of keys a bit more. 'Was it right, what they said in that programme?'

'Some of it.' They'd asked me if I wanted to be interviewed for it. 'A chance to put your side of the story,' they'd said, but I'd refused. For myself, not because I wanted them to trash his reputation. I didn't want everyone knowing who I was, and I didn't want to risk getting upset and making a fool of myself on camera. When I watched the programme, I didn't regret my decision. In any case, the problem with these things is that the people with the real dirt never spill. Joan and Des could both have said a few things if they'd wanted to, but they weren't on it either. Irene des Voeux was, though. 'Wolfgang and I had a very special relationship.' She made it sound like Ronald Reagan and Margaret Thatcher, but it wasn't special enough for her to become the fourth Mrs Blackstock. That prize went to a Grace Kelly lookalike called Virginia French who was ten years younger than she was. I thought, I'll bet my father got a real kick out of telling Irene that he was marrying Virginia. Treating her like he'd treated Angela over Mum, leading her on and then, wham! But Irene did say on that programme that he'd asked her to come and live at Camoys Hall. 'I don't think he ever forgave me for turning him down. And when I got engaged to someone else, I rang him up to tell him and he said, "I see," and put the phone down on me. He was a very masculine man, very possessive.' Simper, simper.

'So which bits weren't true?' asked Jimmy.

'Well, he *was* like a dictator. They interviewed one man for that programme, someone who'd worked for him, and he quoted a line from Auden: "If he'd asked for a pencil, they'd have cut down a whole forest". That was true. But the bit about living with all these women and doing the sort of alpha male bit, that was rubbish. They kept wheeling out that cliché about powerful men having big libidos. I mean, OK – Lloyd George, Kennedy, Clinton. But my father wasn't like that.'

'People in the village thought he was. "All right for some." That's what they used to say. "It's the rich wot gets the . . ." You know.'

'But he wasn't getting it. There was a sort of sexual rivalry, I suppose you could call it that, between Joan and Angela and my mother, and then there was Irene des Voeux, and even his secretaries, in a small way, but it wasn't *for* sex, if you see what I mean.'

'Not really.'

'He wasn't sleeping with any of them. Apart from Mum, I suppose.'

'Weren't you a bit young to know that?'

'I think I'd have realised. Angela's and Joan's rooms were just down the corridor from mine. If they'd been coming and going all night, I'd have known about it.'

Jimmy snorted.

'Sorry. Bad choice of words. But there are no double beds in this house, you know. They're all single. Every one. I know that doesn't prove anything, but . . . Actually, I can't stand it. I'm going to get a double bed. I might put it in here.' Jimmy didn't say anything. 'Well, it wasn't about sex, with my father, it was about power. Women squabbling over him, over his favours, real cat fights sometimes, but he didn't care. He liked it, having people at his beck and call, making all the decisions. Do you see what I mean?'

'Sort of. But why did Joan stay if he was like that? If they'd been married, and he'd divorced her so he could marry your mother? Wasn't it humiliating for her?'

'She loved him.'

'Surely that would make it even worse.'

'I know what you mean, but I don't think he'd met Mum when he divorced Joan. And there was quite a big gap, because he was with Angela for at least three years. I think it must have been different for Joan's generation, with the war and everything. I don't think they expected as much as we do. Most women didn't have careers then, and Joan and my father, they were just sort of used to each other. He could be horrible to her, say really nasty things, but she didn't seem to mind. The way they were with each other, you'd have thought they were still married. An old married couple who've been together for donkey's years . . .'

'Are you all right? I didn't mean to make you talk about Joan.'

'I don't mind. If I'm talking about her, at least I'm not thinking about her.' Or about Mum, either. 'See that piano over there, under the thing?' There was a concert-sized grand piano in one corner of the ballroom, coated like a dog in a linen cover. 'My parents used to play duets on it. In the evenings. He'd put on a black tie and she'd be done up in a long, black velvet skirt and a white lace blouse with a high collar, like real performers. Everyone in the house would come and listen.'

'Very civilised.'

'It wasn't civilised at all. It was more like a bull fight. My father'd been playing for years and he had a talent for it. But Mum was just learning. I mean, she practised the whole time and did her best. She could follow the music and everything, it was just that she couldn't get it together enough to play the right notes at the right speed. He always kept to the tempo, so what would happen was that they'd start together and then she'd slow down because she was concentrating and she'd drop first one bar behind, then two, then three. And in the end she'd be so far behind that he'd have to turn the page and she wouldn't be able to see what to play any more. It always happened like that. Finally, he'd stop playing, and then she'd stop as well, and look at him, and he'd say, "You'd better carry on until you've caught up." So she'd do that, and then they'd start again together, and it would be all right for a couple of minutes, and then . . . same problem. After a while, I'd see her hands begin to tremble and she'd start making mistakes, and then he'd get angry and say, "For God's sake, where's your attention?" Then her lip would go and she'd take deep breaths and I knew she was trying her hardest not to cry. But she never made it and it always ended with him crashing the lid down on the keyboard and her running out of the room in tears. No one ever went after her. Well, Des did, when he was here, but none of the women. They were too concerned about staying in favour with my father. I always wanted to go, but I didn't because I was too scared.'

'What a bastard.'

'I used to pray that Mum would keep up with him. Once, I was concentrating so hard that I had blood on my palms afterwards from where I'd dug in my nails. But Angela and Irene des Voeux, they loved it. You know, how long's she going to last this time? Irene was supposed to be Mum's best friend, for God's sake, but she'd be all agog.' In my mind I could see the whole thing: Mum's slim freckled hand shaking as she reached up to push a strand of hair behind her ear, her eyes huge and glistening with unshed tears, the way she frowned at the keyboard in an effort not to cry. Angela leaning forward, watching eagerly, Irene smirking, and Joan behind them, looking distressed. I felt Jimmy touch my arm.

'Christ, Dodie.'

I waved my hands to try and get rid of the image. 'Yeah, whatever.'

'Look, I could cook for you tonight, if you like. I've got the evening off. Official, this time.'

'You don't have to.'

'I want to.'

'I'd like that. Thanks, Jimmy.'

'I better go and get some food, then. Joan's kitchen cupboards weren't exactly stuffed with gourmet delicacies, from what I remember.'

'Should I give you some money? I mean, if you're going to buy a lot of things . . .'

'It's OK.' He stood up. 'Is there anything you don't like? You'd better tell me, just in case.'

'I'm not mad about watercress soup, but that's about it.'

After he'd gone, I went to Joan's room. I didn't cry, just sat on her bed until I remembered she didn't approve of people sitting on beds, so I went and sat in the armchair instead. Then I thought of another of those ACME codes that Des had taught me. PYTUO. It means collided with an iceberg.

8

Jimmy cooked an amazing dinner. I asked if I could help, but he said no, so I sat on the kitchen table and watched him cook, and we talked a bit. He didn't rush round or get temperamental or anything, he just got on with it. He didn't even have a book to look at. It all seemed to come out of his head. Watching him like that, it was hard to believe he was the same person who'd tried to pollard me with a meat cleaver.

I got out some of the fancy china and set it up on one end of the dining-room table with all the linen and silver and candles, and it looked lovely. I'd have dressed up, too, except I didn't have anything to change into. I'll never be able to cook for Jimmy in return, I thought, but perhaps he might let me take him out for dinner. He'd have to pick the restaurant himself, though.

Jimmy made chicory, Roquefort and walnut salad to start, then chicken with garlic and olives and rosemary, and the pudding was vanilla ice cream doused in hot expresso with cats' tongues to dip into it. Apparently it's called *affogato* when you do that to ice cream.

'It's just as well I chose this because I forgot to buy any ordinary coffee,' Jimmy said.

'Isn't there any in the kitchen?'

'Joan always drinks – drank – coffee essence. They used to keep a special supply for her at the village shop.'

'Oh. Perhaps we should give it a miss, then. That was delicious.'

'Dodie . . .'

'Mmm?' I was looking down at my bowl, wondering if it would be all right to lick it.

'Some people in the village were asking me about Joan's funeral, when it's going to be.'

'What did you tell them?'

'That I didn't know.'

'I'm not allowed to set a date until the death's been properly registered, but it'll be sometime in the next ten days, provided the coroner's done his stuff. The vicar said he'd be willing to do the service here, but the chapel's in such a mess . . . To be honest, I don't really know where to start.'

'I'm sure they'd help. If you asked them.'

'Who?'

'Mrs Bright, Mrs Curtis, Mrs Halstead, all of them. They'd love to help, if you'd let them.'

Mrs Halstead. Same name as that inspector I talked to about Mum. Why hadn't he rung me? 'Who's Mrs Halstead?'

'Sid Halstead had the market garden, remember?'

'Vaguely.'

'Mrs Bright had the village shop before it closed. And you know the Curtises, don't you, the pig farmer?'

'Of course. It's very kind of them, but why?'

'Joan had a lot of friends in the village, Dodie. She was always helping people. She paid for Mrs Bright's new hip – in a private hospital. The old girl would have died before the NHS got their act together. And when my mum had cancer they said she should go into hospital, but she didn't want to. Joan paid for a special nurse so she could be at home with Dad. But she didn't do it in a bad way or anything. It wasn't like Lady Muck dishing out beef tea and Bible readings to the peasants, it was because she really cared about people. I asked her about it once – why she did it – and she said that her mother had told her it was always good to have a bit of money around in case anybody needed help. Sorry, that sounds . . . That's what she said, anyway. But you should go and see them.'

'I didn't know about that.' I didn't want to think about Joan doing those things. It was making me want to cry. I looked at the firescreen in front of the grate. 'It's a shame it's not winter. We could have had a fire.'

66

'I shouldn't think the chimney's been swept for a while.'

'Perhaps I should get them done.'

'What, all of them? Must cost an arm and a leg. It must have been quite an operation, running this place in its heyday.'

'I suppose it was. Joan was brilliant. There were cooks and maids and caterers and people, but that was her *forte*, organising things. You never really noticed, because it all went like clockwork.'

Jimmy grinned. 'Those lists she kept. They must have shortened a bit when your father died.'

'I think she was a bit lost without having him to look after.'

'She was lonely.'

'I know. I wanted to come up and see her, but—'

'Hey!' He reached across and put his hand on my arm. 'I wasn't criticising.'

'No, but I should have. It just got more and more difficult to come back. To be honest, I never really got on with my father. He didn't do much, you know, fatherly stuff, and after my mother disappeared, it got worse. I was at boarding school most of the time, but when I came back – well, it was just awful. He either ignored me or criticised me, and Joan and Angela fought all the time. You know about Angela, don't you?'

Jimmy nodded.

'Anyway, then I went off to university, but he was still there, pulling my strings. He told me which A-levels to do, which course to take, wouldn't let me go to art school. I hated university. I was supposed to be doing economics but I wanted to do painting and design, so I spent most of my time in art galleries. It wasn't that I was stupid or anything, I just hated the course. I got a lower second, which was a miracle, frankly, considering the minute amount of work I'd done. But of course my father didn't see it like that. He was furious. He said I wasn't interested in getting a decent job and I'd end up married to the first man that came along and I might as well have been a typist and he didn't know why he'd bothered to send me to university because all women were the same . . . He'd shouted at me hundreds of times before, and I'd just sat there and taken it because no one ever answered him back, but this time I thought, this man is in control of *my whole life.* And I opened my mouth and started shouting back. I think I was as stunned as he was. I can't really remember what I said – well, not the exact words – but I told him that I wasn't a . . . I don't know . . . a *puppet*, and I didn't need his money, and I didn't need him telling me what to do every five minutes, and . . . Well, that was the gist of it. I remember Joan coming in at one point and gripping hold of my arm and trying to drag me out of the room, and I was screaming at him, "You *bastard*, I hate you, I hate you, it's all your fault." I wasn't talking about me then, I was talking about Mum, that it was his fault about Mum. I know he knew what I meant, because I saw his face and he looked so shocked. Just for a second I saw . . . You know what I said about *The Wizard of Oz*, about getting behind the curtain?'

'This afternoon? Yeah.'

'Well, I saw an old man. He could have been an OAP on a bus.'

'What happened then?'

'It all sounds very noble, doesn't it, me saying I didn't want his money and striding off to begin my life anew and the rest of it, but talk about the babes in the wood. Where was I supposed to go? I didn't have a clue. My father was a lot of things, but he wasn't mean, and all through college I'd had an allowance, money that was paid into my account every month. He'd bought me a flat in London, a car. I'd never looked at a bank statement in my life.' I stopped. 'I know how this must sound to you, Jimmy.' My face was on fire. 'You probably think I'm a spoilt brat, and I wouldn't blame you—'

'I don't think anything. Tell me the rest.'

'Well, I couldn't go back to the flat he'd bought me, so I stayed with a friend for a while and found myself a job on this little magazine. I was hopeless. I couldn't type, couldn't look after myself, my salary was peanuts, and I had no idea how much anything cost – renting a flat, a loaf of bread, a carton of milk, a bus ticket.' I stopped again as Jimmy was laughing. 'It's not funny! I wanted to be independent and have my own life and . . . and . . . You're not going to believe the next bit.' It sounded so ridiculous that I almost laughed too. 'The money I was earning really was nothing, but there I was, buying clothes and all the rest of it, thinking I was doing really well because the bank manager wasn't writing me rude letters, and then – I suppose it was about six months later – I overheard this conversation at work about checking your bank statements, and I thought, right, I should do that. But when I looked, there was this extra sum of money being paid in every month, about ten times as much as my wages. From my father, of course. And I thought I'd been doing so *well.*'

'I'm sorry,' said Jimmy, 'but it's just that most people—'

'I know. Welcome to the real world. That's what's so stupid. So when I found this out, I wrote my father a letter, telling him I didn't want the money. I'd said I had no intention of seeing him so he sent one of his associates round, someone I knew, and he went on about how my father had my best interests at heart. I said, no he didn't, he just wanted to control me, and we had a row which was ridiculous, because it was nothing to do with this man, it was between my father and me. Well, the money was still coming in, only now I knew it was there I tried not to use it, but that didn't work because my salary was so tiny. I kept on eating into it just to pay the rent and stuff, and of course every now and then I'd think, fuck it, and I'd buy some new clothes or something. In the end, I got myself another bank account and asked for my money to be paid into that, so I'd only use that and nothing else. God, I had no idea. I tried to get jobs in the evening, waitressing, working behind bars. I didn't want to spend his money, but it was there. I hated myself for it, because by that time I knew what it was like. I know. Easy for me to say, isn't it?' I looked at Jimmy. He wasn't laughing any more, even with his eyes.

'Go on,' he said, quietly.

'As time went on, I found I was using his money less and less. I had learned how much things cost, I didn't take holidays, I'd cut up my credit cards. I took a part-time design course and got a better job, and then I got promoted, and promoted again, and then I was headhunted, and that was great, because they didn't know who my father was, so it meant that I was treated the same as everyone else. Then I got a mortgage on a flat and bought a car, and for the last two years, I've been . . . well, independent.' It had seemed such a triumph to me, but in front of Jimmy, it sounded pathetic. As if I wanted a medal for doing what everyone else does as a matter of course. 'Look, Jimmy, I'm sorry,' I said. 'I'm just . . . I'm really losing it. Perhaps you should go.'

'I will if you want me to.' I couldn't tell if he was angry or not.

'Excuse me a moment.' I ran out to one of the downstairs loos and sat and looked at the walls. They were covered in pale squares where the paintings had been taken down. Uncle Lawrence's modern art collection, left to my father when he died. My father didn't want them in the rooms he used, so they came down here. There used to be one painting in this loo that I really liked, a small John Minton called *Corsican Cemetery*. I could get it out of storage, I thought, and put it up somewhere.

Thinking about that painting calmed me down a bit, so I splashed some water on my face and went back to the dining room. Jimmy'd cleared the table and was sitting smoking a roll-up. It looked as though it had been under the wheel of a lorry.

'Don't you ever smoke proper cigarettes?' I asked.

'Occasionally. I don't like the taste much. Anyway, these are cheaper. Do you want some brandy? I bought some more.'

'Thanks. And thanks for not going.'

'You should go to bed. I'll tidy up. Don't worry, I'll make sure everything's locked before I go.'

I was glad he hadn't offered to stay. I felt exhausted.

'Dodie?'

'Yes?'

'Do you want me to come back? See how you're getting on?'

'Yes, please. If it's no bother. I mean, aren't you very busy? In the restaurant?'

'They let me out of the kitchen occasionally.'

'Well, I have to go back to London tomorrow to sort some things out, but I'll be back the day after. I'm not sure when . . .'

'I'll ring you from work.' He poured some brandy into a balloon glass and held it out to me. 'Why don't you take this with you?'

'Why not?'

'Sleep well, yeah?' He caught hold of my free hand as I walked past him and planted a little kiss on it.

'Night, Jimmy. And thanks for dinner. I enjoyed it.'

I went into Joan's sitting room and lay down in the jumble of sheets and blankets and cushions on the floor, but I couldn't sleep. I heard Jimmy lock the back door and drive off, and thought, I forgot to ask him for his key back. I put on a bathrobe I'd found in one of the upstairs cupboards and went back down the corridor to the dining room with my empty brandy glass. The bottle was still on the table. I took it into the hall and turned on all the lights and opened the front doors wide. I'd forgotten how quiet Camoys Hall is at night. I sat down at the base of one of the porch pillars. It was covered in lichen and still slightly warm from the sun. I used to stand out here with Des sometimes on summer evenings like this, while he had his after-dinner cigar. He called it his ADC. Joan wouldn't let him smoke them in the house. 'Want to help me with my ADC, Dodie?' We used to look across the front lawn at the cows going home behind the fence and sing 'Goodnight, ladies' to the tune of 'Nice one, Cyril'. The last bit's the hardest, because you have to cram the words in at the end: 'Goo-oo-oo-oodnightladies'.

It's weird, but I kept wanting to tell Jimmy things. I couldn't tell him about Mum as that really would be asking for pity. In any case, it only takes one journalist with one cheque-book to screw up your life completely. Like my friend Tony. His father went ballistic – Tony hadn't even told him he was gay. But there was something I nearly said to Jimmy when we were in the ballroom.

It happened a couple of months before Mum was kidnapped. We were staying at our house in Knightsbridge. It must have been winter because I was wearing my new knee-high suede boots with sheepskin linings. I don't know where we'd been, but afterwards we went into a tube station, which was a sort of adventure because we usually travelled by car or taxi. It was a big station, somewhere in central London. I remember it was quite dark when we walked towards it, with big, blurry splotches of light from street lamps and cars and shops, and lots of people hurrying home from work. I was excited when we went down the escalator, seeing the adverts and film posters, handsome men with guns and cocktails and beautiful women in bikinis, and the people and the smell and the bright colours everywhere.

I thought Mum would stop to look at the map, but she didn't, or perhaps I went into a dream, I don't know, but one minute she was next to me at the bottom of the escalator and the next, she'd rushed away down one of the tunnels that lead to the platforms and all I could see of her was the back of her head. There was a solid wedge of people between us, trying to make their way to the trains. I said, 'Excuse me, please excuse me,' and tried to find an opening among all the thick coats, but they kept saying, 'Stop pushing,' and, 'We're all in a hurry,' and wouldn't let me through. I lost sight of her and called out, 'Mum! Mum!' but she didn't hear me. I put my head down and pushed forward, and then suddenly I saw that the people in front of me were making way for something in the middle of the tunnel, and that it was Mum. She was just standing there looking towards me. The people were pushing past her to get to the platforms, making her rock backwards on her feet, but she just stared straight ahead. I tucked myself in beside her and held on to her arm. A woman trod on my foot and a man's briefcase whacked against my leg. 'Mum, what are you doing? Have we gone the wrong way?' I said. She didn't seem to notice I was there.

Then the crowd thinned out a bit, and I saw that Mum had an enormous leather bag. It was a bit like something in a dream. I hadn't noticed her carrying it. It just seemed to have materialised suddenly. For a moment, I thought that someone must have dropped it in the scrum, but then I noticed that Mum had got it wedged between her feet for safety. I said, 'Please let's go and look at a map so we can go home,' but she squatted down in front of the bag, undid the zip, and started taking things out. Clothes. Hers and mine. The bag was full of them: blouses and dresses, even bits of underwear. I shook her by the shoulder and said, 'What are you doing?' but she pushed my hand away.

A few people came towards us and she stood up and held out some of the clothes. 'Would you like these? They're as good as new.' But they ignored her and hurried on. Then she stepped out in front of a middle-aged businessman and showed him a beautiful lace camisole. 'Take it for your wife.'

The man pushed it back at her. '*Excuse me.*'

She stopped the man behind. 'Take this for your wife.'

'I haven't got a wife.' He carried on walking.

Mum followed him. 'Your girlfriend then. I'm sure she'll like it.'

He stopped. 'I haven't any money on me.'

'I don't want any money. Please take it.'

'All right.' He took it. 'Are you sure about the money?'

'Yes, honestly. You can have it.'

'Well, thanks.' He looked embarrassed and shoved it quickly into his briefcase.

She turned away from him and offered a blouse made of heavy cream silk to a hefty granny-like woman, who fingered the material between her thumb and forefinger and said, 'Oh, g'won, then.' She held her woven-plastic basket open wide as if it was going to receive a pound of spuds. God knows what she thought she was going to do with the blouse, because Mum was a size ten.

Other people came past and Mum gave them things as well, and then a couple of secretaries – or they looked like secretaries – saw what was going on and started rummaging in the bag at Mum's feet, fishing things out and looking at the labels as if they were at the sales. Mum looked down. 'Help yourselves,' she said. 'Take anything you like.'

Commuters began to stop and crowd round us to see what was happening, tightening their circle as the people behind tried to push past them, until they almost fell on top of us. Mum was passing out clothes to anyone who would take them. I kept catching glimpses of things being borne away: a Frank Usher made of hand-painted silk chiffon, a black Balmain, a navy Jean Muir, an oatmeal Kenzo. One of the secretaries at her feet, a skinny girl with heavy black glasses, pulled Mum's floaty white Ossie Clark dress out of the bag. I'd been there when she'd bought it and it was my favourite. I knelt down and tried to grab it but the secretary held on with one hand and pushed me away with the other.

74

'Get off!' she said. 'I want that.' Her bad breath was fenced in by a dozen pairs of legs.

Out of the corner of my eye, I saw my pink skirt lying on the grey, gritty ground, scuffed and trodden on, the fabric torn and soiled. I let go of the dress and stretched between the milling boots and shoes to try and rescue it, but I couldn't get near enough. I toppled forward on to my palms, and someone trod on my hand. By the time I'd got to my skirt, a trail of fallen clothes were being borne away down the tunnel by the crowd. One girl caught the high heel of her boot in an Yves St Laurent halter-neck top and went over on one ankle. I heard her say, 'Ouch! Bloody hell,' and saw the material rip as she yanked it off her foot and threw it on the ground. The two secretaries got up and ran away, giggling, their shoulder bags filled to bursting with Mum's clothes. I don't know how much they cost then, but in today's prices they would have had four or five thousand pounds' worth between them. They didn't even say thank you.

My hand felt as if it was broken. I hugged it against my chest with my other arm to try and stop it hurting. Over my head, Mum was handing a bunch of my T-shirts to a plump mumsy woman. I looked into the bag. There was only one thing left. You know how, when you're a child, you have one piece of clothing that's your all-time favourite? One thing, that no matter how old or worn or grubby it is, you still want to wear? Well, I had a pink and white striped jumper. Des bought it as a present for me from Paris when I was seven, and it was getting too small for me, but it was really special and I loved it more than I've ever loved anything in my wardrobe, before or since. It was the last thing in the bag.

I looked up at Mum. 'Can I keep this?' I held up the jumper for Mum to see. 'It's my best thing. Please let me.'

The surge of commuters thinned to a trickle, and we had a clear view up and down the tunnel. Some of the trampled clothes had been carried to the far end, and the wind from the trains made them skitter about. They looked like bits of rubbish. A woman came along with a girl of about my age. I caught hold of Mum's arm, but it was too late. The jumper was in her hand.

'I think this would suit your daughter,' she said. 'Would she like it?' She turned to the girl. 'Would you like this? You can have it if you'd like it.'

'Mum,' I whispered. 'I don't mind about the other stuff. But let me keep it.'

The mother looked at her daughter. 'The lady's asking if you'd like it, Sandra.' She took the jumper and held it up against the girl's chest and leant back slightly to see how it looked. 'Looks very nice. What do you say, Sandra?'

'Please,' I whispered.

The daughter heard me and smirked. She had big metal braces on her teeth. 'Thanks. I'd love it.' I watched the mother fold it and put it into her bag. The daughter was staring at me, waiting to see if I'd cry.

We watched them go. 'Why did you do that? I asked you not to. I *begged* you.'

'It's only a jumper.'

'It was my favourite. My jumper from Paris.'

'It doesn't matter where it came from. It's just a lot of wool, that's all. It's not important.'

'It is important. It was *my* jumper.'

'Well, if you won't believe me, there's no point in arguing.' She finished zipping up the bag and squatted on her heels, resting her back against an advert on the curved wall of the tunnel.

'I hate you.'

'No, you don't, Dorothy. Of course you don't.'

A London Transport man came along and asked Mum what she was doing. I suppose someone had reported us for causing a nuisance. Mum didn't argue. We followed him to a little grey room and sat there until the police came. The

76

London Transport man offered me a Coke. I thought Mum would say I couldn't have it, but she didn't. There was a black mark across the toe of one of my suede boots which I tried to hide by sitting with one foot on top of the other. The police didn't arrest Mum or press charges or anything, they just took us home.

Joan must have known about it, because she was at the house in Knightsbridge when they brought us back, but I don't think she told anyone. She can't have, or it would have gone straight back to my father, and he'd probably have had Mum certified on the spot. Joan cleaned the scuff mark off my boots with suede cleaner and trotted me round to Harrods to get a new wardrobe, although she never mentioned why I needed one. She even tried to get a replacement for the pink and white striped jumper, but none of them were ever quite right.

I don't know why I thought Jimmy would understand any of that. I don't understand it myself and he's a chef, not a psychiatrist, thank God. It's all shit anyway, all that stuff. My friend Coralie Markham went to a psychiatrist after her third husband left her. It worked – well something worked – but it made her analyse herself the whole time. Honestly, it was so boring it made you wish she'd never stopped taking the drugs.

I was thinking I might ring Coralie about the funeral – she always got on well with Joan – when I heard the noise. The light from the hall pooled out on to the porch and illuminated the pillars and flagstones, but everything beyond was black. Something, or someone, was moving in the darkness. Feet on grass. Leaf rustle. Scrunch on gravel. Too heavy for a fox. A man.

'Hello? Is anyone there? Hello?'

Another scrunch. And then the breath. Close to me. Close enough to hear breathing.

I shot inside, dragged the doors shut and locked them. Someone was out there.

9

It took me about ten minutes to summon up enough courage to go back to Joan's sitting room. The windows at the front of the house are OK because they've got shutters, but the ones at the back haven't. The ones in the corridor don't even have curtains. I kept thinking I'd see a face looking in at me.

The telephone woke me in the morning. It was the registrar from the hospital to say that the coroner didn't require a post-mortem on Miss Draycott, so they could issue a certificate of disposal. I put the phone down and rubbed my eyes. Certificate of disposal. God, you'd think they'd have managed to come up with a decent euphemism for that one by now, wouldn't you? Don't get upset, I told myself. Don't get angry. Don't think about what you're doing. I phoned the funeral parlour about collecting Joan from the hospital and then I left a message for the vicar asking if he could do the funeral on Saturday the 29th, and leaving my London number. I glanced at the calendar. Eleven days. Plenty of time.

On the way to London I dropped in to see Mrs Curtis. The Curtises live in a big pebble-dashed box at the end of the village. I stood on the grey concrete path between rows of bamboo sticks with bits of flappy blue plastic wound round the ends to scare the birds off Mrs Curtis's vegetables, and pressed the bell. No one came. I was just about to go away again when a side window opened and one of the twins stuck her head out.

'Carol?' I called. The Curtis twins are identical, with baby-blue eyes and thickets of unbrushable short ringlets that look like wholemeal *fusilli*, but I usually get them right.

'That's me!' she shouted. 'Sorry, I was on the loo. Come round the back.'

I followed the concrete path past a clutter of dustbins. The kitchen windows were steamed up, and when I opened the door I was met by a head-high row of damp grey tea towels suspended from a ceiling rack.

Carol's voice came from behind them. 'I was just having lunch. You'll have to duck underneath. They won't go any higher, the pulley's knackered.' She was sitting beside the beige Formica worktop. Her nails were ringed with dirt and her fingers were compressing grey marks into the fleecy white bread of her sandwich. She wore no tights and at the side of her skirt a broken zip, fastened at the top by a safety pin, bulged open, showing the edge of a pair of once-white knickers.

'Want a cup of tea?' she asked. 'I just dropped in for lunch. I work at the farm now, so it's easier than going all the way back home.' I was about to sit down when she said, 'Put the kettle on, would you? I've been on my feet all morning.'

One thing I love about Carol and Jackie is that the money thing doesn't come into it. I'm younger than they are, so they boss me around, and they've never been defensive about their standard of living or their house or anything. They're sorry for me because I'm not married.

I fumbled with the electric kettle and opened cupboards in a fruitless search for clean mugs.

'I'm ever so sorry about Joan, Doe. Mum was wondering if you'd come and see us.'

'Is she here?'

'Gone into town with Dad.'

'Could you ask her to give me a ring about the funeral?'

'Course. Have you fixed a date?'

'The vicar hasn't got back to me yet. It's the chapel, getting it ready. Jimmy said your mum might want to help.'

'Jimmy Henessey?'

'Do you know him?'

'Course I do.' She leant forward. 'Is there something going on? Between you and him?'

'No, he just used to go and visit Joan, that was all.'

Carol lit a cigarette. 'Pass us that saucer, Doe.' She pointed to a chipped green one with two wrung-out tea bags on it. 'So, are you living with anyone in London?'

'No.'

'Seeing anyone special?'

'Not at the moment.'

'Anyone you like?'

'No, not really.'

Carol grinned. 'You want to watch that Jimmy,' she said, as if she could read my mind. 'He's gorgeous, I know. But he's got a bit of a name for himself. Just be careful, that's all.' She tapped the side of her nose. 'Don't do anything I wouldn't do, right?' She popped the last bit of sandwich into her mouth. 'I never showed you my wedding pictures, did I?'

Carol got married five years ago. She'd invited me, but I'd made an excuse because I thought I might bump into my father.

'Hang on, I'll get the book. Mum keeps it here so the kids can't get their sticky hands on it.' She shot off and reappeared with a photograph album bound in grubby white satin. The words *Our Wedding* were embossed on the front in silver, surrounded by flying streamers and swinging bells. 'It was a beautiful day,' she said, turning to a photograph of herself in white, squinting into the sun outside the church.

'I didn't know you got married at Camoys Hall.'

'Well, I wouldn't have thought of it myself, but Joan said we should. She had the chapel all done up, paid for the flowers and everything. I always wanted a church wedding. Jackie had hers in a register office, not the same at all.' She dug a dog-eared Polaroid out of a pocket at the back of the

80

album. 'See? She's wearing an ordinary suit. Patrick only gave her that one tiny bunch of flowers. Bit mean, I thought. Not the type of wedding I'd have wanted. Look,' she said, turning back to the pictures of her own wedding. 'Dave's in his uniform and everything. Doesn't he look handsome?' Carol's husband Dave had left the army a year after they married. 'And look, there's Tommy in his little suit. Isn't he sweet? He was so good, I couldn't believe it.' Carol pointed at a photograph of their eldest son. 'Mum had him while we were on our honeymoon. That's where we started Jason.' She laughed. 'Two's enough for me. Jackie's got four now.'

'How is Jackie?'

'Oh, she's doing OK. Still with Patrick.'

'And how's Dave?'

'Didn't I tell you? We split up. I still love him, but I'm with someone else now.'

'And the kids?'

'They're OK. Mind you, Dave doesn't give me a penny for them.'

'Doesn't the CSA—'

Carol laughed. 'That's for men with jobs, Doe. They're not interested in Dave. Want one of these?' She pushed a box of Meltis Newberry fruits towards me.

'No thanks.'

'Watching your weight? You want to put some on, not take it off.' She picked through the top layer of sweets, found nothing she liked and flipped it up to dig into the bottom one. 'Jackie calls him Catweazle.'

'Who?'

'My new bloke.'

I must have looked blank, because she said, 'Don't you remember, on the telly? Oh no, I forgot, you didn't have one, did you?' She looked at me pityingly. 'Catweazle was this character on one of the kids' programmes. He had straggly hair and a beard, like a wizard. Perhaps he was a wizard, come to think of it. Greg – that's his name – he's a bit older than me, so he's got a few lines, and with the beard and everything . . . Jackie says he looks like him.'

'Does he live near?'

'In a caravan. I've never seen it. He's embarrassed. His wife kicked him out when they split up and he didn't have nowhere else to go. He used to be in the army, like Dave. He's always round at mine. You should come over, one night. You'd like him.'

'That would be great. Listen, Carol, I'd better go. Should I leave my number in London in case your mum wants to ring me? I'll probably be back tomorrow, but just in case . . .'

Carol proffered her fag packet and a splintered stump of biro. 'Put it on there. Don't worry, Doe. I'll give it to her.'

I found a stack of mail and seven messages on my answering machine when I got back to my flat in London: Tony Hepworth, wanting to know why I hadn't rung him; one from Des, 'We're seeing Benny at five o'clock tomorrow, so I'll be round to collect you at half past four. I'll fix up a spot of dinner afterwards. Cheerio'; someone called Alex, 'The play's started, I'm outside the theatre, it's ten past eight, if you get this, call me on my mobile.' Then Alex again, 'It's now twenty past eight, it's obvious you haven't got my message. Where are you? If you get this in the next ten minutes, call me.' And finally, 'It's now quarter to nine and I'm going home, so you can ring me there when you get in. I hope you're OK.' I thought it must be a wrong number until I looked in my diary and discovered that a man called Alex Henshall was supposed to be taking me to see *Miss Julie* at the National on Monday night. Just as well I forgot. I'd probably have topped myself if I'd had to sit through a Strindberg. Still, I thought, best to cancel my social life for the next two weeks, just to be on the safe side. There was a message from the vicar at Camoys, saying that Saturday the

29th was fine, and what about 11 a.m.? The last message was from Inspector Halstead. Just a number to call.

I drew the blinds, switched the answer machine back on and retreated into the study with my mobile phone and a large gin and tonic. I fiddled with the computer for about half an hour, then downed the g and t in one and phoned Inspector Halstead.

He answered it himself, which surprised me. 'Thank you for phoning, Miss Blackstock.'

'Have you got some more information?'

'We've done some work with the dental records, and the lady we have here is your mother Susan Carrington, as you thought.'

'Dental records? Weren't they destroyed?'

'They usually are. They tend to keep them longer if you go private, for some reason, but not usually this long, I must admit. We thought it was worth a go, and, well, we were lucky.'

'And it's all the same and everything?'

'Yes.'

'Thanks.' *Thanks?* I'd already made up my mind about it being Mum, but it was strange to hear it confirmed by science or forensics or whatever. All the stuff in my head seemed to have disappeared and left a sort of vacuum. I couldn't summon up any words. I wondered if Inspector Halstead could hear me breathing. 'Why . . . I mean, can you tell me . . . Her death, what caused it? Do you know?'

'We'll be able to tell you as soon as we've had the test results which should be tomorrow, but I'll ring you just as soon as I know anything.'

'You will let me know first, won't you? You won't tell the press before you tell me?'

'Of course not. We wouldn't do that.' I could tell he was humouring me as if I'd said something ridiculous.

'It happens. One of my friends only discovered her stepfather was dead when she saw the headline in the *Sun*.'

'Well, I give you my word it won't happen this time.'

'Because I need to know first, before anyone else. It's important that you tell me first.' I gave him my mobile number and the Camoys Hall number. Then I made myself another gin and tonic and got Joan's tattered old address book out of my bag to make a list of people to invite to her funeral, but I couldn't concentrate. Eventually I decided that Des might recognise more names than I did, so I stuffed the whole lot into my bag to take along to the meeting, and then I went into the bathroom and tried to make myself look presentable. Because I'm so short-sighted, I never knew what my face looked like until I got my first pair of contact lenses. I suppose I must have been about fifteen. I'd got past expecting to see a beautiful fairy princess looking back at me, but the first time was still a disappointment. Because I'd sort of thought, or hoped, that I might look a bit like my mother. People always told me I did, but that was because of the colouring and the hair. What I really wanted was to look in the mirror and see her face staring back at me in a sort of beautiful mist, and marvel. But it didn't happen.

A few years later, I came across this poem. I don't know who wrote it, but I've never forgotten the words.

This face you got,
This here phizzog you carry around,
You never picked it out for yourself at all, at all, did you?
Somebody said, 'Here's yours, now go see what you can do
with it.'

Not much, in my case.

When Des walked through the door, he held out his arms and we hugged each other for ages without saying anything. He had a bit less hair than I remembered, but he looked fit and tanned. He looked at me critically. 'You've gone all boney again. You haven't been on some silly diet, have you?'

'Hardly. You look pretty streamlined yourself.'

'I've been going to some of these health spas. They wrap you up in bales of towelling and bash you about and make you eat bloody carrots for a week. Then of course you sneak out for a cigar and they can smell it a mile off and you creep back in with your tail between your legs and they look all reproachful.' He made a face. 'God knows if it does any good, but it makes you feel *clean*. Perhaps you should try it. Ask them to fatten you up a bit.'

'You'll be using moisturiser next, Des.'

'No, I won't. Anyway, they don't make it for chaps.'

'They do now.'

'God! What's the world coming to! When I grew up, you were a pansy if you put up an umbrella when it rained, never mind putting a lot of muck on your face.'

'Is that where you got the tan? The health place?'

Des looked self-conscious. 'I've been on holiday. South of France. Bought a house down there. It's teeming with grey panthers.' He grimaced. 'Some of them are even older than me, if you can imagine that. You must come and visit. Brighten the place up a bit. Anyway, never mind all this health stuff, the car's outside.'

'Still got the Bentley?'

'Of course. Now get your skates on, or we'll be late.' Des's elderly cream-coloured monster was parked outside. We drove in silence for a few minutes. Then Des said, 'You do know what this is in aid of, don't you?'

I nodded. 'Joan's dead, so the money comes to me.'

'Yes. I know that you . . . Well, that you might not feel entirely happy about it, but there's nothing you can do, I'm afraid.'

'I suppose I can always give it to charity.'

'It's not quite that simple, as you very well know.' Des sounded faintly irritated. 'Anyway, let's get this over with so that Benny can do his stuff.' He paused. 'You'll be the majority shareholder, you know.'

'I do know that, Des.'

85

'Of course. Sorry. Something else I was thinking, about what you said on the phone, this job you've got . . .'

'What about it?'

'Well, you'll have to jack it in, I'm afraid. You know that, don't you?'

'I suppose so, although I wondered if—'

'Dodie, be realistic. It's a question of responsibility.'

'I *know*. Don't give me a lecture, Des. Please.'

'It's not as bad as all that. It won't be a full-time job at Blackstock, after all. No one's going to expect you to be parked behind a desk at nine o'clock every morning, hands on, but you've got a lot of catching up to do, and that's going to take time. Rome wasn't built in a day, you know.'

'No, but Pompeii was destroyed in half an hour.'

Des sighed. 'I've taken care of things up till now, but you're going to have to learn the ropes pretty smartly. I can show you what's what, but I won't be around for ever, you know. I don't know what sort of notice you're on, but I'm sure Benny can square it with your magazine. I'm sorry, my old love, I know you don't want this, but you haven't got a lot of choice, I'm afraid.'

'I know. Can I ask you something, Des?'

'Fire away.'

'When my father died, did you expect him to leave everything to me? Via Joan, I mean?'

Des looked surprised. 'Well, yes. Yes. I'd always assumed he would.'

'Even though we'd had an argument?'

'It was always on the cards, Dodie. It was never actually discussed – to be honest, I don't think your father could imagine Blackstock without himself in the driving seat – but you are his daughter, after all. Besides, you could hardly do that job for ever. You've done your best, but you weren't really making ends meet, were you?'

'Actually, it pays pretty well – by most people's standards, anyway.'

'Yes, well, look on the bright side. Now you can get yourself a decent flat. And a proper car instead of that old heap.'

'I don't know why I bothered trying to make my own life. What was the point? Eight, nine years' work, and it's taken you – what – five seconds to dismantle the lot.'

'I know Wolf wasn't very happy about it, but I always thought it was good for you, striking out on your own.' He patted my knee. 'I'm really quite proud of you, you know.'

After the meeting, when we were back in the car, Des said, 'Now that's over, let's get on to the serious stuff. I thought we might try that new Japanese place I keep hearing about. If someone had told me twenty years ago that I'd be eating raw fish, I'd have said they were doo-lally, but I rather like it. I must have eaten schools of the stuff. Or perhaps that should be shoals. Anyway, what do you think?'

'Can I just go home?'

He looked at me, sharply. 'What's up, Dodie? For most people, inheriting a fortune wouldn't be the end of the world, you know.'

'I know. But when we were in there, and Mr Bennington was explaining it all, it felt like . . . like being buried alive or something. I've known for over six months that this was inevitable, but I suppose – perhaps because I didn't want it to – I didn't believe it would actually *happen*. Do you mind if we don't talk about it?'

'Not at all. But I was rather looking forward to taking you out to dinner. I tell you what, why don't you come back to my house, and Angelina can sort something out for us?'

So that's what we did. Des and his housekeeper Angelina live in one of those beautiful Nash houses overlooking Regent's Park. He bought it for next to nothing in the seventies, which is typical Des acumen. It's true that my father was a brilliant businessman, but Blackstock wouldn't be worth half what it is today if he hadn't had Des to help him, and he knew it. Officially, Des retired ten years ago, but he's still the *éminence grise* at Blackstock – he owns almost ten per cent of the shares, apart from anything else – and he has consultancies all over the place.

Des has the most fantastic garden overlooking the Outer Circle, with wisteria on the walls and a huge archway covered in tumbling white roses. We sat underneath it on a carved wooden bench. 'Now, I want to hear everything you said on the phone again, slowly this time. From the beginning to the end.' He waved a finger at me. 'Deviating neither to the right, nor to the left.'

I told him again about Joan and Mum, and everything else except the bit about Jimmy and the knife. The whole story took about half an hour, during which Des hardly said anything except, 'And then what?' and, 'Oh dear.' When I got to the end, he put his arm round me and patted my shoulder several times, rather awkwardly. 'You poor old thing. You've had a rough time, haven't you? What can I do to help?'

I fished Joan's address book and my guest list out of my bag. 'You could help me with this. I don't know who half of them are.'

Des glanced through it. 'I know quite a few of this lot.' He pulled a silver-cased notebook and miniature pencil out of his jacket. 'When is it?'

'The twenty-ninth. It's a Saturday. The vicar says he can manage eleven o'clock, so I thought lunch afterwards.'

'Right. Why don't I copy down some of these names and start phoning round? Then I can let you know who's coming. That'll speed things up, won't it?'

'Thanks.'

'Have you sorted out the notices for the papers?'

'No.' It hadn't occurred to me.

'I'll do it, then. Now, how are you going to feed all these people?'

'I thought I'd ring one of these.' I showed him the special

section at the end of Joan's address book with the names of all the caterers and florists and wine merchants and decorators and musicians that she'd used for parties when my father was alive.

'Can't go wrong with those. They'll all remember her.'

'It's been a few years since she used any of them.'

'Doesn't matter. She put a lot of business their way. They'll remember that. And people took to Joan. She had a lot of friends.'

'Yes, she did.' I thought of what Jimmy said about the people in the village. 'What do you think about hymns, Des?'

'Well, "The Lord's My Shepherd", that was always her favourite. "Rock of Ages" and er . . . "Abide with Me". She loved Gracie Fields singing that. And how about "Jerusalem"? I always think that's a decent tune.'

I wrote them down on the back of the guest list. 'That was quick. They sound fine to me, but are you sure those are the ones she'd have wanted?'

Des looked sheepish. 'She told me. God knows how it came up, but she said that "Rock of Ages" always made her want to laugh, the way everyone groaned their way through it. Then she said she'd like to have it at her funeral, so I asked her which other hymns she liked, and she asked me . . .' We were silent for a moment. 'When it's all finished – all the preparations and so forth – would you mind if I hung on to this?' He pointed at Joan's address book.

'Of course not. But don't you want something a bit more personal?'

Des looked down at the address book. 'I gave her this. Years ago.'

'Oh, I see. Well, yes, of course you can.'

There was silence for a moment, and then he said, 'Are you going to invite Benny?'

'I hadn't thought of it.'

'You should, you know. He gets terribly peeved if he's left out of things. Do you want me to give him a ring? He was rather taken with Joan, you know.'

'Yes, if you think we should. Is there anyone else I should invite? I mean, anyone who wasn't in the book.'

'There's Joan's sister.'

'I didn't know Joan had a sister.'

'She's several years older. They weren't very close.'

'What was her name?'

'Madeleine. Madeleine Draycott. Never married. Used to live in Bournemouth. It shouldn't be too hard to dig her out, provided she's still alive, of course.'

'Perhaps that's why she's not in the book, because she's dead. But then she'd be crossed out, wouldn't she?' I looked first under D, then M. Nothing. 'Did they fall out?' God, why were there so many things I didn't know?

'I don't think she and your father saw eye to eye.' He stood up and stretched his legs. 'You know the score, Dodie.' He sounded cross.

'Well, even if she doesn't want to come, we ought to let her know. Have you ever met her?'

'Oh, years ago. When we were all young and gorgeous and our knee joints didn't bugger us about.' He leant down and rubbed them. 'What are we going to do about grub?'

'Chinese?'

'Jolly good. There's one round here that delivers. Shall I ask Angelina to order? She always picks a good spread.'

He went indoors, and I walked around and sniffed flowers and thought about Joan. It was hard to imagine her ever having been young, but I've seen pictures, and she was rather gorgeous in an austerity, rolled-up-hair sort of way. I wondered when she and Des had had the conversation about hymns. I bet my father wouldn't have known which hymns Joan liked, and he'd been married to her. Mind you, Des always knows how many children people have got, and what school they went to, and what their dogs are called. I suppose he's the human face of Blackstock PLC. They're always wheeling him out to press the flesh at official functions, even now.

Angelina brought the Chinese dinner into the garden and we ate it sitting under the roses. We talked a bit more about the arrangements for the funeral, but I couldn't concentrate and ended up with black bean sauce all over my list. Des gave me his handkerchief to mop it up. When we'd finished, there was a sort of pause while Des smoked his after-dinner cigar and we watched the windows lighting up in all the houses down the terrace. I'd thought he was miles away, but he suddenly said, 'What's the matter, Dodie?'

'Nothing's the matter.'

'Yes there is. You'll scrub right through that paper in a minute.'

I looked down at the handkerchief. 'Sorry. I'll wash it for you.'

'Never mind about that. What's up? Apart from the obvious, of course: Joan and your mother, inheriting.'

'It's hard to explain, really.'

'Have a go.'

'It's all these things I don't know. Would you tell me things, Des, if I asked you?'

'What things?'

'Things about the past. What it was like, what happened. Just . . . *things*.'

'About Susan?'

'Yes, but about everything, really. I feel I don't understand . . . Sorry, I'm drivelling. But you did ask.'

'Where are you based at the moment? Cambridgeshire?'

'Yes. I only came down for the meeting this afternoon.'

'Why don't I come up and we'll have dinner? Properly, in a restaurant. Next week?'

'Yes, if you like.'

'I wouldn't mind staying at the Fat Hen for a couple of nights, unless they've buggered it about, of course. Better check. I could give you a hand sorting things out.' He got up. 'You are looking a bit peaky, you know. You'd better get some sleep. I'll call a cab.'

Des escorted me to the taxi and leant through the window to kiss my forehead. 'I'll give you a ring. Try not to worry, Dodie. Sleep tight, mind the fleas don't bite.' *Sleep tight, mind the fleas don't bite.* He'd said that to me when I was a child.

It was only nine-thirty when the cab dropped me at my flat, so I thought I'd better start ringing people. I left messages for Tony, Coralie Markham and Alex Henshall, and then I looked at the list I'd made. Des had crossed off at least half the names, which left me with about seventy-five. For some reason, I decided to start at the bottom. Mrs Williams. The woman on Joan's last list. Probably some old dear from the WI. London number, though. Perhaps she *runs* the WI. *Till we have built Jerr-ooo-saa-lem.* I dialled.

'Hello?'

'Hello, is that Mrs Williams?'

'Speaking.'

'I'm calling about Joan Draycott. I'm afraid I've got some bad news.'

'Bad news? Who is this?'

'My name's Dorothy Blackstock. I'm afraid that Joan . . . Well, I'm afraid she died. She had a heart attack. I'm arranging the funeral, and I wondered—'

'Did you say your name was Dorothy Blackstock? *Dodie* Blackstock?'

'Yes. I suppose I'm really – was really – her stepdaughter.'

'I know who you are. Do you know who I am?'

'Well, I've been looking through her address book, you know, to see—'

'My maiden name was Hill.'

'Sorry, I—'

'Maggie Hill.'

I almost dropped the phone. 'Did you offer me orange squash?'

'What did you say?'

'Orange squash. In the kitchen. When the cat was run over.'

'Yes, that was me.' So it was true. The brown velvet trouser suit, the frizzy hair. I hadn't dreamt or imagined it. 'I'm surprised you remember that.'

'I don't understand. Why is your name in Joan's address book?'

'We've been in contact for some time. She wasn't giving me money, if that's what you're thinking.'

'No, I wasn't. Why should—'

'I could have gone to the newspapers. I've had offers. Good ones. But I've never talked to any of them.'

'Look, Mag— Mrs Williams—'

'It's not as if I've got any money, you know. I'm on my uppers, most of the time. But I've never talked to a single newspaper.'

On my uppers. Those boots, held together with elastic bands. 'I want to meet you.'

'To meet me?'

'Yes. Can I come and see you?'

'Well, I don't know—'

'To talk. Look, I'll pay you for it.'

'I don't want your money.'

'I need to talk to you. Please, Mrs Williams.'

'I don't know what you expect to get from me, but if that's what you want—'

'Yes, it is. How about next week? Tuesday evening? Are you free then?'

'Come in the afternoon, if you like. I'm not going anywhere.'

'OK. Two o'clock, next Tuesday. Where do you live?'

She gave me an address in Tower Hamlets. 'It's a rough area. Leave your car at home. And don't wear jewellery and designer clothes and all that, because they'll have them off you.'

'All right. Thanks.'

'Goodbye.' She put the phone down.

It was about ten minutes before I stopped shaking. I went into the kitchen and tried to make myself another gin and tonic, but I sliced the ball of my thumb instead of the lemon. It stung, but not very much. I watched the blood dripping into the lemon juice on the chopping board for a moment, then I dipped the forefinger of the other hand into the liquid and drew little circles on the wooden surface. After a while, I started to think. What Maggie Hill had said about money sounded almost as though she could have blackmailed Joan if she'd wanted to: *Pay me or I'll sell my story to the papers.* Sell them what, though? The news that my mother was still alive? Maggie Hill had gone to prison for seven years, so she must have come out towards the end of 1983 . . . That would be without good behaviour, so it could have been earlier. She couldn't have told Joan about Mum during the time she was in prison, at least, not in the first two or three years, because Joan would have told my father, and Mum would have come back to us and then he wouldn't have married Virginia, and . . . Anyway, what about that photograph, the one Mum had of me at Tony's party? Because what I really couldn't understand was why Mum hadn't come back of her own accord. Unless she'd lost her memory. I mean, she was having a breakdown before she was kidnapped, and that would be enough to push anyone over the edge. But then why would she have had our names in her diary?

I must have stood there for the best part of an hour. Just me, my cut thumb and my gin and tonic. Which was warm, because I'd dropped the ice tray on the floor and all the cubes had popped out and vanished underneath cupboards. Oh well, I thought. Time for bed.

When three o'clock arrived and I still couldn't get to sleep, I got up and started pottering about packing clothes to take back to Camoys Hall. I zipped my laptop into its case and unplugged the fax machine and shoved it into a plastic bag. I was just pushing the unopened post into my handbag when the phone rang. Tony. He's always getting home late from parties and ringing me up to tell me what I'm missing.

I picked up the phone in the hall. 'You're lucky. I'm actually awake.'

Silence.

'Tony?'

'Shut up and listen to me.' A male voice. It definitely wasn't Tony.

'What—'

'You heard me, you rich bitch. Shut up and listen. You think you're nice and safe, don't you?'

'Who is this?'

'Shut. The fuck. Up. All that money, it didn't help your mother, did it? And it's not going to help you either, because I know where you live.'

10

I crashed the phone down, then picked it up again. Tony, I'd ring Tony. He'd know what to do. I dialled. Engaged. I dialled again. Still engaged. Might be for hours. Got to stop my hands shaking. Can't do anything in this state . . . *Christ*. Des. That's it, ring Des. OK, press the buttons, oh-one-seven-one- No. Wait. If the caller knew about my mother, he might know where Des lived too. *I know where you live*. He could be on his way now, coming to get me. He was coming to get me and there was nothing I could do to stop him. I whirled round and stared at the front door. I could almost see the knob begin to turn. *Wait.* Sense, Dodie, sense. Phone Inspector Halstead? No. What could he do, anyway? I had to get out. Get into the car, and put as much distance between me and the flat as possible. Camoys Hall. Nobody knew I'd been there. I hadn't even told my boss where I was going, only Des. And Jimmy. He'd said he'd phone me. I'd be safe with Jimmy. I had to get back to Camoys Hall.

I bundled everything into the car, locked up, and drove as fast as I could through the empty streets. It wasn't until I was halfway down the motorway that I remembered about the prowler. That breath, so *close*. I flinched, slammed on the brakes – no one behind, thank God – and swerved on to the hard shoulder.

I didn't know what to do. I sat there for what seemed like hours, every passing lorry rocking my little car from side to side. I rang Des on my mobile. *Network busy. Please try again.* It might not have been a prowler. It could have been anything – local kids, a fox, the cat . . . Shaanti. I hadn't left her any food. She'd be starving. And whatever had or hadn't been there outside Camoys Hall, the telephone call at my flat was *real*. I could phone Des when I got there, after I'd fed the cat.

At least Shaanti was pleased to see me when I finally arrived at Camoys Hall. She rubbed herself against my legs, purring, while I opened cupboards in the scullery, located a tin of cat food, opened it, and forked the contents into her bowl, gagging at the smell. Doing something as ordinary as feeding a cat made me feel calmer, somehow. I poured some milk into a saucer for her and went through to Joan's sitting room to phone Des.

'It's probably some crank, but it's best to be on the safe side,' he said. 'You ought to have some sort of security up there, in any case. That's what I used to tell Joan, but she was as bad as your father. I told her, things are a lot worse nowadays, but she wouldn't listen.'

'Did you see her much, then? After my father died.'

'On and off. I wouldn't say "much". Anyway, this security business – I know a good firm. I'll give them a ring, shall I? I doubt if they'll be able to come back to you today, but I really don't think you need to worry about this, Dodie. I know it's pretty grim, being phoned up in the middle of the night like that, but they rarely *do* anything, these people. You're not in the phone book, are you?'

'God, no.'

'Sensible girl. As for the other thing – thinking there was someone outside – it was probably just kids larking about.'

'I did think it might have been an animal.'

'More than likely. It's funny how these things take hold of one's imagination, really. I remember one Christmas – must be twelve, fifteen years ago, now – your father and I were in Wales looking at a site, and when we got back to the car, it wouldn't start, and when Wolf's chap looked under the bonnet, do you know what he found? A roast dinner. Potatoes, turkey, brussels sprouts, the lot! It was a bit on the oily side, but neatly arranged, just as if somebody was going to eat it. We never did work out how it got there. Your father said it was Welsh Nationalists. Anyway, it just goes to show . . . But the point I'm making is that strange things do happen from time to time. My advice is to get on with sorting out the caterers and so forth. Take your mind off it. It's always better to get on with things.'

'You're probably right. Thanks, Des.'

'Think nothing of it, my child. I'll give you a call once I've spoken to the security people.'

It was true what Des said about keeping busy. Because the thing was, the minute I stopped doing, I started thinking, and then I started crying or getting scared or depressed. I cleared all the things off the desk in Joan's sitting room and got cracking. He was right about the caterers and people remembering Joan, too. They all did, and they seemed genuinely upset when I told them she'd died. They knew what sort of food she used to order, which flowers went where, everything. I spent practically the whole morning on the phone and managed to organise decorators, cleaners, temporary staff, the lot. And I know this sounds a bit mad, but while I was doing it, I sort of pretended that I was Joan. I didn't imitate her voice or anything, I just tried to do what I thought she'd have done. Because she used to do this the whole time for my father – not funerals, but great big parties with four or five hundred people. I had no idea how much there was to sort out until I sat down and started doing it. My father had a reception or a dinner almost every week, and no one ever helped Joan to fix them up. There are companies that do all the organising for you, and I could have hired one, but I wanted to do it myself. I thought, well Joan, if you can see, I hope you're impressed.

Halfway through the morning I made myself a cup of coffee with Joan's chicory essence. I spat most of it out and wrote a note to myself about buying a coffee machine. I couldn't go back to my flat, so there would have to be a shopping expedition. Then I rang Habitat in Cambridge and told them I wanted the biggest double bed they had, pronto. In a weird way, I was almost enjoying myself.

I was just adding my shopping list to the six others I'd pinned up on Joan's cork board when Jimmy rang.

'How's it going?' he asked.

'Slowly. There's so much to do.'

'Want some help? I could come over tomorrow, if you like.'

'Would you?'

'Yeah, why not? I had a word with Mrs Curtis. She says she'll drop by some time in the morning.'

'Great. Jimmy, I was wondering . . .'

'Yes?'

'The caterers are going to fax over some menus this afternoon for the reception afterwards. Would you mind having a look at them?'

'No problem. See you about eleven, then.'

As I put the receiver down, I suddenly thought, *Mum*. I'd have to do all this for her, too.

I wondered if I'd ever see her again in the after-life – always supposing there is one, of course. I do want to see Mum again. It's funny, I never thought about that at all when Angela died. I was too busy feeling guilty about not liking her. Or when Virginia died. She was supposed to be my stepmother, but I hardly knew her. When I saw her, all anorexic, at my father's funeral, I thought, if you were an animal they'd whip out the humane killer and congratulate themselves on a merciful release. Virginia finally managed to starve herself to death about three months after that. When my father died, I can't say I thought about meeting him again, either. I wasn't glad that he was dead, exactly, I was just so *relieved*. As if I could relax for the first time in my life. But afterwards, finding out about the will and everything, it was as if he hadn't gone away at all, he was still controlling everything. The only difference was, we couldn't see him any more.

I pulled the post out of my handbag and shuffled through it to see if there was anything interesting. Everything seemed to be bills or circulars except for one small Jiffy bag with a printed label. I unpeeled the top and stuck my hand inside, expecting to pull out next month's supply of disposable contact lenses. My fingertips came into contact with something soft. Furry, almost. I looked inside. The jiffy bag was full of hair.

When I upended it, a thick, pale red switch, neatly coiled, fell into my lap. Strawberry blonde. Just like mine. Just like my mother's. *Jesus!* I jumped up and the hair shot off my lap. The impact made it arch and twist for a second like a landed fish as it flopped on to the carpet.

I ran without thinking, out of the room, out of the house and across the lawn. I scrambled across the ha-ha, through the trees and out into a field. I'm not fit. I stopped just before my lungs exploded and doubled over, hands on knees, gasping for breath. Sunshine. Bright, safe sunshine.

He doesn't know I'm here, I told myself. He only knows where I am in London. And it could have been anyone's hair. You only had to look at a photograph of my mother to see what colour hair she had. There were enough of them about . . . except it's not a common colour. And the hair in the package wasn't dyed. When hair is dyed, every strand is the same colour, and these were all slightly different. But it could have been a crank, I thought. Or a sick joke. Couldn't it?

I looked up and realised I was lost. I used to know the estate quite well, but a lot more of the land's been let out to farmers. There were sheep and cows and crops where there never used to be, and some of the trees and hedges seemed to have disappeared. Joan had been left in charge of the estate, not me. Perhaps they'd grubbed up the hedges without telling her. I couldn't believe she'd have agreed to it, but maybe she had. She'd certainly never rung me up to talk about it. Maybe she thought I'd tell her to get lost. Maybe I would have.

After about half an hour's walk I came to the edge of the estate. The Camoys village side. There's only a wooden post-and-rail fence between the fields and the road with a footpath running along beside it. I started walking towards the village, and after about ten minutes I felt more confident about the landmarks, so I clambered over a stile and went through a clump of trees, and, sure enough, there was the old pillbox, encircled by a two-strand barbed wire fence. There'd been some talk of getting rid of it, but it was solid concrete and too big to blow up.

As a child, I'd never liked going inside it much. Something to do with the atmosphere. I wasn't scared that some long-dead Home Guardsman would tap me on the shoulder, but it smelt of wee and the rough grey walls were covered in graffiti. I knew the people who'd written it. Kids from the village. There's no cinema or anything round here, you see, so if you weren't old enough to drive a car or go to the pub and you didn't want to sit with Mum and Dad and watch Saturday night telly, this was the alternative: hanging round a foul-smelling concrete slab in the chilly semi-darkness, boasting and necking and spraying obscenities on the wall. Even if I had been allowed to go out, I wouldn't have wanted to join in.

As I climbed through the barbed wire fence that surrounded the pillbox, I thought, it's part of history now. I can't get rid of it. I read the graffiti. *NF* with a swastika, several times. *Mark woz 'ere. Tracey woz 'ere. Carol loves Pete. Jacki 4 Pete 4 ever 2 gether.* Both twins. Lucky Pete. I suddenly wondered if Jimmy used to come here. I walked round the pillbox looking for his name, then stopped in front of the entrance and sniffed. It wasn't urine, but something else. Bleach? Jeyes Fluid? The village kids wouldn't bring disinfectant up here. Besides, the graffiti was old, not recent. Perhaps they'd found somewhere better to hang out. I peered through the doorway. Except for a pale rectangle where the sunlight came through the gun aperture, I couldn't see anything. There were scuff-marks on the illuminated earth, though, and the edge of a footprint. Human, not animal. Quite a big one. Too big for Joan. Why would she come up here, anyway? She never bothered disinfecting the pillbox in the days when it was being vandalised, so why do it now?

There was nothing else in there as far as I could see. I didn't want to cross the threshold. The roof was too low, the walls too thick. There wasn't a door for anyone to slam and lock me in, but all the same . . . In one of the corners, I could see a shape, darker than the rest of the shadow. I started towards it with tiny steps, holding my breath.

It was grey, soft . . . a dirty white towel. I glanced over my shoulder before bending down for a closer look. What I had thought were grease marks were actually six or seven small batteries. Double-A. But there was no radio or torch. The towel looked lumpy. I lifted up one of the corners. Underneath was a roll of thick black tape.

As I straightened up, I was suddenly aware of someone outside the pillbox. No noise, just a momentary eclipse of the bright patch on the floor, as if someone had moved past the gun aperture. I spun round, barely breathing. Silence. Very slowly, I began to walk towards the doorway.

I looked out at the landscape. Grass, trees on one side, fence and road on the other. More trees in the distance, tiny cows dotted about on the hills. No people. But I knew. Someone was watching me. Someone was there.

I looked across at the trees, half in shadow. A journalist, perhaps? Better than some unknown nutter, but only just. I looked round again. The field was too exposed, the sky was too big. I suddenly felt tiny, as if a giant's foot might come down and squash me at any moment. But this time, I was sure. *I wasn't the only person there.* I started running across the field. I ran out of breath. I felt nauseous and spat out huge gobs of saliva. I got a stitch. But I didn't stop running until I collapsed in a winded heap in Joan's sitting room.

I dragged the curtains shut and wedged the desk chair under the door knob. What good would that do, for God's sake? I could almost see the axe crashing through the door, slashing the panels to strips of kindling, Jack Nicholson's face. Bile in my throat, going to be sick, I need water, I'm going to be sick, roll of black tape, kidnappers, Lesley Whittle in that bloody drainpipe, and I was alone, I was *all on my own.* I looked down. My mother's hair was still there. Curled up on the carpet like a sleeping animal. Our hair is dead, even when we're alive and it's attached to us, it's dead. But when Mum was alive, he'd touched it, he'd cut it off. I couldn't bring myself to pick it up so I nudged it under the desk, out of sight, with my foot. The red light on the message machine was flashing: the voice, the man outside who was going to kill me.

I couldn't listen. I put my finger on the start button but I couldn't press it. *I know where you live.* London, that was in London. But if he was here, if he'd followed me . . . The internal doors to the front of the house were already locked. I went round to the back door and dragged chairs, the hall table and anything else within reach in front of it, and then I rushed round the kitchen and scullery fastening the shutters. I pulled all the dustbins in front of the yard door. They wouldn't actually stop anyone, but at least I'd hear them coming. Then I went back to Joan's sitting room and barricaded myself in for the night.

11

I fell asleep in the end. I must have been tired, because I didn't wake until the back porch bell rang at eleven o'clock the next morning. For a second, I panicked, but then I heard a woman shouting my name outside. Joan's sitting room is on the same corridor as the back porch, so the voice was quite clear. It was Carol Curtis. 'Doe? You all right in there?'

'Just a minute.' It was more like five before I managed to clear a path through the back hall. I undid the latches, but the hat stand was jammed underneath one of the cross bars and I couldn't get the door open more than a couple of inches.

Carol Curtis's face wedged itself in the gap. 'What the fuck is going on, Doe?' She gave the door a hard shove. There was a cracking noise as one of the hat stand's legs broke. 'Christ.' Carol looked down at the splintered wood.

'I hope that wasn't an antique. Can we come in now, do you think?'

'Yeah. Sorry. Hello, Mrs Curtis,' I said, as Carol's mother appeared behind her.

'Hello, dear. We didn't mean to wake you. We just came to talk about the funeral, really, but we can go away if it's not the right time.' She looked round at the deranged piles of furniture, then back at me. 'Are you all right? It looks as if something's been going on.'

'It's fine, honestly. It's very kind of you to come over, Mrs Curtis.'

Carol folded her arms. 'Doesn't look fine to me. What happened?'

'Carol!' said Mrs Curtis. She turned to me. 'If you don't want to talk about it, dear—'

'It's all right. It was last night. I thought I heard a noise, that's all.'

'You must have been really frightened to do this.'

'You know what it's like when you're on your own and it's dark—'

'Well, it can't be very nice all alone in such a big place,' Mrs Curtis said. 'I used to say to Joan, I don't know how—'

Carol interrupted, rolling her eyes. 'Too much imagination, that's your problem. Talking of which, we met Jimmy on the way up. He'll be here in a minute.'

'Oh. Right. Fine. Why don't you go through to the kitchen? I'd better go and put some clothes on.'

'I can shift this lot out of the way, if you like,' Carol offered, 'while you get tarted up.'

By the time I'd got washed and dressed and down to the kitchen, all the shutters were open. Mrs Curtis and Carol were sitting at the table, with the sunlight shining in on their hair, Carol's brown frizz next to Mrs Curtis's white. Mrs Curtis is plump and comfy-looking, with china-blue eyes like her twin daughters and a wind-battered, shiny nose like Rudolph.

'Jimmy's through there,' said Carol, nodding her head in the direction of the scullery. 'Making coffee. Go on, go and say hello.'

Jimmy was holding up Joan's bottle of coffee essence and shaking his head at it.

'Hi,' I said. Why, I don't know. I never say 'hi' to anyone, but I felt so happy to have people in the house. And I was happy because it was daylight and nothing horrible had happened and the sun was shining and the security men were coming – probably. Seeing Jimmy was a big part of it, though. I'm not going to pretend it wasn't. I can't pretend it wasn't in my mind to ask if he'd stay the night either, but I didn't get anywhere near voicing it. 'Want any help?'

'It's OK.' He was loading cups and saucers on to a tray.

'Sorry about the coffee. I should have brought some decent stuff. I was going to go and do some shopping this afternoon.' I suddenly felt a surge of – what? Bravery? Stupidity, more likely. 'I just wondered, well . . . Have you got time for lunch?'

'Yeah. A friend of mine's just opened a new place, down by the river. I've been meaning to go there. I can give him a ring, if you like.'

'Why not?' Not too difficult, said a voice in my head. Easy-peasy, in fact. 'I'll just get an ashtray.' I opened a cupboard and picked out one of the two hundred ashtrays stored inside. What was I supposed to *do* with them all? We went back through to the kitchen to join the others, and Jimmy plonked his tray on the table and patted Carol's head on his way past her chair. She raised an arm to brush him away.

'Gerroff.'

'Sorry, couldn't resist it.' Carol scowled, then smiled at him. They were obviously pretty used to each other. Perhaps they'd slept together. Just because it didn't say so on the pillbox didn't mean it hadn't happened. Carol 4 Jimmy 4 ever 2 gether, I thought. Dodie and Jimmy 4 lunch, though.

'Flowers, that's what you need,' Mrs Curtis announced. 'Little pots. Brighten the place up a bit. I said to Joan, now you're on your own, you should get some nice plants from the market, but she wouldn't. Another thing to worry about, she said.' I looked round the kitchen. Except for the cat, which was asleep on the dresser, all the surfaces were bare. Mrs Curtis leant forward. 'I was very fond of Joan, you know. We all were. We don't want to interfere, but you will let us do something to help, won't you?'

'I don't think . . .' I could feel Jimmy looking at me. *They want to help.* 'Well, there's the chapel. It's got to be cleaned, but I don't know where the key is or anything.'

'Have you tried the little box behind the scullery door?' asked Mrs Curtis. 'Joan kept a lot of keys in there, the ones she didn't use much.'

'I didn't know there *was* a little box behind the scullery door.'

'Have a look.'

I looked, and found a little wooden cupboard perched on the wall. Inside were fifteen or twenty little hooks. All but one had labelled keys hanging from them. Attic 1, Attic 2, Attic 3, Attic 4, Storeroom 1, Storerooms 2, 3, 4, 5. One of them must fit the door of my old room, I thought, but didn't take them. I wanted to remember my room as it was when I had it, not as a jumble of dusty furniture and old suitcases. S's Room. S? Susan's Room. I hadn't been up there, hadn't wanted to. Hadn't it been locked after she went? Surely it had become Virginia's room . . . I couldn't remember. Joan had obviously never got round to changing the label.

Carol stuck her head round the door. 'Found it yet?'

'Hang on.' Chapel. Next to S's Room. I unhooked them both, shut the cupboard and stuffed S's Room into my pocket. 'Got it!'

There were two identical keys on the chapel ring, so I gave one to Mrs Curtis who'd said she'd pop in before she went home to see what needed doing. We discussed Brasso supplies for a while, and whether the aisles could stand a spot of Flash, and I explained where the flowers were going. Mrs Curtis made notes in a spiral notebook and said I could leave it to her and the vicar.

'Thanks, Mrs Curtis. I'm extremely grateful.'

'Like I said, we were all very fond of Joan. Besides, if you can't do something for a neighbour, there's not a lot of point, is there?' She sipped her coffee essence. 'It's a long time since I had any of this. It's not too bad, come to think of it. Mrs Bright used to get it in for Joan specially. It was a shame about the village shop, really. Course, I go up to the supermarket once a week for our big shop, but still, I miss being able to drop in. Norma Bright was heartbroken when she had to close down, but—'

Jimmy looked up from the faxed menus he was reading. 'Is that her name? Norma?'

'Well, that's what people were called in those days. Names like Norma. And Joan. And Shirley, of course, that's my name. That's another one that's gone out of fashion. But they'll come back. Probably be your granddaughters, Carol. Joan. Jean, June, all those names . . .'

'God, I hope not.' Carol grimaced. 'I've got to say it, Doe, this coffee . . .'

'I know. Come back next week, I'll have some decent stuff.'

'All right. Get some instant though. I don't like posh coffee.'

'Peasant!' said Jimmy.

'Oh piss off, Mr Cordon-Blew Henessey.'

Mrs Curtis ignored Jimmy and Carol and carried on. 'Norma – Mrs Bright – didn't have children, so there was no one to take it on when she retired. No one would buy a place like that, not now, the money's not there anymore. But it used to be the centre of the village. I mean, there's the pub, but that's more for the men, isn't it? The older women, they don't go into the pub like the young ones do. Can't see all us old biddies playing dominoes, can you?'

'Dominoes! Sounds like *The Archers*.' Carol made a face. 'Oooaarr, Oi'd better be getting they cows in. You never go down the pub, do you, Mum? Not unless Dad takes you, which he does once a year, about . . .'

I lost the next bit because I started wondering if Mrs Curtis was telling me all this because she hoped I'd subsidise a new village shop. I thought, I *could* look into it, I mean, it would be something for the local community, and it is sad about all those small shops being shut down – better than the begging letters, anyway. I was getting one bin bag-full a week after my father died, from people who thought I'd inherited straight off, but it's calmed down a bit now, thank God. I've kept them all, though I never opened any. Tony thinks I'm bonkers. He keeps asking me why I don't throw them away, but it seems churlish just to ditch them. Might be bad luck. Oh Jesus, I suddenly thought, supposing there's one from my mother mixed up in there that I didn't see? I've got to get them down here, sort through them. I'll have to ask Des, get a courier. There's hundreds of letters, thousands even. I'd have to read them all. I was about to interrupt Mrs Curtis and say I'd just remembered I had to make a call, when I heard her mention something about trouble with Mrs Blackstock.

'What trouble?' It came out like a machine-gun.

Mrs Curtis's eyes widened. 'It wasn't your mother, dear,' she said soothingly. 'It was Virginia Blackstock.'

'What was?'

Mrs Curtis looked as if she wished she'd kept her mouth shut. 'Well, I thought you must know. I thought Joan would have said.'

'Said what?'

'That Virginia used to . . . well, she used to take things. From the shop. Steal them.'

'Did Joan tell you that?'

'Oh, *no*. Joan would never have told me. She was always very loyal to your father, Dodie. Norma Bright told me, just yesterday. She said Virginia used to take the things, but she wasn't very good at it. Mrs Bright told me she thought she was seeing things the first time it happened – Mrs Blackstock stuffing something into her pocket – but of course it was such a small stock, she always knew exactly how many bags of sugar she had—'

'Was that what she stole? Sugar?'

'Well, I don't know about sugar, but it was always food. Packets, tins, that sort of thing. Mrs Bright used to keep a note of what she missed and Joan would settle up at the end of each month.'

No wonder Joan had paid for Mrs Bright's new hip. 'Did anyone else in the village know about it?'

'No! It wasn't like that at all. I only found out yesterday. Norma was saying what a shame Joan had died, she'd always been so good to her. And then she told me about Virginia and how Joan would always see her right. She said she didn't think it was speaking out of turn, now they're no longer with us. I wouldn't have said anything, only I thought you must know . . .' She moved her hand across the table towards me. I jumped up. I couldn't bear to sit there and be patted. The thing about Virginia pinching things from the shop didn't matter in itself. I mean, let's be honest, when did I ever give a toss about Virginia?

I leant against the dresser and tried to look unconcerned. 'Well, I knew Virginia was ill, of course, but . . .' What was it Mrs Curtis had said? *Joan was very loyal to your father.*

'She never looked very happy, did she?' asked Carol. 'You'd think, with all that money . . .' She looked at me. 'Well, it's different for you, Doe. You were born like it.' She made it sound as if it was a deformity.

'There's nothing else we need to talk about, is there?'

Carol put her hands up as if I'd pointed a gun at her. 'Look, Doe, we only came to see if we could help.'

'I don't mean that. Are you sure there's nothing else that everyone knows except me? I feel like the village idiot. I don't know why I don't just go out and stand outside the pub and you can all throw coconuts at me. Give you a good laugh.' Even as I was saying it, I knew it wasn't fair. I mean, there they were, trying to help me, but I just felt so pissed off about everything. I looked at the three of them sitting round the table. Jimmy had his head down, scribbling notes in the margins of the sample menus. Carol and Mrs Curtis were staring at each other. Carol's eyebrows were raised and her head slightly nodding for yes, go on, and Mrs Curtis's eyebrows were knitted and her head almost imperceptibly shaking for no way, absolutely not, don't you dare.

'What?' I shouted. They both jumped. Mrs Curtis got in first. 'I'll just wash these up, then we'll be going.'

'What is it?'

'It's not important. I'm sure you've got things you want to get on with.' Mrs Curtis picked up three mugs together with her fingers and thumb and put them on the tray.

'I think we should tell her, Mum,' said Carol.

'Tell me what?'

'We don't even know if it's true.' Mrs Curtis poured a little bit of milk into the ashtray and swirled it round to make sure Carol's cigarette butts were properly extinguished.

'I saw it, Mum! I wasn't making it up!'

Jimmy looked up. 'Saw what?'

'The man,' said Carol. 'I saw him. Mum wouldn't believe it when Albert said he'd seen him, and when I saw him she said I was just saying it to get attention.'

'Hang on,' I said. 'What man?' I nearly said, is it the man who's been hanging round here, but I stopped myself just in time. I don't know why, I just had this feeling that I shouldn't tell them too much.

'It was a long time ago, now,' Mrs Curtis said. 'A couple of months before your mother – you know . . .'

'End of 1975?'

'I suppose it must have been. Well, Albert kept saying that he'd seen this Land Rover parked up in the lane behind the wood, late at night, with a couple inside. A courting couple, that's what he called it. Well, first we said, so what? But he kept saying he knew who they were, making a big thing out of it. We all laughed at him. We said what you doing spying on people in the middle of the night, you dirty old sod? Because he was like that. But he kept on about it, nearly drove my Fred round the bend. He told practically the whole village, and in the end we thought he must be making it up, or how come he wouldn't tell us who it was? In the end, Chalky, that was the other man we'd got working for us in those days, he was a big lad, he held old Albert over our water trough and said he'd have him in there if he didn't tell him who it was he'd seen. It was around December, and pretty cold, so Albert told him. Chalky said, "You're lying," and dropped him in anyway. Because he said it was your mother, you see. Your mother and a man, in the back of this Land Rover.'

'What man?'

'Albert didn't know. But nobody believed him, that was the thing. We all knew your mother, and she wasn't that sort. Albert got a lot of stick over that, but he wouldn't take it back, even though we told him to his face he was having us on. Anyway, then Madam here . . .' She indicated Carol. 'I didn't think she even knew about what Albert was saying, but she must have been listening where she shouldn't. The next thing is, she says she's seen them, too.'

I looked at Carol. 'Did you?'

'Yeah.'

'I thought she was talking rubbish,' said Mrs Curtis. 'I said to her, "Come midnight you're sound asleep in bed, you and Jackie, not prancing about in the woods," but Carol said the Land Rover was parked down our lane and she'd seen it from the window, with the two of them in there, canoodling.'

'I got a bloody slap for it, an' all,' said Carol.

Jimmy grinned at her. 'Quite right too.'

'Oh, shut up, you.'

'I still think you might have dreamt it, Carol,' said Mrs Curtis. 'You heard Albert going on, and it came back to you in a dream. It was that simple.'

'No,' said Carol. 'I saw it.'

'Well, if you saw it, why didn't Jackie see it too? Always do the same, you two, even now. One's got it, the other's got to have it, an' all.' It crossed my mind that that might include Jimmy.

'I told you, Jackie was asleep. I just woke up and decided to have a look out the window, that's all.'

Mrs Curtis snorted. 'Nothing to see. Pitch black.'

'No, there was a moon, no clouds. Lovers' moon.'

'What did the man look like?' I asked.

'Couldn't see much. I only recognised your mum because of the hair. He had one of those droopy moustaches, though. Hair going over the collar like they all had back then, dark brown or black. That was all I could see, really.'

'Tall? Short?'

'He was sitting down, so I couldn't see how tall he was or if he was fat or thin or anything like that.'

'Were they—'

'He was leaning over her and she had her head right back and he was kissing her. I thought it was the most romantic thing I'd ever seen.'

'And it was definitely my mother?'

'Yeah, honestly.' Carol looked over at her mother, who was prodding inside the sugar bowl with a spoon. 'I wouldn't lie about this, whatever she says.'

'Why didn't you tell me, Carol?'

She lit another cigarette. The milk in the ashtray made her match hiss when she threw it in. 'I couldn't – something like that – I was only eleven, Doe, remember? First I thought I would tell you, because it was this big secret, the biggest secret I'd ever had, but then when I told Mum she said I wasn't to tell stories.'

'But afterwards, when she was kidnapped? Did you tell anybody then?'

Mrs Curtis put the spoon down. 'I'll tell you what happened, Dodie. Like I said, I didn't believe Carol at first, but she stuck to her story and she's never been a liar, so I began to wonder if there might be something in it. And after it all happened, the kidnap and everything, I thought I'd better tell Fred. Well, we talked about it, should we tell Joan or the police or what should we do, and we decided it was better to leave it alone. We didn't see it would do any good, Dodie. It wasn't anything to do with the kidnap and we thought the press might hear about it. It's not right to speak ill of the dead, and besides, it would have just made things worse for everyone, especially your poor father.'

'You mean my poor father who refused to pay the ransom?'

'Well, I don't know about that, Dodie. Perhaps it wasn't the right thing to do, not telling anyone, but we wanted to protect you – all of you – that was why we didn't.' She picked up the spoon and started poking the sugar again.

I thought, OK, December 1975. Longish dark hair. In 1975 half the earth's surface was covered in men with long hair and moustaches. Anyway, Mum's kidnap was political, not personal. It was a gang, not some individual sad act. Get a grip, I told myself. Don't let's jump to conclusions. I mean, all elephants may be grey, but everything that is grey is not an elephant.

12

It's not right to speak ill of the dead. Especially when the dead are still alive, Mrs Curtis. The only person I'd told about Mum was Des. I knew I should start telling people, but I couldn't face it. They'd all ask the same questions, and I didn't know any of the answers. Besides, I still couldn't work out how I felt about it. I was sort of angry and sad and numb at the same time, which didn't really amount to anything much.

I thought about the man Carol saw. The man with longish dark hair and a moustache. Mum must have gone with him willingly, to sit in his car and be kissed and petted in the middle of the night. Skittering down the drive in the warm breeze in her white Ossie Clark dress and matching high-heeled sandals. Except that it was December, so she'd have been frozen. In any case, she had given the Ossie Clark away in the tube station. A fur coat, then. Clutching the collar round her throat with one slightly blue hand which the lover would rub for her between his own warm ones. Big hands, warm and dry. The blow-heater making a racket. He'd clean the Land Rover specially for her, and wind down the window if he wanted to smoke. They'd spread her fur coat across the floor in the back and have sex and lie talking afterwards, propped up on their elbows, facing each other. She'd giggle, complain that his moustache tickled. He'd offer to shave it off but she wouldn't let him. How did she get back? Did he drive her up to the gates? Dangerous, if someone in the village heard the car and came up to their window. Or did she jump out of the car where it was parked and lean into the window to kiss him before she ran away into the dark? He'd whisper 'Will you be all right?' and she'd say 'I love you' and he'd say 'You too' and then he'd sit behind the wheel and watch her disappear and wonder if she'd really been there at all.

Who was he? A moustache. Dark hair falling over his collar. I kept imagining Jason King, except I think that was in the early seventies. God knows why I thought of him, because I only ever saw the programme once, at the twins' house. I hadn't had enough practice at watching TV and films to be able to figure out what was going on, so I kept asking questions and annoying them. If the man was Mum's lover, I thought, she might have run away with him. Or perhaps he had rescued her from the kidnappers and they didn't want to admit that they'd lost their hostage. Perhaps he'd come in his Land Rover and swept her up and driven off with her into the sunset. True love 4 ever 2 gether. True love without me. So why was my name in her diary and not his?

It didn't make sense. I felt like banging my head on the table. Albert and Carol could have *believed* they'd seen my mother in that car when it was just a woman who looked like her. After all, I thought, this is Great Britain. There are women with red hair and pale skin on every street corner.

The Curtises left. ('I'm sorry, Dodie. I didn't mean to upset you. You never know, Carol might learn to keep her big mouth shut one day.') When I came back from seeing them off, I thought Jimmy was going to say something about it, but he just pointed to the menus and asked what I thought of the suggestions he'd made. Afterwards, we went into Joan's sitting room so that he could ring his friend about lunch.

Jimmy put the phone down. 'He's expecting us about half-one, so we'd better get moving.'

'I just need to listen to this message first.' I gestured at the flashing light.

'Right. I'll be outside.'

'No. Wait—' Jimmy stopped at the door. 'Can you hang on a minute? Just while I play it back.'

115

He shrugged. 'If you want.'

It was Des. 'Sorry I've missed you. The security chaps are coming round tomorrow evening. That was the soonest they could fit it in. I've told them it'll be a big job. I've got to go out now, but we'll talk tomorrow. They'll have everything fixed up in no time, don't worry.'

Tomorrow meant today, I thought. This evening. 'Great.'

'That's a good idea.' Jimmy nodded at the answer machine. 'Specially if you're going to keep the place.'

'I don't know if I am. To be honest, I don't know what I'm going to do about anything. I'm sorry, Jimmy, but do you mind if we don't talk about it?'

Actually, I had quite a nice day after that. Jimmy's friend's restaurant was great. The sun shone and we sat in the garden and watched the swans floating about on the river, and Jimmy's friend came out and they talked about covers and commis chefs and things. When the friend asked me what I did, I told him I was between jobs. I felt relaxed for the first time in ages. I even told a joke. Jimmy put his arm round me on the way back to the car.

'Thanks for not telling him,' I said.

'Who you are, you mean? What you said before . . . I thought you wouldn't like it.'

'It's just that people act differently the minute they know who I am. They either try to suck up to me, or they make snide comments to show how unimpressed they are.'

'John wouldn't. He's all right.'

'You'd be surprised.'

'You really don't trust people much, do you?'

'You wouldn't trust people either, if you were me.'

'If I *were* you, who would cook dinner for fifty-eight people tonight?'

'Fifty-eight? Hadn't you better get started? I could drop you off.'

Jimmy looked at his watch. 'I'm not totally indispensable.

I could come shopping with you – only if you want, of course.'

I was pleased that Jimmy would see me doing something normal for a change. As far as supermarkets are concerned, I was a late starter – I hadn't actually been inside one until I was nineteen – but since then I've had lots of practice. Unlike Tony. I remember going to visit him when he was living in New York and trying to do his own housekeeping. He kept forgetting to make shopping lists, so he'd just copy what other people put into their trolleys. When he got home he'd find that he didn't like half of it and the other half wouldn't fit together to make a meal, so he'd end up throwing it all away and ordering take-out instead. His pantry consisted of pasta, old lettuces, and grapefruits which he used to explode in the microwave.

By the end of the shopping, I was feeling really smug – I'd even remembered to get cat food – and then I blew it. We were drinking mineral water in the little coffee bar and watching mothers trying to talk over the howls of toddlers who threw themselves about as much as the straps of their grimy buggies would allow and refused to be pacified with orange juice.

'Why do they bring their children to these places? They obviously hate it, poor little things,' I asked.

'Because they don't have any choice.' Let them eat cake. Well done, Dodie.

'Do you despise me?'

'No. Why should I?'

'For not knowing what it's like when you can't afford to have a choice about bringing your baby to the super-market.'

He shrugged. 'Everyone has problems. Yours are just different, that's all.'

'It's not that simple, though, is it?'

Jimmy sighed. 'Dodie, I'm really sorry, but I can't talk about all this now. I need to get to work.' He didn't say anything on the way back to the car and I thought he was angry. I didn't want to do the what's-wrong bit, because it was such a girly thing. Anyway, I knew what was wrong. Me. He wasn't making it an issue, I was. Des told me once that the Americans had this acronym they used during the war, SNAFU. Meaning, situation normal, all fucked up. Actually Des said all fouled up but he was sure I could guess what the F really stood for.

It got better on the way to the restaurant, though. Jimmy asked me if I'd heard from the fingerprint man.

'God, I'd forgotten about him. He probably didn't find anything worth reporting. He said they probably wouldn't.'

'Still, they haven't asked me for a statement.'

'Well, the burglar didn't actually *do* anything. At least, I don't think he did.'

'You don't sound very sure about that.'

I wasn't. 'Jimmy? It doesn't matter if you're busy, I mean, don't worry, it's not essential, but—'

'What? Come on, spit it out.'

'Can you come round this evening? There's something I want to talk to you about.'

'I don't get off till about half past twelve . . .'

'You could always come for a nightcap. If you're not too tired, I mean.'

Jimmy looked as if he was making up his mind about something. 'All right, I will. Can you drop me round the corner?'

I pulled up outside the back door of The Artichoke. Jimmy leant over and sort of buffeted my cheek with his lips before he got out. I drove home feeling far happier than I had any right to be, under the circumstances.

The Habitat people arrived with the double bed, which turned out to be a tubular four-poster with long muslin curtains. They agreed to take it up to the ballroom and assemble it. I didn't think I could face waking up in the middle of the night surrounded by shrouded furniture, so I stripped off the dust sheets and stuffed them in one of the cupboards on the landing. I can't honestly say that the bed was the most exquisite piece of furniture I've ever seen, and it looked utterly bizarre beside the *chaises longues* and stick-insect thickets of music stands, but it was certainly better than cushions on the floor.

After that, the local police rang and said they understood I'd recently experienced a break-in and please could they come to see me about security later on today. By the sound of it, they didn't even know Joan was dead. I wondered if I was supposed to have phoned them. I would have thought it was the hospital's job, not mine, but if it *was* mine, no one had mentioned it. It was safe, at four o'clock on a sunny afternoon in Joan's sitting room, to imagine the prowler, but all the same, I kept one hand on the telephone. He'd come out at night, in the dark, pushing his way past the shrubs, wet leaves clogging the soles of his trainers. Squatting behind bushes so he wouldn't be seen. Dark anorak, woollen hat pulled down over furtive eyes, dirty jeans, a torch, a knife, the roll of black tape which would sting your lips when he yanked it off and told you not to scream or he'd kill you . . .

Luckily, Tony rang before I could go into paranoia overdrive. 'Darling, I'm so sorry. Why didn't you tell me?'

'You mean about Joan? I did. I left you a message.'

'No, I mean before. You should have called me, Dodie. I'd have been straight there.'

'It's all right, Tony. I've been coping.'

'Have you really, or are you just saying that? You're a runner-away, Dodie, not a facer-up.'

'I'm here, aren't I? And I've been doing all the arranging, for the funeral and everything.'

'Why? For God's sake, get someone else to do it.'

'I want to do it myself. Joan would have.'

'I met her once. Townswomen's Guild?'

'Close, but no cigar. WI.'

'Oh yes, of course. I knew it must have been something to do with jam and backbone.'

'Will you come to the funeral? It's Saturday week.'

'Course I will. I could stay a couple of days if you like, give you a hand. Have to bring the chauffeur, though.'

'The what? Oh, your licence.'

'You can put him up, can't you? That house must have about a hundred bedrooms.'

'No, only twenty five.'

'Well, it's not what you'd call *bijou*, is it?'

'What's he like?'

'Dominic? Gorgeous. He was in the City but it all went pear-shaped, so now he works for me. Have you got satellite?'

'I've only got a black-and-white at the moment. I'm getting another one sent up though. But they've got it in the village pub. Why, anyway? You hate sport.'

'Dominic's mad about it. He'll watch it all day if you let him. He's as straight as they come, of course, but you can't have everything. Actually, I'm wondering if I should go straight. A woman said to me the other day what a great loss it was.'

'Please don't. It'd be terribly confusing.'

'That's it! I could say I'm confused. What a good idea.'

'But that's like me saying I'm going to be a lesbian.'

'Well, you could be a lipstick lesbian, or . . . No, no, no. You'd have to go for the vampire look – dead-white skin and red nails and black clothes. Like a sort of red-headed Morticia. You know, the Addams Family.'

'Yuck. I've gone off it now. Anyway, I haven't got any gay genes or whatever it is you need.'

'Oh bollocks, gay genes. You don't actually believe all that crap, do you? Anyway, if I'm going to be straight, I could sort of bond with Dominic. I could create a sort of bloke heaven for the two of us. Melinda Messenger posters, fridge full of beer, dartboard, football annuals round the walls, we could sit there talking about rugby . . . Oh well, never mind. Listen, Dodie, I've got to go out and do metropolitan things in restaurants. Give my love to the WI, won't you? And listen, if there's anything I can do – anything at all – just pick up the phone, OK? Doesn't matter what time it is, give me a ring. If I'm not here, I'll phone you the minute I get back. Will you do that?'

'You sound like Claire Rayner.'

'Listen, lovey, I *am* Claire Rayner. But will you promise me?'

'Yes. Thanks, Tony.'

'Any time. Love you. Look after yourself.'

As I put the phone down, I wondered why I hadn't told Tony about Mum. Tony's probably my closest friend. I know he thinks it's mad trying to live off my earnings – he's told me often enough – but we get along fine. We've even discussed getting married. It's not such a terrible idea. Tony's incredibly kind, and I know he hasn't got an ulterior motive because a) he's got nearly as much money as I have, and b) he's as gay as anything. I don't know why I didn't tell him, really. Or Jimmy. I'd been over and over it so many times in my head. I suppose I felt I couldn't bear to rehash it all over again.

There was a great slew of paper from the wine merchant's hanging out of the fax machine, and I was about to tear it off when two smiling security men arrived. The one in charge brandished his clipboard. 'We thought you'd prefer to see us sooner rather than later,' he said.

'Oh, absolutely. Shall I show you round?'

'We'd like to start outside, if that's all right with yourself. We're making a report for a . . .' he glanced at his clipboard, '. . . a Mr Haigh-Wood. Is he here at all?'

'No, but I was about to give him a ring, if you want to speak to him.'

'I'd like a quick word, if I may.'

I ushered them into Joan's sitting room and went off to finish putting away the shopping while they talked to Des about patrols and things. I returned just as the clipboard man was saying, '. . . and I think the young lady would like to talk to you.'

'Des? Could you do me a favour?'

'Depends what it is, my child.'

'Could you get my TV couriered up here? In a van?'

'Television? At Camoys Hall? Things are going to be different from now on, I can see that.'

'Joan's always had a little black-and-white one in her room. Didn't you know?'

Des paused for a moment, and then said, carefully, 'I think I did know that, yes.'

'There are some letters, too. Begging letters in bin bags. Could you send those, too?'

'Dodie.' Des sighed. 'I've told you before, giving your money away isn't that simple.'

'That's not why I want them. Honestly.'

'I suppose I believe you. I can send Angelina round there now, if you like. What do we do about a key?'

'My neighbour's got one. Her name's Liza. She works from home, so she's usually about. Why don't I give her a ring and describe Angelina so she knows who to expect? Then I'll ring you back.'

'Fair enough.' By this time the security men were out of earshot, so I told Des about receiving the package of hair in the post.

'Yesterday morning? You mean it was sent to Camoys Hall?'

'No, it was there when I went to my flat.'

'What's the postmark?'

I took the Jiffy bag out of Joan's bin. 'Can't read it. Too smudged.'

'That's no help, then. I suppose it's not beyond the

122

bounds of possibility that it might be one of the people who kidnapped your mother. To be honest, Dodie, I don't really know what to think.'

'There was something else, as well . . .' I stopped.

'I won't know until you tell me.'

'When I said I thought there was someone outside Camoys Hall, that night—'

'I thought we'd decided that was just a bunch of yobs from the village.'

'It might have been, but I'm sure there was someone here yesterday too.' I told him about the pillbox.

'Listen, Dodie. I know you're upset, my old love, but it could have been a farmer. It could have been anyone.'

'You weren't there.'

'That's true. But with everything that's happened . . . You've been having a rough time recently and it's easy to get things out of proportion. The chap from the security firm said they could have their emergency patrol with you by tomorrow evening, and they'll start setting up the whole box of tricks the day after that.'

'Tomorrow evening?'

'Yes. Do you think you'll be able to manage? You could always get someone to stay with you.'

I didn't mention that Jimmy was coming. 'I'll be fine, Des. Really I will.'

'Attagirl. It's only for one night. You'll be snug as a bug in a rug after that.'

I rang my neighbour, Liza, and explained about Angelina needing my key. Angelina's from the Philippines. In case you're wondering, she gets a decent wage, paid holidays, a Christmas bonus and a pension. She's been working for Des for over twenty years and he's never once confiscated her false teeth. I didn't say any of that to Liza. Instead, I told her that Angelina was from work and that I'd left a few things for her to collect while I was away on a photo-shoot in

Ireland. That way, if anyone asked, she couldn't point them in the direction of Camoys Hall.

I'd just put the phone down when it started to ring again. 'Hello?'

'Miss Blackstock?'

'Speaking.'

'Inspector Halstead here. You've been engaged.'

'Yes. Sorry about that.' The room suddenly felt about ten degrees colder. It always says that in books, but it actually happened. It was boiling hot outside, but there were goose pimples on my arms.

'We have some more information about your mother, Miss Blackstock.'

'Yes?'

'As you know, we've managed to establish the identity from the dental records . . .'

'And?'

'Well, we've run some more tests. Toxicology . . . I've got the reports here. They came through this morning as a matter of fact, but I'm afraid I was busy elsewhere.' He stopped and cleared his throat. Whatever those reports said, he didn't want to be the one to tell me. I didn't say anything.

'Miss Blackstock?'

'I'm still here.'

'Well, it would appear – that is, the reports would seem to indicate – that your mother died from a heroin overdose.'

'They *seem* to indicate it?'

'Yes. That is, they do indicate it.'

'I see. Was she a . . .' The word wasn't there. 'I mean, did she have a . . . dependency?'

'We're not absolutely sure. If she was a regular heroin user, she wasn't injecting it. There are other ways, of course. There was apparently only one needle mark, so perhaps it was the first time. However, it's often the case that if someone has taken the drug before, they may not be too fussy about how it's administered. There were a number of other substances found, of a . . . a *chemical* nature. Your mother seems to have taken temazepam. We did find some tablets amongst her effects and I'm afraid that sometimes the combination of drugs . . . There was also a considerable quantity of alcohol, which can't have helped. There will have to be an inquest, Miss Blackstock, and it will be in public. Those are the rules, I'm afraid, but it's usually a verdict of misadventure in these cases. I'm afraid that people who live as your mother did do seem to be more, well, shall we say, susceptible to this sort of thing.' He was telling me they weren't going to do anything about it. Death by misadventure. The End.

'But she hardly drank anything!' Inspector Halstead didn't reply. There wasn't much he could say, really. My mother and the woman who'd turned up dead on the housing estate in Hackney might have inhabited the same body, but they weren't really the same person. The one I knew wouldn't have touched temazepam with a bargepole, never mind heroin. She wouldn't even drink coffee unless it was made out of dandelions.

'Miss Blackstock, have you had any communication with your mother over the last few years?'

'No, I thought she was dead. I told you.'

'You haven't seen her? Spoken to her on the phone?'

'No. I thought she was dead. We all did.'

'All?'

'My father, Joan – er, Miss Draycott, everyone.'

'You never heard anyone talking about your mother?'

'Well, of course I did—'

'But did you ever hear anyone saying that she might be still alive?'

'No, we had no idea.'

'I'm afraid that isn't actually the case, Miss Blackstock.'

'What do you mean, not the case?' Maggie Hill. She must have found out that my mother was still alive, and told Joan. 'Well, it would appear . . . or rather, there is evidence to suggest that in fact Miss Draycott *was* aware that your mother was still alive. A letter was found. From Miss Draycott. We found it among your mother's belongings. It had been sewn into a piece of clothing.'

'What . . . Was there a date on it?'

'Yes, there was. August 1976.'

'What did you say?'

'August 1976. The date. On the letter.'

'Are you sure?'

'That's what it says, Miss Blackstock.'

'But that was less than two months after the kidnappers were arrested.'

'That's right.'

'But it can't be right. The memorial service was in September.'

'Are you sure? After all, it was a long time ago.'

'Yes. I remember because they had to take all the vegetables and things out of the church after the harvest festival—' I stopped. *Joan had known that Mum was still alive when she organised her memorial service.* Inspector Halstead didn't say anything. I felt sick. 'If it is the right date on the letter . . . What does it say?'

'I don't have it in front of me. It's with your mother's personal effects.'

'May I see it?'

'I'm afraid we'll need to hang on to it for the time being. There may be some further investigation into the circumstances surrounding the kidnapping.' He paused and cleared his throat again. 'You see, Miss Blackstock, the letter from Miss Draycott seems to indicate that your father also knew—'

'My *father*?'

'It would appear that he also knew your mother was still alive. That's why we're anxious to interview Miss Draycott as soon as possible.' My father *knew*.

'But you can't.'

'I'm afraid we're going to have to, Miss Blackstock.'

'I mean you really can't. She's dead.'

'I beg your pardon?'

'Joan's dead. She had a heart attack.'

'When did this happen?'

'A few days ago. Sunday.' My father *knew*.

'Why didn't you mention this last time we spoke?'

'Well, it didn't have anything to do with it.' *HE KNEW. HE FUCKING WELL KNEW.*

'I see.'

Inspector Halstead started making vague noises about being difficult to ascertain, and needing to consult people and steps to be taken, but none of it went in. I suppose I must have said goodbye at some point, because I was off the phone when the men from the security company poked their heads round the door and said they'd be off now but they'd contact Mr Haigh-Wood tomorrow with an estimate. Then I just stared at the wall – or rather, I didn't see it, but I was facing in that direction. There wasn't any spare capacity in my brain to look at walls or think or cry or do anything. My father knew she was still alive. That one big fact, filling up the whole world. Like floodwater rising inside a closed room. Roaring in my ears.

13

£10,000,000. DO NOT TELL POLICE OR SHE DIES. Written in blue marker pen on lined paper torn from a spiral notepad. It was wrapped round Mum's American Express Card and posted in Finchley.

It was two days before anyone realised she was missing. She was supposed to be spending the weekend with Irene des Voeux, and that's where we thought she was until

Sunday evening. It was January, freezing cold, and Des and I were playing gin rummy on a folding green baize card table in front of the fire in Joan's sitting room when she stuck her head round the door. 'Dessie? Can I have a word? Outside?'

I started huffing and puffing, because Des had been promising me a game for ages and we'd only just got going, but he laughed and said, 'Stop fizzing. I won't be more than a minute.'

The door was ajar. I used the time to swap a few of the cards round and give myself a better hand, so I wasn't paying too much attention to what was being said outside, but I caught snippets. 'Said she wasn't there . . . A bit much not to phone . . . Irene wasn't very happy . . . Peculiar . . . Well, she has been lately . . . Does worry me . . . Don't really want to bother Wolfie with it . . .' Conversations like that went on all the time at Camoys Hall, usually somebody with a pretence of concern blowing something up out of all proportion in order to gain some advantage with my father. I stuck out my tongue in the direction of the door and called, 'De-es! Come ba-ack!' a few times. He didn't come back though. I heard his footsteps go off down the corridor.

Joan put her head round the door again and told me I'd have to play Patience for a bit because 'Des needs to have a quick word with your father.'

I remember Joan saying afterwards that it was odd Irene hadn't rung Camoys Hall on Friday, and Angela telling her not to be wilfully naïve, because it was ridiculous at her age. Joan said, 'I don't know what you mean.' Angela glanced meaningfully at me and grimaced, and Joan told her not to be vulgar. I didn't have a clue what they were talking about. I tried to look up naïve in the dictionary later, but I couldn't find it because I was looking under ny–. I suppose Angela could have been hinting that Mum was up to no good and Irene was covering for her. Perhaps she meant that Mum was meeting the man in the car.

That evening, I played cards with myself for a while and

then dozed off in the armchair. I must have been asleep for about an hour. When I woke up I was desperate for the loo, but when I tried the door of Joan's sitting room, it was locked. I yelled and hopped about for a while, but nobody came, so I dragged the armchair over to the window and climbed out into the churchyard. It was pitch dark and the wind was icy and I got a huge scratch on the inside of my leg from the window latch, but I felt as if I would burst if I didn't have a wee in the next five seconds. I stumbled along until I found a bush, and crouched behind it with my teeth chattering and the wet grass poking my bum. Then I heard car engines and saw headlights sweeping round the corner and across the side of the church before they came to a halt outside the back porch. Then the porch light came on, and I could see they were police cars and the men getting out were uniformed officers. I heard Joan's voice – something about sorry to trouble you and dreadful weather – and then they all went inside and the door shut behind them.

I ran after them and tried to open the back door, but Joan had locked it so I went round to the front sitting room, where the lights were on, and tapped on the window. I was hoping Des would be in there, but unfortunately it was Joan's face that appeared from behind the curtains. She motioned me round to the front door, let me in, and was just about to explode ('What on earth do you think you're playing at?') when Des appeared and said, 'I don't know what you've been up to, Dodie, but it's turned you purple. You'd better run along to the kitchen and see if they can't give you something to turn you pink again.'

As I ran off, I heard him say to Joan, 'Steady on, old thing. Don't be too hard on her.'

I wanted to have my cocoa in the front sitting room but Des and Joan were in there talking to three policemen. Joan shooed me away and told me to go and sit on a sofa in the hall and she'd be out in a minute. She did come out a couple of times to fetch folders and once for something that looked like a passport, but when I asked her what was happening she just tutted and shook her head at me. In the end, the policemen left and she came and sat down beside me and said that there had been a silly misunderstanding and my mother had got lost, but now everything was all right and she'd be back in the morning. Then she went all brisk and clapped her hands and said, 'Now, up to bed and straight to sleep!' I remember holding on to the edge of the sofa with my hands so she couldn't prise me off it and haul me up the stairs. I knew she wasn't telling the truth. She'd explained it all too quickly for one thing, and when I asked her why Mum hadn't asked a policeman (that school video again), Joan said it was because she couldn't find one. I didn't believe that because the street where we lived in town had a policeman permanently on duty at one end of it, and I thought you couldn't walk more than a hundred yards in London without bumping into a bobby. In the end, Des came back and said that if I went up to bed, he'd tell me a story. Of course I agreed. I was worried that Joan had lied about Mum, but a story was an even better offer than a card game.

That night was the first time I heard *Albert and the Lion*. 'There's a famous seaside place called Blackpule, that's noted for fresh air and fon . . .' I've never heard Stanley Holloway do it, only Des, and I don't suppose his accent was all that good, but I still have every word of that poem by heart. Des sat on the edge of my bed with a glass of whisky in his hand and said he'd stay until I dropped off. I remember him looking into the glass and swirling the liquid round when I asked where did he think Mum had gone and did he think the police would bring her back. He thought for a minute and said yes, and not to worry, because she couldn't have got far. I thought that made her sound like an escaped prisoner.

'Is it because she's gone funny?' I asked.

He said, 'Sometimes people get het up about things and

they need to go away by themselves to sort it out. I'm sure that's all your mum is doing, but it's best to be on the safe side.'

'Does *he* know?'

'Yes, we've told him. He says you're not to worry.'

The kidnap note arrived next morning. It was addressed to my father. £10,000,000. DO NOT TELL POLICE OR SHE DIES. The envelope was postmarked as having been collected on Friday and there was a first-class stamp, so it must have been intended for delivery on Saturday morning but got caught up in the mail. When Joan showed it to me, I went completely berserk. I remember hitting out at her with my hands, thumping her chest and arms, screaming, 'Why didn't you try to find her? You lied to me. They'll have seen the police come. Now they'll kill her! It's your fault, you told a lie, you called the police. You wanted them to kill her.' I thought, they're probably killing her right this minute and no one's doing anything.

Then some men came trooping in through the back door and I heard someone say, 'Hello, officer.'

I charged down the corridor towards them, screaming, 'Go away, go away, they'll kill her!'

One of them tried to pick me up and I flailed about in his grip, twisting from side to side, hands scrabbling for his face. 'Let me go! They'll kill her! I hate you!' I shouted.

A WPC called Rosemary propelled me into the kitchen and shut the door behind us. She was so solid, so firm and calm, I stopped crying in the end and she held my head over one of the sinks in the scullery while I vomited, then wiped my chin and asked me if I'd prefer apple juice or milk. When I said milk, she said, 'It's a good job there isn't a Humphrey about,' which I didn't understand because I'd never seen the adverts. I thought Humphrey must be the name of one of the kidnappers, and that if the police knew who they were they'd be able to save Mum, which made me feel better until I realised it wasn't what she'd meant at all.

WPC Rosemary said I mustn't worry, the police were there to help, and that I could watch them setting up their operations room if I calmed down. I decided the operations room must be like an operating theatre, so I was a bit disappointed when it turned out to be the front sitting room with a bit of extra stuff in it. The police worked in three teams: Red, Blue and Green. 'Like at school,' said WPC Rosemary. Red was based in our house, and they were the ones who talked to my father and Des about what to do. The Blues went out to search the grounds. I'm not sure what the Greens did. Whatever it was, we never saw them.

The Red policemen had a long meeting with my father and Des, and then Joan, Angela and I filed into the room and they gave us a sort of lecture about what was going to happen. The front sitting room was too small for twelve people, really, and Angela insisted on sitting cross-legged at my father's feet, and his chair was bang in the centre of the room so people kept tripping over her knees. Joan perched herself on one of the arms of the chair, and Des and I were squashed on to a two-seater sofa with WPC Rosemary. Everyone was drinking tea out of china cups which rattled in the saucers when they put them down.

It's funny, I can remember how that room looked as clearly as if I had a photograph in front of me, but I can hardly remember anything that was said. It was Detective Chief Inspector Red who did the talking. I've forgotten his real name, if I ever knew it. The first thing he said was that the police's number one priority – that's what he said, number one priority – was rescuing the victim, and that we all had to keep calm. I felt exhausted, stupefied. There I was, listening to this policeman talking about phone tapping and news blackouts and how to get my mother safely home, but he could have been talking about, I don't know . . . bath salts. I tried to make myself listen, but there were words I didn't understand and I'd drift off and find myself looking at something in the room – the way WPC Rosemary's perm was growing out, Angela's watch, which she wore with its face on the inside of her wrist, my father's elder statesman profile against the gold-coloured wing of the armchair as he listened – and then the policeman was asking questions.

'Do you know, Dorothy?' Joan asked.

'Know what?'

'What your mother was wearing when she left on Friday.'

I was scared to speak because of all the policemen. 'Yes.'

One of the policemen said, 'Well, could you tell us?' It sounded like a teacher saying, 'Perhaps you'd like to share the joke.'

'A green jumper. Big woolly coat. Brown. Brown boots. They had high heels. The jumper had a big neck.'

'Skirt? Trousers?'

'I couldn't see because of the coat, but she had a hat. It matched the coat.'

'What sort of hat?'

'A brown hat. It was pulled right down over her hair.'

'A cloche hat?' asked WPC Rosemary.

I didn't know what a cloche hat was. 'I don't know. Like a bobble hat. Without the bobble.'

WPC Rosemary leant over and patted my knee. 'Well done. That'll be a great help.'

Then DCI Red asked Joan if she'd seen Mum on Friday.

'Briefly. We only exchanged a few words. About her going away for the weekend.'

'How would you describe her state of mind?'

'I don't know. She seemed perfectly happy to me.'

My father said, 'She was looking forward to the weekend. Miss des Voeux was a good friend.' He said 'was' as if Mum was already dead. Then he added, 'I think it's time that Dorothy went to bed, Joan.'

There was complete silence while I negotiated my way to the door past all the knees and teacups, and no one said goodnight. I looked at Des, but he was sitting with his head bowed. Joan followed me out and took me up to bed. She waited while I cleaned my teeth and put on my nightdress, then tucked me in briskly. 'Now you're not to worry. Everything's going to be fine.' Then she turned off the light and scooted away to sort out rooms for DCI Red and WPC Rosemary, because they were going to stay in the house.

I can't begin to describe what that night was like. People always say to me, 'It must have been a nightmare,' but nightmare doesn't even come close. You can wake up from a nightmare. If you're awake at 3 a.m. and worrying about something, and you're grown-up, you can say comforting things to yourself like, 'It will look better in the morning,' but when someone's been kidnapped, all that goes right out of the window. Besides, I wasn't grown-up. I was eight, and I was lying in bed in a pitch dark room on my own. Mum had been taken away by these . . . these horrible people, and no one was doing anything to get her back. Of course, *now* I can see that the police were following their special procedures and I think they were probably doing quite a good job until the Suffolk police opened fire on Randall's Farm and cocked everything up. But at the time no one explained anything. WPC Rosemary was kind to me, and so was Des, and Joan, in her way, but no one really sat me down and talked about it, and I was frightened to ask in case someone told me I'd never see Mum again.

The first four days were the worst, while we waited for the kidnappers to get in touch. DCI Red kept saying, 'We can't do anything until they make contact. All we can do is wait, I'm afraid.' WPC Rosemary told me, 'They won't hurt your mum. She's worth too much money to them, and if something's worth a lot of money, you have to keep it nice and safe, don't you?'

My memory of that time is that I am permanently standing in some doorway or other at Camoys Hall, trying to figure out what was going on before someone saw me and turfed me out. Standing there, staring and staring. Watching the detectives, like that Elvis Costello song. Except that I was far from cute. Creepy, more like it, with my bluish-white skin and unblinking gaze from behind my newly acquired pebble-thick glasses, my two eyes never quite moving in the same direction because of my squint.

Men in jeans and sweaters appeared with suitcases full of screwdrivers and lay on their sides under Georgian tables, fiddling with telephone points and unrolling cables. There were other suitcases, small two-coloured ones that looked like Joan's Dansette record player, containing great spools of tape – reel to reel, I think it's called. Dinosaur stuff, compared to today. At first the men tried to talk to me, jolly me along, but I could never manage to answer them, and after a while they gave up. I once heard one of them ask the others if they thought I was 'all there'. They were sitting round the kitchen table eating lunch and didn't realise that I was just outside the door.

The one who answered was called Dave Cook. 'Leave her alone, poor little cow. How would you like it if it was your old mum?'

'Nobody'd take my mum, she'd scare the living shit of out 'em. Tell you what, though, Cookie, I wouldn't mind if they kidnapped my old lady. I'd tell 'em they could keep 'er.' There was a loud burst of laughter, followed by shouts of 'Leave it out' and 'You dozy bastard!' when one of them sprayed the others with masticated crisps. Then the one who'd said about kidnapping his wife saw me standing in the doorway and nudged the man next to him, and one by one they fell silent. They stared at me and I stared back.

Dave Cook held out a triangle of white bread and ham. 'Want a sandwich?' I shook my head. 'Piece of cake?' I shook my head again. 'Very sensible. You don't want to go eating between meals. End up like him otherwise.' He pointed to a fat policeman at the other end of the table. Then he turned back to the others. 'You going to do something about that dodgy microphone?'

From then on, Dave Cook was my hero. I don't think I said more than half a dozen words to him in as many months, but every time he came to Camoys Hall to check the bugging and taping equipment, I followed him everywhere. At some point I overheard someone say it was his birthday, so I made a card for him. I drew a picture of him and his bugging equipment in felt-tip and signed it 'From your shadow' because that's what he called me. If for some reason I hadn't appeared, he'd say, 'I was wondering where my shadow had got to.' I probably drove him mad, but he never showed it.

They'd found Mum's red Mercedes the day before the kidnappers phoned. It was parked just off Elgin Avenue, near Maida Vale. Someone reported it because a couple of the windows had been broken and it was way too smart to belong to anybody local. Those houses are worth a small fortune now, but in those days they were stuffed with four or five families each and falling to pieces, with the porticoes painted in purple or frog-green or bright pink, always peeling, and filthy net curtains or bits of tie-dye cloth hanging in the windows.

The police said it was impossible to tell if anything had been stolen from the car because of the broken windows. Mum's overnight bag had gone, but there was a case of Château Margaux in the boot which she'd taken as a present for Irene. The police towed the car away and did tests and things, but they didn't find anything useful.

On the evening of the day they found the car, I was watching Dave Cook testing his equipment in the sitting room when I heard my father's voice, raised in anger, coming from the front porch. I was standing just inside the doorway, so I backed a few steps into the hall, just enough to hear but not be seen

'It's robbery, that's what it is, extortion and *robbery*! I will not have it,' I heard my father say.

'It might be genuine, Wolf.' Des's voice, very calm. 'The

police think so, and they have done this sort of thing before, after all.'

'The police! They've got no idea of the way that woman operates. I will not be made a fool of. She won't get a single penny.'

'Well, the police think you should tell the kidnappers that you can't afford the ransom. Then they'll lower their demand, and the longer it goes on, the greater their chance of finding her will be.'

'Kidnappers! She has no intention of being found. She's got a great big stick, and she's stirring it up. Trust a woman to do that.'

'Wolf, there's no proof—'

'I don't *need* proof! You've seen her behaviour. There's your proof. What more do you need?'

'Why would she do it?' Des's voice sounded more controlled than I'd ever heard it. 'She loves you, Wolf.'

'She's got you twisted round her little finger like the rest of them. All rushing around like a bunch of fools, dancing to her tune. I will not be dictated to by a mad woman.'

That was how I learnt that my father thought it was all a hoax, and that Mum was behind it. WPC Rosemary had said to me that if things were worth a lot of money, you had to look after them. 'Keep them nice and safe,' was what she'd said. But when the kidnappers found out Mum wasn't worth a single penny to my father, she wouldn't be safe any more. I wasn't angry with Des for not standing up to my father, though. I knew why he hadn't. I mean, I hadn't run outside and shouted, 'It's not true! You've got to help her, she's my *mother*!' I'd wanted to, but I didn't. No one ever did. Instead, I shuffled back inside the door of the sitting room. Dave Cook looked up from his pliers and wires, saw that I was crying, and offered me a Penguin bar.

My father soon locked antlers with DCI Red over whether or not the kidnap was genuine. This was relayed downstairs by Angela, who kept flying up to my father's study 'to comfort him', and being ejected. Of course, the idea that my mother had engineered her own kidnapping in order to get money out of my father was balm to Angela's soul, and she kept mouthing things over my head and making elaborate hand signals to Joan to come outside because she had hot new information from upstairs. Joan ignored most of this, or, when she couldn't, told Angela she shouldn't interfere. I was pretty sure that Joan didn't believe it was a hoax because I kept walking round corners into muttered conferences between her and Des, and I knew he thought it was real.

There were three telephone lines at Camoys Hall, and before the first call no one knew which number the kidnappers would use, so Dave Cook had them all routed through to the secretary's office, and gave her strict instructions to keep the lines clear by telling people we were having a new phone system installed and could they please ring next week because it was having teething problems.

The first time the kidnappers rang and tried to tell my father where to leave the money, he kept shouting, 'Put Susan on the line! I want to talk to my wife!' and wouldn't let them speak, so they hung up on him.

Two days later they phoned again. They refused to speak to my father and insisted that all negotiations must go through Des, or my mother would be shot. I found that out because I was in the corridor and managed to overhear Des and Joan talking on the back porch. One of the good things about living in a house the size of Camoys Hall is that there are plenty of places to hide. This time I'd flattened myself behind the door of the mud room, where the wellington boots were kept and Joan's Jack Russell, Malcolm, had his basket. They must have been walking up and down because I could only hear snatches of what they were saying. 'Lost his temper . . . Still won't believe it . . . Asked if it would put her in danger . . . Too soon to tell, now they've got her they'll probably hold out for what they can get . . . Say we won't pay it . . . I've tried, but he's adamant . . . Never seen him so angry . . . Talk to me from now on . . .'

'Shouldn't we say something to Dodie?' Joan's voice. 'I've got to tell her something.'

'No. We don't have any proof that Susan's still alive. They won't let me speak to her. We asked for a tape of her reading out today's headline from *The Times*, but Friday's the earliest we'll get anything.'

I kept wanting to ask if Mum's tape had arrived, but I couldn't because I wasn't supposed to know about it. It eventually came a day late, in the morning post, and Joan took me into the front sitting room to hear it. We all stood in a circle round the tape recorder and listened to my mother's voice, very quiet, saying the date and a headline about the Concorde factory, and that was it, except that DCI Red didn't get to the button fast enough and I heard a man's voice say, 'Now listen care—' before he pressed STOP and cut him off.

There was silence. Then WPC Rosemary said, 'You see, she's all right.'

'What did that man say?'

'That was a message for your dad.'

I looked at my father, sitting in the wing chair by the fire. If I'd called him Dad I should think the roof would have come off. He said, 'Come here, Dorothy,' and he leant forward and gave me a kiss. 'Off you go.'

Over the next few weeks I heard Mum read out headlines about Angola, the bricks in the Tate Gallery, Harold Wilson and Jim Callaghan, Rhodesia, Princess Margaret's separation, Howard Hughes's death and the Portuguese elections. I remember more news from those few months than all the rest of the seventies put together. That was all Mum ever said, the date and the headline. No personal stuff about I am all right or please send the money. Or if there was, I wasn't allowed to hear it.

Listening to those tapes became part of a weird sort of routine. Unfortunately, the kidnappers' insistence on speaking only to Des made my father more convinced than ever that it was all a hoax, even though the police told him that they could easily have asked Mum for the name of a close family friend. I heard him shout at DCI Red that Mum was giving the kidnappers confidential information about his business affairs and bank accounts. Later I heard Des say to Joan, 'How's Susan supposed to tell them about Blackstock? She doesn't even know the colour of the upholstery, for God's sake. Honestly, Joanie, the way Wolf's going, I shouldn't be at all surprised if he accuses me of kidnapping her myself.'

My father was adamant that the ransom was not to be paid under any circumstances, so Des and the police tried to string the kidnappers along by saying that it was impossible to raise ten million pounds without causing suspicion, and making counter-offers. DCI Red told Des that the more he could prolong the negotiations, the greater would be their chances of rescuing Mum. He wrote out notes in thick black marker pen on big sheets of paper for Des's phone conversations with the kidnappers. They were pinned up on the walls of the front sitting room so Des could see them easily while he was talking. Sometimes they left them up there. They said things like:

NO POLICE HERE

WORRIED ABOUT SUSAN

MORE PROOF — USUAL WAY

MOVED HEAVEN AND EARTH TO GET MONEY

CAN PAY £6M — OUR BEST OFFER

It was always the same man who rang. I heard his voice only once, by accident. I'd left a book in the front sitting room after we'd been listening to one of Mum's headlines, and when I went back for it afterwards no one was there and the tape recorder was still on the table with the tape slotted into it. I pressed PLAY, and I heard a man's voice saying, 'We're sick of being messed around, Blackstock. We know you can afford it. We'll start cutting off her fingers. One a week until you pay. Don't worry, you'll get your proof. Look in the post, Pig.'

Then silence. I couldn't move. Everything just sort of stopped and I was locked inside myself. I stood there looking at the little wheels of the tape going round and round. I don't know how much later it was that Des came in. He didn't say anything, just sat me down on the sofa and put his arms round me. I heard someone open the door and felt the motion of Des's chin against my hair as he shook his head at them. The door clicked shut.

'I'm sorry you heard that, Dodie.'

'They're going to cut her fingers off.'

'No, they're not.'

'They *are*. He said – he said—'

'I know what he said, but it's not going to happen. Your mum's been all right up to now, hasn't she?'

'I suppose so.'

'If they were going to do anything bad to her, they'd have done it already. Look, if you're with someone for a long time, you get to know them. Like you and me, we know each other, don't we?'

'Yes, but—'

'No buts. If you got to know someone, you couldn't hurt them. You couldn't cut my fingers off, could you?'

'N-no. Of course not.'

'Well then. Nothing's going to happen to her.'

I *had* to believe him. I was only five when Paul Getty had his ear cut off, so I didn't know about that, thank God. I don't know what happened to those tapes. I suppose the police must have taken them away.

Even though my father didn't believe the kidnap was genuine, he took me out of the village school when the

141

police told him there might be an attempt to snatch me as well. I missed two terms in the end, and went to a boarding school in the autumn. Joan didn't tell the village school why I was leaving, just that my father had decided to have me taught at home. No teacher ever materialised, which left me with a lot of time on my hands. I used to spend hours looking at photographs of Mum. Fashion shots, commissioned portraits, wedding pictures, family snaps, anything. I'd sit on the floor in the middle of my room and lay them out in front of me on the carpet. Joan asked me if I wanted an album to put them in, but I said no. I liked to see them all together, side by side.

Des used to sit with me sometimes, or we'd go into my mother's little kitchen and drink tea and eat pink and yellow Battenberg cake. We'd clink the mugs together and he'd say, 'Mud in your eye.'

Once I asked him, 'Des, what was I like when I was little?'

'Well, you squawked a lot, but I suppose all babies do.'

'Yes, but later.'

'When you were a tot, you mean? Well, you had a purple suede hippo called Timothy. You used to take him everywhere, and if anyone tried to take him away, there'd be *howls* of dismay.'

'How old was I?'

'Three or four, I suppose. You used to walk round the garden without a stitch on, with this *repulsive*-looking animal tucked under your arm and a big beam on your face.'

I'd forgotten about Timothy. I must have made poor old Des tell me that little anecdote fifteen or twenty times. Joan remembered Timothy, too. She eventually ran him to earth in the back of a cupboard and I reinstated him on my pillow.

The other thing Des and I used to do was sing. 'Two Little Girls in Blue', 'The Stately Homes of England', 'Lily of Laguna' and all the other songs he remembered from when he was a young man. I know all the words like other people my age know Beatles songs. It's funny, because really they're part of Des's past, but they've sort of become part of mine as well, even though I wasn't even born when they were popular. We'd stand on the porch after dinner, belting out, 'She's-my-lai-dy-love, she is my own, my own true love', and Des would pretend to be drunk and sing 'Kiss Me Goodnight, Sergeant Major'. He'd throw his head back and bellow, 'Sarn't Major, be a muvvahhhh te-oo meeee . . .' I'd howl with laughter and Joan would come fussing out and tell us to keep the noise down, for heaven's sake. But that was before they bungled the drop.

The threat to cut off Mum's fingers seemed to convince my father that the kidnap wasn't a hoax, probably because he remembered the incident with the Getty boy, and he agreed to pay. By then it was early June, and Des had managed to negotiate the ransom down to £6,000,000. The kidnappers told him that they wanted notes in certain denominations, which Dave Cook took away to be micro-filmed. They were packed into a suitcase which was fitted with a special device so that it could be located. A huge row blew up because my father wanted to put real money on the tops of the bundles and fake notes underneath, but DCI Red told him that Mum might really have her fingers cut off if the kidnapper realised he'd been tricked.

Des lost his temper, too. I heard him shouting, 'For God's sake, Wolf! You do *want* her back in one piece, don't you?'

The kidnapper told Des that he had to carry the suitcase, and that he must go to a phone box at a service station on the A12 at midnight to get instructions about where to leave it. He said that one of the gang would be watching every move he made, and they'd kill Mum immediately if he tried to trick them. There was an unexpected storm that night, and the rain came down in sheets. The kidnappers made Des go on this mad sort of treasure hunt, driving round half of Suffolk looking for phone boxes with sets of directions hidden in them, which would tell him to go to the next phone box, and the next, and eventually to the one which told him where to leave the money. I can imagine him getting out of the car in the driving rain and climbing up some drenched bank, headlights left on so he wouldn't end up in the ditch, mac saturated and water cascading off his hat-brim when he bent his head to read felt-tipped instructions in some piss-smelling phone box. It was pitch dark and Des didn't know the area, so he got completely lost in a tangle of country lanes that were little better than tracks. An unmarked police car was supposed to be following at a distance, but they kept losing the signal from the suitcase and by the time Des reached the actual drop at 4 a.m., they were miles away.

The drop was a disused Baptist chapel and Des was supposed to walk round the side and leave the suitcase in the back porch. He ended up coming at it from the wrong direction, and he said afterwards it was a complete fluke that he found it at all. He was just about to leave the money behind the building opposite, which was a cattery, when he bumped into their sign – a five-foot-high cut-out ginger cat – and realised his mistake.

At that point, the whole thing turned into a farce. The Blue kidnap team set up a surveillance operation at the chapel, but no one came to collect the money. The local police hadn't been told what was going on, so when the village bobby discovered a suspicious-looking suitcase in the chapel porch, he immediately decided it must be an IRA bomb. This was 1976, remember, eighteen months after Guildford. His superiors agreed with him, and they cordoned off the area, called out the army, and tried to arrest our surveillance team when they crawled out from under the rhododendrons to explain the situation.

That was the beginning of the end, really. The pouring rain worked to our advantage, because the Blue team came across an abandoned Ford Anglia van stuck in a muddy gateway a few miles down the road from the chapel, and Mum's brown coat was in the back. The car was littered with so much hair and fluff and fingerprints that the police thought someone must have been living in it. They even found toenail clippings in the ashtray. They got a match for one of the sets of fingerprints: Steven Joseph Moody, shoplifter and petty thief.

The woman who ran the cattery had complained to the local police about the car. She told them she'd seen the couple who'd abandoned it, and gave them a description of Mick Martin and Maggie Hill. Suffolk in 1976 being one of those places where you're a newcomer unless your great-grandfather was born in the village, they'd been noticed by quite a few people and, after about a week, the Blue team pinpointed Randall's Farm, which was about five miles from the chapel.

The Blue team also established that Randall's Farm didn't have a phone, so they bugged the call box in the nearest village by pretending to be repair men. That was the phone Mick Martin used a few days later when he rang up Des and screamed that we were a bunch of liars and pigs and he was going to stick Mum like a pig and let her bleed to death because that was what she – and we – deserved.

I know that was what he said because I overheard Des tell Joan. The Blue team sat in the back of a laundry van parked across the road from the phone box and listened to every word. What I never understood is why they didn't arrest Mick Martin the moment he stepped out of that phone box, but I suppose at that stage they didn't know how many other kidnappers there were, or that Steven Moody was still in London. They might have thought that Mum would be killed if Mick Martin didn't return, but . . . Well, let's just say that if things had just worked out differently, then, *even then*, everything might have been all right.

Finally, one of the local police – who by then were totally at loggerheads with the surveillance team – caught sight of

Mick Martin in the lane outside Randall's Farm and thought he might be the man who'd abandoned the car, so he tried to apprehend him. (That was the word he used in court, I swear to you.) Mick Martin saw him, panicked, pushed him into the hedge and rushed back inside to warn Maggie Hill. Of course, the policeman immediately got on his walkie-talkie and summoned every single unit in Suffolk. Within twenty minutes, Randall's Farm was ringed by armed police.

On the newsreel, it says that the kidnappers fired the first shot, but everyone was so hyped up it may well have been a trigger-happy police marksman. But whoever started it, by the time the Blue team arrived, there was a miniature war going on. The name Randall's Farm makes it sound terribly agricultural and grand, but I shouldn't think it had been much of a farm even in its heyday, and all that was left by 1976 was a sagging cottage with an overgrown garden beside it, and a derelict barn. The newsreel shows a row of police marksmen crouched behind the crumbling stone wall of the front garden, their guns trained on the upper windows because they couldn't see the ground-floor ones for grass and weeds. When the police finally stormed the house, some of them went in through those bottom windows and the sills collapsed beneath their weight. They brought Mick Martin out in handcuffs and refused to take them off, even though his purple shirt was soaked in blood and it must have been obvious that he was dying. They laid a tartan blanket across the front path and made him lie down on it. You can't see that on the newsreel because the path is partly hidden by the stone wall, but it was mentioned in most of the newspaper reports. But you see them bring out Maggie Hill afterwards, and you see her start to scream when she realises who it is lying bleeding on the ground. Maggie Hill was wearing a blue halter dress and you can see the blood on her arm quite clearly, but it was only a flesh wound and it must have healed up before the trial because she wasn't wearing a sling or anything in court. As the policemen took her away she kept craning her head round to look at him and screaming, 'Help him! You bastards, why doesn't somebody help him?' But when the ambulance finally came it couldn't get through because all the lanes were blocked by journalists' cars. The coroner said that if the wounded policeman, Tim Corrigan, had got to hospital sooner, he would have survived. Des attended his funeral on my father's behalf.

14

While this shambles was taking place, we were playing Monopoly. I'd gone to bed, but Joan had come and woken me up and brought me downstairs in my nightie to sit in the front sitting room with the others and wait for news of Mum's release. It was WPC Rosemary who suggested that we play a game. 'We're mad keen on board games in my family. Well, it's nice to have something you can all do together, isn't it?'

For a moment I thought my father was going to explode. He would have done if Joan or Angela had said that. Instead he said, 'It's many years since I had a game of Monopoly.' It was rather like Professor Stephen Hawking saying he'd like to re-sit his Physics O-level.

Joan started to say, 'But Wolfie, we haven't got a—'

'But you've got one, haven't you?' My father smiled at WPC Rosemary. 'Why don't you fetch it and we'll all have a game?' Even while we were waiting for news of whether Mum was alive or dead, he just couldn't resist making WPC Rosemary his favourite for the evening, setting her up against Angela and Joan.

Angela made a great show of moving out of the way so

that WPC Rosemary could go and fetch the board. She'd taken to sunbathing on the roof where the journalists couldn't see her, and she was burnt almost black. I remember her kneeling on the carpet, leaning against one of my father's knees, dressed in a white cotton robe and leather flip-flops, with a dozen bracelets clanking up and down her arms. Her shining jet-black hair was pulled back into a great big pouf thing on the top of her head.

In the five months since the kidnap, WPC Rosemary's perm had grown out until her brown hair was dead straight with little squiggles at the ends. She was wearing a denim skirt and patterned nylon slippers with bands of raggedy pale blue fur across the fronts.

When she'd gone, Angela said, 'I don't know how she can bear to wear those dreadful slipper-slopper things. Man-made fibres are disgusting. The skin can't breathe.' And she stuck one dark brown leg out of her robe to show us that her skin was breathing nicely, thank you.

My father put his hand on her shoulder. 'Why don't you go and make some tea?'

'The kitchen staff have gone home, Wolfgang, and I don't know where anything is.'

'Find it, then. Make yourself useful for a change.' He aimed a not-very-gentle slap at her bottom as she got up. I wondered for a moment if he might get rid of Angela so that WPC Rosemary could take her place. It didn't occur to me that she might not want to. I remember thinking that she'd have been much nicer to have around than Angela because she was specially trained in stuff like how to stop people shouting at each other. She probably thought that Mono-poly would be a normal sort of thing to do in stressful circumstances. Mind you, you'd think by that time she might have guessed that for us, playing Monopoly under any circumstances was about as normal as a trip to Pluto.

Periodically, DCI Red would poke his head round the door and motion for Des to come out into the hall. When

Des came back a few minutes later, my father would raise his eyebrows at him and Des would shake his head very slightly, and the rest of us would pretend we hadn't noticed. My father won the Monopoly game in the end, although WPC Rosemary gave him a good run for his money. Des wasn't bad either, except that he had to keep going out to talk to DCI Red and forgetting that he was the boot and moving my dog by mistake.

WPC Rosemary patted my hand. 'I bet you're looking forward to seeing your mum again, aren't you?'

'Let's just hope she turns up, shall we?' Des said. He'd smoked all his cigars and started cadging cigarettes from Dave Cook, but Joan didn't even frown at him.

When the game was finished, Des and I went outside and tried to sing a bit, but it didn't really work.

I said to Des, 'She'll come back, won't she? They will bring her back?'

He turned to look at me and I could see he was just about to say 'Of course they will' or something like that, when he stopped. 'I don't know, Dodie. I honestly don't know. I hope so.'

We stood on the front porch and faltered our way through 'My Old Man Said Follow the Van' until I started to cry and he put his arms round me and said, 'I'm sorry, my old love.'

Then we heard car wheels scrunching on the gravel and Angela flapped the angel sleeve of her white robe out of the door and hissed, 'Journalists! Get in!'

When we got back to the sitting room, Joan was closing the shutters. I don't know how long we sat there after that, listening to the sound of the journalists congregating in the drive. No one said anything. Joan started making a list and WPC Rosemary read *Woman's Realm*. I eventually fell asleep with my head against Dave Cook's shoulder. Nobody woke me up to tell me that Mum had been rescued, because she hadn't.

And that's how I remember it, pretty much. But that wasn't how it was, was it? Or perhaps it was then, but not afterwards, when they were searching for Mum. Because my father knew she was still alive. He knew, but he didn't tell the police or they'd have called off the hunt. And he didn't tell *me*.

And Joan. I thought she loved me. Surely she'd have told me Mum was still alive, if she loved me? But she loved *him* more. I heard Mrs Curtis's voice again in my mind: Joan was always very loyal to your father. That knowledge was the ultimate secret she could share with him. I could imagine the special little chats it must have occasioned, the 'Something important I have to say to Wolfie. In private, if you don't mind,' and being able to shut the door, with smug legitimacy, in Angela's face. The everlasting trump card.

I moved so fast I practically fell up the back stairs to Joan's bedroom. I pushed the door open with both hands so that it flew back and crashed against the side of her wardrobe. I pulled the chests away from the walls, upended the drawers, yanked the cushions off the chairs, destroyed the bed and swept the books off the bookshelves. Within about thirty seconds the carpet was covered in a tangle of bed linen, splayed paperbacks, burst lavender sachets and old lady's tuna-coloured underwear, with Joan's lists scattered over the top like giant snow flakes. When I knelt down to examine it all I thumped one of my knees squarely down on the bristle side of an unseen hairbrush. It nearly went through the window when I threw it out of the way. I sifted through pincushions, little flasks of Yardley's lavender, leather jewellery boxes, chiffon headsquares, embroidered spectacle cases and packets of monster, loop-ended sanitary towels. STs, Joan called them. It must have been years since she'd needed one. There was a yellowing belt to go with them, neatly wrapped in a brown paper bag.

But there were no letters, no postcards, nothing to

indicate that Joan knew my mother was still alive. I picked up one of the lists. *Window cleaner. Why no groceries Fri? Batteries for wireless. Book chiropodist for W. asap. Sew button on blue cardigan.* She never did anything unless it was on a list. One of them would say *Write to Susan.* Or, more likely, *Write to S.*, in case Angela saw it. I'd have to read through them all. I started gathering them up in handfuls and dumping them in an empty drawer.

Joan often accused Angela of going into her room when she wasn't there and 'poking about'. If Mum had written to her, perhaps she'd hidden the letters elsewhere. This house is full of all sorts of crap, I thought. And it's vast. I could search for days and still not find anything. I looked round at the mess on the floor. If Joan saw it, she'd be horrified. Still, it would serve her right for being such a hypocrite, pretending to be Mrs Do-good-put-everyone-else-first when all the time she was living a great big thumping lie.

A dozen books were sprawled in front of me, lightly dusted with loose face powder from a broken compact. Joan wasn't much of a reader. She thought it was a waste of time. I looked at the spines: Agatha Christie, Ngaio Marsh, Margery Allingham. Only one Dorothy L. Sayers. I hide things in books, sometimes. I picked up *Death on the Nile*, held it upside down, and shook it. I did the same to *Surfeit of Lampreys*, *Murder Must Advertise*, *The Father Brown Stories* and *The Pickwick Papers*. Nothing there.

Underneath the detective stories was a copy of *The Cloud of Unknowing*, which didn't seem a Joan-type book to me, more an Angela-type one, although her thing was eastern religions, not Christian mystics. But it was beardy and weirdy enough. Perhaps Joan had pinched it from her room to annoy her. Angela's shelves were always full of stuff like *The Way of the Sufi* and the *Bhagavadgita*. Not that I ever saw her reading any of them, she just left them on the side tables for effect. The book's black spine was unbroken – in fact, it looked as if it had never been opened.

I upended and shook it, like the others, but nothing fell out. I was just flicking through the book and wondering where I should look next when I saw the edge of a black-and-white photograph that had been stuck between the pages.

I must have looked at it for a full minute before I realised that it was a wedding picture. A man and woman, standing together: she laughing, in a pale-coloured suit with a corsage, he raising a wineglass to toast the photographer, in some sort of uniform – blue, perhaps? Only the bouquet in the woman's hand gave it away. During the war? After? There was a little mark on each corner of the photograph where it had once been mounted in an album. The people looked sort of familiar, like when you meet a TV actor: you've seen the series and you feel as if you know them, when of course— It was *Joan*. The man didn't look like my father, though. His hair was fair not black, and anyway my father was never in the services, unless that's something else I don't know. I screwed up my eyes to blur the picture. Less wrinkles and crinkles, but the features were the same: Des. He must have been their best man. He had that special old-fashioned hair, like frozen ripples. Funny, I thought, still to be wearing his uniform in 1950, he must have been demobbed before that. I turned the photograph over. There was a date written on the back: March 16, 1946. And underneath, scribbled with a flourish, *Mr and Mrs Desmond Haigh-Wood!*

I stared at it. Joan was married to *Des*?

15

I suppose I should have guessed, really. The way they talked to each other, Des asking me if he could have Joan's address book, and knowing about the hymns she liked. They were married in 1946, but by 1950 Joan was married to my father. What had happened? Did he come along and woo her away from Des? But if he *did* . . . Well, you don't stay friends with someone who's stolen your wife, do you? I couldn't imagine Joan going in for adultery, either. It didn't make sense.

Something else to ask Des. One more topic for the grown-up conversation he'd promised me. I thought, I won't actually ask him, I'll just produce the photograph and see what he says. It had to be something bad, or he'd have told me before. Or Joan would. Or Angela, if she'd known.

It all made me feel terribly unimportant, somehow. I obviously meant so little to Mum that she hadn't bothered to see me again for twenty years. She hadn't even said goodbye. I remember standing in the back hall watching her put her coat on, and she gave me a kiss and told me not to come out and wave her off because it was cold. And that was it. And now Des. What was it that he had said? 'I'm grateful that you still want to talk to me.' Well, I thought, I'm bloody *amazed*. I wanted to walk out of the house and throw the key away. To walk away from the whole lot – all the secrets, all the lies – and leave it to rot. I stood in the debris of Joan's room and shouted, 'What about me? What about *me*?' There was a second's silence, and then I heard the bell clanging in the back porch.

It was an avuncular bobby called PC Russell. 'I was sorry to hear about Miss Draycott, Miss Blackstock.'

'I didn't know you knew about that. The policeman who rang me up didn't.'

'No, he wouldn't. The hospital notified us, though. The break-in was along this corridor, wasn't it?' I took him to the repaired window and we stood in front of it as if it was an exhibit in an art gallery.

'You got someone in to fix it, then?'

'Yes.'

'This was where Mr Henessey found Miss Draycott, was it?'

'Yes. The man surprised her. When he broke in. If it was a man, that is.'

'Big feet, if it was a woman. We found a footprint here.' He pointed to the table.

'Can you tell anything from it?'

'Not really. Some sort of trainer. They're two a penny. Well, not a penny, they're bloody expensive, I've just bought some for my daughter.' He sighed. 'Look, Miss Blackstock, as I said, I'm sorry about Miss Draycott, but there's not a lot we can do. We only found the one footprint, and that's not enough to go on, I'm afraid.'

'Oh, well. That's it then, isn't it?'

'To be honest, Miss Blackstock, it's often kids that do the break-ins, round here. For a laugh, mostly. The young people who live in these villages, there's not a lot for them to do, I'm afraid, so they end up hanging around and getting into trouble. I'm sure you know what I mean.'

I thought of the pillbox. 'I suppose so.'

'Once they find out you've no security . . . To be honest, Miss Blackstock, I'm surprised you haven't had this sort of trouble before now.'

'I don't know if we have. I haven't lived here for years.'

'Nothing's been reported. Big property like this, I'd get it secured straight away if I were you. There's the insurance to think of for one thing. I shouldn't think your contents insurance would be valid with the house wide open like this.' I told him that I was about to turn the place into Fort Knox, which obviously pleased him. What I didn't tell him was that Camoys Hall and its contents might not be insured at all. I remembered DCI Red asking my father if we had any cover for kidnapping and getting a flea in his ear about how all insurance companies were thieves. Joan would undoubtedly have followed his lead.

'You here on your own, are you?'

'I am at the moment, yes.'

'Must get a bit lonely, all on your tod.'

'I'm used to it. I have heard noises, though. I mean, I think there's someone—'

'Have you seen anyone?'

'No, but I'm sure there was someone there. Outside.' I sounded like some old spinster who thinks there's a burglar under her bed. 'I suppose I might have imagined it, but I really don't think I did.'

'Probably just kids, like I said. I shouldn't worry. They might make a bit of a mess, but they're not going to hurt you. A bit of outside lighting would help, though. Still, I'm sure your security firm will be advising you on all that.'

I let PC Russell out and went back upstairs to Joan's bedroom to look at the mess I'd made. Then I picked *Sleeping Murder* off the floor, went downstairs to the kitchen and made myself a gigantic vodka and tonic and took them both to my new bed in the ballroom. It was only six o'clock, but I thought, I've had it for today. I don't want to be awake any more. I'd hoped Agatha Christie would send me to sleep, but I'd forgotten how much I hate Miss Marple. If I was a character in one of those books, I'd kill her and then I'd say, 'Now solve *that*, you old bag.'

I put the book down after a while and just lay there, thinking about things. In the end, I drifted off to sleep.

I woke up because the bell was ringing. I still had all my clothes on. My eyes felt glued together because I hadn't taken out my lenses. It was dark outside. Midnight. From a window in the passage I could see a man standing under the porch light. *Jimmy*. I couldn't believe I'd forgotten he was coming. He was pantomiming something at me. I opened the window. 'Shall I let myself in?' he shouted. He held something up. The keys. Shit, I thought, I must get them back.

'I'll be down in a minute. Wait for me in the kitchen.' I shot into the nearest bathroom and stared at myself in the mirror. My clothes were crumpled and there was a red score mark down the side of my face from the edge of the mattress. I took my top off in front of the basin and flicked water under my armpits, then I poked around in the cupboards for a clean comb to pull through my hair. I splashed water on my face. Wearing only my knickers, with the rest of my clothes bunched up in front of me, I sprinted back down the passage to the ballroom. I dug a dress out of my bag, looked round for shoes, failed to find any, and went downstairs barefoot. Jimmy was standing in the kitchen with a tin-opener in his hand.

'Nice dress.'

'Thanks. It's Ghost.' God, what a stupid thing to say. Jimmy looked nonplussed, as well he might.

'Did you feed the cat?' he asked.

'No, I've been asleep.'

'She must be starving. I'm surprised she hasn't come in.' He opened the back door.

'Shaanti! Foo-ood! Shaanti!' He handed me the opener. 'Put some out. I'll go and see where she's got to.'

I got out one of the tins of cat food we'd bought at the supermarket and held my nose while I upended it in Shaanti's bowl. I could hear Jimmy moving about outside, shouting, 'Come on! Nice tasty morsels of mechanically recovered offal! Bloody cat, where are you?'

I got a glimpse of my reflection in the window as I was washing my hands. Des would have said I looked peaky. I was just wondering if there would be enough time to rush upstairs and slap on a bit of make-up when Jimmy returned, catless. 'Never mind,' I said, 'I'm sure she'll come back when she's hungry.' I picked up the bowl to put it down beside the door. 'How can cats eat this stuff? It smells disgusting.'

'Dodie . . .'

'She'll be fine. Come and have a drink.'

'She's not.'

'What do you mean, she's not?'

'She's not fine. I've found her.'

I looked round. 'Where?'

'You don't want to see this, Dodie. Why don't you let me deal with it?'

'Deal with *what*? What's happened to her?'

'All right, then. I'll show you. But you asked, OK?'

I followed him through the kitchen yard and round the side of the house to the front porch, walking on the grass because the gravel hurt the soles of my feet. Shaanti was lying on her side in front of the big doors. There wasn't much light, and at first I thought she was part of the mat. Her grey fur was covered in dirt and little stones, as if someone had dragged her across the drive.

We stood there, side by side, and peered down at her.

'Look.' Jimmy indicated the cat's head with the toe of his boot.

It looked as if it was about to burst; the eyes were bulging and the mouth gaping open as if the skin had been pulled from behind. When I bent down, I noticed there was some sort of cord, a black and white stripey thing like you'd get on an old hairdryer, round her neck. It was pulled so tight you could barely see it for fur. She'd been strangled.

16

Jimmy did everything. I just stood there shivering. When we got back to the kitchen, I started to cry.

'Why don't you go into the dining room and get the brandy?' he said.

When I came back, Jimmy had taken the coffee-machine box out of the bin and was lining it with newspaper. He went outside with it, reappeared a minute later and took it through to the scullery.

'What did you do with her?' I asked when he came back.

'One of the empty fridges. I can bury her later.' He plonked two balloon glasses down on the table and waved his hand at the brandy bottle. 'Go on, slosh it in.'

'You sound like Des.'

'Who's Des?'

'He's a—' I was going to say, he's an old friend, but I thought, fuck it. 'I'm surprised Joan didn't mention him. He was her first husband.'

Jimmy frowned at me. 'I didn't know she had a first husband.'

'Nor did I, until about six hours ago.'

'I don't understand.'

'It's ironic, really, because I've always thought . . . Well, in a way, Des and Joan acted more like my parents than my real ones. Now it turns out they were married.' I laughed. 'I've just thought . . . I could have been their daughter. I *should* have been. They should have stayed together and had me.' Jimmy was looking dangerously sympathetic. I stopped before I started to cry again. 'Stupid, isn't it?'

'How did you find out?'

'I found a wedding photograph. In Joan's room. Just before the policeman came. He said it was just kids, but it can't be, can it. Why would they kill the cat?'

'Hang on. He said what was just kids?'

'Whoever it is who's been here. He said it was just kids.'

'Has someone been here?'

I found myself telling him everything. About the men finding Mum's body, and Maggie Hill, and Joan knowing, and my father knowing, and about the voice on the phone and being sent the parcel of hair and what was in the pillbox. The lot.

When I'd finally stumbled to a halt, he said, 'Let's get some air.' So we went and stuck our heads out of the back door. 'Sorry,' he said, 'but I feel slightly sick.'

'Was it the brandy?'

'No. What you just told me. Christ.'

'Do you mind if I say something else? About what I just told you, I mean.'

'Go on.'

'Well, the cat thing. It wasn't as if Shaanti was my cat. But that other cat, the one that got run over, it sort of started the whole thing.'

Jimmy looked confused. 'But he couldn't have done that, could he, your father? I mean, he couldn't have got the cat to cross the road just at the same time—'

'No, I didn't mean he could have done *that*, but later, perhaps he could have found out who those people were, and set them up to kidnap Mum, and—'

'But you told me you'd heard him say to whatshisname – Des – that it was all a hoax.'

'Yes, I did, but that could have been to throw him off the track or something. Oh, I don't know. I feel so confused, that's all. I suppose it does sound a bit ridiculous.'

Jimmy put his arm round me. 'Look,' he said gently. 'I know your father was rich and powerful and all the rest of it, but he wasn't God. Besides, even if he could have done all those things, why would he want to? If he wanted to end the marriage, what's wrong with getting a divorce? He got a divorce from Joan, didn't he?'

'That was different. Joan stayed. Mum was getting away from him, she had a lover and she was going all funny, and . . . Perhaps he wanted to punish her in some way. That would make sense. He wanted to scare her. I told you he was a complete bastard.'

'I can't believe he was that much of one.'

'He *was*. You didn't know him! If Mum left him, she'd be free to marry someone else, and then—'

'But his first wife, whatever her name was, they got divorced, didn't they? She probably went off and married someone else, so why didn't he mind about that?'

Betty Carroll. I hadn't mentioned her. I shot out from under Jimmy's arm. 'How do you know about her?'

'It was in the *Public Image* programme. Don't be so paranoid all the time.'

'You'd be pretty fucking paranoid if it was you that—'

'Stop, stop. Sssh, sssh . . . Come here.' He put both arms round me and practically suffocated me against his chest. 'I know. I'd be paranoid too. It was a stupid thing to say. I don't blame you for feeling like this, but you've got to keep calm, OK?'

I grunted.

Jimmy stroked my hair. 'Don't grunt, Dodie. Are you all right, sweetie?' He stepped back to inspect me. 'I can't see properly in this light. Let's go back into the kitchen.'

I followed him, gasping. 'I'm fine. I just couldn't breathe.'

'You should have said.'

'I couldn't.'

'Sorry. I didn't mean to squash you. Perhaps you'd better have some more brandy.'

He peeled off his enormous jumper and lowered it over my head. 'That's better. You were shivering.' He sat down at the table opposite me and started rubbing my hands. 'Now, where were we?'

'First wife. Betty Carroll. I don't know what happened to her. My father could have had her killed and buried under a clump of roses. He probably did and Joan knew about that as well.'

'So why didn't he have your mother killed? You're saying he thought he was above the law . . .'

'He wanted to punish her, like I said. And, you know what, Irene des Voeux could have known about it too. Mum was on the way to see her, and she lived in Knightsbridge, which isn't a million miles from where the car was found. She could have asked Mum to pick up one of the kidnappers—'

'Why?'

'I don't know. To give them a lift. She could have said it was a friend or a friend's son or something. She could have lied to the police—'

'But why would she have done it? I thought she was your mother's best friend.'

'She was desperate to get in with my father. She'd have done *anything*. Jimmy, Irene des Voeux was a gold-digger. Women like that see other women as rivals, not friends. You have to understand, Mum could be very naïve. I didn't really see it at the time, but she accepted people at face value. Anyway, the point is, she thought Irene was her friend, but she might not have been.' I stopped. Mum thought Irene was her friend. I thought you were my friend, Joan. Joan and Des. Oh God, Des. Surely he hadn't known? Those evenings standing on the front porch, singing songs, had he just been pretending? Lying to me and pretending to be concerned when he knew she'd never come back? Perhaps my father had told him and Joan so that they'd be as guilty as he was. Oh God. It felt as if someone had pushed the FAST FORWARD button inside my head. The wheels were spinning round and round androundandroundandround. I closed my eyes tight and shook my head to try and get it to stop.

'Are you OK?'

'Yeah, I . . .' I opened my eyes. Jimmy was staring at me, concerned. 'Is there any more brandy?'

He leant over and poured enough into my glass to paralyse an elephant.

'But what I don't understand,' he said, 'is even if your father did want to punish her, well, in a way, he got punished too, didn't he? When the story broke, every news-paper in the country was running pictures of your mum looking stunning alongside articles saying what a bastard he was because he hadn't paid up. And you do look like her, by the way.'

'He wanted to punish her for being barmy, too. He hated madness. Do I really look like her?'

'Yes.'

'Why did you say that?'

'Because I suddenly thought of something.'

'What?'

'Well.' Jimmy looked down at the table, then up at me. 'I know this isn't really the time, but I was thinking . . . how much I want to go to bed with you.'

'Oh . . . Look . . .' I felt myself beginning to blush. 'I'm terrible in these situations. Anyway, I'm no good in bed.'

'Well, that's very romantic, isn't it?' He leant forward and aimed a slap at my hand. 'That jumper cost me sixty-five quid. Stop unravelling it.'

'Sorry.' I'd been picking at the sleeve without knowing I was doing it.

'Anyway, I don't believe you're no good in bed. Unless you don't want to, that is.'

'It's not that, it's just that I'm really not very—'

Jimmy practically leapt across the table and held his hand in front of my mouth. 'Enough. Come on.' He scooped me off the chair and into his arms, managing to bang only one of my knees on the underside of the table in the process, which was pretty good, considering. 'Oops. Sorry about that.'

'I shouldn't worry if I were you. My legs already look like overripe bananas, so one more bruise isn't going to make a lot of difference.' I leant sideways, picked up my brandy glass and held it up. 'Hang on, I'm getting hiccups.'

'How delightful. Try not to chuck brandy all over me, there's a love.'

'Are we going upstairs now?'

'That was the general idea. If you'd like to.'

'Yes.'

'Are you sure?'

'Yes. I want to. I'd like to.'

17

So there I was, sitting up in my new double bed in the ballroom. The morning sun was streaming in through the white muslin hangings and falling in thick stripes across the white piqué bedspread and showing up the itty-bitty freckles on my arms and shoulders and the whole picture was to die for. There was just one little problem, apart from my headache. I was the only person in the bed. Jimmy'd gone.

I'll share it with you, if you like. We got undressed and into bed and everything, and that was all fine. But then, well, I don't know why, maybe it was the brandy or Shaanti or maybe because I'm just fated to screw everything up, but I started to cry and I couldn't stop. Jimmy was lovely. He lay there and cuddled me and said nice things about how it didn't matter and not to worry, but that wasn't exactly what was supposed to happen, was it? When I realised he'd gone, I thought, now I'll never see him again. Depressed, I wrapped myself in a sheet and wandered out on to the landing to have a look at Uncle Lawrence.

'We left all the lights on.'

I spun round, got my feet caught in the sheet, and fell over.

Jimmy was standing there with a tray of tea. 'You'd better stay put until I've got rid of this,' he said.

I jerked my legs about, but my feet were so tangled in the sheet that I couldn't manage to stand up without taking it off altogether and I didn't want Jimmy to see me naked in daylight. I mean, lamplight and brandy are one thing, but sunshine and hangovers . . . Besides, I was starting to feel a bit sick.

'The white linen maggot.'

'Oh, thanks.'

'Keep still!' He swatted my legs with a tea towel. 'You'll tear it.' He unwrapped one of my feet. It was so pale I was surprised he could tell where the sheet ended and I began.

'There, that's better. You look rather nice like that,' he added as I scrabbled about trying to cover myself up. 'It's a shame I've got to go to work.'

'Can't you even stay for breakfast?'

' 'Fraid not. I really have got to go, Dodie. I'll give you a ring, OK?'

I staggered to my feet. 'Sorry about last night.'

'It doesn't matter.'

'I told you I was hopeless.'

'It really doesn't matter. And you're not hopeless at all.'

'Really?'

'*Really.* Don't worry about it.' He kissed me on the forehead. 'I've buried the cat, by the way.'

I leant over the rail and watched him walk down the stairs. He stopped on the turn and blew me a kiss before he disappeared out of sight. God, I thought. No sex, and he still buries the cat in the morning. The man must be a saint. Either that or he's completely demented.

I'd just about managed to get dressed when Des's van turned up with my TV and the bags of begging letters. Six bulging dustbin liners. More than I remembered. The driver lugged them into the back hall.

'Would you like a cup of something?' I asked.

'No thanks, love. I'll only have to stop on the motorway if I do. Oh, before I forget, there you go.' He handed me a brown envelope. 'It was on your mat.'

Miss D. Blackstock, Camoys Hall. Private. I waved the driver off and went into the kitchen to make myself some tea. The envelope was handwritten. I slit it open with a fruit knife and glanced at the letter, expecting a note from the vicar. There were two sheets of pale pink stationery with *Forever Friends* teddy bears in each corner. Not the vicar, then. The handwriting sloped backwards. Carol Curtis, perhaps?

It wasn't Carol.

You think your very clever but your a parasite that prays
on the blood of the working class like your mother and
the rest of your family. I got her and now Im going to get
you. I thought she loved me when she was working for the
capitalist conspiracey all the time. Well I showed her.
Your family paid the pigs to shoot us. She thought I was
stupid but now she knows different doesnt' she? I will not
write any more but I tell you YOU ARE GOING TO
PAY
PS I know the spelling is poor but it is from bad
education. A devise by capitalists to make the working
class think their stupid when their not
Don't tell the pigs like you did last time. You thought you
could escape from me but I will know if you tell them
because I am here on the spot

Almost before I realised what I was doing I'd ripped it in
four. I couldn't bear to look at it, even at the torn bits. I put
a tea towel over them while I was retrieving the envelope
from the bin and then I wrapped the whole lot in tinfoil and
shoved it into the little key cupboard behind the scullery
door. I wondered what to do. If I rang PC Russell he'd
probably tell me it was just kids having a laugh. Jimmy'd
used that door. It couldn't have been there when he left or
he'd have noticed it. For God's sake Dodie, get a grip.
Daylight, security men coming, everything OK. Everything.
Is. Going. To. Be. OK. Cup of tea. Nice hot tea. Calm down.
Boil kettle. Sugar. Got to have plenty of sugar. The bag of
demerara slipped through my shaking hands and exploded
on the flagstones.

I hoisted myself up onto one of the draining boards and
sat looking out at the old coal shed, trying not to cry. Then I

limped across the spilt sugar in my bare feet and went into Joan's sitting room to phone Tony. I got the answering machine. 'Tony, pick up the phone, please, if you're there, it's Dodie. Tony, you have to be there, I've got to talk to you, pick up the bloody phone—'

His voice cut in. 'I'm here, darling. What's going on?'

'Will you come up tonight?'

'*Tonight?*'

'Please Tony, just come. I really can't be alone. I can't bear it, for God's sake.'

'I've only just woken up, for God's sake. I need to look at my diary.'

'Bugger the diary. Tony, *please* . . .'

'*Bugger the diary?* My social life may not mean much to you, but it's all I've got. Besides, I've got to tell people if I'm blowing them out, haven't I?'

'Oh, thank you, Tony. Honestly, I wouldn't ask, but I just feel . . . I'm scared, Tony. I'm so frightened. I—'

'Look. Stay calm. I'll get dressed and I'll come straight up.'

'The people—'

'I can do the blowing out in the car. Now, stop flapping. Have you got some booze?'

'I think there's some brandy left.'

'Good. Go and drink it. I'm on my way.'

I felt a bit better after that. I didn't take Tony's advice about the brandy, but I did manage to pick most of the grains of sugar out of the soles of my feet before the cleaners arrived. There were five of them, in particoloured jumpsuits with vacuum cleaners strapped on their backs, hauling gargantuan floor-polishing machines. I asked them if they wouldn't mind starting upstairs, and then went back to the scullery to have another go at making myself a cup of tea.

I couldn't stop thinking about the letter. In the end, I got the square of tinfoil out of the cupboard, shook the pieces out on the kitchen table, fitted them back together and sellotaped them into place.

'Sorry to disturb you,' said a woman's voice. One of the cleaners. I hadn't heard her coming. 'We just need to know if we can come through here. For the steam cleaner. We need to empty the water.'

'I'm sorry?'

'It's for the carpet.' She laughed. 'Miles of it, you've got here. So that's all right then? We can bring it down?'

My mother ran away, I wanted to shout. 'Yes, go ahead, whatever.'

'Thanks.' The woman disappeared.

The tent in the garden. I suddenly remembered it. The summer before she was kidnapped, Mum had started sleeping in a tent on the front lawn. It would have been easy to slip away from the tent to see a lover. I knew it was during the summer, because I could see myself sitting in a deckchair beside the tent, wearing my school uniform and cracking walnuts and putting the shells into my straw boater. She let me sleep out there too, sometimes. It was only a small tent, no windows or anything. She couldn't have got up and gone out in the middle of the night without my knowing, could she? Albert and Carol didn't see her with the man in the car until months later, but she wouldn't have been sleeping outside in the winter; it would be too cold. I remembered how she'd woken me up at dawn to see a family of hedgehogs. A mother and six babies. We'd sat in the tent opening and she'd put her arm round me and we'd watched them walk across the lawn . . . *Oh, Mummy, I love you so much. Why did you leave me?*

I heard Mrs Mop coming back and had to grab the letter and dash next door into the old butler's pantry till she'd gone. Then I sat down at the kitchen table and looked at the letter again. Two of the kidnappers were men: Mick Martin and Steven Moody. Mick Martin had been killed. That left Steven Moody. Mick Martin and Maggie Hill were students, but Steven wasn't. If he really was my mother's lover, then she'd rejected me in favour of a pathetic Baader-Meinhof wannabe who could barely string two words together. Her man who waited in the car, who rubbed her hands to warm them, whose moustache tickled her and made her laugh – was that *him*? Had they planned the kidnap together, in the car, so that she could go away with him and be a different person and never see any of us again? If she did, she must have planned her own disappearance, her own death. With Steven Moody. Who'd killed her and was going to kill me. Except that he was released in 1987, so why hadn't he surfaced before? Carol Curtis had said that the man in the Land Rover had a moustache and 'brown or black hair going over the collar'. Surely it would have been too dark for her to see the colour properly? Steven Moody hadn't had a moustache at the trial, but it would have been easy enough to shave it off . . . *Your family paid the pigs to shoot us.* I shut my eyes. Faces spun in front of me in a hideous carousel: Steven Moody, Maggie Hill, Mick Martin, Mum, Joan, Des, my father, round and round and round . . .

'Are you all right?'

I opened my eyes. The cleaner was standing there, the motherly-looking one in the cardigan who'd asked about the carpet machine. 'You were rocking backwards and forwards.' She leant across the table. 'Is it your tummy?'

'No, no. I—'

'Are you sure? You looked as if you were in pain.'

'I—'

'Would you like me to get you something? I could make you some hot milk if you like. I'll put some honey in it. That'll settle your stomach.'

I nodded, more to get her out of the room than anything else, keeping my head down so she couldn't see my eyes. I could hear her pottering about in the scullery, running water and clattering saucepans. 'I always used to make it for my children when they were poorly.'

She came back and put a saucepan on the Baby Belling. 'I hope you don't mind me saying this, dear, but you look as if you could do with a square meal. You're not on one of these silly diets, are you? Those model girls, they all look half-starved if you ask me. You don't want to be like that. You'd be ever so pretty if you weren't so pale. There you are. That'll put roses in your cheeks.' She set a mug of milk on the table in front of me. 'I'd better get back upstairs before they send out a search party. If I were you, I'd drink that and then I'd go and have a lie-down.'

'Thank you.'

'That's all right. You look after yourself, now.'

I kept my eyes on the milk until she'd gone. A skin was forming on the top. The shiny puckered surface and the warm smell made me feel sick. Put roses in my cheeks. English roses. *Mum . . .*

I held my nose and drank the milk, and after a while I went to the loo next to the mud room and vomited. I poured a bottle of bleach down the pan after I flushed so the nice cleaner wouldn't know I'd been sick.

I went upstairs and stood outside the door of my mother's room. I listened to my heart pound for a while before I unlocked it. It was empty except for a wooden chest of drawers under one of the windows. A Victorian chest in solid pine, with round porcelain knobs for handles. I didn't remember it. Its top was thick with dust, and the window sill was a flies' graveyard. The room looked as if it had been unused for two centuries, not two decades.

All the drawers were empty except the deep one at the bottom. There, all by himself, lay Timothy, the purple suede hippo. I picked him up and blew on him and brushed off the dust. His suede skin was grubby, but his seams were intact and so was his special hippo half-smile of round contentment. Perhaps I could refurbish him. Clean the bits of sawdust out of his ears with Q-tips. Send him to a leather specialist. The nice cleaning lady might be able to recommend someone.

God, I thought. Is this what happens when you go bonkers? Does clcaning a toy hippopotamus become the most important thing in the world? I patted Timothy on the head and we both looked out at the garden until I heard the back door slam and Tony shouting my name. I looked at my watch. Four hours seemed to have passed since I was sick. I heard his footsteps coming up the corridor.

'Come into the garden, Maud, For the black bat, night, has flown, Come into the garden, Maud, I am here at the gate alone . . .' he was singing.

I didn't have the energy to go out to him, so I leant against the chest of drawers and waited for him to find me. I almost wished I hadn't asked him to come.

He stopped dead in the doorway, his arms full of flowers. 'There you are. What's going on? There's cables everywhere. I nearly broke my neck coming up the stairs.' He moved closer and peered into my face through a mass of arum lilies and stephanotis. 'Uh-oh, Dorothy. Looks like we're not in Kansas any more.'

'It's the cleaners. For the funeral.'

'Are you all right?'

'Thanks. For coming.'

'You're not all right, are you? You're covered in cobwebs for one thing, your clothes are filthy, and your feet are *black*. What have you been doing? Rolling in mud? You look like an absolute urchin. You'll have to have a bath immediately.'

I let him take me down the corridor in search of a clean bathroom, and then sat down on the mat while he dumped the flowers in the basin, turned on the bath taps and rummaged in the cupboards for unguents.

'Look, Badedas. D'you remember those adverts? *Things happen after a Badedas bath.* She's standing there on the balcony catching her death wearing nothing but a towel and there's a gorgeous man in britches and ruffles prancing about with a coach and four in the driveway. I wonder if they still make this stuff?' He sniffed it. 'I hope it hasn't gone off, I've poured it in now. Oh well, at least it's bubbles.' He pulled me to my feet. 'Come on, get your kit off.' I got it off. 'Have you eaten *anything* this week?'

'I thought you said one couldn't be too thin.'

'You've succeeded. Go on, get in. I'm taking you out to a restaurant tonight and you're going to eat yourself senseless, even if I have to ladle it down your throat.'

'Can it be tomorrow, Tony? I'm too tired.'

'All right, but I'm sending Dominic out for provisions. Now, you just sit there and soak, and I'll go and arrange things. Who did you say all those people were?'

'Cleaners.'

'I'll get them to sort out our rooms. Dominic can take the things up. Where are we supposed to be sleeping, anyway?'

'I hadn't thought. Anywhere you like, really.'

'Goody. Dominic can go next to me. I want to be on hand in case he decides he isn't straight after all. Now, don't lock the door. I'll be back in a minute.'

He came back with a bathrobe, a magazine, a joint and a gin and tonic. 'There you are. We'll have to share it. I couldn't carry two.'

'The flowers are lovely.'

'Lots more downstairs. I've deployed people to look after them. What's this?' He swatted Timothy on the nose with a piece of sea holly.

'I had him when I was little. He needs cleaning.'

'Shame he can't get into the bath with you, really.' He passed the joint to me. '*So, follow me, follow, down to the hollow, and there let us wallow in glor-or-or-orius muuuuud.*'

'I am glad to see you, Tony.'

'Only because I give you drugs. Have you seen this?' He stuck his magazine in front of me and pointed at one of the photographs. 'Top left.'

'What is it?'

171

'*Tatler*. You think you've got problems. I look like some mental queen and that's a fact. Do you think I could sue?'

'It's not *that* bad.'

'Yes it is. It's a travesty. Anyway, we can worry about that later. You've got to tell me what's going on, Dodie. When you phoned . . . I've never heard you like that before. You were so distressed. You sounded like a virgin in a troopship.'

'Male or female?'

'Either. Both. And you look like shit.'

'Gee, thanks.'

'And I'm not letting you out of this bath till you tell me what's wrong.'

18

So I told him. The lot. By the time I got out of the bath I was a bit puckered round the edges and red round the eyes but I felt a whole lot better. I put on clean clothes and took Tony down to the kitchen to look at the pieces of letter I'd stuffed back in the key cupboard behind the scullery door. The cleaners had gone home but Tony's new chauffeur and general factotum, Dominic, was sitting at the kitchen table with the guard from the security company and his long-haired Alsatian, which lay under the table, panting and gazing at us with greedy black eyes.

Dominic turned out to be quite nice in a golden retriever sort of way. Tony always goes for men who look like young John Kennedys – heavy pink chops and buttery blond hair. Not my cup of tea, but there you go. Dominic fetched an Indian takeaway for us while we gave the security guard – whose name was Dave – the makes and colours of our cars. Neither of us could remember our number plates, much to his disgust. I wrote out a list of everyone I could think of who might be visiting Camoys Hall in the next few days. After that, Dave and his dog went outside on patrol for the night and Dominic took himself off to the pub while Tony and I had dinner.

Tony agreed that I should have a serious conversation with Des about the past, and said that if I *was* going to meet Maggie Hill, I should take someone with me, just in case. After that, we talked about other things, thank God. Still, the less said about trying to sleep, the better. The merry-go-round of faces wouldn't leave me alone. Every time I closed my eyes they were there staring at me, individual features thrusting towards me as if they were trying to burrow into my head. I went up to Tony's room at about two o'clock to beg for sleeping pills, and he told me to get in with him. Dominic found us there when he brought Tony's tea in the morning. If he was shocked, he hid it well.

We spent most of the day in the dining room. Tony sat at the table, surrounded by bin liners, reading the begging letters, and I lay on the floor in a patch of sun under one of the long windows and sorted through Joan's drawer full of lists. *Hairdresser. Flowers Wed not Thur. Worm dog. Laundry man £15.00.* Riveting.

'Some poor old duck here who hasn't had a holiday in fifteen years . . . *My husband has a nasty temper. He pushed me downstairs and my right shoulder is broken. My son is writing for me because it is hard to use the hand . . .* Ooh, she's put in a photograph of her son. He's rather gorgeous. Can I keep this?' He waved the photograph at me.

'For God's sake, Tony. He's about twelve.'

'Fifteen, it says on the back. Sixteen by now. They should lower the age of consent, anyway. The father sounds a complete bastard. You might send her a cheque, Dodie.'

'Why don't you send it? You're the one who's after her son.'

'She might think I was a pervert or something.'

'You *are* a pervert.'

Tony was just launching into 'Hallelujah, I'm a pervert' to the tune of 'Hallelujah, I'm a bum' when Dominic stuck his head round the door.

'I got through to the restaurant.' He smiled at me. 'They were fully booked, but as soon as I mentioned your name, they miraculously produced a table.'

'Which restaurant?'

'The Fat Hen.' Tony looked smug.

'How did you know—' I'd thought of getting a table there so that we could do a recce for Des.

'I told Des we'd check it out.'

'What do you mean, you told Des?'

'I rang him.'

'Hang on. *You* rang *Des*?' Des and Tony aren't exactly kindred spirits. Des normally refers to Tony as 'that poofter chap'.

'Last night, after you'd gone to bed. Don't look so surprised.'

The minute Dominic had closed the door, I said, 'What did you talk to Des about?'

'Well, I told him about the letter and the cat. Dodie, this is serious. I had to tell him. Oh yeah, and I phoned Della Ewart, too. She's coming up tomorrow morning. I told her it was a matter of life or death.'

'I don't believe this.' Della Ewart is my hairdresser.

'You want to look nice for Joan, don't you? Anyway, it's my treat.'

'Yes, but . . . Oh, never mind. Thanks.'

'Don't mention it.'

'Tony?'

'What?'

'When you spoke to Des, did he say anything about calling the police? About the letter?'

'I don't think so.'

'Then . . . doesn't that mean he knew about the whole

174

thing? He'd hardly want the police to go searching for this man if he could say that Mum had gone with him because she was part of a plot, or that my father had set him up, or . . . Oh, God, I don't know.'

'We don't know that either of those things happened, Dodie. Anyway, I don't see what good the police would be. They're hardly going to call out the whole force to patrol the grounds, are they? And they can't do anything about threats unless you've actually been murdered, or at least mussed up a little. Don't you remember when Coralie was getting all those nuisance calls from her second husband, after they separated? They didn't lift so much as a truncheon. That's what the security guard is for. In any case, as soon as the inquest is over, five billion journalists are going to be jumping up and down on your doorstep, whether you like it or not. That ought to deter your letter-writer, even if he's an out and out lunatic. He's not going to risk anything with that lot around, never mind posses of tattooed ex-squaddies with attack dogs.'

'How did he sound?'

'Des? Concerned. He's worried about you. We both are. You weren't thinking of going to the inquest yourself, were you?'

'I don't have to, do I?'

'No. And I don't think you should. You'll be mobbed.'

'Someone should, though.'

'Des will. He told me. He's going to ask your solicitor to make a plea for privacy on your behalf.'

'Fat lot of good that'll do.'

'It's worth a try. I still think you should send some money to that woman with the gorgeous son. Where's your sense of female solidarity, woman? You should be sympathetic. Your father was a wanker, wasn't he?'

'So's yours.'

Tony rolled his eyes. 'Thanks for reminding me. I've got to go up to Scotland next month. He'll be yomping all over the heather gralloching everything in sight. It's displacement activity, of course. It's me he wants to gralloch. You know he's bought another castle, don't you?'

'*Another* one? He's already got two.'

'I know. It's ridiculous. Six months ago he didn't know a laird from a gillie, and now he's prancing around in tartan and tossing cabers all over the place. I can't imagine why my mother married him.'

'How is she?'

'Playing Cowboys and Indians in Arizona. I might go out there for Christmas. More fun than Scotland, anyway. She's gone a bit mock croc, though. Too much sun. I keep telling her she ought to get the face done, but she says she can't be bothered. Now, what's this? Postgrad in modern American Literature. Can't get funding. I'm not surprised. This one's from a woman whose son wants a new football strip.'

'Tony?'

'Mmm?'

'Have you found anything that looks as if it could possibly be from my mother?'

'Nothing. I'm on the last bag. Oh, darling, I'm sorry. But it was a bit of a long shot, you know.'

'I know.' I picked up a handful of Joan's lists and let them flutter to the floor. I'd tried to get them into date order, but it was impossible. Half of them didn't have dates, just Wednesday or Friday or whenever it was. *Dry Cleaning. Ask Driscoll's when curtains ready. Phone Annie re. church flowers. Paracetamol.* I turned the paper over, expecting another list, but it wasn't. It was the draft of a letter. It didn't say who to, just: *I am sorry to hear that you haven't been well. I hope you are looking after yourself. I recently bumped into a friend of Dodie's who told me that she is very well and happy. He gave me this photograph, which I enclose. I am sending more money to the usual place.* Mum. Joan was writing to Mum. Sending her money. I got up and went over to the table.

'Tony? Did you give Joan a photograph? When you met her. Did you give her a photograph of me?'

'Yes, actually, I did. I know you don't like them, but she really wanted one. It was from my Christmas party. Paul Ackroyd left them at my house. I can't think why I had them with me. I only kept the ones with Raoul in.' Raoul was a male model who Tony'd been in love with at Christmas.

'Did the one you gave Joan have Raoul in it?'

'Must have done. I binned the rest. It was weird really. I mean, we weren't talking about anything in particular and she suddenly asked me if I had a photo of you. Have you just found it or something?'

'Joan sent it to Mum. It was one of the ones the police showed me. The photographs were what made me think it really was her.'

'That's one mystery solved, anyway.'

'It's not a *game*, Tony.'

'I know. Sorry.'

I looked again at Joan's letter. It was formal, not affectionate, as if Mum was someone she didn't know very well. 'The usual place' sounded as if she was transferring money to a bank account, but the police hadn't mentioned finding one. Perhaps they hadn't looked.

'Tony? When you met Joan, did you tell her I was "well and happy"?'

'I might have done. Well, you were, weren't you?' He swept the last of the begging letters back into their bin bag and stood up. 'Come on, it's time we got tarted up for Ye Olde Henne or whatever it's called. We can pretend we're reviewing it for a Sunday paper.'

19

In the morning, as soon as Tony and Dominic had left, I rang Des to tell him about the Fat Hen. It hadn't changed at all. They'd got pretty much the same menu, and they'd kept on all the old staff. I can't have been there for at least seven years, but everyone remembered me. The new owner even came over and insisted that our drinks should be on the house, which was very kind of him.

I told Des that it was worth eight points on the Haigh-Wood scale (ratings: one to ten), and he said, 'I'll get booked in for tomorrow night. Do you want to meet me there?'

'Yes. You know I said I wanted to have a talk?'

'Yes . . .' he said cautiously.

'Well, there's other things too now. Things I need to know.'

'I'll try and help you—'

'It's not a question of *try*, Des. You've *got* to help me. I have to know. For God's sake, I have a right—'

'Dodie?'

'What? Please don't start trying to put me off.'

'I'm not. I may not be as much use as you think, that's all. I haven't got all the answers.'

'You must have *some* of them.'

'I've been doing a lot of thinking lately, and I don't think I've got the answer to anything. I'm not terribly good at all this talking stuff, Dodie, I haven't had much practice. But I'll do my best.'

'Promise?'

'Promise.'

'Because there's been rather a lot going on. Apart from the letter, I mean.'

'So I gather. That friend of yours gave me a brief outline.'

'Tony?'

'That's the one.' Des knows Tony's name, but he can't bring himself to say it. 'Eight o'clock suit you? In the bar? It's still got a bar, I take it?'

'Of course it has.'

'Well, you never know what they're going to do to these places. Put in a discotheque or something—'

'No, it's all right. Everything's still where you left it. I'll see you tomorrow, Des.'

The sun was blazing down by the time Della arrived, so after she'd washed my hair we took a chair out to the front porch and she cut it there. Jimmy and Carol turned up halfway through.

'I thought I'd come up and see how you were doing,' said Carol. She turned to Jimmy, 'Go inside and get us a chair.'

'What did your last servant die of?'

'Not doing what I said. Oh, go *on*.' When Jimmy'd gone, she said, 'I met him on the way up. How's it going?'

'How's what going?'

'You and him.' Della didn't say anything, but I could practically hear her ears flapping.

'It isn't going.'

'Come off it! It's all right for some.'

'Why? Is there something wrong with . . .' I couldn't remember his name. '. . . your wizard man?'

'Greg? I don't see him for a couple of days, and I think, oh well, nice while it lasted, and then he comes back and it's all, you know . . . I'll take you here Carol, I'll take you there, we'll do this, we'll do that, and then I turn round and he's gone again. To be honest, I'm beginning to wonder if I can be arsed. I mean, what with the farm and the kids—'

'There you are, your ladyship.' Jimmy plonked Carol's chair down and turned to me.

'Hello.'

'Hello.' I could feel a horrible hot blush coming out all over my face and wished he'd stop staring at me.

'Do you mind if I get myself a drink, Dodie?' he asked.

I nodded, and Della sighed and readjusted my head.

'I'll have a beer if you've got one,' Carol said.

'Anyone else?'

'Not while I'm working,' Della said, primly.

'There's mineral water.'

'Thanks. No ice.' I could hear 'How does he know what's in the fridge?' ricocheting around inside Della's head.

'Dodie?'

'I'm OK, thanks.'

Della gave my cheek a little shove with her palm. 'Stop moving your head.'

'Sorry.'

'And there's another thing,' Carol continued. 'Do you remember George Day? We used to call him Daisy. He went out with Jackie for a couple of months.'

I didn't. 'I think so.'

'Well, his brother, Wonky—' I heard Della snort behind me. 'Wonky was in the army with Dave, yeah? Dave's my ex,' she said to Della. 'Anyway, Wonky was in the pub and Greg was there, and they started talking about the army and what it was like and everything, and he reckons Greg was talking bollocks. He doesn't think Greg's ever been in the army. Jimmy said he probably made it up because of Dave.'

'How do you mean?'

'Well, he thought I must like soldiers, so I'd be more likely to go out with him if he said he was in the army. Quite flattering, really.'

'He must have known you'd find out.'

'Yeah. But he doesn't think of things like that. He never really makes any plans, you know? He's always telling me we're going to this place or that place, but we never do any of it. Even if we go to the cinema, I have to arrange it all. Anyway, it's not like he's saying to me, "Carol, I love you, let's get married," is it?'

'Oh Carol, I am just a fo-o-ol,' sang Jimmy. He came across the porch and twirled his tray of drinks expertly on one hand between Della and Carol.

Della was visibly impressed. 'Where did you learn to do that?' she asked.

'I used to be a waiter.'

'Oh.' She sounded disappointed. I nearly said, Where do you think he learnt it? On a fashion shoot in Morocco? But I didn't want to give anyone any more ideas by leaping to his defence.

Carol stuck two fingers up at Jimmy and looked suspiciously at her bottle of beer. 'I suppose I ought to be grateful you didn't stick some poncey piece of orange peel in it.'

'Lime.'

'I *know*. I was just winding you up.' Carol turned back to me. 'The stupid thing about it is that I couldn't give a monkey's. I mean, if you like someone, it's for them, isn't it? Not their job or what they've got.'

Luckily, Della pushed my head forward right at that moment so I couldn't see Jimmy's expression, and, more importantly, he couldn't see mine.

There was a few seconds' silence, and then Carol said, 'Well, *I* think it is, anyway.' Jimmy was sitting on the flagstones opposite her, and she reached out a foot and gave his leg a nudge. 'Roll us one of your cigarettes, Jimmy, I've run out.' She rooted in her plastic bag and produced a very flat purse. 'I'll have to see if I've got enough for ten Rothmans. One pound twenty, thirty . . . Shit. Got to be some more in here somewhere.' She upended the bag and a roll of loo paper fell out and trundled off across the drive, trailing a pink streamer in its wake. 'Dad never has any at the farm. It's disgusting.'

Jimmy picked up a grubby My Little Pony, also pink. 'Do your kids play with that?'

'Course not, stupid, they're *boys*. Must belong to one of Jackie's. Here we go.' She picked up a half-eaten Meltis Newberry fruit with fifty pence sticking to it. 'Oh well. Waste not, want not.' She peeled the sweet off the coin and popped it into her mouth.

Della muttered, 'Yuck,' into my hair.

'Funny. I could have sworn I had a picture of Greg in here. I was going to get a frame for it. One of the kids must have had it. Oh, well, never mind.' She got up and shovelled everything back into the carrier. 'Got to go. I'll be at the pub later.' She nudged Jimmy with her foot. 'You coming down?'

'Sorry. Too busy.'

'Shame. See you soon, Doe.'

When Della went off to find an extension lead for her hairdryer, I said to Jimmy, 'Did you go out with Carol, once upon a time?'

'Sort of.' He was fiddling with his Rizla papers, not looking at me. 'Not exactly.'

'You just seem . . . You know.'

'It was a long time ago. Besides, it wasn't just me. Lots of us did, in the village. I mean, Carol wasn't special, or anything.'

'You mean a sort of teenage Saturnalia?' I sounded like Robert Robinson. As soon as it was out of my mouth, I wished I hadn't said it. Jimmy looked embarrassed.

'No! Oh, you know . . . It must have happened with your friends. You have a thing with someone, then someone else, and you all know each other. It's like a sort of game.'

'Did you ever do it in the pillbox?'

'No. That place stank.' He stood up. 'Look, I've got to go over to my brother's. I told him I'd babysit.'

'When will I see you?'

'I'm busy the next couple of days. I'll give you a ring.' He didn't kiss me or anything, just went.

Dodie Blackstock, the woman whose father sponsored the Chair of Communications at Aberystwyth University. What a joke.

When Della had gone, I went down to Mr Molloy's cottage to ask him to order some herbaceous borders and things to tart up the area round the church in time for Joan's funeral. Mr Molloy used to be the head gardener. Now he's the only gardener, poor man, and there isn't a bedding plant in sight.

'It isn't right, all this instant gardening. Still, we can't choose when we go, can we?' he said.

'No, we can't.'

'Just as well, or some of us ud never go at all. Don't worry, Miss Blackstock. I'll make it look nice for Miss Draycott. Be glad to.' I was just about to leave when he added, 'Are you going to keep the house then, for yourself?'

'I haven't decided.'

'It's just with the cottage and everything, Miss Blackstock . . .'

I assured him I wouldn't turn him out and asked if he'd like to take on some help over the next few months. He muttered a bit about lads not being properly trained nowadays, but he seemed quite pleased.

Mr Molloy's cottage is almost a mile away from the house. I suppose the Victorians who built it didn't want the sight and smell of the peasantry to interfere with their gracious living. I took a bit of a detour on the way back, because it was lovely and sunny and I knew I wouldn't be able to settle down to anything anyway. There was such a jumble of stuff inside my head – Joan's funeral, and Mum, and Steven Moody, and what had happened, and why – and it had receded into a permanent background clamour, like a dog whining a few rooms away. I felt depressed about

Jimmy too. He hadn't even stayed around to see me with my new hair.

I thought, if I could just lie down and go to sleep, I could blot it all out, at least for a couple of hours. But I'd already checked all the bathrooms for sleeping pills and found nothing. I wondered if Tony had got rid of them. I wandered across a couple of lawns and down a rough overgrown track. At the end was a small Nissen hut, its curved corrugated walls almost obliterated by brambles. Beside it, the carcass of a washing machine lay on its back in a clump of nettles. There was a small square of mossy cobblestones in front of the hut. Its battered wooden doors, secured with a snarl of orange baler twine, were covered in graffiti. The only words I could make out were *Motorhead*, written in careful Gothic script, and underneath, *Watch out, P. Graham is Bent*. The whole building looked as if it was ready to give up and sink into the ground.

I suppose I must have known the hut was there, but I couldn't remember it being used during my childhood. In fact, I couldn't recall ever having been inside it. If I wanted to sell the place, I'd have to ask Mr Molloy to get rid of it. He was over sixty, so if I did sell Camoys Hall, the new people wouldn't want him. I pictured Mr Molloy standing in the doorway of his pretty cottage, with his honeysuckle and his neat rows of prize vegetables, and then I imagined him and his wife at the window of a raw red brick house on a council estate, looking out at stunted trees and turd-covered grass, frightened and hating it.

I peered into the washing machine. There was a discarded horseshoe lying inside the drum. I fished it out. The horse who'd worn it must have been huge. A cart horse, like Boxer in *Animal Farm*. Hardworking Boxer, faithful and true, whose reward was a one-way trip to the glue factory. The Molloys on a council estate. *YOU ARE GOING TO PAY*. That's what the letter had said. *I am here on the spot*. I jumped as if someone had come up behind me, and almost lost my footing on the skiddy green stones. The thought of messing up my clothes made me angry. 'If you are here on the spot, you bastard, then you're trespassing,' I muttered. 'It's my house, my land, and my Nissen hut. I'll go where I like.' But the silence was eerie. I wished Malcolm was with me. Joan's dog. Bright and alert and hopping about on three legs the way Jack Russells do. He was white, with black ears and a patch of black over one eye, and his tummy was round and pink. I don't know why I thought of Malcolm. Just wanting to be near something warm and alive, I suppose. Except that Malcolm was dead. Joan told me, in one of the letters I never answered.

I set to work unpicking the loop of baler twine. I thought the doors would open easily once I'd untied the knot, but they sagged and stuck on the bumpy cobbles and I could only get them to move a couple of inches. In the end I turned sideways, breathed in, and squeezed through the gap. Complete darkness. Tentatively, I took a step forward. My knee whacked into something hard. I stuck my hands out in front of me and groped about. There was nothing at eye level, but low down I could feel something big and solid, covered by a heavy cloth. I leant backwards as hard as I could against one of the doors and almost fell over when it gave way, flooding the shed with dusty sunlight.

It was a car. I squatted down in front of it and lifted up the dust sheet. The number plate was gone but the radiator grill had a familiar horizontal line running across it. *Oh God, it can't be, it can't.* My hands were trembling. The middle, find the middle. There it was, the three pointed star. My heart was thudding as if I'd run a race. *Please, please, please.* I pushed the cloth up and I saw a dull red gleam. A Russian red Mercedes. I was looking at my mother's car.

I slithered down the narrow gap on the passenger's side, pulling the cloth with me, and tugged at the door handle. It wasn't locked. I flung the cloth across the car in an explosion of dust, and scrambled round and lowered myself on to the passenger seat. The springs groaned but the beautiful cream leather still smelt the same. The car was dark inside because the hard roof was in place, and the windscreen so dirty I could barely see through it.

I put my head back and shut my eyes. If you were going to commit suicide in a car, this would be the one to use. Not by driving it into a wall or anything, because that would ruin it. But with the exhaust. Carbon monoxide, from the exhaust. You'd have to have a tube or something. I leant over and felt around the ignition. No keys. I opened the glovebox to see if they'd been left in there, but there was nothing except a packet of cigarettes. Gitanes, with the swirly blue dancing girl. Only three left. Mum hadn't smoked. Perhaps they were *his* cigarettes. Why hadn't the police taken them as evidence? I shook one out of the packet, split the paper with my thumbnail and rolled the tobacco between my fingers. It wasn't dusty or crumbly, and it smelt fresh. I couldn't remember the car being brought back. Maybe I had been away at school. I twisted myself round until I was in a kneeling position and pushed my head and shoulders between the front seats to feel around behind them. My fingertips touched mud and grit and bits of straw on the rubber mats.

I was trying to free my skirt from the handbrake and get back the right way round when I sensed something behind me. I swivelled round and caught a glimpse of someone's face between the doors of the shed. The smudgy windscreen made it look like the Turin shroud, beige and fuzzy, with hazy brown features and hair almost like smoke. It was there and gone so quickly I could almost believe I'd imagined it. But I knew I hadn't.

I am here on the spot.

20

He made no noise at all. I couldn't tell whether he'd actually gone, or whether he was waiting for me outside the shed. I didn't even know if he'd been able to see me through the dust on the windscreen. If he'd been following me, I thought, surely I'd have sensed him? I slid off the seat and curled up in the cramped space under the dashboard. I was covered in dirt and grit and my calves were stuck to the backs of my thighs. My head was jammed between my knees and my shoulders felt as if they were on fire, but I stayed put.

He might come back and drag me out of the car. If he'd seen me. If he was the letter-writer, he might kill me. I couldn't do anything except wait. The effort of keeping still made me tremble all over.

The sun was setting when I finally staggered out on to the cobbles. I saw the keys immediately. Silver at my feet, the Mercedes symbol gleaming in the weakening light. Her keys. He'd dropped her car keys. Or left them. I felt my knees buckle and half-knelt, half-sprawled on the slimy cobbles, trying to rub the circulation back into my legs. Her car keys, her hair.

I thought of all the people who could have had those things. The kidnappers – Mick Martin, Maggie Hill, Steven Moody. Either my father or Joan could have had the car keys and the hair – could they have *given* them to somebody? Joan was in contact with Maggie Hill, after all. But why would she . . . Mick Martin was dead, so it could only be Maggie Hill or Steven Moody. Margaret Susannah Hill and Steven Joseph Moody. Their full names, I remember them from the court reports. *You are going to pay.* Steven Moody was going to make me pay – if he was the one who had written the letter.

I suddenly felt not angry, but irritated. Pissed off. What have I ever done? I can't help being Wolf Blackstock's daughter, can I? I didn't choose to be born into this family. I scrambled to my feet and tested my legs. If whoever it was did decide to come back and murder me, running away was going to be out of the question. So much for one security man and his dog. Still, there'd be reinforcements coming soon. But the strange thing was, I wasn't frightened. I was irritated, annoyed, even. Mainly, I just felt very very tired.

When I finally got back to the house, I dragged myself up the stairs to my favourite bathroom and had a long hot soak. I ended up sitting in a moat of dark grey water with little trails of pink from where I'd collided with various brambles on the way back. Then I sat on the end of the bath, soaked a wad of cotton wool with some elderly Dettol I'd found in the cupboard and dabbed it on to my cut legs, wincing. I flipped my ruined skirt into the bin with my toe. Still, at least it was the skirt that was in shreds and not me.

I went to bed after that. I'd hoped to get straight off to sleep, but of course it didn't happen. I tried to read some more of the Agatha Christie I'd taken from Joan's room, but I just got irritated, so after a bit I got up and went in search of something else.

I walked straight past the green baize door that led to my father's rooms, or what used to be his rooms. I hadn't been in there since I came back, and I didn't want to. He despised novels, said they were nothing but dreams. That's probably why I like them so much.

I paused outside Joan's bedroom but I couldn't bear the thought of all that mess on the floor. Part of me wanted to rush in there and stamp on everything, but the other part felt sorry. Joan hated untidiness and disorder. She'd have been straight in there with her sleeves rolled up, setting it all to rights again. Des sometimes called her the Little Red Hen. It was from a story he'd read me when I was three or four.

None of the other animals in the story would do anything, and at the bottom of every page it said, 'Very well,' said the Little Red Hen, 'I'll do it myself.' And he used to call me the Fierce Bad Rabbit when I was naughty. That was from a Beatrix Potter story. The Fierce Bad Rabbit kept grabbing all the other rabbits' carrots. 'He doesn't say thank you, he just takes it.' Nice safe memories. I stood in front of Joan's door and tried to hang on to them, but my mind kept slipping back to Mum and all the other stuff I didn't want to think about.

My old room was locked. I remembered the row of keys in the scullery cupboard. I thought about fetching the five storeroom keys and trying them in the lock, but what was the point? Going into Mum's room had been bad enough – except for Timothy the hippo. The memory of my room would be something nice to hold on to, like Beatrix Potter.

The door to Angela's old room wasn't locked. When she died, Joan had taken most of her books to the Sue Ryder shop, but there were two left on the shelves. One was an *A to Z*, and the other was *Magick, in Theory and Practice*, by Aleister Crowley. Joan must have decided it wasn't appropriate for a charity shop. Perhaps Angela was casting spells to make my father love her. Or to make my mother disappear. I thought of her, sitting cross-legged on the bed surrounded by incense and trinket-boxes, with expensive hippie jewellery twined round her orange wrists and throat, and I felt almost sorry for her.

Next to Angela's room was a door to one of the staircases that led up to the attic. Locked. Perhaps the contents of Mum's room had been taken up there after she'd gone. But when? I thought. If Joan and my father knew Mum was alive, surely they expected her back, at least to collect her belongings. Anyway, I thought, what did it matter? All I wanted to do was go to bed.

At the end of Angela's corridor were the Dead Stairs. A short downward flight, cut off by a wall like an Escher painting. The rest of the flight was demolished when alterations were made to the main part of the house. The builders put the wall up, but for some reason they never got round to removing the top of the stairs. The banisters were still there, with a heavy mahogany bookcase in front of the whole thing to stop people falling down them by accident. There were no windows at that end of the corridor, and it was dark even at midday, so Joan had put a lamp on top of it. I switched it on, tilted back the shade and held it up to the row of books. My A-level texts, mostly. *Othello, Tess of the D'Urbervilles, Mansfield Park.* And there at the end, spineless and disintegrating, was *The Diary of a Nobody.* Des had given it to me. It was his favourite book. He'd winced at Mr Pooter's awful puns, but his own were just as bad. I took it back to bed with me. Reading would be safe, as long as I concentrated. Like walking a tightrope across the Niagara Falls. One thought a fraction out of place, and down you'd go. *Have we got lodgers, dear? The garden's full of borders.* Old, well-worn jokes. I pretended that Des was sitting on the bed, reading to me. Steady the Buffs, old thing. Keep it on the island.

After about ten minutes I gave up and just lay there thinking how can I get out of this mess? I kept remembering Mum's car, wondering if I could get it started. I wasn't really considering suicide, not in an emotional sense. It was more . . . well, the logistics, really. I kept worrying about it. Would the car start? Could I use a length of garden hose or would it be the wrong diameter? I couldn't remember if carbon monoxide made you turn pink, or if that was just gas. I kept trying to jump-start the sensible bit of my mind, but then I thought, things are already as bad as they *can* be. They can't get any worse than this. Anyway, I couldn't go back to the Nissen hut in case *he* was there. At that point, I sat up in bed and laughed. Because we had exactly the same aim, he and I: doing me in. The moral is, I told myself, learn to delegate and you'll save yourself a lot of bother. I must have fallen asleep then, because I was woken up at 9.30 by the cleaners banging about on the landing.

I spent most of the next day on the phone in Joan's sitting room, finalising arrangements for French polishers and orders of service and things. Above my head the cleaners banged their huge machines round the corners and stomped up and down ladders with feather dusters stuck in their belts.

The nice lady stuck her head round the door, her bright blue woolly cardigan clashing hideously with her green and orange jumpsuit. 'I just came to see if you were all right.'

'I'm fine, thanks.'

'Because you did worry me on Friday. I didn't know if you'd still be here this morning, to be honest, you seemed that distressed.'

'I'm OK now.'

'Are you sure?'

'I'm fine, really. One of my friends came down.'

'That's nice.' She looked at me doubtfully. 'At least let me get you something. Would you like a cup of tea? It's no bother.'

'Thanks.'

After that, she brought me six more cups of tea without asking. I've never heard of anyone dying of a tannin overdose, but by the time I went upstairs to change for Des I thought I might be the first case. Being fussed over like that was nice, though. I wondered if I should ask Woolly Cardigan if she'd like to be my housekeeper. It'd be better than being a cleaner. For one thing, she wouldn't have to dress up in a clown's outfit. And I could give her more money. All she'd have to do is organise a few things, and be nice to me, and . . . and *be Joan*. Then I thought, God, what am I doing? I haven't even decided if I want to keep the bloody place.

I ordered a car to take me to the Fat Hen, got dressed in something I thought Des would approve of and put his wedding photograph into my handbag. He was there when I arrived, chatting to the barman about cricket. Des loves restaurants. In the old days he ate at home about twice a year, and even then he'd hire one of those directors' lunch types to cook three courses and dish it up with linen and silver so he could pretend he was at Le Gavroche. Actually, I don't think Des really cares whether the restaurant is posh or not, just as long as the food is good. I suddenly remembered how, when I was seven or eight, he'd started taking me out to the Jade Palace in Cambridge if my father was away, and we'd smuggle sweet and sour pork balls back in the napkins for Joan's dog.

When he saw me, he said, 'That's a nice outfit. Very sedate.'

'Thanks.' I hugged him.

'You look civilised enough to be seen with. I might even buy you a drink. What would you like? I've got some nice blue gin here.'

'It doesn't look very blue to me. How much have you had?'

'Bombay Sapphire,' said the barman. 'The bottle's blue. I'd recommend it to anyone who drinks gin.'

'Sounds fine.'

'Stop hopping about on one leg.' Des patted the bar stool next to his. 'You'll wear yourself out. Sit down. I know you've got a chap from the security firm there at the moment, but I'll be coming over tomorrow morning with the manager so that we can go over their report. About lighting and sensors and so forth. It'll only take a few hours to go round the place, but I thought I might stay on for a couple of days. That chap who phoned seemed to think you were in need of a spot of company.'

'Do you mean Tony?' I asked innocently.

Des frowned. 'You know jolly well I mean Tony. I'd

better have a look at that anonymous letter too. God knows, one doesn't want to get the police involved, but . . . Well, anyway, let's cross that bridge when we come to it, shall we? *If* we come to it. There'll be reporters, of course. They'll be down here like a shot after the inquest. The security will help to keep them at bay, but it's not going to be very nice, I'm afraid. I'll go to London on Wednesday morning for the hearing, but I really don't think you ought to come. It's up to you, but it's going to be pretty grim. You might as well enjoy the peace and quiet while you can.'

'I am going to see Maggie Hill, though.'

'When?'

'Tomorrow afternoon.'

'Are you coming back here afterwards? I really don't think you should be anywhere near London on Wednesday, Dodie.'

'I'll come straight back. I'm taking Tony with me.' Des raised his eyebrows. 'His chauffeur's coming along too, so you don't have to worry.'

'Fair enough. I meant to ask you, have you still got that wireless in the kitchen?'

'Wireless!' Des still refers to JFK as Idlewild, believe it or not. 'Yes, you'll be able to enjoy the Light Programme or the Home Service.'

'Very funny. There's a test match, that's all.'

'Des, there's something I want to show you.'

'I see.' He'd stopped looking at me and was staring into his gin and tonic. I took the wedding photograph out of my bag and slid it on to the bar beside the glass.

'Mr and Mrs Desmond Haigh-Wood, 1946,' I said.

He looked at it without speaking for a moment. 'Where did you find this?'

'Joan's room.'

Des put a palm on the bar and swivelled himself round on the stool so that he was looking directly at me. 'Look, Dodie, there's quite a lot . . .' His eyes fell from my face to the floor. I said nothing. 'Dodie. This isn't . . . It's not as . . . There's more to this than . . .' Out of the corner of my eye, I could see a patch of peacock blue waistcoat approaching us.

The waiter inside it said, 'If you'd like to follow me, sir. Your table is ready.'

Neither of us said anything more until we'd ordered our food and unfurled our napkins. I thought again of the sweet and sour pork balls in the Jade Garden and wondered how it was that we hadn't got sauce all over our laps, because those napkins had been made of paper.

Des gave a few warming-up coughs and then he said, 'You people nowadays, you're very articulate, but it's all you seem to do. Talk. We just got on with it.' He chuckled and shook his head. 'And I suppose all we do now is talk about how we just got on with it. During the war and all that. All this . . .' He flapped his hand, searching for the word. '. . . counselling. Everyone has to have counselling. I've hurt my little finger, I need counselling. Everybody, all the time, squawk, squawk, squawk. But I suppose it's harder for your generation. God knows what the world's going to be like by the time you're my age. To be honest, I'm bloody glad I'm not going to be around to see it. Sorry, I've gone off on a tangent. Well, no, I haven't. All I meant was, some things . . . sometimes it can be better not to know. Easier. There's no sense in kicking up a whole lot of dust. One has to be practical—'

'You sound like Joan.'

'Well, that's my age, I suppose. And Joan was always sensible.'

'Don't talk to me about being sensible and not kicking up dust.' Suddenly I felt furious. 'You – all of you – you've created a bloody *sandstorm*. Let's keep everything under wraps, let's tell lies, or better still, don't let's talk about it. That's why I'm in the middle of this mess and I don't have a clue what's going on. And you're sitting there telling me that it's making things easier. Well, I've got news for you. It's making them a hell of a lot harder.'

'I think you're probably right about that.'

'I know I'm right. Des, when I phoned you, whenever it was, the first time, you told me you were amazed I was still talking to you, so you must have had some idea of how I felt—'

'Look, I'll do my best, Dodie. I can't explain everything, but I'll try not to make excuses. And if you decide you don't want to talk to me after that, well . . .'

There was a cough above my head, and I saw the waiter's black-trousered thighs next to the table. 'Your wine, sir.'

Des took a sip. 'Fine.' He looked up at the waiter. 'That's absolutely fine. Splosh it about.' Another waiter flourished a basket of rolls at us. 'Go on,' said Des. 'Take one. It'll give you something to shy at me.'

I kept my head down until the waiter had retreated. 'It isn't funny.'

'I know it isn't, love. I'm sorry.'

'Tell me about you and Joan.'

'We met during the war, when I was on leave. Then I got captured, and I was stuck in Germany for three years. She used to send me her chocolate ration. And she wrote marvellous letters. Very funny.'

'I've never thought of her as being funny.'

'Well, she was. Marvellous sense of humour. I got home a month or so after the war ended, and we were married about a year after that, I think.' He pulled the photograph out of his pocket and turned it over. 'March. I thought it was later. It was a very warm day, I remember that. More like June than March. To be honest, I've often wondered if it wasn't the distance; whether we'd have kept it up if we'd seen more of each other. I don't know.'

'Didn't you want to get married?'

'I didn't know what I wanted. I'd just spent three years as a prisoner of war. I suppose I thought I should get back into the swing of things. For three years, in the camp, all I could think of was getting back home, but when I got here it seemed such a let-down. People talk about the marvellous welfare state and all the rest of it, but it was bloody awful. Everything was grey: grey faces, the rationing going on and on, and everything seemed sort of . . . shrunk. Or dismantled. Or bombed out of existence. I suppose I'd been imagining England as it was in the thirties, and it wasn't the same country any more.'

'But wasn't there a depression in the thirties? Unemployment?'

'Yes, but—' Des stopped and looked at his plate. 'But I was a boy, and anyway, it didn't affect my family. That's what it boils down to, I suppose. Everyone remembers the good times, don't they? And I suppose I thought, well, that Joan had been through the war in London, so she knew what to expect, and somehow that would help me, and we could manage together. So we were married, and everyone said, "Good luck," and we set up house, and all the time I had this sensation . . . as if I was trapped under something heavy. A great big stone or something. I could never quite crawl out from under it.' He stopped as the first course was lowered in front of him. 'I can't understand why they do this,' he said, when the waiter had retreated. 'Great big plate, minuscule pile of food, right in the middle. What's that they've sprinkled on yours?'

'Parsnip chips. Want one?'

'No thanks.' He shuddered theatrically. 'You're welcome to them.'

We had a few mouthfuls and I thought he might not carry on talking, so I said, 'Did my father come to your wedding?'

'No. I barely knew him in those days. I started working for him at the end of forty-six. December. One of those chance things, you meet someone who knows someone. He was looking for a chap who was trained in accountancy, which I was. I went to see him for a chat, and we hit it off, and, well, Bob's your uncle.' I opened my mouth to interrupt, but he waved his finger at me and carried on. 'You have to understand, that was the most exciting time of my life. There'd been the war – until I was captured anyway – but working for Wolf . . . We were going to rebuild the country, you see. No more slums, no more Victorian monstrosities, everything clean, and new, and far, far better than before. A lot of people didn't have bathrooms and lavatories. There was a certain sort of house, built in a terrace, with no back door, so if you wanted to use the lavatory, you'd have to go out of the front door and walk for two hundred yards. And you were sharing it with thirty-odd people, so there'd be a queue when you got there. This was everybody – old people, invalids. You had these rows of tiny little houses with families crammed in, no room to swing a cat, water coming in through the walls, bed bugs. That was what life was like for a lot of people. You simply have no idea. It's easy for people who don't remember to look back now and make clever remarks, but then . . . it was the future. It was exciting. A new beginning. A better life. It was the war that did that. People thought, we didn't go through all this for nothing.'

'But my father wasn't doing all this because he felt sorry for people, was he?'

'No, that's not how the world works, you know that. There were huge contracts, the money started coming in, slowly at first, but then – yes, your father made money. We all made money and that was part of the fun, I don't deny it. I'm just trying to explain to you how exhilarating it was, not just the new houses, but offices, towns, new places to live and work. We'd stay late, we'd be there talking, making plans . . . What I said before, about the heavy weight, well, it was gone. Wolf – your father – he inspired people, Dodie. One felt there was a vision there, something to work towards. Strive for. It's good, this.' He prodded his calves' liver with his fork. 'Joan used to make me sandwiches. To take into work. Used to put them into my briefcase. I missed that. God knows why, because I went out for lunch most of the time. Meetings. Chaps always want to take you to restaurants, and of course one didn't exactly complain. But I did miss the sandwiches.'

'You and Joan. What happened?'

Des sighed. 'I suppose you have a right to know.'

'I think I have.'

'Of course you have. Just bear with me a moment, will you?' He got up and went in the direction of the loo. He was gone a long time. I could imagine him staring into the mirror as he washed his hands, turning them over and over with the soap on them, careful not to get it on his cuffs, and wondering how to say whatever it was he was going to tell me.

His return coincided with the arrival of the next course, and we sat in silence while the waiter put down plates and topped up glasses. When he'd gone, Des said, 'How much do you know about your father's first wife?'

'Her name was Betty Carroll. They were married in 1948 and divorced a couple of years later. Then he married Joan. That's all.'

'You've never heard anyone talk about her?'

'Des, I didn't know she even *existed* until I read it in one of the obituaries.'

'She was a redhead, like you and your mother. Well, not red exactly, that's too crude. Strawberry blonde is what they used to call it. She was rather lovely. Lots of what they used to call SA.'

'What's that?'

'Sex appeal. She was still very young, but she'd been a singer with one of the all-girl dance bands during the war. They used to go on tours. I think they even went to Africa at one stage.' Des cleared his throat. 'Betty had, well, she had a past. There'd been quite a few other men. Your father was very much in love with her. I'm not sure how much he knew, but I suppose he thought she'd settle down once they were married.'

'You mean she had affairs? Afterwards?'

'Yes.' Des was staring at his plate. He hadn't even picked up his knife and fork.

'Des?'

He raised his eyes. He looked as if he was about to lay his head on the block. 'Yes?'

'The affairs. Was one of them with you?'

'Yes.'

'Why?'

'I told you I wouldn't make excuses, Dodie, and I won't.'

'Were you in love with her?'

'No. It wasn't anything to do with love.'

'Was she in love with you?'

'God, no. Betty liked intrigue, and she liked sex. In those days, she'd have been called promiscuous. To her, it was exciting. I don't think she understood how much pain her behaviour would cause – not at the time, anyway. It was just, well, just how she was.'

'So why did you do it?'

'Because I was stupid, I suppose. I made a mistake. It was part of the excitement. If I'd thought about it, about betraying Wolf, I wouldn't have done it, but she made it seem like a joke, a prank. One was drawn in. Look, Dodie, I said I wasn't going to make excuses, and I'm not. It wasn't Betty's fault. It was mine. I didn't have to do what I did. But I did do it, and I'm, well, I'm very sorry.'

'Was it because of Joan? Didn't you love her?'

Des sighed. It was a peculiar sound, almost like a rattle. 'I enjoyed being married to her very much. She liked looking after people, but she wasn't so keen on the other stuff. I think she didn't really understand why people were interested in sex. But I'm not blaming Joan.'

'You aren't, are you?'

'I hope not. It wasn't my intention.'

'Des, we'd better start eating. The waiter keeps looking.'

We had a few mouthfuls, and then he said, 'You know, your father never knew.'

'But surely—'

'Not about me. It was one of the others he found out about. Joan knew. I told her, but I think she knew already. She kept it to herself. She and Wolf . . . Well, we all saw a lot of each other. Social things, of course, and she used to come to the office sometimes . . .' He tailed off, and I thought again of what Mrs Curtis had said. *Joan was always very loyal to your father.*

'Joan and my father; did they become lovers?'

'I don't know. It was more that they had a sort of understanding. She felt sorry for him. When she said, you know, that she was leaving, going to be with Wolf, I didn't try to stop her. I felt so wretched. I've often thought, if it hadn't been for my stupidity, we could have made a go of it.'

'Didn't you want children?'

'Yes. Unfortunately, it wasn't possible. Betty had a son, though. She always said he was Wolf's child, but Wolf didn't believe it. He didn't want anything to do with the boy, and she didn't make an issue of it. I saw her a few times, after—'

'Is she still alive?'

Des shook his head. 'She died in 1974. She wasn't very old. She never remarried.' He smiled. 'There were always lots of dancing partners, right up to the end. Wolf didn't want her name mentioned. I think, when he heard the rumours about your mother, well, I think he saw history repeating itself.'

'Did he say that?'

'No. He never talked about that time in his life. I think he thought, by not talking about it, he could sort of cut it away. As if Betty deceiving him had never happened. But it stayed with him. He'd loved her very much.'

'But you were party to the deception, didn't you—'

'I'm not proud of it, Dodie. I admired your father very much. If I wanted to work at Blackstock and have his company, then that was the price. Knowing I'd betrayed him.'

'I heard a conversation you had, when Mum was kidnapped. He said all this stuff about women stirring things up, how it was all Mum's fault.'

'He said those things because of Betty. He'd trusted her, and when she betrayed him, that was it. I don't understand all this relationship stuff they go in for nowadays, but I can tell you this: it comes down to trust. If you can't trust someone, well, you might as well not bother. With Joan, once she knew about Betty and me, that put the kibosh on the whole thing.'

'So when she married my father, you just accepted it?' Des suddenly seemed transfixed by the food on his plate, and a ruddy flush suffused his tan.

'Des? Are you all right?'

He put his fork down and looked straight at me. 'I may as well tell you, Dodie. They weren't married.'

'But all the obituaries—'

'People believe what you tell them. They don't ask to see a certificate. Joan and I were divorced, and she wanted to marry Wolf, but he wouldn't. I thought it was because the love wasn't there, but looking back, I think he was afraid. I think he very much wanted a woman who would love him *entirely*. But he didn't believe it was possible, after Betty. The ideal and the reality, I suppose. I think that was the reason he was attracted to your mother. She was beautiful, of course, but she was young, that was the thing. Innocent. She didn't have a past.'

'She didn't have much of a present either. Or a future.' I pushed back my chair. 'I'm sorry, Des. Will you excuse me a moment?' My legs felt stiff and I had to force them forwards across the carpet as if I was walking on stilts. My shoulder felt like a big numb block as it pushed against the door of the Ladies'. I filled one of the basins with cold water and stood hanging on to the edge, staring into the mirror. *This here phizzog.* I barely recognised it. I thought, I should be feeling something. Anything. But I wasn't.

When I got back to the table, my barely touched main course had been removed. 'I ordered coffee. You didn't want pudding, did you?' Des said.

'No. Thanks.'

He stretched across the table and patted my hand. 'Chirp up, chicken.'

When the coffee had arrived, I said, 'I don't understand. He was surrounded by all these women who adored him, fought over him.' I stopped, remembering how it had been. 'It was like a competition, all the time. And that was the big thing Joan always had over Angela, that even if Angela had supplanted her, she'd been married to him and Angela hadn't.'

'I know. Joan used to call herself Mrs Blackstock – until Wolf married your mother, of course. She went back to her maiden name after that. I realise that people live together all the time, nowadays, and no one seems to mind, but for someone of my generation . . . I never thought it was right. Not that I was in a position to do anything about it. I did sometimes wonder whether Joan hadn't actually come to believe that the marriage had taken place. Angela certainly didn't know they weren't married.' Des chuckled. 'Joan would never have heard the last of it if she had.'

'I thought the reason he wouldn't marry Angela was because she was Jewish. Joan told me that was why she wasn't buried in our churchyard.'

'I don't think so. I didn't know that Angela was Jewish. If she was, she kept it pretty quiet.'

'That was because he didn't like Jews.'

'It's true he didn't have much time for them. But some of

the top men in the firm were Jewish, and he didn't discriminate against them. Not in business.'

'Why? Was it because his mother was German? I mean, was she anti-Semitic?'

'I don't know, but I doubt it would have made any difference. Rather the opposite, if anything. Your father and your Uncle Lawrence were born just before the First World War, remember. People didn't like the Germans much in those days, and some of it was pretty irrational. Banning Wagner and kicking dachshunds, that sort of thing. And in the middle of all that, your grandmother insisted on having them christened Ludwig and Wolfgang. There must have been some pretty nasty taunts. Makes you wonder what sort of woman she was, really.' He stopped and nudged the plate of *petits fours* in my direction. 'Have one.'

'No thanks. By the way, I found the car.'

'Which car?'

'Mum's Mercedes. In a Nissen hut on the estate.'

'What was it doing there?'

'I was hoping you'd tell me.'

'I can't help you there, I'm afraid. Perhaps they just wanted it out of the way. The police must have brought it back at some point, I suppose, but I don't remember.' Des pushed back his chair. 'I think it's time for my ADC.'

There's an enormous herb garden at the back of the Fat Hen, lit up at night by strings of tiny white bulbs draped over the hedges and trees. The paths are edged with huge clumps of lavender that brushed against our legs and released their smell as we walked up and down.

'There's no mystery, Dodie. Your father thought the kidnap was a hoax, but it was genuine. Even he had to admit that, in the end. The odd thing was, we'd discussed the possibility of a kidnap before, when the Getty boy was taken. I'd been trying to get Wolf to take out some insurance, but he wouldn't. We thought *you* were the one who'd get snatched, not your mother.'

'Oh, great. And I suppose if I'd got kidnapped, he would have decided that I was taking the mickey and not done anything about it either.'

'No, he wouldn't, Dodie. You know that.'

'Do I? The police found a letter from Joan in Mum's stuff. It was dated August 1976. That was about six weeks after the kidnappers were arrested, in case you don't remember.'

'Yes, your friend Tony told me about that.'

'Did he tell you that the letter made it clear my father knew as well? And don't bother telling me he didn't, because I won't believe you.'

'I can't tell you anything, Dodie, because *I don't know*. That honestly is the truth, whether you believe it or not. I told you I wanted to make it right, if I could, but I can't invent things. I don't know what happened. Be reasonable.'

'Reasonable!' I didn't want to get angry, but I couldn't help it. 'Oh, fine. You lot can do anything you want and fuck everyone else's lives up in the process, and I'm supposed to take it all like a lamb and *be reasonable*. I mean, let's face it, it's not as if I've spent my life surrounded by role models. Well, is it?'

'I don't know what to say. Except that I'm very, very sorry.' Des held his cigar at an angle and flicked at it with his thumb and finger, but the ash stayed where it was. 'I was thinking about what your – what Tony said about Joan writing to your mother. And I think you're right. If Joan knew, then your father knew as well. Joan was a certain type of woman, Dodie. An old-fashioned type, if you like. Women like her, they have to . . . Well, they have to give their loyalty, their *care*, to something. It could be to their children, or the WRVS, or the church, or to, well, anything really. Joan didn't have children. That was her tragedy, I think. And somebody had to be the recipient of her care, and that person was your father.'

'But she didn't even tell *me*.'

'That surprises me. As I said, misplaced loyalty. It's the

only explanation I can come up with, Dodie.' He paused. 'When you first told me that Susan's body had been found, I thought you meant, well, a skeleton. I had no idea that she had been alive for so long.'

'But you knew about the lover, didn't you?'

'We'd heard rumours, that was all. Wolf believed them.'

'Did you?'

'No, I didn't.'

'Why not?'

'Well . . .' Des thought for a moment. 'If Susan had a lover, she had a funny way of showing it. I mean, not that one would necessarily *know*, but she seemed preoccupied. Abstracted. She just seemed, well, *odd*.'

I nodded, remembering the strange mealtimes we'd had. 'Well, that could have meant that she was thinking about someone else.'

'I suppose so. But it was more as if she was withdrawing into herself.' Des sighed. 'If you want the absolute truth, I think she was just very unhappy.' We were walking through a pergola of white roses towards a round raised pond. When we got there, Des sat down on the brick surround.

'I was very fond of your mother, you know. You're very like her.'

'Barmy, you mean?'

'I mean you look like her.' He smiled at me. 'You're quite presentable, you know.'

'Huh.' I sat down beside him.

He shot his cuffs and leaned forward to put his elbows on his knees. I sensed that he was doing it to avoid looking at me. 'You know, Dodie, your father . . . at the end he was lonely. The house was full of staff, but he would only see the two of us, Joan and me. He missed you.'

'I can't think why. He'd never given me much attention before. You did, but he didn't.'

'He regretted it. That he hadn't been more approachable. Hadn't got to know you. Joan used to ask him if he wanted her to telephone you, see if you'd come down. But he always said no. I think he was afraid you'd refuse.'

I didn't know what to say. The truth was, I probably would have refused. Before I could stop them, my eyes filled up with tears. I had nothing to wipe them with. I tried to sniff them back, but it didn't work.

'It's always a good idea to do these things . . . before it's too late.' Des sounded muffled. I looked at him sideways and saw that he had his head in his hands.

'Des?'

'Mmm . . .'

'Can I have a go of your handkerchief?' He didn't look up, just stuck out his hand. His handkerchief was still folded into a neat oblong, but one side was wet. I dabbed my face as carefully as I could, but there was a glob of black mascara on the white cotton when I'd finished. 'There you are.'

Des groped for it, spread it out in front of his face and made an awful choking sound. I sat and looked at the herringbone brick paving between my feet. After a couple of minutes, he blew his nose and straightened his back. He gave me a crooked smile. 'All mopped up?'

'Yes. You?'

'Yes, thanks.'

'Actually, Des, I think I'd better check you for make-up. Some of mine got away.'

'God, yes. Don't want people thinking I'm a pansy.'

I took his chin in my hand and turned his face towards the row of white tree lights. 'Nothing to worry about. Quite presentable, really.'

We began walking back to the restaurant. I touched the top of a rosemary bush as we passed, and held my hand up to his nose. 'Smell this.'

'No point asking me to smell it. My hooter is purely ornamental, as you once pointed out. Too many of these.' He waved his cigar at me.

'When did I say that?'

'When you were a tot.' He patted me on the head.

'Get off!'

'Out of the mouths of babes . . .' He lifted my arm and put it through his, keeping it there with his other hand. Under his breath, he began to sing, '*O, we all walk the wibbly-wobbly walk, And we all talk the wibbly-wobbly talk . . .*'

'We can't sing here,' I said. 'They'll throw us out.' But, automatically, my feet were mimicking his, two steps and a little skip, just as we'd done when I was little. 'Des?'

'Yes, my child?'

I wish you were my father. 'Thanks for dinner.'

21

When we got back to the terrace, the waiter told me that the car I'd ordered was waiting. Des waved me off. I lay back in the squashy leather seat, closed my eyes, and let the driver take me home. Des and I hadn't had the conversation I'd imagined we would, and I'd said hardly any of the things I'd been rehearsing in my head for so long, but it didn't matter. It was better, in a way. None of the things I'd learnt had gone into focus. They were just *things*. They could have been stories about people I didn't know. It was as if I was staring in through the window of a stranger's house.

Only one thing stood out clearly: I had to find out about Mum. When Des told me he hadn't known she was still alive, I believed him, and I still believed him when I got home. He isn't a liar. He hadn't told people things, but those were more, well, sins of omission, really. Besides, I thought, what would be the point in lying now?

'*Oi! Do you mind?*' The taxi driver's shout made me jump. We'd stopped. For a second, I was blinded by torch-light, then the beam was switched off and I saw Dave the security guard standing beside the Camoys Hall gate. His hairy Alsatian had its front paws up on the driver's door and its nose was poking through the open window. 'Get that thing off my paintwork.'

The dog barked. 'He doesn't think much of your air freshener,' said Dave. 'Sorry, Miss Blackstock, I didn't realise it was you in the back there.'

'I don't think much of his breath, mate. Go on, get out of it!' The driver made shooing movements with his arms. The dog licked his hand. It looked as though it was smiling.

'What's his name?' I asked.

Dave looked faintly embarrassed. 'Treacle. My little girl's idea. He's ever so good with kids.'

'He is actually a guard dog, is he? I mean, he doesn't look terribly fierce, that's all.'

'Best dog I've ever had, this one. He may look like a pussy cat, but if I say the word, he'll do the business.' He drew a finger across his Adam's apple in a cut-throat motion.

'Oh, good. Is everything all right?'

'Yes, very quiet. You've got four of us on duty now, and they're starting with the gates and that tomorrow, so you've got nothing to worry about.' He clicked his fingers for Treacle to get down and gave the top of the car a slap. 'Off you go, mate. Sleep well, miss.'

I gave the taxi driver an extra-large tip to make up for the dog, let myself in, and then wandered around the house for a bit, thinking. I didn't feel scared any more. It wasn't just having the security guards. Maybe it was because I'd learnt something. Knowing things makes you feel powerful, somehow. When I looked at my watch, it was quarter to two. I wondered if I should give Tony a ring and tell him what I'd discovered, except that I thought he might not be in. If he was, he'd be asleep by now. Anyway, I'd be seeing him in the morning.

On the way to bed, I suddenly decided to visit my father's

old rooms. I'm not sure why. I stood for a while with my hand on the knob of the outer door. I'd switched all the lights off, but the moon was shining through the glass panels in the huge landing window, and I could see the grain of the wood. I thought of all the times I'd waited outside looking at those knots, waiting to be summoned in to give an account of myself; my school reports – marks that were good, but never good enough. Once I got ninety-eight per cent in a Latin exam, and all he said was, 'Why didn't you get a hundred?' I remembered the butterflies in my stomach and always promising myself, this time I won't cry, but never succeeding; Joan waiting outside, pulling a string of pink paper tissues from the sleeve of her cardigan to mop me up. The peaceful feeling I'd had inside broke into jagged pieces. Shit, shit, shit! I clenched my fists. 'He's not in there,' I said out loud. 'He's *dead*.' I twisted the knob and opened the door.

I blundered around in the dark for what seemed like an hour before I found the light switch. I'd thought Joan would have swathed everything in dust sheets, but she hadn't. In his sitting room, the armchairs and little tables were just as they always were, the cabinets with photographs on top: fifty, a hundred images of my father, in colour and black and white, shaking hands over and over again with Henry Kissinger, Edward Heath, François Mitterand, Margaret Thatcher, Charles Clore, Pablo Casals, Charlie Chaplin, Viv Richards, the great and the good and the wonderful and the marvellous. In his private dining room, the candelabra were still on the polished walnut table and the silver bon-bon dish was full of nuts, the crackers placed beside it. Everything was the same as when he was alive.

His bedroom smelt cabbagy. A vase of wilting stocks, foxgloves and delphiniums stood on the bedside table. Joan must have put it there the week before. I took it into the bathroom, emptied the flowers into the bin and rinsed out the viscous yellow water, wondering if she'd come up here much after he'd died. It was probably just another task on the list, *Fresh flowers for W's room*, the only difference being that he was no longer there to see them. On the same day, each week, Joan would walk across his bedroom with a fresh offering, her cardigan draped round her shoulders so that the sleeves hung down like redundant arms. She'd remove the old vase, put the new one in place, and give the arrangement a few tweaks before going out again. She wouldn't be lingering and sentimental, touching things and crying; just in, out, and on to the next thing, because that was her way. God, I thought, she was so strong. She'd been the engine of the house, its heart, the strongest muscle in the body, the one that makes everything else work. Misplaced loyalty, Des had called it.

There was a photograph beside the vase of my mother and me, wearing identical *matelot* shirts with blue and white horizontal stripes. Mum's hair is blowing across her beautiful face, and she's hugging me. Blue sky behind us. We must have been happy because we're laughing. I didn't remember it. I didn't remember the bedside table, either. It was small and square, made of cheap dark wood, with barley sugar legs and a scalloped edge. It didn't go with the rest of the bedroom furniture. Neither did the bed. Unmade, it had a hospital look, with a steel frame and a thin mattress covered in a khaki-coloured waterproof material. Three pillows were neatly stacked at the end, beside a pile of heavy pink blankets with satin edges. My father must have died on this bed. I prodded the mattress. It sprang back immediately, bouncing my finger off. There was a commode underneath, an ugly green box mounted on white tubular legs. I imagined my father painfully manoeuvring his grey-white old man's legs over the edge of the bed, with Joan standing by to help. He wouldn't have let a nurse help him.

I thought he had had all the power, but it wasn't true. The little boy with the German name, shielding himself from flying stones. The cuckold. The man who was scared of rejection, scared of madness, scared of what people would discover about him. I'd never have described my father as a coward, but he wouldn't have had the courage to do what Des had done tonight, to tell me those things, to admit he'd been wrong.

As I turned away from the bed, my eye caught the photograph again. My face was in profile, half against Mum's chest, and the wind was trying to tug the hair out of my ponytail. If my mother *did* have a lover – I wasn't sure if I believed Carol Curtis's account of that, or Des's, but if she did – he drove her to it. And he hadn't forgiven her, either for betraying him like Betty Carroll – if that was what she'd done – or for going mad. He'd judged all women by Betty. He'd even judged me that way in the end.

'You bastard!' I shouted. 'You owe me an explanation. You owe me that!' I ran into the sitting room. The silver-framed photographs crashed and splintered round my feet as I swept them off the surfaces, and the cabinets tottered on their gilt legs as I yanked open door after door. I didn't know what I was looking for. I tried the hall stand, the secretaire, the medicine cabinet in the bathroom, even the grandfather clock. All empty. Joan had cleared out the lot.

Back in the sitting room, I looked down at the slew of teeth and smiles, the outstretched hands, the slapped backs, the dinner-suited moguls surrounded by pretty women and the debris of expensive meals. They were probably all as bad as he was, with their wives and mistress and intrigues and lies. I'd felt so good, walking round the house. Floaty. Detached. Free. Not angry any more. And then it all came back. I poked the photographs with my toe and felt my anger congeal and harden until my whole body felt like a stone. I can't forgive him, I thought. I'm not going to, ever.

I snatched our photograph from his bedside table, smacked the lights out, slammed the door and ran across the landing to my own room.

22

I was too angry to sleep, and *The Diary of a Nobody* didn't help. I dropped off eventually and woke again at four, worrying about the meeting with Maggie Hill. I got out of bed and went over to the vast centre window of the ball-room to watch the sun rise. My heart was pounding and my stomach felt like a small hard ball being squeezed by a giant's hand. I decided to ring Maggie Hill and make an excuse. I'd switched on the mobile and was about to dial the number when I remembered what time it was.

I was up and dressed and on my fourth cup of coffee by the time Des arrived. I left him drinking tea and talking to the nice cleaning lady while I went upstairs to gather up the stuff I wanted to take to London.

Des came outside to wave me off. 'You'll be back tonight, won't you?'

'Yes. Don't worry, Des, I'll be fine.'

I can't have sounded very convincing, because he said, 'Well, I'll be here. I want to make sure you get back in one piece. That chauffeur of Tony's, he's all right, isn't he?'

'He's fine, honestly.'

'And he's going to wait for you while you talk to this woman?'

'Yes.'

'Have you got a phone?' I held it up for inspection. 'It works? You've recharged it?'

'Yes.'

'Good. Well, look after yourself.'

'I'll do my best.'

'Dodie?'

'Yes?'

'Just be careful, that's all. This Hill woman . . . You don't know what she might do.'

'I know, Des. But Dominic's going to be there all the time.'

'Fair enough, but what this woman says, it won't necessarily be true. She's got her own axe to grind. You probably don't remember, but they were a weird bunch, and what they came out with in court was a lot of gibberish. Capitalist conspiracies and God knows what else. I know you want to find out what happened, but she'll have her own take on it. She's had plenty of time to think, get herself into a stew about it. She's been banged up in prison for quite a few years, and people like that always want to blame somebody else. They haven't got a job or money, and it's always somebody else's fault, or else it's the system's. All I'm saying is, you're not bound to believe what she tells you. It won't be gospel truth.' He held up the tinfoil envelope that I'd made for the anonymous letter. 'For all we know, she might have written this herself. I'm not saying she *did*, but there's a possibility.'

'I know.'

'Well then, remember what I've said. Got enough petrol?'

'Full tank.'

'OK. Drive safely.' He opened the car door for me with a little flourish. 'In you get.'

I lowered myself into the driver's seat, started the engine, and slid the window down. 'Des?'

'I'm still here.'

'I do love you, you know.' I didn't stop to see his reaction, just let out the handbrake and went.

All the way to London, I felt sick. Every time I came to a junction, it was all I could do not to turn round and drive straight back to Camoys Hall, and the nearer I got to London, the worse it became. I did pull over once, and walked up and down on the hard shoulder, trying not to think about where I was going or what on earth I was going to say when I got there. In the end I rang Tony.

'Where are you?'

'In a lay-by. Tony, I don't know what I'm going to say to her.'

'You don't have to do this, you know. You can phone her and say you've changed your mind. I can phone her, if you like. What's her number?'

'I don't know.'

'Haven't you got it?'

'Yes, but—'

'If you've got her address, I can look it up. You have got her address, haven't you? Dodie? Dodie? Are you still there?'

'Yes. I dropped the phone, that's all.'

'Have you got her address?'

'In the car.'

'Well, go and get it and call me back.'

'No. I've got to go and see her. I have to do it, Tony. I'll be at your house in . . . in three-quarters of an hour.'

'All right, but don't go mad.'

'Is Dominic there?'

'Yes, he's got his flak jacket on and he's just about to go and put the armour plating on the car. It's *Bonfire of the Vanities*, darling. We're *living* it.'

Tony opened the door wearing a back-to-front baseball cap.

'It doesn't do anything for you.'

'Oh, thanks. I've got one for you too. And Dominic. Help us blend in. Come on through.' I followed him down the hall and out to the mews where he keeps his cars. Dominic was sitting behind the wheel of a grey BMW.

'Is that one of yours?'

'No, it's Dominic's. He insisted. He says it'll be good for a quick getaway, if we have to.'

'Oh, stop it.'

'Sorry. Do you want to go in the front?' He opened the door for me, and climbed into the back.

214

'All set?' I asked Dominic. 'Have you got a map? I mean, we won't be able to ask anyone, and . . .'

Dominic looked at the address I'd handed him, and then at me. 'It's OK. I can handle it.' He started the engine and backed the car across the cobbles and out into the street.

'I'm glad someone can.'

From the back, Tony said, 'Dodie, I told you, you don't have to do this.'

'I'm doing it.'

He sighed. 'It's your funeral. Any time you want to stop the car, just say.'

'Can we talk about something else?'

'Whatever you like. Do you want my James Bond car?'

'The DB5? You're selling it?'

'I've told him he's mad,' Dominic said. 'It's beautiful.'

'I can't think why I bought it. It's revoltingly straight. Gives all the wrong signals.'

'I shouldn't worry, Tony,' I said. 'No one would mistake you for a heterosexual, even if you drove a tank.' Dominic laughed.

'Anyway,' Tony said, 'it's a pig to drive. No wonder James Bond always smashes everything up. I'm sure gay men cause far fewer accidents than straight ones.'

Dominic grinned at me. 'Don't listen to him. It handles like a dream. I can drive it to Camoys Hall for you, if you like.' We were going east, away from the parts of London I know. 'I used to live near here.'

Tony thrust his head forward, over my shoulder. 'Did you? Where?'

'Islington.'

'This isn't Islington, is it?'

'Down the road. It was when I worked in the City.' Dominic gestured at the rows of tower blocks. 'Stack-a-prole. That's what they call them in Russia.'

'God.' Tony shuddered. 'I'm terrified already.' He thrust a hip flask under my nose. 'Want a drink?'

'No, thanks.' There were walls of corrugated iron down each side of the road. I caught sight of a wasteland behind padlocked chain link gates. Rectangular concrete blocks scrawled with graffiti lay on their sides in the rubble. A revolution in public housing. Des's hope for the future. Perhaps it was the place where they'd found my mother's body. In my mind I saw the photograph from the magazine article, 'English Roses'.

'I've got my eyes shut,' said Tony. 'Why have we stopped?'

'Traffic lights,' I said. On one corner of the junction was a boxy red brick pub with boarded-up windows. Someone had spray-painted the word STRIPPERS across the plywood, and underneath it MEGA JUGS IN YOUR FACE.

'Whose face?' I asked Dominic. 'There's no one here.'

He gestured across the road. 'There's a shop.' It was nameless with metal grilles locked down over the windows. I could see stacks of fizzy drinks and white sliced bread behind them. A fat woman in a grubby tracksuit shoved a baby buggy round the corner and went in. 'Perhaps she's the mega jugs,' he said.

The lights changed and we drove past deck-access flats with polythene sheets stretched over the roofs; huge, furious dogs imprisoned on tiny balconies; rows of sagging shop-fronts plastered with so many layers of posters that they'd curled away from the windows like crusts of stale bread; a burnt-out litter bin, its melted plastic casing flopping outwards; Indian women splaying their high-heeled sandals on a pavement strewn with fag packets, newspapers, take-away chicken cartons and cans of Special Brew.

'Imagine,' said Tony, 'this could be your life.'

I didn't answer him. It had been my mother's life. This, or a place just like it.

'It should be just off here.' Dominic turned left between two rows of tower blocks mounted on massive concrete stumps. 'What's that one called?'

'Can't see. Shelley, I think.'

'*Ozymandias,*' said Tony. 'In a thousand years' time, it'll be four concrete legs in a desert of melted tarmac. All the rest will have disappeared. Look on these works, ye mighty, and despair.'

'What name are we looking for, Dominic?'

'Byron. It can't be far away. Let's try in here.' He turned off the road into a parking area. The shadows cast by the giant blocks surrounding it made it dank and chilly. A group of teenagers in hooded sports tops came out of their huddle in a doorway to stare at the car. One of them began walking towards it.

Tony leant forward. 'Oh God. Keep moving. He's got a chain in his hand. He's going to kill us.'

'It's a dog lead.'

'I don't care what the fuck it is, Dominic. I just don't want to fucking die, that's all. For Christ's sake put your foot down.'

'I'll run him over.'

'I told you this would be a disaster, Dodie, I warned you. Oh God.'

The boy was standing right in front of the car, arms raised, palms towards us.

Dominic stopped. Tony grabbed his shoulder. 'Just don't open the windows, whatever you do.'

The boy walked round to Dominic's window and tapped on it.

'Don't open it. Just drive on,' Tony hissed.

The boy gave the window an open-palmed slap and pointed downwards with his forefinger.

'Dominic, if you want to carry on working for me, don't even think about it!'

The boy slapped the glass again. Dominic lowered the window.

'Oh, Jesus.' Tony scrambled as far away along the back seat as he could.

'Want something?' The boy was white – well, greyish-pink – but his voice sounded black. He looked about sixteen and very, very hard.

'Byron House. Do you know it?'

'What you after?'

'We're looking for a woman called Maggie Hill.'

'Williams.' I leant towards him. 'Maggie Williams.'

'Make your mind up,' said the boy. He looked round the car, and said, 'Never heard of her. You want Byron House, though, you've come in the wrong end. Down there on the left.'

'Thanks.'

He shrugged and stood back from the car. 'Go on, then.'

We drove past Wordsworth, Coleridge and De Quincy in silence. Byron was right at the end. Its car park was deserted. Dominic pulled up outside one of the slabby scrawl-sided staircases that turned corners into dripping, ominous darkness.

'What are you going to do?' I asked.

'Stay here,' said Dominic. 'Unless you want me to come with you.' I looked over my shoulder at Tony, who was staring into his lap.

'No. I'll be all right by myself.' I opened the door.

Tony looked up. 'Wait a minute. Shut the door. Is your phone switched on?'

I nodded, opened the door and began to get out.

Tony lunged forward and grabbed my wrist. 'Give me your watch.'

'What is this? A practice mugging?'

'It's a Patek Phillippe, for God's sake. Take it off before someone sees it.'

I fumbled with it and dropped it on the seat. 'Happy now?'

'Come here.' He brushed his lips across my cheek. It felt clumsy and not like Tony at all. 'Just be careful, OK?'

23

The lift was broken. On the way up the eleven flights of stairs I passed a stooped pensioner with a dull red face and blue lips, wheezing as he heaved himself up one tread at a time. Perhaps he'd fought in the war and hoped for a better world, like Des. If I turned Mr Molloy out of his cottage, would he end up like that, imprisoned in vertical concrete and scarcely able to breathe?

A single strip of light flickered on and off above my head as I stood in the windowless hallway, waiting for Maggie Hill to open the door. Maggie's was Flat D. A sign on the wall said A–H, but the hall had been bricked up halfway down so you could only get as far as E. There was only one exit, the way I'd come up. I saw myself cornered between the door of flat E and the breeze-block wall, screaming against the stabbing blur of a knife. None of the doors would open to save me. I thought, if I get killed, it'll be my fault. I shouldn't be here at all.

Maggie Hill took so long to come to the door that I decided she wasn't at home. I was on the point of going back down the stairs to the car when I heard footsteps. I looked up and down the hall while she made scraping sounds with bolts and chains and almost jumped out of my skin when she finally swung the door open and stood in front of me.

I hadn't really thought about what she'd look like. I suppose I'd expected to see the slim girl in the brown velvet trouser suit, scratching her frizzy yellow hair with the stub of a pencil. She was older, of course she was. The frizz was still there, but grey. Her cheeks and nose were red, as if she'd been walking in a cold wind, and a hundred crinkles dredged in blue powder and lined with kohl seemed to radiate out from her eyes, which were far larger than I remembered. And kind. Her eyes looked kind.

'I didn't think you were going to come,' she said.

'I nearly didn't.'

'Well, you're here now.' She motioned me inside and turned to lock the door behind us. She was wearing a tight turquoise T-shirt and a long, limp, grey tube of a skirt. She'd hardly put on any weight. Stripy thick-soled flip-flops on her feet. Silver rings on her toes and fingers. 'Go on through. I'll put the kettle on.' She slithered through a half-open door and disappeared. The hall was dark and empty, with newspapers spread haphazardly across red and white lino. I took a few steps and peered through the only open door.

I saw a sitting room, a tiny box with a thick salmon-pink carpet, patterned with semi-circular impressions like un-finished corn circles. In the middle, a *chaise-longue* with a fleur-de-lis pattern in faded cream and blue was half hidden under an enormous orange cat who stared at me through slitty yellow eyes. The *chaise-longue*'s legs were scored with claw marks, and chunks of grey stuffing were hanging out of the bottom. Opposite were two dark brown corduroy armchairs, their seats flecked with ginger hairs, and a wall-mounted electric fire surrounded by pale green tiles. On the floor in front of it sat a leather-cased Roberts radio, which looked easily the most valuable thing in the room. There was no television, no bookshelf, and no pictures on the walls. The only decoration was a collection of African violets, begonias and geraniums in pots lined up against the skirting board.

I was bending over to look at them when Maggie Hill reappeared with two mugs of tea. 'Do you have milk?' she asked.

'Yes.'

'That's good, because I put some in. Sugar?'

'No thanks.' I took the mug. 'Lovely plants.'

'I get them in Columbia Road. Sunday morning. Bit of a crush, but if you wait till the end you can get stuff cheap.'

I said, 'That's nice,' and I could see Maggie thinking I was being sarcastic, but she didn't say anything, just bent sideways and batted the orange cat off the *chaise-longue* with one hand before subsiding into one of the armchairs.

'That's Napoleon, by the way. Ignore him. Sit down.' The cat stalked past me to the door, looking offended.

'He's a nice colour.' I lowered myself into the other armchair, trying surreptitiously to brush the orange hairs out of the way of my skirt.

'Same colour as Arthur Lowe's moustache. That's why he's called Napoleon.'

'Sorry?'

'In *Dad's Army*. That's what Bill Pertwee used to call him. The air raid warden, remember?'

I didn't. 'Oh. Yeah.'

Maggie gave me a where-exactly-did-you-park-your-spaceship look and shook her head. 'Why did you come here?'

'Because I wanted to know what happened. I was so young, and nobody would tell me anything. I just wanted to know, that's all.' Maggie stared into her mug. 'Why was your name in Joan's address book?'

'She got in touch with me. About six months ago. I think she must have got a private detective to find me, because I'd got married by then and changed my name. Not even my parents knew where I was. Well, they didn't want to know, did they? Not after I was arrested.' She paused. 'I'm sorry she's dead, by the way. Joan. I liked her.'

'Thanks.'

'She was nice. I thought she was going to have a go at me, you know. I mean, I wouldn't have blamed her. I wouldn't blame you, either.'

'I'm not going to have a go at you. Look, Maggie . . .' I stopped. 'Can I call you that? Is that what people call you?'

She looked surprised. 'I suppose it is. What shall I call you?'

'Dodie.' It was ridiculous, but I felt as if we should shake hands.

Maggie said, 'Williams is my married name, like I told you. We got divorced, but it was too much hassle to change back. Anyway, it was easier.'

I wondered if she'd been going to say it was easier because people recognised her other name. 'Do you ever tell people? What you—' I was about to say, what you did, but instead I said, 'What you were part of?'

'No.'

'You know my mother's dead, don't you?'

She looked puzzled. 'Well, yeah. I mean, I didn't *know*, but I always thought . . . I thought it was Mick. I thought he'd arranged it before we went to the farmhouse—'

'You thought Mick had killed her?'

'Well, I wasn't sure, but I suppose I did think that. I never asked him. Well, I couldn't. And I was scared it was true, so I didn't want to find out. After we were arrested – Steve and me – they wouldn't let us talk to each other. I knew she'd disappeared, but that was all. Well, I was hardly going to make it worse for myself, was I?'

'She died a couple of weeks ago.'

'Are you certain?'

'Positive.'

'God, I had no idea.' Maggie stared into her mug again. 'Poor Susan.'

'She was found near here.'

Her head jerked up. 'What?'

'Her body was found near here.'

'Oh *Christ*. I don't know what you're thinking, but I had nothing to do with it. That's why you're here, isn't it? I told you, I thought it was Mick. All the time I was in prison, I kept expecting somebody to come and tell me they'd found her body, and I thought, they're bound to think I had something to do with it, because Mick was dead so they'd want to put the blame on me and Steve, and I used to think, if that happens I'm going to be in here till I die, because they'll never believe me—'

'She died of a drug overdose.'

Maggie looked straight at me, but the words can't have registered because she said, 'And now it's all going to start again, and we'll be blamed.'

'Have you seen Steve? Since you came out?'

'No. And I don't want to, either. I can't believe this is happening. All I've ever wanted was to put all this behind me, get married, have kids. I wanted kids so much. I just wanted to get on with my life.'

'I can't get on with my life.'

'Look, what do you want me to say? If I could make it different, I would, of course I would, but there's nothing I can do, is there?' Maggie got up and squeezed behind her chair to get to the window. Although she was upright, her blind, blundering movements reminded me of Joan's Jack Russell, Malcolm, during a thunderstorm, terrified and scrabbling to hide himself in the tiny space between the washing machine and the wall.

I said, 'I want you to tell me what happened, that's all.'

She stood in front of the window. Her back was towards me, but I could see the angle of her cheekbone through her frizzy hair and the silver-ringed thumb of one hand, the nail chipping at the edges of the row of popped paint blisters on the wooden sill.

After a moment, she said, 'They wanted to try us separately, but we'd agreed before, if anything happened – if we got caught – we'd take our chances together, as a group. I did it for Mick, really, because he was the one who made us promise. My lawyer told me I'd have got less time if I'd been on my own. They might not have charged me with conspiracy.' She bent over behind the chair to put her mug on the floor and looked straight at me on the way back up. 'And I could have told them the truth.'

24

'It started when I moved into that flat, the one where you came,' said Maggie. 'At the beginning I was sharing with a girl called Maureen, and we needed someone else to help with the rent. That was how we met Steve Moody. He was the odd one out, really, because he wasn't a student like we were. He did odd jobs on building sites, but he was signing on as well. The dole.'

'I know what signing on is.'

'Well, it was Maureen who introduced me to Mick. At a party. The first time I saw him, I was stunned. He was so, well, so beautiful, I suppose. I just thought, *my God*.' She stopped, as if she'd just remembered who she was talking to. 'Sorry.'

'It's OK.'

'If I'm going to tell you how it was, I need to make it clear. How I felt. I need . . . not to make it sound different to how it was. Not to lie about it.'

'It's OK. Go on.'

'I started going out with him, and then Maureen met someone and she wanted to move in with him, so Mick came to live at the flat. That must have been about . . . oh, about three months before the thing with the cat, something like that. The politics, that was all Mick, really. That's what he'd studied for his degree, and Steve was really into it as well, so they used to talk about it a lot: Marxism, the Black Panthers, how to make the revolution happen, you know. I'd never thought about it much. I was a music student, and we didn't really talk about things like that, but I'd been along to a few meetings and demonstrations. It was just part of it. Going to university. Everyone did it.'

'Did you believe in it?'

'What?'

'Changing the world. We will overcome. Whatever.'

'I suppose I did. It was different then. It just seemed . . . It seemed possible, you know? That we could change things. All that stuff about the workers' revolution, well, it happened in Russia, didn't it? But I didn't think too much about what it would mean if it really happened in this country. I suppose I just thought it would be better if things were more fair.' She stopped and looked at me. 'Because it isn't fair, is it, the way things are?'

'No. But nothing ever is. What happened to my mum wasn't *fair*.'

'No, it wasn't.' She leant forwards over the back of the armchair and tipped it slightly towards her. I noticed that her arms were starting to go saggy at the top. 'I think about it a lot, you know. Every day. I'm sure you do, too.'

'Yes, I do.'

'Do you want me to go on?'

I nodded.

'Well, Mick used to tell me about stuff. Politics, mostly. I'd listen to him, and I'd think, God, he's so *real*. When he talked about capitalism, and how the ruling class were making the people work for next to nothing in their factories, and then they had to spend their wages buying back the same shit they'd been forced to make, he had so much passion. I loved that. I used to think, if I could just have some of that in my playing – you know, my cello . . . Because that's what the great musicians have, that immense feeling. Like Paul Tortellier. He did these masterclasses, ages ago, on television.' She saw me look round the room and said, 'I used to have one, but I gave it away. Too much violence. I suppose you think that's funny, coming from me.'

'Lots of people think that.'

'Anyway, I didn't have it. The passion. When I played, it was good, I mean, technically it was fine, but I was pretending. The feeling wasn't really there, and I—' She stopped and hung her head, and then released the armchair so abruptly that its front legs came down on the carpet with a thud. 'Excuse me,' she whispered, and barged past the furniture and out into the hall.

A few minutes later, she came back with a box of Kleenex in her hand. 'Sorry about that. Emergency supplies.' She dropped the tissues on the *chaise-longue*. 'D'you want some more tea? I'll put the kettle on.'

I sat and looked at the plants again while Maggie clattered about in the kitchen. 'I used to have them on the window sill, but the frame's disintegrating.' She put the mugs of tea in the middle of the carpet and sat down on the *chaise-longue*. 'Help yourself. The wood's rotting because of the damp. It's like a fridge in here in the winter. We have at least two pensioners die every year – pleurisy, pneumonia, hypothermia. The council won't fix it. Costs too much. Still,' she bent down to pick up her tea, 'it's one way to keep the numbers down, isn't it?'

I ignored the challenge in her voice. 'You were saying before, about the music . . .'

Maggie frowned. 'It was stupid, really. Mick hated classical music. If I was playing Elgar or someone, he'd say he couldn't believe I was naïve enough to spend my life warbling out bourgeois rubbish to make the arch pigs feel superior to the working class.'

'Arch pigs?'

'That was how he talked. Arch pig. Chief pig. High pig.'

'He called us pigs. On one of the tapes.'

'Did he?'

'Didn't you hear them?'

'No. Mick always did them on his own. Well, him and Susan. He said I only liked classical music because I'd been told I ought to.'

'But you must have realised that was bullshit, didn't you?'

'I was in love with him, Dodie. I didn't want to piss him off, so I used to go to the practice rooms at college, but that

226

meant dragging the cello into town on the bus, plus you had to book in advance, so that was a hassle, and after a while, well, I just gave up on it. It didn't seem very important any more.' She paused as the orange cat curled itself round the door and jumped into her lap, turning round and paddling with his toes for a foothold. 'All right, but don't dig your claws in, OK? The bow got broken when the police raided the farmhouse. Snapped. They did it. It was an expensive one as well, but I didn't get any compensation.'

'Have you still got a cello?'

'No. I haven't played for years. I used to listen to my CDs, but they got nicked when the flat was broken into. Now it's just Classic FM.' She winced as the cat dug his claws into her thigh. 'Owowowow. Bloody cat. Get *off*. Look,' she sounded irritated, 'it's not like some great loss to the world or anything. I mean, let's face it, I wasn't going to be the next Jacqueline du Pré.' She dumped Napoleon on the carpet and leant towards me, arms on her knees. 'You probably think I was just a doormat, but you've got to understand, where I grew up, my family, it was all "Don't raise your voice, don't bother your father, don't upset your mother." You couldn't get excited about anything, scream, cry, throw your arms in the air, because it would be too loud, too messy. When I met Mick, it was as if someone had suddenly turned the volume up and I could hear properly.'

'What was his background like?'

'Middle class, like mine, I suppose. He didn't talk about it much, none of us did. I think his parents were dead. He'd been left some money – not masses, but enough to live on. He was always telling us he was hard up, but if there was something he wanted, he'd buy it.'

'What sort of thing?'

'Well, if he wanted new clothes, he wouldn't go and buy just one jumper or one pair of jeans, but four or five things, quite expensive. He used to tell me he'd nicked them, but then once he came back with some stuff still in the carrier bags with receipts and everything, and another time I saw him in a shop handing over money, so I think he always bought them. He was the one who rented Randall's Farm and paid the deposit. That was what made me think he was serious, when he told me he'd done it.'

'Serious about the kidnap?'

'Yes. He must have done it a month before. He'd been talking about it for ages, and then when he said he'd rented this old farmhouse, I thought, God, he really means it. But sometimes he'd say one thing and do another, like with the clothes. And the food.' She smiled and shook her head. 'There was a Chinese restaurant round the corner from where we lived, and Mick would take Steve and me there every couple of weeks and order an enormous meal, far more than we could possibly eat, and he'd pay for all of it. He and Steve were always going on about conspiracies to poison our food with chemicals so we'd be too weak to fight the ruling class, and saying we should be vegetarian because it was exploiting animals, but they'd both sit there wolfing down the chicken chow mein with the MSG and all the rest of it. Or they'd go to the Wimpy and order a hamburger. Steve would eat anything. We used to call him the dustbin. Susan was always giving him her food.'

I looked down at my mug, and for a second, the thick brown tea became water, with watercress leaves floating on top like lily pads. 'Mum was fussy about food. Only in the months before the kidnap, though. It happened so suddenly. She seemed to go vegetarian overnight. And she wouldn't mix things. I used to think, what difference does it make, it all gets churned together in your stomach, but she said the flavours needed to be separate.'

'Yeah, she was a bit weird.'

'My father thought she was going mad. She did other things too. Once she went into the underground with a suitcase full of clothes and just started giving them to people.'

'God, so she actually did that, did she?'

'I was there. She gave away some of my things as well. How do you know about it, anyway?'

'Steve told us.'

'Steve?' Steven Moody. The lover. *The man who'd written the note.* 'Was he . . . was he the one?'

'Yes.'

'He came to our house in the country. People in the village saw them together in his Land Rover.'

'That belonged to Mick. Steve used to come back and tell us about it, what they'd done, what she'd said, you know . . .'

I pictured them all, lounging in their dirty kitchen, laughing about my mother. Randy rich bitch. 'So he didn't love her. It was all just a . . . a set-up.'

'No.'

'Look, we come to your house by accident, then six months later my mum has an affair with someone she met there, and then six months after *that* she gets kidnapped by the same man – and you're sitting there and telling me it was a coincidence?'

Maggie sighed. 'I'm trying to explain. It really wasn't a set-up – not in the way you think. It's true it was Mick's idea.' She held her hand up. 'I know you're thinking, well, she would say that, wouldn't she? But when Mick came to share the flat, he sort of took it over. Like he was in charge.' She shrugged. 'Strong personality, I suppose. Looking back, I think he did things deliberately to reinforce it, like when we'd go to the Chinese restaurant and he'd pay for the food. And he was the only one with a car, so that was another thing. Steve was pretty much under his thumb, but that was as much about class as anything else. It's funny when you think about it, because there we all were, going on about how class barriers must be smashed, and Steve was in awe of Mick because his posh education had made him articulate and confident and all the things he wasn't because he'd grown up in a council house and been to a state school. He used to argue with Mick, though. He'd educated himself quite a lot, mostly from television, and he used to get obsessions about things. Self-educated people often do, I noticed it a lot in prison. With Steve it was who killed Kennedy. He could talk about it for hours, but he usually kept quiet if Mick was there because it irritated him. They'd had this massive row at some party when Mick said whoever shot Kennedy ought to get a medal because he was a warmongering pig who'd got the Americans into Vietnam so all the blacks would be killed and that would solve the race problem. Steve just went ballistic. He would have gone for Mick if someone hadn't grabbed hold of him. But most of the time, if Mick said do something, he'd do it. Like with Sus— With your mother.'

'So he told Steven to contact her? How did he know where to find her, anyway?'

'She'd given us your address.'

'Did she? I don't remember that.'

'We were in the kitchen. Perhaps you weren't in there.'

'It must have been when Steven was telling me about the mannequin.'

'God, you remember *that*? I really hated that thing. I was always tripping over its feet.'

'What happened when we left?'

'Mick was out somewhere, and when he came back I told him about you and your mum so he'd know to keep a look out for the cat, in case it needed to go to the vet. I told him I'd stuck the slip of paper with the address into my diary, because that's where I put phone numbers and things. And that was it, really. It must have been a couple of weeks later, he was looking in the diary for a number and he found the paper. He came racing into the kitchen shouting, "Don't you know who this is?" I told him I had no idea what he was talking about, and he said, "Look at the name! She's married to the number one pig. Wolf Blackstock is an enemy of the people, and this woman is his *wife*!" He was so excited he was pacing up and down, and he kept stabbing the paper with his finger and saying, "I can't believe it!" Then he took us out for dinner. All through the meal he kept saying, "I can't believe it! I'm not passing up a chance like this." But he didn't mention kidnapping, not then. I just thought he had some scam in mind, like getting money out of your mother by saying we'd had to pay for the vet to come out and see the cat or something. He didn't say anything more about it for a couple of weeks, but he kept the address. I know because it was in the pocket of his jeans when I took them to the launderette, and he went *mad*. He came storming in and tried to wrench open the door of the machine while all the stuff was still going round. You could still read the writing, though, just about, so it was OK. Then he started saying to Steve, "Why don't you phone this woman up? You could do with a sugar mummy." Steve brushed it off at first, but Mick kept going on about it, and I think Steve must have said Susan was beautiful or something, because Mick started on about how young women who married rich old men were randy as hell and how they were always having it off with the chauffeur because they never got it from their husbands—' She stopped, looking defensive. 'Sorry, but I'm only repeating what he said.'

'Don't worry. Just go on.'

'Well, Mick wouldn't leave it alone. It got so bad that Steve said, "Look, why don't you phone her yourself, if you're so interested?" I got worried in case he did, but he just kept going on at Steve. It was weird, I mean, I could see Steve didn't really get it – well, neither of us did – but he was flattered at getting the attention from Mick; that Mick thought he could have this fantastic woman.

'I think that was really why he rang her up. He only told us after he'd done it. I think he was scared that she'd tell him to get lost, but she didn't. How I know about her giving away the clothes is because he used to be sort of, well, boastful about it. That he was influencing this woman to think about what a privileged life she had, about how other people needed clothes as well. He wanted Mick to see how clever he'd been.'

The anger in my chest and throat made me feel sick. 'So it was his suggestion to give away her clothes?'

Maggie nodded. 'And being vegetarian. But all that business about separating the flavours, that wasn't him. I mean, he cared about the politics of food production, but he wasn't interested in . . . diets. That was totally her.'

'But he was treating her like a performing poodle! He was like some . . . *ringmaster* with you two applauding every time she balanced a lump of sugar on her nose. How could you treat someone like that? What did she ever do to you? For God's sake, you knew what kind of person she was! You'd *met* her!'

Maggie was silent for a moment after I'd stopped shouting. Then she handed me the box of tissues and kept quiet while I blew my nose and got my eyes under control. 'It was only like that at first, Dodie. And it was only Mick who was egging Steve on, not me. He was always asking questions about Susan, what was she wearing, what was her hair like, things like that. I thought he was asking Steve all this stuff because he was falling in love with her himself. She was beautiful, rich – let's face it, she was everything I wasn't. I used to lie awake at night, thinking I'd lose Mick because I wasn't good enough. But it wasn't that at all.' She leant forward, elbows on her knees. 'I can't believe how blind I was!' She cupped her palms over her temples and shook her head. 'I mean, what the fuck was I thinking? All that stuff Mick used to spout about the distribution of wealth on an equal basis was utter balls. He didn't give a toss about the downtrodden masses, he just wanted to be *rich*. He was totally fascinated by it – the money, the lifestyle, everything. Let me tell you something, Dodie. Later on, when your mum was . . . when she was with us, Mick used to do what he called "interrogation sessions".'

'Stop it!' All the images of torture I'd managed to wall up in the back of my mind burst out. 'You're going to say you hurt her, aren't you? He – Mick – he hurt her, didn't he? He—'

'*No!*' Maggie shouted it. 'No. We didn't hurt her, Dodie, you've got to believe that. Listen to what I'm telling you. Please. Nobody hurt her. Even if Mick had wanted to, which he didn't, Steve wouldn't have let him. He loved her.'

'But you said he only did it because—'

'Later, he really did fall in love with her. What I was saying about the interrogation thing, Mick told us he was asking your mother about how much money your father had, how many shares . . . It used to happen in the after-noons, they'd go into one of the rooms together, just the two of them, and talk. We were living in Alfriston Road in Cricklewood by then. It was only a small house, so we'd have heard if he'd been shouting at her or anything. The door was closed, so you couldn't hear what they were saying, just the tone, and it sounded like an ordinary conversation. They'd be in there for ages. There was one afternoon when Steve was out, and I went and listened at the door. I was jealous, because Mick was spending so much time in there with her. You know what they were talking about? A hotel in Paris. She was telling him about this fancy hotel where she used to stay with your father—'

'The *Georges Cinq*?'

'Yeah, it's the most expensive or something. She was describing what it was like inside, the rooms and everything, and he kept asking questions about the decoration and the food. It was like *Hello!* magazine. That was the "interroga-tion". Getting her to tell him about hotels and yachts and cars and the people she knew and . . . and who made your father's shoes, for God's sake. And Mick was lapping it up! He *loved* it! And I didn't realise, even then. I didn't get it.' She laughed, suddenly. 'Christ Almighty!' She was shaking.

'Are you OK?'

'I'll be fine in a minute. I've gone over and over this in my head, and now actually saying it to you, telling you . . . you know? No, you don't know, do you? Why should you even try to understand, after what happened? God, Dodie, I'm so sorry. I can't even start to tell you. I'm just so sorry!' She was sobbing. I went over and put the Kleenex into her lap. She didn't pick out a tissue, or make any effort to stop crying, so after a moment I perched myself on the side of her chair and put my arm round her. I thought, was this what I came for? To see her break down like this and feel triumphant? But I didn't. I just felt confused. After a bit, she said, 'Let's have a drink, shall we? I think I've got some gin left. We could have it with orange juice.'

'Shall I go and get it?'

'I'll come with you.' She got up and led the way to the kitchen, and we stood opposite each other, leaning against the fitted cupboards, our toes almost touching in the tiny space.

I put my hand into my pocket and felt the anonymous letter in its tin foil wrapping. 'What did you mean when you said Steve fell in love with my mother later on?'

'What I said. At first, he used to come back from seeing her and talk about it, and Mick would ask questions, but then, after a while, he stopped telling us things. I thought it was because Mick was annoying him, but it wasn't just that. He wanted it to be private. Their meetings. He didn't want to share them with us any more, because it was special. Romantic.' Maggie stared down at her feet.

Romantic. Steven Moody and my mother.

'It just seems so unlikely. I know he was your friend and everything, but it's hard for me to understand what she saw in him.'

'Well, he was sympathetic for one thing. Paid attention to her. She didn't have much confidence in herself.'

'That's true.'

'She felt she'd never done anything on her own. She said her mother had pushed her into being a model, and after that there were always people telling her where to go and what to do. She was quite frightened of your father, Dodie. She'd thought she was really in love with him when they were married, but afterwards she realised that part of it was because it meant she could give up modelling, which she hated. She told me she couldn't stand the way people looked at her. I think she wanted some sort of purpose, a validation. She said your father wasn't interested in what she thought and never talked to her, and she felt like she was starting to disappear. She couldn't see the point of her life.'

'She told you all that?'

'Yeah. When we were washing our hair. The bathroom in Cricklewood didn't have a shower, so one of us would stick our head in the basin and the other one would pour jugs of water on it. We used to end up completely soaked.'

'You make it sound as if you were friends.'

'We were. I liked her. When she stopped being frightened, she was great.'

'What do you mean, frightened? There's something you're not telling me, Maggie. Did Mum go with Steve of her own accord, is that it? But if it was Mick's idea like you said, how come—'

'It *was* Mick's idea. He only told me, not Steve. We were having this conversation one night, quite soon after Steve had started going to see your mother, and Mick was saying it was a perfect illustration of how the system worked, that thousands of people were suffering so that this one man could have millions of pounds. I was getting a bit tired of it all, to tell you the truth, so I said, "Well, what are you going to do? Bomb their house?" Mick was really getting under my skin, so I started being really sarcastic and saying, "Maybe your friends in the Angry Brigade would help us," because Mick had been going on about—'

'Hang on. The Angry Brigade?'

'Sorry. It was in the early seventies. They were this group of people, anarchists. They used to do bombings: police chiefs' houses, government ministers, things like that. Against state repression.'

'And Mick knew them?'

'He *said* he knew one of them. I don't think he really did, he'd just met some guy once who'd had something to do with it. But he was always talking about people like them or the SLA, they were the ones who'd kidnapped Patty Hearst in America.'

'Was that what gave him the idea?'

'It might have been. But when I mentioned bombing, Mick said that was a stupid idea. He said it wouldn't help to redistribute wealth because if we bombed your father's house he'd just buy himself a bigger one. That was when he suggested kidnapping. He said it like he'd just thought of it, but I think he'd probably had it in his mind right from the beginning. I didn't take him seriously, but he was really into it. He kept saying it was the perfect way of redressing the balance, of the people taking back what was rightfully theirs. He said we could use the money to found a revolutionary workers' movement. He kept going on about it whenever Steve wasn't there, and one day he came in and told me he'd rented this farmhouse in Suffolk; and then suddenly he had this whole plan worked out.'

'And you never tried to stop him?'

'Half of me was thinking he wouldn't do it, that if I just ignored him, he'd get bored and start talking about something else.'

'What about the other half?'

Maggie hesitated for a second. 'I'd have done whatever Mick wanted. But it wasn't just that, Dodie. This plan he had, it just didn't seem real. Even when it finally happened, it was like I wasn't involved, I was just there, watching.'

'How *did* it happen?'

'We didn't snatch her or anything. Steve was already trying to persuade Susan to come to the house. Although the house in Cricklewood was small, it was nicer than the place you saw in Muswell Hill, better decorated. I suppose Mick must have put the idea into Steve's head originally – about her coming, I mean – although I don't remember him saying anything about it. Then Steve came back from seeing her one day and told us she was coming for the weekend. They'd got this plan that she was going to say she was staying with a friend, but instead of going there on Friday night, she'd stay the weekend with us and go on Sunday night instead.'

I nodded, remembering. Irene des Voeux. Simpering away to that TV interviewer. *Wolfgang and I had a very special relationship*. Not if he knew she'd provided an alibi so that Mum could spend the weekend with her lover, they didn't. I thought, perhaps he worked it out later and married Virginia to pay her back.

Maggie continued. 'I started tidying up and Mick said, "Why are you hoovering for that rich bitch? She's no better than we are." So I thought, fair enough, and left it as it was. But it was so weird seeing her sitting at our kitchen table. We were all there, drinking tea, and it was like Mick and I were Steve's parents, and he was bringing his girlfriend home for the first time. It was really stilted. Susan was trying to make conversation, but I couldn't think of anything to say back. I just kept looking at her and thinking, surely Mick's not going to go through with it? Even though I'd met Susan before, I'd sort of built her up in my mind as being really assured, you know . . . But she wasn't like that at all. She looked so *young*. She had this beautiful green mohair jumper that matched her eyes, and her hair was falling down over her shoulders. Steve was holding her hand under the table. Mick didn't tell Steve about the plan until the next day – Saturday, after we'd sent the note. Steve and your mum had, you know . . .' She suddenly looked embarrassed.

'Spent the day in bed?' I suggested. It was so ridiculous I nearly laughed.

'Yeah, they did. Do that. Sorry. Anyway,' she hurried on, 'Steve came out of the room about eight o'clock, I think. We were in the sitting room. Mick said, "Where's Susan?" and Steve said, "She's asleep," and then Mick made some crack about how she must be tired and Steve told him to shut up. I knew what was coming. I was sure there'd be an almighty row and I didn't want to be there, so I said I was going to do the washing-up and left them to it. When I was in the kitchen I kept thinking, any minute now one of them's going to storm out and slam the door, but it got later and later and neither of them did. I started inventing things to do – not that it didn't need doing, but stuff I didn't do normally – like taking all the tins and things off the shelves and wiping them. I'd been so certain that it wasn't going to happen, but the longer Steve stayed in that room with Mick, the more I started to think, *shit*, it really is going to happen. Let's have that drink, shall we?' She started faffing around opening cupboards, pulling things out and grimacing at them. I knew she didn't want to tell me the next bit.

'Maggie?'

She turned round looking flushed, a bottle of gin in her hand. 'This seems to be all I can find. What were you going to say?'

'I'm not going to get angry, I promise you.'

'I know. Well, I don't mean I *know*, it's just . . . Look, there's some orange juice in the fridge. Unless you want it plain. It's all I've got.'

'It's *fine*.'

'OK.' She stepped around me to fish two glasses out of the sink, and kept her back to me while she dried them. 'It did cross my mind to go to Steve's room and wake Susan up, but at the same time I kept thinking, you don't know what they're talking about in there. For all I knew it could have been the football results . . . Mick would have been furious if I'd woken her up, really angry. So I just kept on finding myself jobs to do. In the end I started making tea. I was thinking, maybe Susan would like some. I even got two mugs out and put tea bags in them, I got that far with it. It was pitch black outside and we didn't have curtains or anything, and I could see my reflection in the window, standing in front of the sink with this tea. I didn't turn round when Mick came into the kitchen. I could see him in the glass. He just said, "It's on." He looked so handsome, and I knew, I *knew*, that if I was going to have any chance of staying with him I'd have to go along with it. So I did. I'm not proud of it.' Maggie turned round and busied herself pouring the drinks. 'Say something, for God's sake.'

'I'm glad you're being honest with me.'

'Yeah, well.' She took a mouthful of her gin. 'I don't know what Mick said to Steve exactly, but it was like, well, Steve thought that he was going to sort of rescue Susan from your father. Like a knight on a white horse. They'd just ride away into the sunset and live happily ever after. He was sitting there telling us how the two of them were going to live in a cave on a Greek island and grow oranges—'

'Wait a minute, Maggie. You're saying that my mother was part of the plot? Is that it?'

'Not exactly. She was very confused. We were all really on edge and nobody knew what was going to happen.'

'But what about when you sent the ransom note? The first one?'

'She didn't know about it.'

'But she must have found out. You sent us her credit card. With the note. So she must have known.'

'She didn't. Steve told me that she'd agreed to stay on for a couple more days. She wanted to think about what to do,

OK? I thought he would have explained what we'd planned, but he hadn't, and I'm sure Mick didn't speak to her, either. Well, he can't have done, because a couple of days later she was looking in her bag for something and she discovered her credit card was missing, and that was when it all came out. Mick had taken it from her purse when she wasn't in the room.'

'But didn't she just . . . didn't she . . .'

'It was awful. She started crying, and she was saying to us, "Why are you doing this to me? Why do you hate me so much? What have I done to you?" Nobody said anything, not even Steve. We just sat there and watched her. I wanted to tell her it was all right, we weren't going to hurt her or anything, but Mick told me to go and make her a cup of tea, and I thought that would be something, anyway, to help. I stood outside the door and listened. She had some money in her bag, twenty pounds or something, and she was offering it to Mick, trying to give it to him. He kept telling her it wasn't her money we wanted, but your father's. She was so upset. She was sitting on the sofa, and when I went to give her the tea, she sort of flinched away from me into the corner. I'll never forget the way she looked at me, I don't think she could believe what was happening to her, what we were doing. Mick asked me if I'd take her upstairs and put her to bed in my room. I put my hand out to her like you would to a child, and she took it, she didn't try to resist. When we got to my room she just sat down on the bed and didn't move. I had to undress her. I was scared in case she got upset again and Mick heard her, so I told her I was going to get some hot milk because that gave me an excuse to go back downstairs. When I went back up, she was in the bed. She asked me where Steve was, and I told her I didn't know. Then I said, "I've got to lock the door," because Mick had told me to. She just looked at me. She was so pale, her face on the white pillow. As if all her blood had been drained away. She kept on saying, "I don't understand." '

'God, poor Mum.'

'It was just . . . *bizarre*. Looking back – I've thought about it a lot, and it was all so weird. You say "poor Mum", but it wasn't like she was terrified *all* the time. OK, so she was our captive, and she couldn't go out or anything, but often it was more like she was a schoolgirl who'd stayed the night with her boyfriend and was scared in case her mum and dad found out. That sort of scared, not petrified by fear or anything.'

'What about the tapes?'

'She never heard any of that threatening stuff. She wasn't there. At first I thought she was putting on an act so we'd start to trust her and then she could escape. I mean, that's what I would have done, but when she did—'

'So she did try to escape?'

'Well, sort of. She didn't do it in secret or anything. It was in Cricklewood, one afternoon, I was in the front room and I heard the door click, so I looked out of the window and there she was, walking down the path. I told Mick and he went after her. He caught up with her at the bottom of the road – I was watching from the front garden – they talked for a couple of minutes and then she came back with him. He'd got his arm round her, but it didn't look like he was pushing her or forcing her to come or anything. There was nobody about, but she'd got her hand in front of her face like she didn't want anyone to recognise her, and she ran straight upstairs as soon as they got through the door. I asked Mick what he'd said to her and he was all sort of "piece of cake", you know, but afterwards he said he'd told her that if she went back she'd be arrested, that the police would think she was in on it too, because of Steve. He kept telling her afterwards that she'd go to prison, and talking about Patty Hearst, because she'd been found guilty of taking part in that bank robbery, even though it wasn't her idea or anything. You probably won't believe this, but up until then, when Mick told me that, it was the first time I really understood that there was a chance that I could go to prison if we were caught.

'We went to Randall's Farm about two weeks after that. Steve and Susan came with us, but Mick got suspicious about the Suffolk police so when we came back to Cricklewood to collect the rest of our stuff, they stayed behind. We were sure that Susan would be too scared to go to the police, and anyway, Steve wouldn't have let her. He was in cloud-cuckoo-land most of the time, talking about how they were going to get fake passports and go to Greece. Susan had a Post Office account with a few thousand pounds in it that she'd saved when she was modelling, and Steve had some mad plan about changing it for drachmas so it couldn't be traced. I tried to explain to him that he'd be arrested the minute he tried to take any money out, but he wouldn't listen.'

'But you said you thought that Mick was going to kill her.' My voice was as steady as I could make it.

Maggie wiped her hands over her face. 'I don't know what I thought. Everything was getting out of control. After Mick told Susan she might go to gaol, she practically stopped talking to anyone. Steve didn't even notice, he was on another planet with all this crap about Greece and orange groves, and Mick was obsessed with getting the ransom money and totally paranoid about the police.' Maggie's words were getting faster and faster. 'He had this gun! Just came home one day and *waved* it at me. He said a man from the Angry Brigade had given it to him, that they were going to help us like they helped the Basques when they machine-gunned the Spanish Embassy, they were going to give us back-up and, I don't know, that's what he kept saying. I didn't believe him. Even I knew that the Angry Brigade had fallen apart in 1972 and half its members were in prison. We argued about it all the time, and I didn't know what to do. Mick kept shouting that I was a bourgeois turncoat. He picked on everything I said, and I just kept thinking, what am

I doing here? I used to think about my parents, how they'd paid for my cello lessons so I could go to college, how I'd betrayed them. But even then – even then I still loved Mick.'

Maggie slid down the front of the cupboard she'd been leaning against until she was squatting on the floor. She put her head back and shut her eyes. 'Randall's Farm was a pigsty. The toilets were blocked, so we had to use the garden. We had no fridge, and all our food went rotten. Remember how hot it was? There was this huge pond, right next to the house. It was stagnant and teeming with mosquitoes but Mick made me leave all the windows open so he could shoot if the police came. I was covered in bites, I couldn't stop scratching – some of them even got infected. I've still got the scars on my legs. Look!' She hiked up one side of her skirt to show me. She was shaking.

So was I. My legs felt like rubber. Slowly, careful not to touch her, I lowered myself on to the floor beside her. There was just room for the two of us to sit side by side on the tiny piece of lino.

'Maggie?' Her arms were resting on her knees and her head was bowed. I couldn't see her face. 'Maggie? I'm grateful to you for telling me this. I'm glad . . . that I know . . . what you told me. But there's one thing I don't understand. OK? One thing.' She looked up. 'If my – if Susan was in London, and Mick was setting the trail for the money in Suffolk, how was he going to give her back to us? If it had worked?'

'He was going to give directions where to find her. Where the house was.'

'But you said Steve wanted to take her to Greece. He might have taken her away.'

'Mick said it didn't matter, because we'd have the money by then. I don't know what happened, Dodie, I really don't.' She sounded exhausted. 'You'd have to ask Steve.'

Ask Steve. Steve who said he'd killed my mother. Who wanted to kill me. *You are going to pay.*

'How did the police find out about the house in Cricklewood?'

'They found the address when they went through our stuff. It wasn't difficult.'

'I see.' We sat in silence for a couple of minutes, and then I said, 'We thought it was about politics. But it wasn't, was it?'

'*I* thought it was about politics. I know this sounds stupid, but for me, it was about, well, it was about love. In the end. And look where it got me.' Maggie got to her feet and held her hand out to help me up. 'Come on,' she said. 'Time to go home.'

I stood in the narrow hallway while Maggie picked bits of fluff and cat hair off my back.

'This is probably a stupid question,' I said, 'but you haven't been sending me things, have you? Through the post?'

Maggie came round and stood in front of me, eyes on a level with mine. She looked baffled. 'No. Why would I? In any case, I haven't got your address.'

'Of course not. It doesn't matter. You don't know where Steve is, do you?'

'No. I had an idea that he might have gone to Australia, but I don't know. He always said he wanted to travel. Look, Dodie, I know it's not up to me to say this, and of course it's your decision, but—'

'What?'

'Well, I don't think you should try and contact Steve. I'm really sorry about your mum, and I know you want to know where she was and everything, but she wasn't with him. I mean, he was in prison, wasn't he? And to be honest, Steve was always a bit of a no-hoper. He lived in his own world. I know I'm not one to talk, but I just don't think it'll get you anywhere, that's all.'

'Yeah, well . . . There's something I ought to tell you.

244

They're going to release the details about Mum in a couple of days. It'll be in the papers. But if you think of anything else, anything you remember, will you let me know?' I scrabbled about in my bag for a pen and paper and wrote down the Camoys Hall address and telephone number.

'Yeah. But I've told you everything.' She paused, looking at what I'd written. 'This is where Joan lived. I remember the address. When she came, she asked me all the same questions you did.'

'Did you tell her what you told me?'

'Pretty much.'

'She was going to ring you. The day she died. Do you know why?'

Maggie shook her head. 'Are you sure it was me? We hadn't been in touch. I told you.'

'Oh, well. Mystery.'

'Yeah.' We looked at each other. 'You need to get home.' She stepped past me to unbolt the door. 'First left, straight down the stairs.'

'Goodbye, Maggie. And thanks. Thanks for . . . you know.'

She smiled. 'Take care, Dodie. Enjoy your life.' I stepped into the hall, and she closed the door behind me.

Steve was always a bit of a no-hoper. I was too tired to be frightened any more. I made my way down the stairs, leaning on the handrail, and sat down on the bottom step. A few seconds passed before I noticed some writing on the wall, to my left. Separated from the graffiti, lower down. DRY RISER INLET, in large white capitals. And next to it, on a small plaque, DESIGNED BY CLAUSEN PARTNERS, BUILT BY BLACKSTOCK LTD, 1961.

My father had built Maggie's flat.

The next time I looked up, Tony and Dominic were running across the car park towards me.

25

Dominic dropped Tony off at his house, then drove me back to Camoys Hall in his BMW. I slept most of the way. Neither of them asked me any questions, and I didn't feel like volunteering much. I needed to think about the things Maggie'd told me. My head was full of images, snippets of how I imagined it was. Men with long, dark brown hair and droopy moustaches putting the world to rights in maroon and orange rooms, swearing, slogans, jargon, tank tops and flares. And in the middle of it all, my beautiful confused mother.

It was hard to get my thoughts into any kind of order, but two things seemed clear. One was that neither my mother, my father nor Joan had anything to do with the kidnapping itself, and the other was that Steve Moody was almost certainly the person who wanted to kill me. This didn't seem wildly significant. It was just something to take on board. That's how exhausted I was.

Des was waiting for me in the kitchen at Camoys Hall. I sat at the table and tried to stay awake long enough to drink a cup of tea while he and Dominic shifted around behind me and mouthed things at each other over my head.

When Dominic left the room, Des said, 'He's going to stay the night. Seems a nice chap. Used to be in the Coldstream Guards.'

'I thought Tony said he was something in the City.'

'Before that.' Trust Tony to employ a guardsman, I thought, and smiled. 'I know his father. Very decent man,' Des said reprovingly.

'I'm sure he is.'

'I've had a talk with the security people and it's all shipshape. They told me you'd given one of their chaps a list of people who might come and see you, so there shouldn't be any trouble about that. They can always contact you, anyway, if there's any doubt. Oh, and they've put something called a panic button beside your bed. It makes the most dreadful racket.'

'It was really strange, Des. I liked her.'

Des shook his head at me. 'Tell me tomorrow – if you want to, that is. I'm having a meeting with Bennington after the inquest, but I should be back here about eight. You look done in. Why don't you scoot off and get some kip?'

'All right.' I hauled myself upright and began tottering towards the door.

'Oh, and Dodie . . .'

'Yes?'

'I'll get Benny to make a plea for privacy, but I'd give up answering the phone for a few days, if I were you.'

As usual, once in bed I found myself wide awake, my head full of images: Maggie in grey-white underwear, in a grotty bathroom, sluicing Mum's head with a tooth mug; a basin surrounded by cracked avocado-green tiles, black mould in the grouting; a cracked sliver of pink soap with two or three curlicues of hair stuck to it; Mum and Maggie splashing each other, laughing; Steven Moody, holding Mum's hand under a flimsy table in a strip-lit kitchen; Mum like a little girl, excited and solemn at the same time, her eyes huge, then curled in silent misery in a knot of brown synthetic sheets. Maggie'd said Steven Moody was too wrapped up in his fantasies about Greek islands to notice that she wasn't talking any more. She'd told Maggie she was afraid she'd disappear. She'd been afraid of that at Camoys Hall, but in Cricklewood she really did disappear. For twenty years, into thin air.

I wondered if it had really been like the pictures in my head. Everything's changed so much, even in twenty years. Not just how things look, but what people assume, what they believe, how they think. It's no use trying to turn back the clock.

I'll never get Mum back, I thought. I'll never have my childhood back, either. I imagined my eight-year-old self, skinny and pale, hovering forever on the threshold of a room, waiting to be included. If only I could talk to her. 'Everything's going to be all right.' That's what I'd have said. 'Don't worry. It's going to be all right.' I stared into the heavy fuzzy darkness, and wished I believed myself.

26

Des and Dominic were long gone by the time I surfaced. The cleaners were having their elevenses when I walked into the kitchen, huddled together round a tabloid newspaper spread out on the kitchen table. When they saw me, the paper was whisked out of sight, but it didn't happen quickly enough for me to miss the words MYSTERY DEATH beside a three-quarter-page print of the same photograph of my father and mother that I'd identified at the morgue. Thanks a bunch, Inspector Halstead. So much for trying to keep it quiet. 'Please don't get up,' I said, but the jumpsuits made excuses and scattered, towing their gadgets behind them.

Only Woolly Cardigan Lady stayed put. 'Why don't you go in that nice little sitting room, dear? It'll be quiet in there, away from all this bother.' She waved a pink knitted arm at the now-empty kitchen. 'Have you had your breakfast?'

'Not yet, no.'

'Then I'll bring you some toast. Now, off you go.'

I did as I was told. There was another great scroll of fax paper lolling out on to the floor, but I couldn't face looking at it. I played back my messages. The first one was from Tony: 'You'll probably get this tomorrow morning, Dodie. In case you didn't speak to Des last night, we've had a chat and I'm lending him – and you – Dominic for a few days.

We're both worried and don't think you ought to be on your own. Listen, I'm going to come up tonight, on the train. I'll get a cab from the station. Anyway, we'll sort something out. *Ring me.*'

Then Des calling from the court. 'We're about to go in. This place is like a madhouse, journalists everywhere you look. Dodie, my old love, I hope you don't think I'm interfering, but I've asked Helen Bain to come up. You probably don't remember her, but she used to be my secretary at Blackstock. Very efficient. You don't have to worry about putting her up, I've told her to book herself into the Fat Hen. Someone's got to handle the phones, and she can see to all of Joan's business.'

God, the funeral. I'd almost forgotten about it. I glanced at my *Things to Do* list. The words *Choose clothes for Joan* were ringed by big red stars. I could hardly ask Helen Bain to do that.

I thought I'd better phone Liza, my neighbour in London. She sounded hysterical. 'I knew it was bollocks about you going to Ireland. What am I supposed to do, Dodie? Every single journalist in London must be camped outside your door and they keep asking where you are. What am I supposed to say to them?'

'I'm sorry, Liza. Do you know what's going on?'

'All I know is, I can't leave my flat. Anyway, how would I know what's going on? I didn't even know it was your family until I heard them say your name on the radio this morning. Thanks for telling me, by the way.'

'I'm really sorry.'

'I'm sure you are, but in the meantime, what about all these tabloid fuckwits on my doorstep? I'm not the one who inherited God knows how many million pounds. I mean, I actually *need* my job, you know?'

I felt like saying, 'So do I,' but ended up apologising yet again. I tried to calm her down, and all the time I was thinking, if you only knew how much I want to be like you.

I was about to call Tony when the phone started ringing. I stopped myself picking it up just in time and waited for the answering machine to start.

'Doe? It's Carol. Mum's just got the papers, and there's lots of—'

'I'm here, Carol.'

'Have you seen the papers, Doe? It's everywhere, about your mum.'

'I know. I didn't think it would happen so quickly.'

'Have they started bothering you?'

'Not yet, but it's only a matter of time.'

'Is there anyone there with you?'

'Just the . . . No, not really.'

'Do you want me to come over? Mum only bought a couple of papers, but I think you should see— Hang on a minute. What? Oh, Mum says, is there anything she can do?'

'That's very nice of her, but I can't think of anything at the moment.'

'Listen, I'll be with you in ten minutes.'

'Yes. Fine. I'll be here.'

'Mum's saying it's disgusting. Ten minutes, OK?'

'See you then. Oh, by the way, Carol—' I was going to warn her about the security guards but she'd already put the phone down.

Woolly Cardigan Lady's head appeared round the door. 'Only me.' She put a tray of tea and toast down on the desk. 'I don't want to disturb you.'

'Thanks. I'm sorry, but I don't know your name.'

'Vera.'

'Vera. Thank you.'

'You ought to try and eat something, dear. I'll be in the kitchen, so if there's anything else you want, just give me a shout.' She closed the door behind her.

I stared at the teapot and the row of brown triangles poking through the silver ribs of the toast rack and wondered what I was supposed to do with them. I ate a sugar lump and wondered when the journalists would get to Maggie. Perhaps they already had. I was almost certain she'd been genuinely surprised when I'd told her about Mum's death. I tried to play back her reaction in my head for confirmation, but I couldn't remember it clearly enough. I found her number in Joan's address book and dialled it, but she didn't pick up. I left a message on her answering machine for her to call me, explaining about how I wasn't answering the phone so I'd have to ring her back. It wasn't till I'd put the phone down that it occurred to me she was probably doing the same thing.

Any offer Maggie gets from a newspaper, I thought, I can top it. I'd have to know about it first, though. I thought of asking her if she wanted to come and stay at Camoys Hall until the feeding frenzy had died down. She would be protected from the press, and I'd definitely know if they tried to contact her. Whatever Maggie'd said to me on the phone about not wanting any money, if I offered enough, she'd take it. I thought of her in that horrible flat. She must have known that my father built it, but she hadn't mentioned it to me. Perhaps she'd assumed I already knew.

I was on the point of leaving another message on Maggie's answering machine when it suddenly occurred to me that I was thinking like a rich person. Thinking I could buy her. Like my father, I was using money to control people. If Maggie lets me give her money, I thought, then I'll have power over her. Like I have power over Mr Molloy, because of his house, and over Blackstock Holdings, because I'm the majority shareholder. If you'd asked my father about power, he'd have come straight back at you with responsibility and service. But let's not kid ourselves, he *revelled* in it. The more he had, the better. And he didn't just control people through money either, but through love. Because if someone's in love with you, that's the most power you can have over anyone, isn't it? And he used it to control Joan, Angela, and even Des, in a way. Was it because Betty Carroll had hurt him? I could find out every last detail about his life, but I'd never really know. He probably hadn't known himself.

Vera's head appeared round the door. 'There's someone here to see you.'

'Who's that woman?' Carol Curtis barged the door open with her shoulder and plonked a couple of tabloids face down on Joan's coffee table.

'Do you want some tea?'

'Yeah.' She felt the teapot. 'Not this, though. It's stone cold. I'll go and make some more, shall I?'

'Vera might make it for you, if you ask her nicely.'

'Doubt it. Bossy cow. Anyway, I brought my own tea. Yours is disgusting.' She ferreted around in the pockets of her torn elderly waxed jacket and produced two scrunched-up tea bags. 'See?' She turned to go and I saw that the back of the jacket was covered in bits of straw.

'What have you been doing? You look like a haystack.'

'Wouldn't you like to know? It's all on again, with Greg. He was being really nice last night.' She grinned at me and then frowned. 'Honestly, Doe, what they're saying, it's bad. Libel. You could sue.'

'I'd better read it first.'

'Yeah, of course. What do you want to start with, the *Tit* or the *Bum*?'

'Whichever's on top.'

She picked up the *Sun*. 'You won't believe what's in it. Those people are the biggest pieces of shit that ever walked the earth.' She held the newspaper out to me. The headline said, BODY FOUND: IT'S SUSAN BLACKSTOCK SAY POLICE. Beside it was a photograph of my mother wearing a ball gown. I couldn't take my eyes off it.

'Doe? I'll be back in a minute, OK? They're bastards, they really are.'

The newspaper lay flat on the desk in front of me. I didn't

want to touch it. Feeling scared and sick, I listened to Carol going down the passage. Then, without wanting to, and almost not knowing I was doing it, I began to read.

The body of Susan Blackstock has been discovered – 20 years after she was declared dead, it emerged last night. The stunning ex-model wife of multimillionaire property tycoon Wolf Blackstock was kidnapped by left-wing terrorists in 1976. They were caught after a shoot-out that left a policeman and one of the kidnappers dead. But Mrs Blackstock had disappeared, like Lord Lucan. After a national manhunt she was declared dead. Until police found her two-day-old corpse 12 days ago in London's East End.

Husband Knew

But new evidence shows that Wolf Blackstock knew his wife was alive all along. The ruthless businessman refused to pay the £10m ransom. He bargained the kidnappers down to £6m, but never intended to part with a single penny to save her life.

Cruel

Blackstock, who was well known for his string of beautiful mistresses, married again in 1980. When he died in 1995 he left his £400m fortune to his only child, Susan's daughter, Dorothy 'Dodie' Blackstock.

Blackstock divorced wife number 4 in 1989. Anorexic Virginia Blackstock died earlier this year. One source said yesterday, 'He was so cruel. She died of a broken heart.' His last years were spent alone in his vast mansion home near Cambridge. He was kept a virtual prisoner by secretive second wife Joan Draycott and long-term business partner Desmond Haigh-Wood, who would not allow his daughter to visit him.

Disappeared

Reclusive Dodie Blackstock, 29, identified the body. Dodie, who has never married, was quizzed by police about her mother, who was kidnapped when she was only eight years old. Our reporters were at her London flat yesterday, but daughter Dodie has disappeared.

KIDNAP PLOT Unfaithful Wife Had to Go on page 16
HOW COULD IT HAPPEN? Tragedy of Bungled Police Raid on page 18
POOR LITTLE RICH GIRL Dodie Blackstock's Tragic Life on page 20
WHY I STILL MISS DAD by Dead Shoot-Out PC's Son on page 22

I turned to page 20 to find out more about my tragic life. There was a grainy photograph of me. At least, that's what the caption said. *Camera-Shy Dodie: Did She Know?* Behind the shielding hand and the black insect-eye Jackie O sunglasses it could have been anyone. It could have been a man in drag. There was a blurred picture of my flat and next to it, boxed off from the rest of the text, was the photograph of me as a toddler that Inspector Halstead had found in Mum's things. *This photo was found in the plastic bag where tragic Susan kept her few remaining belongings*, read the caption.

I turned back to KIDNAP PLOT on page 16, but I couldn't take it in. The letters slid about in front of my eyes, and single bold words bounced out at me. **Jealous. Lover. Hoax.** Running along the bottom of the double-page spread was a rectangular box with the heading THE MANY WIVES OF WOLFGANG and photographs of all of them, including Betty Carroll. I'd never seen a picture of her before. Upswept curled hair, Joan Crawford lips and glossy bare shoulders, crooning into an old-fashioned microphone. *Wife Nò. 1 Forces Sweetheart Betty: Too Sexy For Wolf?* Next to her was Joan in a plastic rainhood, looking old and jowly. *Wife No. 2 Joan: Did she plot to get rid of Susan and win back love cheat Wolf?* Mum, tawnily glamorous in mink, was to her right. *Wife No. 3 Tragic Susan: Murder victim?* Finally, there was Virginia, looking impish in a Peter Pan collar. She must have been about fifteen when it was taken. *Wife No. 4 Child-bride Virginia died of anorexia. 'Wolf made her ill,' claim friends.* Beside them, under the heading MISTRESSES, were photographs of Angela, Irene des Voeux and some American woman I'd never heard of called Kitty Jarrell Gardner who claimed she'd had an affair with my father in Singapore in 1957.

I put the paper down. I didn't want to read any more. It's always the same old stuff. People have to be served up to us as simplified versions of themselves: they have to have bits trimmed off to make them fit a stereotype, or exaggerated to make a caricature, and then their behaviour can be summed up in a series of bullet points.

I felt horrible. Disloyal. To my father, my mother, Joan, Des – all of them, even Angela. Because they were my family, my life – all I'd got, really. I was disgusted with myself for looking at the paper, for even asking Carol to bring it into the house. I don't mean that I'd suddenly decided my father was a saint, or anything. I just had this sort of undertow, this feeling that I wanted to protect them. Whatever privacy or dignity there was – or would be – left, I wanted to protect it. I thought of Joan's bedroom upstairs, the mess I'd made. All at once, I wanted to go and fold the clothes up and make it neat again. She wouldn't be there to see, but it would be something to make up for the way they'd written about her. And the photos I'd knocked down in my father's room, I'd put them all back, put new flowers by his bed.

The phone rang and Des's voice came on the answering machine. I grabbed the receiver. 'Have they finished?'

'Yes.'

'What did they say?'

'Death by misadventure. There wasn't much else they could say. Have you seen a newspaper?'

'Yes. Carol brought one round. I read some of it.'

'Well, I shouldn't read any more. I'm bringing Benny back with me tonight to discuss it. He'll know what action to take. We'll try and stop the worst of the speculation, anyway.'

'They'll find me, though, won't they? Camoys Hall was mentioned in the paper. Not by name, but it said Cambridgeshire mansion or something. I'm surprised they're not here already.'

'I should think you'll be all right for a couple of hours yet. You've got the security people, but all the same I'd stay in the house for the time being, if I were you. The girl who brought the papers, is she there with you?'

'Carol? In the kitchen, I think.'

'Why don't you ask her to stick around for a while? I'm sure she won't mind.'

'OK. Des, it will be all right, won't it?'

'Don't worry, my old love, we'll get through this. And we'll come out the other side. Worse things happen at sea, you know.'

'I can't think what.'

'No, I'm sorry. Silly remark. But Benny will know what to do.'

'I hope so.'

'That's what we pay him for. We'll sort it out, I promise. I'm not sure what time we'll be back because we've got some things to tie up here, but I'll ring and let you know.'

'All right. Speak to you later.'

'Good-oh. Chirp up, chicken.'

He put the phone down and I went out to the kitchen to find Carol. She was sitting at the kitchen table with a man in combat gear. It was a hot day but underneath his camouflage jacket he was wearing a hairy brown jumper which looked as if it had been knitted out of his beard. I was about to ask if he was from the security company when Carol jumped up.

'I was just coming to see if you were OK, Doe. This is Greg, by the way.'

'Hello, Greg.' Greg made a noise like 'ump' and took one hand off his mug of tea.

'Known to his friends as Catweazle,' she said, blowing him a kiss. 'It's all right, Greg, Doe didn't have a telly when she was little.'

Greg looked at me, surprised. 'Didn't you?'

I shook my head.

'You don't mind him being here, do you?' Carol asked. 'The security bloke got really stroppy about it but it was OK in the end. They had my name on a list. Did you give it to them, Doe?'

'Yes. They wanted to know who might be coming to the house.'

'Oh. Right. I just brought Greg because otherwise I won't see him till next week. He's off to Bristol.'

'That's nice,' I said automatically. 'Business or pleasure?'

'See my brother.'

'So is it OK if he stays for a bit?'

'Fine,' I said. 'Safety in numbers. Actually, Carol, I was going to ask if you wouldn't mind hanging around for a while. I'm a bit worried about people coming here – journalists really.' And murderers, I thought.

'Don't worry,' said Carol. 'They won't get past us. Greg'll see them off for you, won't you, Greg?'

Greg nodded, then bared his teeth and made a growling noise.

'Did you look at those papers?' Carol asked.

'Enough.'

'I can't believe they'd print that stuff. They're bastards. You've got to sue them, Doe. They can't do that to your family and get away with it.'

'No, they can't,' I said as confidently as I could. 'Look, I need to go up to Joan's room to sort some things out. If the phone rings, just ignore it.'

'Fair enough. We'll be down here. Jimmy said he might drop by later, by the way.'

'Did he?'

'He came in the pub last night.' She stretched out one of the stubby little corkscrew curls from her fringe and squinted up at it for a minute before letting it bounce back. 'He really likes you, Dode.'

Greg saved me from having to reply. 'I need a slash.' He disengaged himself from his mug, put both hands palms down on the table, and rose from his chair in a sort of vertical press-up.

'Turn right out of the right hand door, and it's at the end of the passage.'

'Cheers.'

Carol waited until he'd gone then said, 'He's gorgeous, isn't he?'

'He seems . . . very nice.'

She made a face. 'Just cos he's not called Cedric or Humphrey or something.'

'I don't know anyone called Cedric or Humphrey, Carol.'

'You know what I mean. Anyway, *I* think he's gorgeous.' She started sorting through her hair again. 'Have you got anyone in London?'

'No, honestly.'

'Jimmy's a nice bloke.'

'I know. Are you going to be all right down here?'

'You're not going to tell me, are you?'

'There's honestly nothing to tell, Carol. I'll be in Joan's room.'

'What shall I do if Jimmy comes?'

'Tell him where I am.'

Carol gave me a knowing smile. 'OK, if that's what you want. Just don't do anything I wouldn't do.'

I left before Carol could say anything else. All she needed was a bow and arrow, some stick-on wings and a blindfold. Maggie Hill had said my mother had loved Steven Moody; although he didn't agree with her, judging from the letter. And now Jimmy and me. I wondered what Des would make of Jimmy. My father said that the only reason I – or any other woman – wanted to go to university was to find a husband, but it wasn't. You know how people talk about finding themselves? Well, I wanted to find that I was some-body *else*. I kept on hoping it would just happen and then when it didn't, I got depressed. That lasted nearly three years, before I had the row with my father. Situation normal, all fucked up. As Des would *not* say.

I stood in the doorway of Joan's room and looked at the mess on the floor. At least the newspapers didn't know that she and my father weren't married. She'd have hated that.

After a while I knelt down on the carpet at the edge of the muddle and started sifting through it, re-folding things and putting them in piles, concentrating really hard to stop myself wondering about what Des was doing, what Maggie Hill was doing, what Steven Moody was doing . . . I kept thinking about Jimmy, too, whether he'd turn up and what I'd say to him if he did. Jimmy'd been so nice about the cat, and when I had cried. It would be so much easier if there was somebody to be with. Even though I had Des and Tony – and Carol, of course, downstairs – they weren't there at night; and that's when it's worst, being alone.

After half an hour I'd managed to divide everything into six big piles, with a mound of loose lavender seeds and dried rose petals in the centre. I knelt in front of Joan's tallboy, pulled out the bottom drawer, and was about to start putting her blouses back when I noticed a bump in the lining paper. I lifted up the edge and found, encased in clear plastic, three little sacks tied at the top with pink ribbons. They were painted to look like Victorian housemaids in frilly aprons and caps, one with a tray of tea, one with a saucepan, and one with a feather duster. Across the top of the package was a strip of cardboard which said *Three Little Maids from the National Trust.* Joan's supply of emergency lavender bags.

Well, I thought, Joan would have considered this to be a five-star emergency. The plastic wrapping wasn't sealed. I shook out the three little maids on to a *broderie anglaise* blouse and bent over to sniff them. The lavender was still working. It gave me such a strong impression of Joan that I actually turned round to see if she'd come into the room.

As I did so, my eye was caught by something glinting underneath the chest of drawers. The bottom of the lowest drawer wasn't more than two inches off the ground, but there was a gleam of silver from behind one of the round stubby feet. Thinking it must be something that had fallen out of Joan's jewellery box when I'd messed up the room, I leant across to retrieve it.

It was a key. I picked it up. It had a white plastic label, like the ones in the cupboard behind the scullery door. *D's room*. I held it in the palm of my hand and thought, it's as if I was meant to find it. As if Joan were still looking after me.

27

It hadn't been turned into a storeroom after all. I closed my eyes for a moment to remember it: the tall windows, the dapple-grey rocking horse with his beautiful painted eyes; the pink carpet with splashy flowers, specially chosen from Sanderson's; the white Lloyd Loom chairs. That was how it was when Mum was kidnapped, but when I came back after my first term at university, Joan had had it redecorated. 'I thought you'd like it a bit more grown up,' she'd said. It wasn't that I didn't like it, Joan. It just didn't seem to be my room any more.

Could there be something in there? I picked the key up, leapt to my feet, opened the door of Joan's room and cannoned straight into Jimmy.

'Are you—' he began.

I held up my hands to stop him. 'Just don't ask me if I'm all right,' I said. 'Please.'

'OK, I won't. But Carol said—'

'I've found a key. Look!'

'Great. What's it for?'

'My room. The room I used to have.'

'Why would it be locked?'

'I don't know! That's what we've got to find out.'

'Hang on a minute. Why should there—'

'Just listen to me, OK? Just a minute.' I tried to explain

the events of the past three days as clearly as I could, but I was so excited that I couldn't get the story in a straight line. By the time I'd finished, Jimmy looked punch-drunk. I grabbed hold of his hand and started to pull him down the corridor.

'Calm down!'

Arrested, I ran on the spot in mid-air for a second, still hauling on his hand.

He laughed. 'You look like a cartoon character!'

'I *feel* like a cartoon character! Come *on*!'

'Am I allowed to give you a kiss first?'

'Oh . . . Yes, all right, if you like.' I turned round to face him, suddenly embarrassed. 'It's just, if there's anything to find out, I've got to know what it is. There's a man out there trying to kill me, for God's sake.'

'No chance. You must have more security than the Queen, Dodie. Honestly, all you need are a few of those blokes in bearskins.' Guardsmen. I thought of Dominic and smiled. Jimmy leant forward and kissed me on the cheek. 'I thought you'd be upset – depressed, Carol said – what with the papers and everything. But you seem all sort of jiggly.'

'You sound like Des.'

'Is that bad?'

'No. It's rather nice.'

Jimmy kissed the other cheek. 'Now you're symmetrical. Let's go.'

I hesitated in front of the door to my room, and Jimmy said, very gently, 'Dodie, there might not be—'

'I know. If there isn't anything in there . . . all that stuff I told you – getting that horrible note, and what Des told me, and meeting Maggie Hill . . . What if it's all just a great big mess? And what if—' I was thinking, what if Mum hadn't come back because she felt we'd all let her down and hated us, and I was part of that? 'It's just all this *stuff*, like a rollercoaster, and I just can't bear to think—'

'Dodie, you were eight years old. It wasn't your fault.'

'It wasn't, was it?'

'Of course it wasn't.'

There was silence for a few seconds. Then Jimmy said, 'I'm sorry I didn't come back before, it was just seeing you in front of this great big house, and knowing it belonged to you, and there was your hairdresser who'd come specially. It really brought it home to me how different your life is. And then there's all this going on. But when I bumped into Carol in the pub, and she was just talking about you as if—'

'As if I was a normal person?'

'Yes.'

'Well, that's all I am really. Sorry to disappoint you.'

Jimmy said, 'You're very beautiful, you know.'

'No, I don't. I mean, I'm not. Beautiful.'

'Yes, you are. I think I'd better give you another kiss. Just quickly.'

It was a longer kiss this time. When Jimmy let go of me, he said, 'I think you're doing really well. And you *are* beautiful.' He put his hand on my cheek and rubbed my nose with his thumb. 'I love freckles.'

'I do have quite a few.'

'Good. Now open that door before you explode.'

I unlocked it, and the door swung open. 'Careful, there's a step down.'

'What a lovely room!' said Jimmy. It was. The sun shone in on the white Lloyd Loom chairs, the white-painted chest of drawers, and the brass bed with its candlewick bedspread. My pyjama case, a white horse with a zip in its tummy, was lying on the pillow. The rocking horse had gone and the pink carpet had been replaced by rugs on the wooden boards, but the room was less changed than I remembered. Surely there'd been a different bed, different chairs. Joan must have put some of the old furniture back.

'I'm surprised you haven't been in here before,' Jimmy said. 'I know what you said about not wanting to use any of the bedrooms, but—'

'I thought Joan was using it for storage.'

'That's what my mum did. I thought she might be a bit upset when I told her I was leaving home, but all she said was, "Oh, great, now I can have your room." Mind you, this house does have a *few* more rooms than ours.'

I touched the top of the bookcase. Hardly any dust. The brass knobs on the bedstead shone as if they'd just been polished. It couldn't have been the cleaners, because they didn't have a key. There were flowers, too, on the chest of drawers: a big bunch of alstroemeria. They looked fresh. 'Joan must have come in here,' I said. 'She must have put those flowers here. There were flowers in my father's room, too. Stocks, but they don't keep so well.' I imagined Joan, week after week, putting fresh flowers in empty rooms.

There was a single photograph on the mantelpiece. Jimmy picked it up. 'This is the one she showed me.'

'That's Malcolm. Joan's dog.' I must have been thirteen or fourteen – post squint, anyway, thank goodness. I was standing in front of the house with the Jack Russell, un-comfortable but resigned, in my arms. I thought of Joan standing in front of his little grave in her sturdy outdoor shoes, a trowel in her hand, looking down at the smoothed soil, freshly dug for spring bulbs. I blinked but it didn't work. I shoved the photograph into Jimmy's hand and went over to the window. He didn't say anything, but a second later I felt his arm go round my shoulders.

'God, Jimmy, she must have been so lonely.'

'Yes, I think she was.'

We stood in silence for a moment, looking out of the window. I could see Mr Molloy's two new helpers stagger-ing down the ramp of an enormous lorry underneath what looked like a fully-grown tree. A security guard stood watching them, his head on one side like a parrot, oscar-sierra-rogering like mad into his walkie-talkie. The pews from the church were ranked on the lawn as if the vicar was going to preach an outdoor sermon. Six elderly ladies in flowered pinafores sat on the front one, drinking tea out of thermos flasks.

'What are they doing here?' asked Jimmy.

'The Brasso brigade. For the church. It's really kind of them. I'll have to go down and say thank you.'

Jimmy gave my arm a little squeeze. 'Look there's Mrs Curtis. And Mrs Bright. They've seen you. Go on, give them a wave.'

'I feel like the Queen.' All six ladies waved back.

'Bit better now?' asked Jimmy.

'I'm OK. I think.'

'Ready to have a look around?'

We looked. There was nothing in the wardrobe, nothing in the desk and nothing in the chest of drawers.

'There's nowhere else.' I sat down on the bed. Jimmy bent down to peer beneath the bedspread. 'Anything?'

He straightened up, shaking his head.

'Oh, well.' So much for Joan looking after me. I couldn't hide my disappointment. 'I really thought there was going to be something.'

'Yeah, I know. I'm sorry.'

Jimmy sat down beside me on the bed. 'Hello, horse,' he said to the pyjama case. 'It's sweet that Joan didn't get rid of this.'

'His name's Hector. Des gave him to me. I was about twelve. We'd been learning about the Trojan War at school, and I must have told him about it, because he put his old lead soldiers in Hector's tummy and said he was the Trojan Pyjama Case. I thought it was funny. Joan didn't. She had to wash him out afterwards.'

Jimmy handed him to me. 'Go on,' he said. 'Open it.'

I put Hector on my lap. His head, neck and legs were stuffed and fairly hard, but his body was flat and empty. When I rubbed it between my finger and thumb, there was a faint crackling sound. 'God, Jimmy!' I undid the zip and stuck my hand inside. 'Come on, Hector, show me your secrets.'

I pulled out a flat package, wrapped in newspaper. I was about to tear the paper off when Jimmy said, 'Wait a minute. Turn it over. Look for the date.'

'Friday, June the fourteenth, 1996. That was the day they found my mother's body. Two days before I came up here.' Underneath was a brown paper grocer's bag with DOROTHY written across it in black ink. The bag was sealed with sellotape.

I started to slide a nail underneath it, but Jimmy said, 'I think you should look at that on your own. It might be . . . you know.'

'Something terrible? If that's the case, I'd rather not be on my own.'

'Not necessarily terrible, but something about your family. It's got your name on it. I bet Joan didn't want anyone to see it except you. That may have been why she put it inside him.' He nodded towards Hector. 'She was a very private person, wasn't she?'

'You're right.'

'Listen, I promised my brother I'd help him move some furniture. He's decorating, and I told him I'd do it this afternoon, so why don't I go off and do it now? Then you can read whatever's in Hector the Hero, and . . . you know. Moving this stuff's not going to take more than an hour or so, then I'll be back. If walkie-talkie man lets me through.'

'You're on the list.'

'I'll tell them I'm coming back anyway. It shouldn't be a problem. Then I'll cook for you.'

'I don't think there's very much *to* cook.'

'I'll improvise. I know you're dying to read it, so *go*.' Jimmy propelled me out of the door, kissed me on the forehead, and disappeared down the stairs singing 'Walkie-talkie Man' to the tune of 'Hoochie-coochie Man'. He actually managed to sound like Howlin' Wolf.

I locked up and went down into the kitchen. There was a scrap of paper on the table. *Hi!!! Gone home got to put kids to bed. Don't worry back later. Carol xxx PS Your out of milk.* There was no sign of Vera. The cleaners must have gone home. I opened the paper bag with the kitchen scissors very carefully, imagining Joan's hands smoothing it straight, folding it neatly and tucking it under the broad elastic band with all the other bags. I could almost hear her: 'It may seem daft to you, Dodie, but they always come in handy.' Perhaps she'd wanted to destroy whatever was inside it, but the habit of saving things was too powerful to break. Even though my name was on the bag, I felt as if I ought to ask her permission before I looked inside it.

I shook the contents out on to the table. There were seven sheets of paper, held together with a clip. On the top was a lined page torn from a spiral notepad. My mother's handwriting, faint in pencil.

Please help me, Joan. I know I have no right to ask, but I want to see my baby again. I never stopped thinking of her. Perhaps you thought I was dead. Perhaps you even hoped I was. I don't blame you if you did. I'm sure the police will have told you what happened, that they came to the house in Alfriston Road and I wasn't there. It was Steve who got me out. He pushed me out of the back door and told me to run. There's an alley beside the house and I went down there. It was so easy. I never even looked back. We'd cut my hair and dyed it so no one would recognise me. I thought it wouldn't work. Steve and the others said the police would arrest me if they'd found me there. This sounds so stupid, but if I could just talk to you and explain how it happened – writing won't work, I could never make you understand and I'm no good at it anyway. If I've ruined everything then it's my fault, and I accept that. I want to ask Wolf if he will forgive me. I know we can't go back to how it was before, and in a way I don't want to. But I do want my daughter. I had a bit of cash left, so I went to the Blue Bird Hotel in Bayswater. That's where I'm writing from. It's horrible, full of prostitutes, but they don't ask questions. Joan, if you don't want to help me, please at least write and tell me how Dodie is. I miss her so much.

Susan

PS I told them my name was Susan James.

PPS I miss you, too.

There was another letter underneath it, this time in biro.

Dear Joan,
Thanks for sending the money. I'm going to move to a different place, better. I'll send you the address. I don't understand what you mean about Wolf saying he knows who Mick Martin is. He's the man who kidnapped me. I know nothing more about him than that. Please tell me what you're accusing me of. I agree it's all my fault, but what I told you is true. I was never part of any plot about anything. I don't understand what you want from me. You didn't even tell me about Dodie. How is she? Please, please let me know. If Wolf doesn't want to have anything to do with me, I understand. *But I want to know when I can see my daughter again.* Please Joan, don't be angry with me. I feel so desperate, it's like being buried alive. I don't know what to do. I went to Irene's house yesterday. I thought I'd go and see her, but when I got there, I couldn't do it. She's on Wolf's side. I know you are too, but please try to help me. There's no one else I can turn to.

Susan

Why hadn't she written to me? Perhaps she had. Perhaps I'd been away at boarding school and Joan had intercepted the letter. Perhaps she'd torn it up or burnt it. I looked at the next letter. Mum to Joan again, this time on hotel paper. *Canberra Lodge, Kenniston Road, London N19.* This one was dated *September 3rd, 1976.*

Dear Joan

I can't believe Wolf is doing this to me. Dodie is my child as well as his. I've got to see her. I just can't believe it. If I could hear it from him, then I might. Have you really told him about me? Honestly? I haven't hurt you, Joan, and yet you can just calmly sit down and write threatening that Wolf won't leave any money to Dodie if I try to see her. I think you're lying to me, or that's what I want to think, but I know Wolf as well, how cruel he can be. I grew up poor and it was no fun, just a constant struggle to make ends meet, and Wolf knows I wouldn't do that to our daughter. Before I got your letter, I'd just read in the paper that Patty Hearst was sentenced to seven years. I thought, well, if that's what it takes – because I'm in a kind of gaol anyway. Being in a real one won't make any difference. But then when you told me that Wolf would disinherit Dodie, I knew I couldn't do it. I miss her so much. Can't you arrange a meeting? Just once? You don't have to tell him. Dodie is all I think about. I can't believe she's happy at that school. I never wanted her to be sent away. Wolf must be doing it to get back at me because he knew I didn't want her to go. I know you love him, Joan, but you love Dodie too, and you're doing this to her as well as me, putting her through this hell. Why won't you meet me? Then I could try and convince you. I don't know what to do. Perhaps I should just kill myself. I want to. I'm sure it would come as a relief to all of you if I did, or if I had died. I might as well be dead. But what would you say to Dodie? That would be your decision, not mine. But it would still be MY FAULT.

Susan

Thank you for the baby picture of Dodie. Try and send another one, if you can, more recent.

Tucked behind it was a grubby brown envelope covered in frantic scribble. The date *30/9/76* was scrawled across the top.

Joan,
I read about my memorial service in the paper. What do you want me to say? Thank you so much for saying nice things about me? What I said before – that I felt buried alive – now I know what it really means. You've taken my life away. Now I don't exist.

S.

It's no good even trying to explain what reading those letters was like. It was overwhelming. I just sat there, looking at my hands holding the letters. All that was left, just those words. I felt as if someone was trying to pull out my heart, but at the same time, it was as if a light had been turned on. A bright, clear, horrible light, and I suddenly understood. Mum had never done anything off her own bat in her entire life. Other people were always there to run it for her, like she'd told Maggie. There'd been her pushy mother, then the modelling agency, then my father and Joan, and then Steve and Mick and Maggie; and then, all at once, they were gone. She had no one. She'd been there all along, desperate to see me, and I . . . I didn't know. She could have gone to the police and said, 'Look, I'm still alive.' Anyone would have done that. But she wasn't anyone, she was *Mum*. Maggie'd said they told her she'd be arrested, and then she thought my father would disinherit me. Oh, God, why didn't you do it, Mum? Why didn't you come back? I could have managed without the money. That's the stupid thing. I can do without it. I actually know I can do without it. Christ!

My fault, she'd written in the letters. MY FAULT. That's what Joan and my father had been telling her, and she thought the police would be on their side. When she was kidnapped, I used to worry about her being tortured or starved, but this was almost worse. Because it wasn't someone else doing it to her, she was doing it to herself, inside her own head. She thought she was a criminal, an outcast. She couldn't even come to me. And Joan, all those letters she wrote to me at school, all that drivel about how the garden was looking and how the dog was keeping and the bloody WI, and never *one single word*. I couldn't believe it. How could someone so good be so hard? She'd left me these letters, so she must have wanted me to know, but only when it was too late. Des could never have known she'd done this, not in a million years.

There was one more letter from Mum to Joan. A sheet of lined paper from an A4 pad, punch holes in the left margin. No address, but a date, December 2nd, 1995. Almost a month after my father's death.

Joan,
I have made a decision. I don't want you to tell Dodie about me. Especially not about the problems with the drugs. I've hurt her enough as it is. I don't want her to see me like this. I'm grateful that you got me into this place, everyone is very kind, but my life is impossible. Steve came here. I don't know how he found out where I am but he claimed to be a relative so they let him in. He kept shouting at me until one of the volunteers heard and made him leave. Now he says he knows where I live. I know I can't stay here for ever, but I'm frightened to go back because of him. Joan, you get to a point where you can't ask why any of it is happening any more, and you might as well be dead. That's where I have got to. I told the counsellor, I want to climb into the white dot on the TV screen and be sucked into nothing, except there is no

white dot. I kept looking but it's not there. I can't sleep any more. Steve's gone but I can still hear his voice inside my head. He brought back things I didn't ever want to remember. I wish I could say, give my love to Dodie, but you know why I can't. I've been to her office a couple of times. I got the address from one of those magazines you sent me with her work in it. I didn't go inside, just stood round the corner and waited till she came out. She didn't see me, but I knew it was her immediately, she's so like I was. I'm so proud of her. But she's got her own life, Joan, and I won't go back on my decision. If she has any good memories of me, then that's better than what there is now.

Susan

Oh, Mum. That day, the impression of her in my mind, the feeling that she was actually *there* . . . It was because she was saying goodbye.

28

There were two more pages. Light blue Basildon Bond. Joan's handwriting, with the date January 2nd, 1996:

To dear Dodie,
I'd be telling a lie if I did not say that in many ways, I am writing this in the hope that you will never read it. But if you are, then you will have read the other letters too. It might be foolish to say I hope they have not upset you too much, but I feel that it is only fair that you should know what has taken place. All my life, I've wanted people to get on with each other. It hasn't always happened that way, but I've tried to do what I could, and I honestly thought that I was acting in your best interests. I know you must

have felt – and must still feel – angry and confused, and I'd like to try and put that right if I can.

The man who organised the kidnapping called himself Mick Martin, but that was not his real name. You may not know anything about this, but your father's first wife, Betty, gave birth to a son soon after they were divorced. The reason for the divorce was that Betty was unfaithful to your father, and although she said it was his child, he never believed it. To my knowledge, Betty never pressed the matter, but your father did receive several letters from this young man Brian Carroll, making various threats and asking him for money. Those letters were not answered. Your father gave them to the police during the kidnap investigation, and they found some fingerprints which matched those of Mick Martin. Your father requested that this information did not become public, and it was not thought to be relevant in the court because Mick Martin was not on trial. We had heard some rumours from the village that your mother had been seen with a man, and your father was quite convinced that it was Betty's son, and that he and your mother were engaged in a plot to extort money from him. I want you to know, Dodie, that I never believed this, but I was not able to dissuade your father. I tried to show him the letters you have seen on several occasions, but he refused to read them. I did not persist because I didn't want to make him angry. I think now that I should have done.

There is no real proof that Mick Martin was your father's son. He certainly believed that he was. I had some acquaintance with Betty, and whatever her faults may have been I'd say that she was, on the whole, a truthful person. In any case, she died before any of this happened. Mick Martin's body was cremated, so there was no possibility of any tests being made to show paternity. Even had there been, I doubt your father would have allowed them to take place.

There is a favour I want to ask of you, Dodie. It concerns Desmond Haigh-Wood. He knows nothing of this. Your father would never discuss Betty after the divorce. Even to me, he said very little. I promised him that I would never speak of it to anyone, which is why I did not, but there is another reason, and I will tell you what that is: I am ashamed of what I've done. It has taken me a very long time to admit this, Dodie, but it's true. As I've got older, I've become aware of a need to clear up certain things – to get them off my chest, if you like – before I die. What I ask is, that you do not repeat to Des what I have said in this letter.

Last year, I spoke to Maggie Hill. I employed a private detective to find her and went to see her. I was rather fearful about what to expect, but she seemed decent enough and genuinely sorry for the part she played in the kidnapping. Maggie told me that she had been in love with Mick Martin all the time. Incidentally, she still thinks that he was Mick Martin. I did not tell her his real name. But our conversation left me in no doubt that your father was mistaken. Although it is true that your mother had some involvement with the kidnapper Steven Moody, she was a victim of circumstance, not part of a conspiracy. She says in her letters that it was her fault, but that isn't true. Your father and I were more at fault than she was. Wolf made a terrible mistake which I compounded, against my better judgement, by not acting to set it right. You'll know by now why your mother did not try to contact you after your father's death. I am afraid, Dodie, that her addiction can also be laid at our door, or, more specifically, at my door. Susan needed help and support, which my feelings for Wolf made me unable to give. That, I think, is why she turned to drugs. Remember, Dodie, she never knew you as a grown-up woman. I think she imagined that you had become like your father, and that you, too, would be unable to forgive her. Please believe me when I say that I tried to persuade her. She would not change her mind, but she loved you so very much, and that is what matters in the end.

I was frightened for you, Dodie, and for Wolf, that he would lose you as well as everything else. I know that what I did was wrong. If I had been honest, with myself and everyone else, there might have been a reconciliation between you and your father. Wolf was a very proud man, and in many ways it was his strength, but he could never allow himself to appear weak. A couple of days before he died, he told me how much he loved you, and he said, 'I wish we could have been friends.'

I hope that, in the fullness of time, you will be able to forgive me, Dodie. I loved your father, and, whatever you may think, I love you, too. I wish you well.

Joan

Underneath was a postscript, dated 14th June:

I have been receiving peculiar telephone calls recently. I pick up the receiver but no one speaks. I think someone has been in the garden at night too. I am not a fanciful person, but I am beginning to wonder whether these things may have some connection with your mother. Some people might say that the chickens are coming home to roost.

I stared at the letter for a long time. I was shivering. I couldn't stop myself. It certainly wasn't cold, so I suppose it must have been shock. After a while I thought, Jimmy's coming. He's going to cook. And Carol. Carol's coming back. Perhaps she'd like some dinner, too. And Des. Des was coming. And Tony. Everyone. I felt exhausted. It was too much even to think about. What am I supposed to do? I thought. They can't just troop in and find me here like this. And the letters. I couldn't let them see the letters. I must change my clothes, I thought. Go upstairs. Have a bath. Change. Get myself sorted out.

I picked up the letters, put them back into the paper bag and took them upstairs to the bathroom. I turned on the taps and sat down on the mat, waiting for the bath to fill. *If Dodie has a good memory of me . . .* If I'd been allowed to see her, I could have told her all the things I remembered, the good things, and even at the end, when she didn't want me to see her, I could have held her hand and just talked to her, told her about my life. Joan had written that she thought I'd grown up to be like *him*. All those years, not telling me, not letting me see her . . . I thought suddenly of Des, our dinner at the Fat Hen, what he'd said about Joan. The way he'd talked about her. She had asked me not to tell him what she'd done.

'I won't tell him, Joan,' I said, out loud. 'But I'll be doing it for his sake, not for yours.'

Des had had an affair with Betty. He said my father didn't know. But Joan knew. Perhaps that was another reason she didn't want me to tell Des. She'd said there wasn't any proof of paternity, so perhaps Mick Martin – or Brian Carroll, or whatever his name was – perhaps he was Des's son. Had my father guessed? Those photos in the papers – you couldn't really tell what people looked like, but what if Betty's son had sent my father a photograph of himself, a good one, and he'd seen the likeness? When I'd asked Des if he'd wanted children he said it wasn't possible, but that could have been because Joan couldn't have children. Perhaps my father couldn't bring himself to admit that he'd been cuckolded by his best friend. Or perhaps – just *perhaps* – he never confronted Des with the fact that the man who'd kidnapped my mother, the man who was ultimately responsible for her death, was his child. Oh God, I thought, that can't be true. It *can't* be. I can't even allow myself to think that it might be.

I looked up and saw that the bath was almost over-flowing. I took off my clothes and got in. Steven Moody had known where Mum was. It would have been so easy to kill her. The policeman had said it was heroin and something else, but he wouldn't have needed anything else. If it was purer than the stuff she normally had, or if there was just more of it . . . Steven Moody wouldn't even have had to give it to Mum himself, he could have just passed it along to somebody else and got them to give it to her. Drug addicts aren't interested in where the stuff comes from. I thought suddenly of the Fierce Bad Rabbit in the Beatrix Potter story, snatching the carrot. 'He doesn't say thank you, he just takes it.'

Mum's last letter sounded as if it had been written from some sort of clinic. She was seeing a counsellor, but she'd given up. Because of Steve? He'd made her think of things she didn't want to remember, that was what she'd written. Terrible things.

I must have forgotten to lock the door. I didn't hear it open, just felt a draught on the side of my neck. I was in one of the small guest bathrooms, and the bath takes up the whole of one side so the door opens next to the head end. I was sort of half-sitting, half-lying in it, with my eyes closed. I thought the draught must have blown the door open, so I reached out with one hand to push it shut again, and my arm hit something solid. Not the edge of the door but cloth. Material, and underneath it, flesh.

My heart stopped. I opened my eyes and lunged towards the shape, but one of my legs slipped and my chin came down hard on the porcelain edge of the bath. An inch away from my face was a wall of splashy khaki camouflage. Trousers. Legs.

'It's just the two of us.' The man's voice seemed to come from miles above my head. 'There's no one else in the house.'

I looked up. It was Carol's boyfriend, Greg. Standing in the doorway. He was holding a knife.

29

He sat on the side of the bath, his bottom next to my head, and looked down at me. Close up, I could smell him. Pungent, accumulated sweat. I had a mental picture of his brown crusted armpit hairs against the woollen underarms of his jumper. I wanted to be sick. His thick fingers held the knife against his thigh. 'It's called a *kukri*. The Gurkhas use them. They have a rule: you don't put it away until you've drawn blood.'

'But you're not . . . not a Gurkha.'

There was a second's tight silence, and then he exploded. 'Shut the fuck up!' The words and the edge of his knife burst into my face together and I jerked away from them, slamming my elbow into the tiles on the wall. I hugged it to my chest in agony, eyes closed, rocking backwards and forwards, shaking, trying not to cry.

'Don't bother, you've nothing to hide,' he said contemptuously. I heard his knife clatter on to the floor and – too fast for me to duck away – felt the pressure of his hands on my head and shoulders, forcing me downwards. My head slammed backwards into the tiles behind the bath and my body shot forwards in a wave of grey soapy water. I tried to get a grip with my feet on the other end of the bath, but it was just too long and they kicked uselessly for a second as I saw, out of the corners of my eyes, the edges of water closing in round my face. Then, before I had time to breathe, I was underneath. The heel of his hand ground into my right eye socket and for a moment I thought my head would burst open, and then I was jerked to the surface again, gagging and choking, a burning waterfall of soapy water and snot flowing out of my nostrils and down the back of my throat.

My eyes felt as if they'd been sealed shut. I pawed at them and felt a sideways movement against one eyeball as my contact lens slithered across it and fell out into the bath. The other one was still in place, and when I managed to open my eyes I saw Greg's face in front of me. I could hear nothing, but the yellow teeth were opening and closing inside the beard, the pink tongue in the centre wet and moving. There was a *waaa!* sound of air inside my ear and then there were words, and inside them, somehow, a voice in my head: the water, stop the water, get the water out. I looked at the other end of the bath and saw, draped over the hot tap, the few inches of snapped-off chain that should have connected to . . . I saw a round shape, wavy in the dirty water. The big brass plug.

I put my hands on the sides of the bath and tried to pull myself forward to reach it but my body was quivering, too weak, and Greg's hands clamped down on my arm, spinning me round towards him again. I slipped and kicked, my feet thudded against the side of the bath with no purchase and the grey water curved above me and splashed on the floor.

Greg wrenched me backwards by my hair. 'You still don't get it, do you?'

I could barely speak. He jerked my head backwards, sending the scalding, viscous remains of the liquid in my nose cascading down into my throat. 'Please—' The word came out in a bubbling whisper. 'Please, just tell me what you want.'

'You got the letter, you stupid bitch.'

'You sent the letter?'

'Yes.'

'The hair? The phone call?'

'Me.'

'I didn't . . . recognise your voice.'

'You wouldn't. We all sound alike to you, don't we?' He yanked hard on my hair. 'Do you know what we used to call you lot? Pig family. Susan used to talk about you. She wanted me to meet you. I told her, you don't need your pig family and your pig daughter. Forget about them. But she couldn't, could she?' His eyes were squeezed tight shut and he was shaking his head violently. 'She told me she *loved* me! You pigs! You don't understand what love means! All you understand is money!' He jerked on my hair and bellowed into my face and I choked as my throat filled up again, drowning from the water inside me, scarcely able to breathe. Then he let me go and I retched and retched, my whole body throwing itself forward with every spasm. I couldn't stop.

'Look at you,' he said. 'All your money. What's it going to do for you now? It can't help you now, can it? I said, can it?' I shook my head, and he grabbed hold of my chin, twisting my face towards his. The yellow teeth seemed to spring towards me. 'CAN IT?'

'N-no.'

'I *saved* her.'

'I'm sorry . . . I don't understand.'

'I'm sorry, I don't understand,' he repeated, mocking my voice. 'Of course you don't understand, you stupid cow. You people think you're so wonderful, with your money, and your houses, and your cars, and your planes, but you're all *dead*! You're decaying, rotten with money, you *stink of it*! You don't have feelings.' His face was an inch away from mine, and his breath seemed to cover my head like a hood as his voice dropped to a whisper. 'You can't even fuck.' His hand clamped on to the back of my neck, shoving my face into his. I felt the furze of his beard on my chin, the scrape of his teeth against mine and then his tongue was inside my mouth, twisting, curling. A warm, wet web of sputum coated the back of my throat, choking me. He pulled away and I coughed and spat, trying to breathe.

'God, look at you.' He knelt on the floor and rested his arms on the edge of the bath, trailing one hand in the water as if he was bathing a baby. I suddenly thought of Carol, putting her children to bed. Had she known who he was all along? 'Frigid,' he said. 'Like mother, like daughter. What a surprise.'

I drew my knees up to my chest and hugged them, trying to stop shaking. Tears were coursing down my face, and I could feel the snot spilling out of my nose to join them, bearding my chin with a thin mucus. I put my hands up to my eyes and felt my remaining lens, dislodged by the water behind it, pop out into my palm. Greg's – Steve's – face went suddenly out of focus and the rest of the room became a blur of indistinct shapes and colours. He mustn't realise, I thought. I mustn't let him know I can't see.

He was talking again. '. . . when the police raided the house, it was me who told her to run. They were all round the place, but I kept them busy so she could get away. I thought she'd be back for me. All the time, before the trial, I thought, she'll come, she loves me. She'll come back for me. I thought she'd tell the police how she'd wanted to come with me because we were going to be together, how it wasn't a kidnap at all. If she'd done that, they'd have had to let me go. She could have done it easy, but she didn't. I *saved* her and she just walked off and left me like she didn't even know who I was! She did that to *me*! I thought I'd opened her eyes to what was really happening. It didn't matter if she'd sold out because she could change, I'd help her change. I saved her from all that capitalist shit. I *freed* her! The stupid worthless bitch. Because when it comes down to it, she was just as corrupt and filthy and disgusting as all the rest of you. We were going to live together. We were going to Greece, to live in a house on the beach. That's what you people can't understand. You fly round and round in your private planes, you pollute the atmosphere so we can't breathe, but you don't care because you can buy your own private oxygen supply. You'd like that, wouldn't you? If you could own the air we breathe. Because that's what it comes down to with you lot. You can slum it and pretend to be radical and then you can go back to your nice safe homes with the guards on the gates to keep the poor people out! You wouldn't want us coming too close, would you? Like your housekeeper – she dropped like a stone when she saw me come through that window, poor cow. I went through her bag and found your address. Because it was you I was after – at least you showed up. Nineteen years I waited for Susan – eleven inside and the rest trying to find her. I couldn't believe it when I saw the state she was in. She was at this shelter. It was one night when I didn't have a place to sleep, and when I went in, she was just sitting there. I was looking at her for five minutes before I realised who it was. She was too out of it to recognise me. I never spoke to her, but I talked to a few people who said she'd only been there a day, and that she'd been kicked out of her flat. This one woman said Susan was going to try and get herself cleaned up – she'd told her she was going to some posh clinic in Gloucestershire. She thought Susan was just another junkie like the rest of them, talking bollocks, but I thought, no, and I went off to the library to look it up – that took bloody ages, finding the right place – but sure enough . . . So I went up there. They've got it all set up so it looks like one of those health places, but it's full of rich weirdos and drug addicts. I told them I was her brother, and do you know what?' He laughed. 'They believed me. They only fucking believed me. When I got in there, I said to Susan, "I did time for you, you bitch." I said, "I must have been out of my fucking tree, thinking I loved you." She was crying and saying, "Leave me alone," and all this, going on about how she'd been punished as well, but she was just saying it to get rid of me. You only had to look at her to see their poxy treatment wouldn't work; she was in there six months and using the week after. Well, I made sure she got what she needed, didn't I? But it's funny, isn't it? When you think about it, she'd have been a lot better off if she'd stayed with me.' His voice rose into a plummy squeal. 'When you

consider it, I think you'll find, that's very fucking funny.'
He took hold of my shoulders and jerked me towards him.
'Ver-ry fuck-king fun-ny, isn't it?' He began pushing me
back into the water with a series of jabs. 'Isn't that ver-ry
fuck-king fun-ny?'

I grabbed hold of the sides of the bath to try and brace
myself but he smashed his elbow down on my wrist and I
screamed with pain, and then I seemed to lose control of
everything and he plunged me down into the water, my
heels, thighs and buttocks skidding and banging against the
hard white porcelain, making the water roll and pitch in
great waves that overflowed the bath and slapped down on
to the floor. I opened my mouth to take a breath but I was
too late and, as he pushed me under, the scummy tide of
water flowed into my throat, my ears roared and I couldn't
breathe and everything began to close in on me and the last
thing I remember thinking was, *I'm starting to die.*

30

I was heaving, my body pitching forwards, vomiting gallons
of thick molten liquid out of my nose and mouth. Skeins of
mucus hung down my face, slathering the curtain of clogged
hair that flapped in front of my eyes every time I retched.
The inside of my chest was on fire. I wouldn't have been
surprised to see the spiky, little red trees from inside my
lungs uprooted and gushing out of my mouth.

My bottom felt as if it was glued on to something. I
looked down. A patchwork of blue towels was spread across
my legs and stomach, and where they stopped, white and
shiny, curving upwards on either side of me, the bath. My
brain shot into panic. I was still in the bath. The water,
the water, would cover me up . . . Something soft pressed

against the back of my neck, across my shoulders, pushing me down.

'No!' I threw myself backwards, lashing out with my arms.

'Dodie! It's all right, darling. Calm down. It's all right. Sssh, sssh.' Tony's voice. I felt the thing – the towel, that's what it was, a towel – go round my shoulders and a hand rubbing my back through the material.

'The water . . . Get it out . . . Help me.' My throat was like sandpaper, the sound hardly there at all.

'No more water. All gone.'

Someone thrust a length of toilet paper into my outstretched hand.

'Try and blow your nose. That better? Nod for yes.' I nodded. 'Come on, let's get your hair off your face. Now you can see what's going on.'

I could see Tony's face reasonably clearly, but the room behind him was fuzzy. There was a human-sized assembly of colours blurring into the darkness of the doorway.

'Who's that?'

'It's only Dominic. You can't see properly, can you? God, she's probably concussed. Dodie, can you remember who the Prime Minister is?'

'My contact lenses came out.'

'Oh Christ, and you're completely blind, aren't you?'

'Where are your glasses?' said Dominic from the doorway. 'I'll go and get them.'

'In my bedroom – the ballroom.'

'I'll get them for you. Back in a minute, OK?' The fuzzy column disappeared from view.

'What's he doing here?' I asked.

'He was with Des, remember? He's here too, and your solicitor. They're with the police, downstairs. Jimmy's down there with them.'

'Jimmy?'

'He saved your life, Dodie. He bashed the guy on the head

with a Le Creuset frying pan. That knocked him out, then Dominic sat on him and Des called the police. I was trying to sort you out. I thought you'd stopped breathing – you were dead white and your mouth was blue. I've changed my mind about the lesbian vampire look, darling. It's not you at all.'

'Thanks for telling me. I won't try it again.'

'Sorry you're still in the bath. The doctor's on his way. We thought you'd better stay put until he arrived. Nothing feels broken, does it?'

'I don't think so. Just achy. Have they got him?'

'The man who was trying to murder you? Yes, darling. He won't come back.'

'His name's Steven Moody.'

'He wrote that letter, didn't he? Christ, Dodie, I'm sorry. We should have called the police.'

Dominic came back with my spectacles and a huge pile of pillows. 'Something to lean on. Sit forward a bit.' He stacked them up behind me. 'More comfortable?'

I nodded, and put the glasses on. 'God, I must look completely mad.'

'You could be a famous eccentric. Edith Sitwell or somebody. It's a shame you're not a writer. You could do your work in the bath and the magazines could come and take photos.'

'Wasn't there a famous novelist who wrote in the bath?' Dominic asked. 'Wasn't it Proust?'

'That was in bed,' said Tony. 'The bath is much more original. The doctor should be here in a minute. I'd give you some brandy but there'd only be a fuss.'

'Tony?'

'What is it, my lamb?'

'Don't let's talk any more.'

He patted me on the shoulder. 'All right.'

The doctor arrived after a while. He peered down my

284

throat and into my eyes and asked questions and felt things to make sure they weren't broken, and then he said I ought to try and get up, so Dominic was despatched for my dressing gown and then there was a bit of a hiatus with towels falling off and everyone being polite and trying not to look, but I was past caring. I just wanted to be out of that bath.

I shuffled down the corridor to my room, Tony propping me up. To be honest, I was sort of surprised to find the rest of the house was still there, unaffected. What had happened to me was just this sort of isolated thing, in one room. While it was going on, the rest of the house, the things in it, had stood there, just the same. They'd be the same even if Steven Moody had killed me. All the stuff that had always been there, the floorboards and walls and the radiators and furniture, it all looked so normal, somehow. When we got to the ballroom, I got into bed and the doctor gave me some painkillers, and after that I went off to sleep.

I woke up when somebody knocked on the door. I heard it open a fraction, and then a voice said, 'Can I come in? It's Jimmy. I thought you might like some breakfast.'

'Wait a minute!' I sat up gingerly, groped for my hand-bag, dredged up my compact and peered into the dusty mirror. My right eye was a puffy splurge of red and purple, the bruises spreading down my cheek and into my hair line. My hair hung down over the whole mess, ratty and tangled. Swamp Thing. Nothing I could fix. I toyed briefly with the idea of trying to poke in one contact lens, gave it up, and cast about for my glasses instead. Moment of truth. 'Come in!'

Jimmy didn't scream or drop the tray. He just swiped the door shut with his foot and put my breakfast on the bed. Smoked salmon, scrambled eggs and cold bread-and-butter pudding.

'Sorry, I look terrible.'

'You look a lot better than you did last night. How are you feeling?'

'Awful. My head, mostly. But at least I'm alive. Thanks to you.'

'Yeah, well . . .'

'Tony told me you saved my life. With a frying pan.' My throat hurt too much for laughing, but I wanted to.

'To tell the truth . . .' He tailed off, looking embarrassed.

'Yes?'

'I've always wanted to do that. Either that or smack a bald man on the head with a ladle. It would make such a satisfying noise. Splack!' He mimed whacking someone with a ladle.

'You're mad, do you know that?'

'Probably. But there's this bit in *Fawlty Towers* where Basil does it to Manuel. With a spoon. He rubs it all round his face, and then he goes thwock! on his head. It's just something I've always wanted to do.'

'Well, I'm very glad you've achieved your ambition, for both our sakes.'

'Is it all right if I stay for a bit?'

'If you can bear to look at me.'

'Don't be stupid.' He sat down on the side of the bed. 'Want some tea?'

'Yes, please.'

'It's Earl Grey. Mr Haigh-Wood called it "poofter's tea". He whispered it to me so Tony wouldn't hear. He's nice, isn't he?'

'Yes, he is.'

'He was brilliant last night. He's downstairs now, with the secretary, sorting out the press and everything. I just rang up my brother and he said he opened his door this morning and found them taking pictures of his garden.'

'Oh, for God's sake.'

'Mind you, they were Japanese. But he said he couldn't see your gates for cameras and those fuzzy sound things on sticks. It's all right though, they can't get in.'

'The secretary . . . she's called Helen Something, isn't she?'

'Helen Bain. She's so efficient, it's scary. She's got this really fierce look, like you've got your flies undone. Tony said the same thing. Mr Haigh-Wood says you're not to worry about anything, because they're dealing with it. Actually, he told me to call him Des but I haven't quite got round to it yet.'

'Sounds like pandemonium. What time is it, anyway?'

'About eleven. We didn't know if we should wake you.'

'I'm glad you did. Jimmy, this all looks lovely, but can I just concentrate on the tea for now? I'm very thirsty.'

'Yeah, whatever you like. The bread-and-butter pudding's from last night, I'm afraid. Should still be good, though. I made it with brioche.'

'You made it last night?'

Jimmy shrugged. 'I'd done my bit with the police, Tony was upstairs seeing to you and everyone else was sorting things out, so I thought, we'll have to have dinner sometime. We had it in the kitchen. It was quite fun really – except for being worried about you; but the doctor said you'd be all right if you got some rest.' He stopped and looked at me. 'Carol came back, Dodie. She'd seen the police racing through the village and everything. The security guard wouldn't let her in. It was a different bloke and the other one hadn't given him the list when he went off duty. Anyway, Carol went and got her dad. You know how big he is? He came bursting into the kitchen *wearing* this security guard round his waist like a belt or something. When she heard what had happened, she was in a real state. She said she'd left you a note about putting the children to bed—'

'She did. I assumed she'd taken Greg with her.'

'Apparently he said he'd stay here till she got back, make sure everything was all right. She said she'd thought it was a good idea, because he'd met you and everything. I honestly don't think she knew, Dodie. I mean, I'd met him a couple of times, and I didn't think there was anything odd about him. Well, I suppose he was a bit weird, but I didn't think he was . . . you know.'

'Out of his tree?'

'Yeah. He was a bit quiet, that's all.'

'Kept himself to himself. They always say that when some maniac's gone on the rampage with a shotgun.'

'You ought to talk to Carol, though. Tell her it isn't her fault.'

'Not today, though.'

'Mr Hai— Des, I mean. He said he'd be up a bit later, and the police will want to talk to you at some stage.'

'I suppose so. Oh God, Jimmy, I've just thought of something. The paper bag we took out of the pyjama case, I left it in the bathroom—'

'It's OK, I've got it.'

'Nobody else saw it, did they?'

Jimmy shook his head. 'It was on the floor so I stuffed it in my pocket. It's a bit crumpled, I'm afraid, but it's all there.' He put it down on the bed. 'I haven't read it.'

'Thanks.'

'Was it OK? Joan's letter, or whatever it was?'

'It's weird, but I suppose you could say it *was* OK, in a way. I'm glad we found it.'

'Good.' Jimmy smiled at me. 'Is there anything else you need?'

'Just to say thank you. You saved my life. You and your frying pan.'

'Any time. You can thank the frying pan later. Now then, where can I kiss you? Most of the bits I can see look as if they hurt.'

'You could try the end of my nose.'

So he kissed it. Then he picked up the hand that wasn't

bandaged and said, 'This bit looks quite healthy,' and kissed that as well.

'Jimmy?'

'Mmm?'

'Everything will be all right, won't it? It's just that I feel like I've come to a stop. A sort of conclusion. I just want everything to be all right. Oh, God, now I sound like Joan.'

'Well, that's not so terrible, is it?'

'No, I suppose it isn't.'

'For what it's worth, I think it's all going to be fine. I know you've got lots of things to sort out, but last night, when I went into that bathroom and you were lying there in the water, and I thought, it's too late, she's dead, and you were so *white* – apart from the bruises. And then when you started coughing like that, it was just . . . it was like . . . like the best thing I've ever seen.' He fiddled with the edge of the sheet, looking embarrassed.

'Was it . . . was it better than your best soufflé?'

'Yes, it was. Actually, there was this fantastic chocolate one I made a few weeks ago. I'll do it for you, if you like. When you feel better.'

'Will you? Will you be . . . around?'

'Course I will. I mean, if you want.'

'Yes. I do. I do want. Very much.'

'Good. Now, are there any other bits that need kissing?'

31

Five to eleven. Jimmy, Tony and Dominic were standing in the hall, admiring each other's black suits. I stood in front of the mirror, adjusting my hat.

Jimmy came up behind me and planted a kiss on the back of my neck. 'Nice legs, shame about the face.'

'I still look like Quasimodo, don't I?'

'Your deportment's slightly better. No, honestly, you're not that bad.'

'She *is*,' Tony said. 'She's been at it all morning. More slap than Lily Savage. I nearly went and asked the gardener for a spade.' He handed me a glass of sherry. 'Go on, get that down you. And put your sunglasses on, for God's sake. There might be small children out there.'

'Oh, up yours.'

Des stuck his head round the door. 'Are you ready?'

'As I'll ever be.'

'Well, everyone's here, so put your best foot forward.'

I've never seen the church looking so good. The stone floors were scrubbed white, the pews were polished, you could see your face in the brass and the flowers were spectacular, even by Joan's standards. There wasn't an empty seat. The whole village had turned out, and the WI, and there were lots of people I remembered from twenty years earlier – craggier faces and greyer hair, but still straight backed and smartly suited. When I looked round at them, I thought, these are the men and women who won the war, like Joan and Des. That almost made me cry, but I didn't. I sang, instead, as loud as I could. Everybody sang, in fact, really well, and the organ sounded better than I've ever heard it. I caught Des's eye during 'Rock of Ages' and he gave me a crumpled smile.

When the vicar started speaking about what Joan had done for the community and how she always put others first, I remembered how Joan had blamed herself for what happened to Mum. I thought, I could spend the rest of my life hating her and my father, but it wouldn't bring Mum back. When Des asked me what I wanted to do about her funeral, I said just him and me and the vicar. I don't want some great circus with flowers and press, and people who hardly knew Mum saying what a tragedy. She had that twenty years ago, at her memorial service. She deserves some dignity, and it's the only thing left that I can do for her. She feels closer to me now than she's ever done, but it's not a *raw* feeling. Not like a fresh wound. I suppose it's not surprising. I've had twenty years to get used to missing her, after all.

I looked round at all the old faces and remembered the breathless pensioner struggling up the stairs at Maggie Hill's flat. Perhaps I could do something for him, or for people like him, anyway. That makes it sound like St Paul on the road to Damascus – deciding I was going to be a better person – but it wasn't like that really. I'd been thinking a lot while I was lying in bed. The police came to interview me about Steven Moody and Helen Bain got a rail-full of black dresses sent up from London for me to choose something for the funeral, but apart from that, I just lay there and thought about things. I can't just forget about the past and sail off into the future like a film or something, but at least now I know what happened. And the reason I know is because of Des and Maggie Hill and Joan. Because they were brave enough to tell me the truth.

It was boiling hot when we came out into the churchyard, not a cloud anywhere. After the burial, we went back to the house for lunch. The caterers had set up a buffet in the front hall, and people drifted out in groups and sat on the lawns to eat.

Des and I stood on the porch with our drinks and watched them for a bit.

'It's nice, isn't it?' I said. 'You wouldn't know it was a funeral, except for the clothes, of course.'

Des patted me on the shoulder. 'I'm sure Joan would be pleased. Have you had anything to eat?'

'Not yet. I'm not very hungry. I thought I might just go back to the churchyard for a minute. Do you want to come?'

'If you like.'

Joan's grave was beside my father's, as I'd wanted. We stood in front of them.

'Thanks for sorting everything out.'

'That was Helen, not me. I told you she was efficient. Joan was very fond of you, you know. Very fond indeed.'

'I know. She wrote me a letter.'

'I thought she might have done something of the sort.'

'Des, you know when we had dinner at the Fat Hen? When you said you wanted to put things right? Well, Joan did, too. That's why she wrote the letter. And I'm glad. That she told me, and that you told me. I can't go on nursing myself through life, shying away from things. I have to go forward, and . . . Sorry, I'm not explaining it very well.'

'Sounds all right to me. There was something Joan said to me, once, when we were married – I think her mother had said it to her – anyway, she said to me, you should never let the sun go down on your anger. And she was quite right. We rather lost sight of that, I'm afraid. But you're fortunate, Dodie. Most people don't realise it until they're my age, and by then it's too late.' He smiled. 'That's the worst thing about being old, you know. Everybody bloody dies. Look, whatever Joan put in her letter, that's between the two of you, but if there's anything else you want to ask me, fine. You'd better think of it quick, mind you, before I conk out.'

'You can't die, you're too important. But thanks. I've still got a lot of thinking to do, I know that.'

'Well, don't wear yourself out. I think somebody's calling you.'

We turned in the direction of the sound and saw Jimmy standing at the gate, holding a glass of wine. 'Everyone keeps asking where you are. I brought you this. Shall I bring it over?'

'No, I'll come out.'

'Off you go, my child.' Des patted me on the bottom. 'I'll stay here for a while.'

'Are you sure?'

'Sure I'm sure. Be off with you.'

I gave him a kiss and began threading my way through the graves towards Jimmy.